ALSO BY JOHN SANDFORD

Rules of Prey

Shadow Prey

Eyes of Prey

Silent Prey

Winter Prey

Night Prey

Mind Prey

Sudden Prey

The Night Crew

Secret Prey

Certain Prey

Easy Prey

Chosen Prey

Mortal Prey

Naked Prey

Hidden Prey

Broken Prey

Dead Watch

Invisible Prey

Phantom Prey

Wicked Prey

Storm Prey

Buried Prey

Stolen Prey

KIDD NOVELS

The Fool's Run

The Empress File

The Devil's Code

The Hanged Man's Song

VIRGIL FLOWERS NOVELS

Dark of the Moon

Heat Lightning

Rough Country

Bad Blood

Shock Wave

MAD RIVER

JOHN SANDFORD

G. P. Putnam's Sons

New York

PUTNAM

G. P. PUTNAM'S SONS
Publishers Since 1838
Published by the Penguin Group
Penguin Group (USA) Inc., 375 Hudson Street, New York, New York 10014, USA •
Penguin Group (Canada), 90 Eglinton Avenue East, Suite 700, Toronto,
Ontario M4P 2Y3, Canada (a division of Pearson Penguin Canada Inc.) •
Penguin Books Ltd, 80 Strand, London WC2R 0RL, England • Penguin Ireland,
25 St Stephen's Green, Dublin 2, Ireland (a division of Penguin Books Ltd) •
Penguin Group (Australia), 250 Camberwell Road, Camberwell, Victoria 3124, Australia
(a division of Pearson Australia Group Pty Ltd) • Penguin Books India Pvt Ltd,
11 Community Centre, Panchsheel Park, New Delhi–110 017, India •
Penguin Group (NZ), 67 Apollo Drive, Rosedale, North Shore 0632, New Zealand
(a division of Pearson New Zealand Ltd) • Penguin Books (South Africa) (Pty) Ltd,
24 Sturdee Avenue, Rosebank, Johannesburg 2196, South Africa

Penguin Books Ltd, Registered Offices: 80 Strand, London WC2R 0RL, England

Library of Congress Cataloging-in-Publication Data

Sandford, John, date.
Mad River / John Sandford.
p.   cm.
ISBN 978-0-399-15770-7
1. Flowers, Virgil (Fictitious character)—Fiction.
2. Government investigators—Minnesota—Fiction.
3. Teenagers—Fiction.   4. Spree murderers—Fiction.   I. Title.
PS3569.A516M33   2012   2012025454
813'.54—dc23

Printed in the United States of America
1   3   5   7   9   10   8   6   4   2

BOOK DESIGN BY AMANDA DEWEY

I wrote this book in cooperation with my friend Joe Soucheray, a Twin Cities newspaper columnist, author, radio personality, and a roughly 52-handicap golfer with whom I have played at least a hundred rounds of golf, and witnessed the man's only hole-in-one, which he will tell you about at the drop of a hat. Or even if you don't drop your hat. He is the only man I know who has a urinal in his garage, the better to keep him busy on the old MGB he's currently fixing. We were thinking about dedications, and came up with "To all our grandchildren," of whom we have many.

—JOHN SANDFORD

MAD RIVER

1

JIMMY SHARP STEPPED BACK from the curb and impatiently waved the car by, waved it by like a big shot, like he couldn't be bothered to assert his rights to the pedestrian crosswalk.

"We shoulda parked closer," Tom McCall said. "I'm freezing my ass off."

As the car went by, a woman driver peered out at the three of them. The overhead reading light was on, and she was wearing an overcoat, wool hat, and one black glove. Her bare hand was holding a cell phone to her ear, and she was talking as she looked at them. A multitasker, headed for a three-car smashup somewhere down the line.

"One big problem there—somebody would have seen it, and put two and two together, and then we got a witness," Jimmy said. "Besides, the walk will warm you up."

"Glad I got the gloves," McCall said.

Becky Welsh said, "It's April, you fool. You don't need gloves for the cold. Just walk."

Jimmy had smoked a Marlboro down to the filter, and he snapped it into the street and bent into the task of climbing the hill, Tom and Becky on his heels, the three of them throwing splashy shadows in the pale April moonlight. Halfway up, Jimmy stopped to catch his breath, turned, and said, "That's a pretty sight of the town."

They all turned to look, the Bigham business district spread out below them, the county courthouse with its eternal flame, a few cars turning corners, flashing red lights on an ambulance heading into the hospital. The Minnesota River was down there, a black ribbon at the foot of downtown, not much more than a creek, really. They'd left Jimmy's Firebird in an apartment parking lot at the base of the hill, where they could get to it in a hurry.

"It *is* pretty," Tom agreed. Puffs of steam came out of their mouths, dissipating in the night air.

Jimmy took another cigarette out of the pack and tapped the tobacco end on a thumbnail, then cupped his hands to his mouth and lit it with an old Zippo lighter that left behind the stink of lighter fluid when he sparked it off. His square jaw looked yellow in the light of the flame; the trace of a ladder-stitched scar showed up on his chin, from the bad old hay-humping days down in Shinder, when a piece of wire from an ancient baling machine lashed him like a whip.

He was wearing a green army field jacket that he'd bought at a flea market, with the collar up under his ears, and a blue Dodgers baseball cap with a big white LA on the front. He'd never been to LA, but he planned to go, someday soon. He'd manage Becky's career, and they'd both get rich and buy a Winnebago and tour around the country.

"Diamonds tonight," Becky said.

Tom said, "I don't know about this. It don't feel entirely right to me."

Tom was tall and wiry, and wore silver-rimmed glasses that he got from the three weeks he was in the navy. At the end of three weeks, one of the RDCs noticed the scale on his arms and asked, "Is that the heartbreak of psoriasis I see there?" It was, and Tom was out.

On this cold night, the psoriasis was concealed by a thin blue work shirt and an uninsulated leather jacket, the sleeves too short to cover Tom's bony wrists. With his black jacket and black jeans and black hair and glasses and big nose, he hovered around Jimmy and Becky like a cartoon crow.

"Don't be a pussy," Becky said.

"It's diamonds," Jimmy said. He rolled the words around the cigarette as he studied Tom's pinched face. "What's the matter with you? You look nervous. You nervous?"

"Naw, I'm not nervous, I just want things to go right," Tom said.

They crossed the top of the hill, heads down, hands in their pockets, around the curve and past George, past Arroyo. They were in the dark, with nobody around, a quarter to two o'clock in the morning, a sharp eye out for prowling cops. Jimmy had a pistol stuck in his waistband at the small of his back, and he reached back under his coat and touched it from time to time, a talisman of power. He'd never had one of those.

"Getting close," Becky said. Now she sounded nervous. They passed a streetlight, and in the pool of light, which fell on them like a mist, she said, "Stop a minute, Jimmy." She caught his arm and pulled his cigarette hand out to one side, and kissed him, and put her tongue in his mouth, and pressed her pelvis against him. He tasted like nicotine and french fries.

Jimmy said, "Baby," and stepped back, and took a drag and tipped his head into a dark side street and said, "Let's go."

They were going over to Lincoln, to a dark wood-frame house with a wide front porch and bridal wreath bushes down the sides: good cover. They'd scouted it earlier in the day, Jimmy and Becky, arm in arm down the sidewalk, Becky spitting, "Fuckin' Hogans, they think they're so hot-shit. Like, *not*."

"O'Learys," Jimmy said. "O'Learys, now."

Marsha Hogan had grown up in Shinder, out on the prairie, her father the town pharmacist. Hogan had sent his virgin daughter up to St. Kate's, the big Catholic girls' college in St. Paul, and hoped for the best. A nice Catholic boy, he hoped, from St. Thomas, who might even be a . . . pharmacist.

He succeeded beyond his wildest dreams. Marsha had met John O'Leary, a biochemistry major who had ambitions in medicine. She'd married him a week after their graduation, lived with him in dark apartments as he worked through medical school at the University of Minnesota, and then through an internship in Milwaukee. Back in Bigham, John joined a prosperous practice and Marsha bore him two daughters, Mary, named after her mother, and Agatha, named after his, and four boys, John Jr., called Jack, and James, Robin, and Franklin.

Marsha was fifty-three years old when she went back to Shinder for her thirty-fifth high school reunion. She'd been on the court of the homecoming queen, back when, and had been her homeroom representative to the student council, had organized a school-wide charity to help support the county animal-rescue program. She still had friends in Shinder, though they mostly saw her in Bigham, which was only thirteen miles away.

For the reunion dance, she wore her twenty-fifth anniversary necklace, possibly the most expensive array of diamonds ever seen in Shinder. Everybody commented on it, both approvingly to her face, and jealously behind her back. The homecoming queen, who rumor said was an alcoholic down in Des Moines, didn't show, so Marsha was the belle of the ball.

And had been served a square of chocolate sheet cake by Becky Welsh, the prettiest and hottest girl ever to come from Shinder, a girl who'd never had a diamond, or much of anything else.

Becky had seen Marsha O'Leary in a Snyders drugstore right after they hit town, had recognized her immediately, though Marsha hadn't shown a flicker of interest in Becky. She mentioned the diamonds to Jimmy, but he hadn't been interested until that night, when he showed her a gun and said, "Let's go get you them stones."

Lincoln Avenue was quiet and dark. Jimmy, Becky, and Tom sauntered along, looking far too casual for people on a midnight stroll. If a cop car had come along, they might all have died, for Jimmy had said he'd never give himself up to the law, and he meant it, which Becky felt was one of the exciting things about him. *He meant it.* No cop car came.

They slowed as they came up to the house, taking a last look around, then Jimmy said, in a whisper, "Quick now."

They crossed the lawn in single file, their feet crunching on the blades of grass that had stiffened in the night chill. They stepped between the bridal wreath bushes, now invisible to the street, took cowboy handkerchiefs from their pockets and tied them over their faces. Becky and Jimmy pulled on the same type of cheap brown cotton work gloves that Tom already wore. Jimmy took out his pocketknife and unfolded the main blade, and in the dim light from the street, he led the way down the side of the house, checking out the windows.

The windows were new, made of wood, some dark color that they couldn't make out but that still smelled faintly of the paint. The house was old, and wood, and carefully preserved with its antique hardware, because the O'Learys were that kind of people, concerned with historical preservation. At the back of the house, Jimmy stopped at a window that was a little higher than the rest, and a little smaller. The blade went deep into the crack between the window and the sill and it lifted as though greased.

Becky, surprised by the ease of it, said, "Whoa."

"I ain't to be involved in anything but diamonds and cash, and gold rings," Tom said, in a hoarse whisper that was way too loud.

"Shut the fuck up," Becky said.

"Both of you shut up," Jimmy said. "Give me a boost."

Tom made a stirrup with his hands. Jimmy disappeared through the window headfirst and found himself on a kitchen counter. The kitchen was not quite dark, with bare illumination coming from a variety of LEDs on the refrigerator, stove, clock, coffeemaker, and dishwasher and a hard-wired telephone. The granite counter was slick under the cotton gloves, but solid, and he levered himself the rest of the way through the window, to his knees, and then cautiously lowered himself to the wood floor. The kitchen smelled of stew meat; he stood in the dark for a moment, letting his eyes adjust. When he could see again, he leaned across the counter and whispered, "Back door," then made his way to the back door and unlatched it.

Becky and Tom, waiting there, followed him into the house.

Jimmy had a flashlight he'd brought from the car, but didn't need it yet, as the streetlight shone through the lacy curtains over the front windows into the dining room, and the front room on the other side of the center hall. The light threw bent shadows of armchairs across the soft thick carpet underfoot, and Becky noticed that the smell of the place had changed, from food to floor wax and fabric. The staircase going up to the bedrooms was on the other side of the front room. As they were crossing it, a grandfather clock struck two, soft gongs from a bell that shocked all three of them, Jimmy dropping into a fighter's stance, Tom and Becky freezing.

Jimmy breathed, "Shit," and Becky giggled.

Tom said, "Just the diamonds now."

Jimmy waved a hand, hushing him, and they began climbing the carpeted staircase, feeling with their feet the slightly worn area at the center of each tread. In front of the window at the landing, Jimmy took the pistol out of his belt and continued up. The pistol was an old .38 Smith & Wesson Hand Ejector, Military & Police, with a six-inch barrel, once a good gun, but now a corroded piece of shit; and the only gun they had.

Jimmy turned to the front of the house. The carpet had ended with the stairs, and he was on a wooden floor now, and it creaked under their weight as they made their way down the hall. There was a door at the end, which couldn't be anything but a bedroom, and as he came up, he saw a darker edge, and realized that the door was open just a bit.

And then he heard a female voice, in an urgent half-whisper, half-cry.

"Ag, Ag, get up. There's somebody in the house."

"You're dreaming," another voice said. "Go back to sleep."

"No, Ag, there's somebody in the house." Then, louder, "Is that you, Jack? Are you messing with us?"

Ag. That would be Agatha O'Leary.

Jimmy pushed open the bedroom door, into a rush of girl-smell, perfume and powder and clean bedclothes. He put his flash-light up, next to the barrel of his gun, clicked it on. There were two beds, side by side, a girl sitting up in one, the other still lying flat, eyes open but sleepy, now widening quickly.

"It ain't Jack," Jimmy said quietly. "You two keep your traps shut. We're only here to do a little stealing. You scream, you're dead."

"Jesus, God, please, Jack!" It was a little girl's voice, with noth-ing behind it.

"I told you, it ain't Jack. Now shut up. Are you Ag?"

Tom said, "Let's get out of here."

The larger of the two girls, the sleepy one, rose out of her bed and shouted, "Get out of here. Get . . . !"

Jimmy reached out with the flashlight and cracked her across the head, and she went down.

Mary said, "Please, please, don't hurt us." She reached toward the girl on the floor. "Oh, my God, Ag . . ."

Tom said, "It's gone wrong, let's get out of here," and he turned and ran, pounding down the hallway to the stairs.

Becky said, urgently, to Jimmy, "I hear somebody."

Jimmy said, "Shit," looked down at Ag, who'd gotten to her knees. He could have changed his mind then, and everything that came after would have been different. He hesitated, then pointed the gun at Ag's head and pulled the trigger.

The Smith flashed in the dark, Ag went down, and Jimmy ran after the others.

Tom and Becky had already gone through the front door, which stood open to the streetlight, and as Jimmy crossed the front porch he heard the other sister scream, "Mama! Mama! He killed Ag, he killed Ag."

THE THREE OF THEM ran across the lawn and across the street in the still night, another block, then across Dannon Avenue and down the hill, through the park, following a gravel track barely visible as a dark thread in the moonlight, then heard the first of the sirens, another block in another thirty seconds, across White Street, running hard, single file, into the parking lot, into the Fire-bird. Jimmy jammed the key in the ignition and turned it, and nothing happened.

Nothing at all. "Motherfucker," he groaned. The car started

about half the time. Given a few minutes, he might have gotten it started. Now, half-panicked, he said, "Come on, come on . . ."

At that moment, Emmett Williams walked out of the side door of the apartment complex and, absently whistling an unrecognizable tune, strolled down the side of the building to the street, where he'd parked his brother-in-law's Dodge Charger.

Tom said, "Somebody's coming."

Jimmy tried the ignition again. Nothing. He'd put the gun back in his pocket, but now he pulled it out again, said, "Come on."

Williams was walking away from them. He pointed the ignition key at the Charger, pushed a button, and the car's light flashed back at him; the last light he'd see. Jimmy was leading the line of runners, and he ran straight at Williams and when Williams looked up, the pistol flashed again, from six feet, and Williams went down, and Jimmy dragged him around the front of the car and dumped his body on the grass next to the sidewalk, turned toward the car, turned back, took Williams's wallet out of his back pocket. Becky piled into the passenger seat and Tom in the back. Jimmy took the wheel, and five minutes later they were headed out of town.

"Where're we going?" Becky asked.

"Get the fuck far away from here," Jimmy said. "Rest up, figure out what to do. Maybe head for LA, if we can get a car."

"That girl back there, is she hurt bad?" Tom asked.

"She's dead," Jimmy said. "She should be dead, anyway. If she ain't dead, I'll go back and shoot the bitch again."

Tom looked out the back window and said, "I think the black guy is dead too."

Jimmy said, "Yeah?" He reached out and turned on the radio, and the satellite came up, Outlaw Country, Travis Tritt singing "Modern Day Bonnie and Clyde."

"Ain't this some fuckin' car?" Jimmy asked. "Ain't this a ride?"

2

VIRGIL FLOWERS WAS STANDING under a streetlight outside the Rooster Coop in Mankato, Minnesota, at the mouth of a long cobblestone alley that led down toward a curl in the Minnesota River. He was talking to Cornelius Cooper, the proprietor of the place, about who, exactly, was the best country singer in America, at that very moment.

They agreed that while Ray Wylie Hubbard was a leading candidate, there was no question that it was not Ray Wylie but, in fact, Waylon Jennings, who wrote and sang the best song ever written, which was "Good Hearted Woman." How could you be the best country singer if you weren't responsible for the best country song?

Waylon was at a disadvantage, though, being dead.

And then there was always Willie, who was the best country singer in a lot of years when Waylon wasn't, *but at that very moment?*

Ray Wylie had been around a long time, too, long enough to

write the National Anthem—known to downtown cowboys as "Up Against the Wall, Redneck Mother." That was good, but not nearly enough to make him the best country singer, but he'd followed that up, many years later, with stuff like "Wanna Rock and Roll," and "The Messenger," and "Resurrection," and "Snake Farm," some genuine poetry, with a taste of blues and the salt of humor.

"But in fact, it is not Ray Wylie who sings 'Wanna Rock and Roll' the best," Cooper said, "but Cross Canadian Ragweed."

"That's true," Virgil said. "But what song, *right at this moment*, is as good as 'Resurrection'?"

"But he didn't write 'Resurrection.'"

Virgil said, "No, but he sings it, and he did write . . ." He broke out in a gravelly baritone imitation of Ray Wylie's "The Mission."

Cooper said, "Jesus Christ, keep it down. People will think you're drunk. And what about Guy Clark?"

Guy Clark. What could you say about "Rita Ballou" or "Homegrown Tomatoes" or "Texas 1947" or "Cold Dog Soup" or "L.A. Freeway"?

But then, what about "Sunday Morning Coming Down"? And if "Sunday Morning" was that good, right up there at the top, and the *same guy* wrote "Me and Bobby McGee," which actually was pretty good, despite being some sort of hippie shit, shouldn't Kris Kristofferson be considered? They thought about that a minute, then simultaneously said, "No," because, when everything was said and done, Kristofferson just wasn't country enough, down in his heart.

Billy Joe Shaver? Good, very good. There was a lot to be said for "Georgia on a Fast Train" and even, they agreed, "Wacko from

Waco," which testified to a certain genuineness of the lifestyle. Then there was "Old Five and Dimers Like Me," covered by the likes of Bob Dylan, backed by Eric Clapton. What about that? What could you say about the second-best country song ever?

They were still working through it, each with a Leinenkugel longneck in his right hand, and Cooper crowned with a black hundred-beaver cowboy hat from Santa Fe, New Mexico, when along came a Mankato cop named Bob Roberts, who everybody called Bob-Bob, and who said, "Hey there, Virg."

Virgil asked, "Is Ray Wylie the best living country singer?"

Bob-Bob hitched up his duty belt and said, "Well, hell. Let me think. How about . . . Emmylou Harris? Or maybe Linda Ronstadt?"

There was a moment of silence, then Virgil said to Cooper, "You miserable sexist piece of shit. You never even considered a woman."

"I'm sorry," Cooper said. "I apologize to all women. For everything."

"I don't think that's good enough," Bob-Bob said. "You'll have to come down to the station for an application of pussywhip."

Virgil, trying to smooth over the awkwardness, said, "I think we can all agree that the Texas guys write very smooth stuff."

"In other words, not tin-eared Nashville whining violin Martha White Grand Ole Opry banjo bullshit," Cooper said.

"And at this very moment, I say Ray Wylie leads the pack— nothing against the women," Virgil said. He held out his bottle, and Cooper hesitated only for a moment, then clinked his bottle against it, and they both said, "Ray Wylie." Cooper tipped his bottle up, finishing the last of the brew, and then looked down the alley and said, "See that net?"

They couldn't, because there was no net. What there was, was a hoop, with a sixty-watt bulb flickering just beyond it, where the kitchen staff shot baskets on slow nights.

"Sort of," Virgil said.

"One shot each, for five dollars."

"You got it," Virgil said.

Cornelius carefully gauged the distance—just about a free throw—then arced the bottle toward the hoop. The bottle clanged off the rim, ricocheted down the alley, and shattered on a cobblestone. "Shit," he said.

Virgil finished his beer, and Bob-Bob said, "I got two dollars says you don't even hit the rim."

Virgil said, "You got that, too," and lofted the bottle down the alley; it dropped gracefully through the hoop, the neck just ticking the steel as it went down, and then shattered on another cobblestone. "That's what you get when you go head-to-head with a natural athlete, you ignorant small-town hicks," Virgil said. "Pay me."

"I been set up," Bob-Bob said, as he dug two dollars out of his pocket. "By the way, Virgie, this BCA guy, Davenport, is trying to find you. He said you don't answer your phone, but he knows you're around here. He called at the station house and Georgina said she'd seen you down here. She sent me down to tell you to call in."

"I told you, you shouldn't have been hittin' on her," Cooper said.

"I was just being social," Virgil said. To Bob-Bob: "Did Davenport say what he wanted me for?"

"Not to me," Bob-Bob said. "But calling at this time of night . . ."

They all reflexively looked up toward the moon: it was after midnight. A call after midnight meant there'd probably been a murder somewhere. Virgil fished the cell phone out of his pocket, turned it on, found three messages from Davenport.

"Goddamnit. I got home from vacation at six o'clock, and he's already on my ass."

"You look like you're tanned," Bob-Bob said, squinting in the bad light. "You didn't get that here. Where you been?"

"Bahamas," Virgil said. "Bone fishing."

"Bahamas," Bob-Bob said with amazement, as though Virgil had said Shangri-la.

Virgil pushed the button to call Davenport, who picked up on the first ring.

"We got a bad one in Shinder," Lucas Davenport said. He sounded sleepy, and maybe bored. "You better get over there."

"I'd blow about a ten-point-three right now," Virgil said. "Can it wait until morning?"

"They're holding everything for you," Davenport said. "Get some coffee, and when you're down to a seven, take off. I'll find out where the highway patrol is, and you can dodge them. I'm putting Crime Scene on the road, soon as I can."

"Still probably three hours before I can get there," Virgil said.

"Three hours is better than anybody else we got," Davenport said. "And you know that country."

"How many dead?"

"Two. Man and a wife, named, uh, let me look . . . uh, Welsh.

Shot in their kitchen, probably last night or early this morning. The locals got nothing, except maybe their dicks in their hands."

"I'll go," Virgil said. "But I'll be a little slow."

"You know about what happened Friday night?"

"Friday night I was on Grand Bahama," Virgil said, "fishing all day, and at night, playing beach volleyball with women wearing bikini bottoms."

There was a moment of silence, then Davenport said, "I might have to kill you. It was snowing up here."

"Yeah, well, what happened Friday?"

"There was a double murder over in Bigham. I don't know if these two are connected, but they're over in the same corner of the state. Haven't been four murders, that close, in that corner, in a hundred years."

"Who caught that?"

"Ralph. But there wasn't much to do after the crime-scene crew got finished. Nobody had any idea of what happened."

"Okay. Send me what Ralph got."

"I will," Davenport said. "When you say they were wearing bikini bottoms, they were also, like, wearing the tops, right?"

"Nope, just the bottoms," Virgil said.

"Fuck me," Davenport said. "Anyway, you bring anything back home?"

"Jesus, I hope not," Virgil said.

"I meant fish," Davenport said.

"Oh. No. No, I didn't."

Cooper offered Virgil a ride home, but Bob-Bob said, doubtfully, "That don't sound like a real good idea," and Virgil said, "Thanks, anyway, Cornelius. I can use the walk."

. . .

VIRGIL LIVED THE BEST part of a mile northeast of downtown, a cool walk in early April, but he was wearing an insulated Carhartt jean jacket over a black Wolfmother T-shirt, jeans, and boots, and was comfortable enough as he ambled along through the dark. He lived in a small two-bedroom frame house with a double garage. A fishing boat was usually parked in the driveway, in this case, an almost-new fishing boat, a Ranger. The boat had been purchased with some fear and trepidation about ethics, from a friend of the governor of the state of Minnesota.

Virgil's previous boat had been blown up by a mad bomber. Virgil had crawled away from the wreckage, unhurt, by the very skin of his teeth. The governor had offered to help out by locating the Ranger, two years old, but with only thirty hours on the motor. Virgil initially declined, because he thought that the boat broker might be doing a favor for the governor, some kind of political deal, and he didn't want a part of that.

But the governor had come back to him, said he appreciated Virgil's ethical conundrum, and insisted that there was no deal, he'd only done it because he imagined that he and Virgil were friends and he felt bad about the bomb. No payback was expected or required from anyone. Virgil got a letter from the director of the BCA saying it was okay, and he bought the boat, because, the fact was:

He hungered for it.

It had been love at first sight. A Ranger Angler, red with black and gray trim, eighteen feet, six inches long with a ninety-eight-inch beam. There was a rod case under the front deck with space

for six rods, plenty of storage in the side lockers, a Minn-Kota
trolling motor on the bow, a 175 Merc on the back.

Virgil had to put up the whole insurance payment on his old
boat and motor, plus he'd financed twelve thousand dollars over
four years through the state credit union. That was cheap, he
thought, when it came to true love.

And now, as the saying went, he could pad his ass with fiber-
glass, a big change from his old aluminum boat.

VIRGIL WAS A TALL MAN, an inch or two over six feet, slender,
with blue eyes and blond hair worn long for a cop, but not too long
for farm country, where he usually worked. Like country people,
he had a tendency toward ball caps, barn jackets, and cowboy
boots, especially in the spring, when he needed to be mud-resistant.
He'd been born out on the prairie, in Marshall, Minnesota, where
he'd lettered in football, basketball, and baseball. He still looked
like a competent third baseman.

He got back to the house around twelve-thirty, clear of mind
if not fresh of breath. He patted the boat on the nose and said,
"Hey, baby," went in the house, started a pot of coffee, brushed his
teeth, threw a few days' worth of shirts, jeans, and underwear in a
satchel, along with a dopp kit. He got his pistol and a shotgun out
of the gun safe, and some ammo, took the whole pile of gear out
to his truck, a Toyota 4Runner, and packed it away. That done, he
hooked the truck up to the boat, backed the boat into the garage,
unhooked it, and locked the garage door behind himself.

Back inside the house, he poured a cup of coffee, put the rest in a thermos, sipped at the coffee, and went back to the second bedroom he used as a study and dug out his Minnesota atlas.

Shinder was a small farm town of a few hundred people, ordinary enough, as far as he knew, out on the prairie in western Minnesota. It was only thirty miles from Virgil's hometown of Marshall, and probably seventy-five or eighty from his current home in Mankato.

Though he'd been past Shinder a hundred times, he'd never stopped, because there wasn't anything to stop for. He wasn't even exactly sure what county the town was in—it was right where Yellow Medicine, Lyon, Redwood, and Bare came together. He thumbed through the atlas and found that it was just inside Bare County, five miles from the Yellow Medicine line.

Virgil said, aloud, to his empty house, "Ah, man."

Bare County was run by Sheriff Lewis Duke, known to other local sheriffs as the Duke of Hazard. He believed in Guns, Punishment, Low Taxes, and the American Constitution. If he wasn't the source of all those things—the Almighty God was—he was at least the Big Guy's representative in Bare County.

Among other things, he'd tried to set up a concentration camp on the site of an old chicken farm, complete with barracks and barbed-wire fences, for minor criminals. He believed that an actual indoor Minnesota jail was simply pampering the miscreants. He figured to rent space in the concentration camp barracks to other counties that wanted to unload expensive prisoners, and even make a profit for his Bare County constituents. The state attorney general's office, backed by a court order, stopped the concentration camp.

But no court order could stop Lewis Duke from being an asshole.

AT TEN MINUTES after one o'clock in the morning, ninety-eight percent sober, Virgil pulled out on the street and rolled away in the dark toward Shinder. His phone rang on the seat beside him, and he picked it up: Davenport, who always stayed up late.

Davenport asked, "How're you feeling?"

"Stone-cold sober, if that's what you mean," Virgil said. "I just pulled out of my house—I'm on the way."

"Good. It'd be best if you were gunned down in the line of duty, and not killed in a drunk-driving accident."

"Anyhooo . . ."

"The crime-scene truck is leaving town now," Davenport said. "They'll be an hour and a half or maybe two hours behind you. If you're going over on 14, you don't have to worry about the patrol, so you can let it roll. Watch out for town cops."

"I'll do that," Virgil said. "You think Ray Wylie Hubbard is better than Waylon Jennings?"

"I don't know, but they're both better than any of the Beatles," Davenport said. "I'm going to bed. Hesitate to call."

One good thing about a long drive in the dark, when you didn't know anything about where you were going, or what you were going to do when you got there, was that you had lots of time to think.

Virgil had for years worked a sideline as an outdoors writer, a freelancer for the diminishing number of magazines that were actually about the outdoors, as opposed to outdoors technology. He knew which brands of fishing rods he liked, and what reels, and he knew something about guns and bows and snowshoes and about boats and canoes, and not as much as he would have liked about dogs—his job made it almost impossible to keep a dog—but not much about technology.

He wasn't much interested in arguing whether a .308 was better or worse than a .30-06 on whitetail, or a Ranger a better boat than a Lund or a Tuffy, or a Mathews Solocam a better bow than a Hoyt or a PSE. He couldn't have found his own ass with a GPS. He just did what most guys did, which was talk to his friends and try a few things out. The fact was, most of the known names worked pretty well, and you got used to what you had; you could punch all the half-inch holes in paper that you liked, but the fact is, when it came to hunting, anything in the bread box would do the job.

So when he wrote, he looked for *stories* instead of technology. He usually sold them. He'd even sold a two-part crime story to *The New York Times Magazine*. Now he was stepping up. Maybe.

A few months earlier, Davenport's daughter had been shot in the arm, and he'd gone to see her in the hospital, and had seen her afterward at Davenport's home. Her name was Letty, and she had been adopted by the Davenports after her alcoholic mother was killed on a case that Lucas Davenport had worked in northwestern Minnesota.

Virgil had known that she had been a dirt-poor country girl, but he hadn't quite understood how bad it had been, and what she'd actually done to survive. One thing she'd done was wander around the countryside with a bunch of leghold traps and a .22, trapping raccoon, mink, and muskrats—mostly rats. She'd sold them to a local fur buyer for enough money to keep the family's head above water. Had done this when she was ten years old . . .

He'd gotten pieces of the story when she was recovering from the wound, and somewhere along the line, it occurred to him that it was a terrific story. Here was what appeared to be a stylish young high-school girl, who'd shot a cop—the same crooked cop—on two different occasions, and recently survived a shoot-out with two Mexican narcos, leaving the narcos dead. He talked to Davenport about it, and then Letty, and wound up doing five long interviews, on five consecutive weekends, during the fall, as well as some research up in the Red River Valley.

He'd spent the next two months writing a girl's short memoir of a nightmarish rural life—though she hadn't at the time thought it particularly nightmarish, it just *was*—and sent it off to *The New York Times Magazine*, to the editor who'd bought his earlier pieces.

The editor had gotten right back and said that while the *Times* wouldn't buy it—it was simply too long—he'd sent it to a friend over at *Vanity Fair*, and they were definitely interested.

The problem was, *Vanity Fair* wanted to send Annie Leibovitz out to the Red River Valley with a ton of photo equipment to shoot Letty and Lucas Davenport, as part of a major editorial package. Both Letty and Davenport had the faces for it, and Letty loved the idea of meeting Leibovitz, who was one of her media heroines, but the Davenports had gotten their knickers in a psychological twist about what the attention would do to their daughter, about the whole gestalt of *Vanity Fair*, about how Letty had already had way too much attention from the press, and blah blah blah . . .

That all had to be worked through. Virgil didn't want to piss anybody off, and the Davenports were good friends of his, but he really wanted the piece in *Vanity Fair*. *Really* wanted it. Maybe not as much as he'd wanted the Ranger, but it was like that, the same order of magnitude: about an 8.4 on the Richter scale.

Something else. He suspected that *Vanity Fair* liked the idea of having a gun-toting shit-kicking cop as a roving reporter. If he could nail down that job . . .

DURING THE DRIVE OUT to Shinder, he considered a half dozen calming approaches he might take with the Davenports; he thought he might point out that all of the stories about Letty had been sensationalized TV trash, while his work was a sensitive re-telling of the girl's actual history. . . .

And when he was done thinking about the Davenports, he thought a bit about God, and whether He might be some kind of universal digital computer, subject to the occasional bug or hack. Was it possible that politicians and hedge-fund operators were some kind of garbled cosmic computer code? That the Opponent, instead of having horns and a forked tail, was a fat bearded guy drinking Big Gulps and eating anchovy pizzas and writing viruses down in a hellish basement? That prayers weren't answered be-cause Satan was running denial-of-service attacks?

HE WAS STILL THINKING about that when he came up to Shin-der, running fast, and west, on State Highway 68. The Welshes, if that was actually the victims' name, lived in the northeast part of town. Virgil knew that because he could see, across the barren, yet-to-be-planted prairie, a cluster of cars with their lights on, gathered around a house, and a bunch of houses with their lights on, all on the northeast corner of town.

He came to the intersection leading into town, turned north, rolled past a roadhouse and a gas station, and a line of grain elevators that went off at a diagonal to the northwest. He was on April Street, and took it north across Apple, Cherry, Peach, Pear, and Plum, to Main, where he took a right, crossed May, June, July, and August, turned left, and crossed Aspen, Birch, Cedar, Elm, Maple, and Oak toward the pool of light, realizing, as he did so, that the east-west streets south of Main were named after fruits, and alphabetized, and the east-west streets north of Main were named after trees, and alphabetized.

At the same time, the north-south streets were named after the months, apparently starting from the west edge of town and marching east. That meant that if a parent were told her kid was acting up at the corner of Pear and April, she would have an instant appreciation of the kid's precise location. What would happen if the town built more than twelve north-south streets, Virgil couldn't guess. In any case, it all seemed a little anal, even for Minnesota.

THE STREET LEADING up to the crime scene was closed off by cop cars. Virgil parked, put on a baseball cap, because it was chilly, and climbed out of the truck. He was in what he thought must be the workingman's corner of town—small white prewar clapboard houses, some of them crumbling badly, most of them with small front porches, most with one-car garages converted to rooms, with larger, newer, metal-sided garages in back. The neighbors were out sitting on the porches, wrapped in blankets or wearing their winter coats, watching. Some had brought out aluminum lawn furniture, including one recliner.

The cops had set up work lights to illuminate the house, and Virgil could see a half dozen people walking the lawn, like soldiers policing up cigarette butts. *Looking for evidence,* he thought. A young deputy walked toward him, thumbs hooked on a duty belt, and as Virgil came up, he called, "This is off-limits . . . who are you?"

"Virgil Flowers. I'm with the BCA."

The cop looked him over: Virgil hadn't changed clothes and was still in the jean jacket, open over the band T-shirt, jeans, and the cowboy boots. "You got any ID?"

Virgil had seen the sheriff, Lewis Duke, come out on the porch of the death house, and he said, "Sure," and waved his arms in the air and shouted at the sheriff, "Hey, Lewis—it's me, Virgil."

The cop turned and saw the sheriff, an annoyed look crossing his face, wave Virgil over. The cop said, "So you're a wiseass."

Virgil said, "Maybe."

"Don't much care for wiseasses in Bare County," the deputy said, as Virgil walked past him.

Virgil said, "Like I could really give a shit." He himself didn't much care for officious pricks.

. . .

LEWIS DUKE WAS A SHORT, barrel-chested man who looked like he spent his spare time doing bench presses. He had a square, dry prairie face, thinning sandy hair, a short nose under glassy blue eyes, and a brush-cut mustache. He wore the same uniform his men did, but with five stars on the collar, and a Glock in a military-style thigh-mounted holster. He nodded at Virgil and said, "Agent Flowers."

Virgil said, "Sheriff. I've been told you've got a bad one. Actually, I've heard you had two bad ones."

"That's correct," Duke said. "The first one was worse—they were good folks. This whole family was white trash, but still, pretty gol-darned unpleasant."

"Let's take a look," Virgil said.

"This way."

Virgil followed Duke inside, along a path through the narrow living room demarked by two lines of blue masking tape. Duke said, "We put down the tape to keep people from wandering off into other parts of the house. We cleared it, of course, but nobody's been in the rest of the house since then. We're hoping your crime-scene specialists can pick up some DNA."

"Smart," Virgil said. Never hurt to flatter a sheriff, for those who needed it. The inside of the house was a reflection of the outside: poorly kept except for a gigantic LG television that sat against the only wall big enough to take it, with a couple of green La-Z-Boy imitations facing it. A green plastic bowl sat between the chairs, as though it might have contained popcorn; the house didn't smell like popcorn, but like years of bacon grease and nicotine.

Duke led the way to the kitchen. A fat man in a white T-shirt lay on the kitchen floor, looking up at the ceiling—eyes wide open—with a big bloody splotch in the center of his chest. A broken coffee cup lay on the floor beside him, with a damp brown splatter stain on the floor that probably had been coffee, but might have been something like apple cider. A woman lay in a doorway leading through what looked like a mudroom. She may have been running for the back door, but had been shot before she got there. She was facedown.

"Who found them?" Virgil asked.

"Neighbor lady. She'd been trying to talk to Miz Welsh all day, about changing shifts at the nursing home," Duke said. "She walked over and knocked on the back door, about the fifth time she'd done it, and then peeked inside and saw Miz Welsh layin' on the floor. She called us."

"I'll need to talk to her," Virgil said.

"Sure. But she doesn't have much to say."

Virgil squatted next to each body, one at a time, and looked at them closely. The woman gave him nothing, but the man's dark pants showed a flash of white against the floor. Virgil got his nose right down on the kitchen linoleum and saw that it was an inside-out back pocket. When he stood up, he found Duke and a deputy staring at him, as if he was about to pull a rabbit out of a hat.

"Have your guys figured out when this might have happened?" Virgil asked.

Duke said, "Well, George, there, was seen walking out of the

Surprise market between nine and ten o'clock last night. Uh, Friday night. We haven't been able to find anybody who saw him today. I mean, Saturday."

"You know what he bought at the Surprise?"

Duke looked at the deputy, who said, "Well, no, I guess we didn't ask that."

The deputy was wearing plastic evidence gloves and Virgil asked, "You got any more of those? The gloves?"

"Yeah . . . don't you?"

"In my truck. I'd rather not go back, if you've got some handy," Virgil said. Another prick; it always had something to do with the training.

The deputy glanced at Duke, who nodded, and the deputy said, "Two seconds." He left, and Duke said to Virgil, "Haven't seen much of you."

"I've been busy back east. Besides, do you really want to see the likes of me?"

"Maybe not," Duke conceded. "Not when it's on this kind of business."

They looked at the bodies for a few seconds, then the deputy was back and handed Virgil a pair of yellow plastic gloves. Virgil pulled them on, and stepped over to the kitchen sink and pulled open the cupboard beneath it. A trash can was there, and he pulled it partway out, found a plastic grocery bag near the bottom of the can, under a bunch of empty beer cans. He opened the bag, found a receipt from the Surprise with a time stamp that said 8:45 PM. It also said that $10.25 had been charged on a Visa card with a number ending in 4508 for a twelve-pack of Miller High Life.

"He bought the beer at eight forty-five," Virgil said. He tipped the trash can back and forth a few times, digging around, found five Millers, plus three empty Bud Lights.

"Huh," he said. He stood up, stepped to the refrigerator and pulled open the door, expecting to see the rest of the Millers. No beer. He said to Duke, "No beer."

Duke asked, "What does that mean?"

"I don't know. Maybe the killers took it with them." He looked around for a few more seconds, then peeled off the gloves and said, "So, you said this family was trashy?"

"That's what I've been told. Darrell here covers this area."

Darrell, the deputy with the evidence gloves, said, "George never managed to hold a job for long. I guess Ann was down at the nursing home for quite some time now. George has anger issues, argues with the neighbors, doesn't keep the place up. That sort of thing. You think that's important?"

"What about kids, or in-laws?"

"Got a daughter, named Rebecca, she's up in the Cities, as far as anyone knows. That's the last we heard. Haven't tried to get in touch with her yet, but we're looking around for a contact."

"Mmmm." Virgil took another quick look around, then said, "I'll tell you, Lewis, it feels like a domestic to me. This George guy bought a bunch of beer Friday night, and he and the old lady—or somebody—drank five cans of it, and maybe three more Buds. He's wearing a T-shirt, and it's been pretty cold out. He shaves, because I can see a little shaving nick under his ear, healing up, day or two old, but he's not shaven here. Ann is wearing slippers. That all makes me think they'd been up late drinking Friday night, probably watching TV, got up Saturday morning and hadn't been up long. They were killed early in the morning, while they were having coffee, before George had a chance to shave or Ann got completely dressed. No sign of a break-in, or anything. And if you were a robber, would you pick this place?"

Duke looked around and shook his head. "I guess not."

"Whoever did it, took George's wallet, I think. We'll have the crime-scene guys check around for Ann's purse, but I'll bet it's either gone, or the money's gone. It looks to me like somebody came here, somebody they knew, but who might have been unwelcome. They have an argument, and boom. Whoever it was needed money, because they took the time to rob the bodies, even though they couldn't have had much cash—I mean, George charged a twelve-pack on his Visa card."

"So . . . an argument about money, with somebody that they knew," Duke said.

"Feels that way to me," Virgil said. "Somebody who might have expected to get some money. I think we've got to take a real quick look at this daughter . . . though, mmm, I'm not sure a daughter would have brought a gun in, to kill her parents. That doesn't feel quite right."

"We've got the names of a couple of her friends. We can find out where she is," the deputy said.

"If she's in the Cities, I'll have somebody run over and talk to her," Virgil said. "At the same time, we need to look at other possibilities. Friends, other relatives. People George has been hanging out with."

"We can do that," Duke said.

"I talked to the neighbors," Darrell said. "I don't think he had much in the way of friends. I can check out Ann, down at the nursing home."

"Not much more we can do tonight, though," Virgil said to Duke. "I'll want to talk to the woman who found them. Have some of your people close the place up until Crime Scene gets here. They're on the way, should be here in a couple of hours."

Duke nodded and said, "I'll take you over to the neighbor lady's. The one who found them."

THE NEIGHBOR LADY was named Margery Garfield, and she didn't know anything. She'd wanted to talk to Ann Welsh about trading shifts at the nursing home the next Monday night, so she could go to parent-teacher night at the school, and had been trying to find Welsh all day. "I seen their car was still in the garage, but I never did see them. I was knocking on the front door, and I felt something funny might be going on, so I went around to the back, and peeked through the glass, and I could see Ann on the floor. I didn't know it was a body, at first, but then, my eyes got adjusted, and I was pretty sure it was a body, so I ran back home and called the sheriff."

"You didn't touch anything?" Virgil asked.

She shook her head. "I never went inside. I did put my hand on the window glass, trying to see in better."

He talked to her a few more minutes, and finally ran out of ground; and she asked, "I suppose Crime Scene will be coming around?"

"Pretty soon," Virgil said.

"They oughta be able to figure it out," she said.

. . .

VIRGIL AND DUKE said good-bye, and they went outside and Duke asked, "You get annoyed by that? The Crime Scene thing?"

"No. People watch TV. No way to stop that," Virgil said.

"It'd get under my skin, after a while," Duke said. "So, you're going to stick around?"

Virgil nodded. "Sure. I'll run over to the Ramada in Marshall. I'll call back to the Cities tomorrow morning and see if I can get somebody to look for the daughter. I'll give you my cell phone number, if you come up with anything overnight. Main thing is, we get the scene processed. But we won't get much going at four o'clock on Sunday morning."

Duke said: "Okay. I'm heading home. I'll have my men seal up this place. I'll be going to church in the morning, and I'll be back here right after."

"I'm planning to do that myself," Virgil said. "The worship service starts at eight o'clock. I'll be out here by nine-thirty or so."

Duke tipped his head: "Little surprised to hear you're church-going, Virgil, but I certainly approve. I'll see you at nine-thirty, unless something breaks."

3

VIRGIL CHECKED INTO the Ramada across the street from Southwest Minnesota State University at a little after four o'clock in the morning, set the alarm for six-thirty, and was asleep as soon as he lay down. He'd slept on the plane from Miami to Minneapolis Saturday morning, had taken a nap after he got home on Saturday afternoon, and was still young enough that he could deal with a day on two hours of sleep.

Although, when the alarm woke him up in what seemed like an instant after he went to sleep, he would, he expected, be fairly cranky by early afternoon.

He sat on the bed for a minute, getting oriented, then picked up his cell phone and punched the menu item for "home." His mother never slept past six o'clock on any one day in her life, and at that moment, he thought, would be looking into the kitchen cupboard and calculating how many pancakes to make that morning.

She answered immediately, an edge of horror in her voice. "Virgil: What happened?"

"Nothing happened, Ma, except some people got killed over in Shinder and I'm looking at them. Right now, I'm here in town, at the Ramada, and I thought I'd run over and get some pancakes if it's not too much goddamn trouble to expect that from your mother."

She was delighted: "Get over here, Virgil. Your father's already up and raving in the study."

"I gotta take a shower. I'll see you in a half hour."

RAVING IN THE STUDY—the old man was practicing his sermon. Feeling more awake, Virgil cleaned up and got dressed, and headed into a sunshiny morning that felt like it might even get warm later in the day. It didn't, but it felt that way.

Virgil's father was the lead pastor of the largest Lutheran congregation in Marshall, a town with several species of Lutheran. Virgil had grown up in a redbrick house across the street from the church, and had gone to church services every Sunday and Wednesday of his life, until he went to the University of Minnesota. He'd since given up churchgoing, but not some fundamental belief in the Great Architect.

When Virgil pulled into the driveway, he was ambushed by his father, who'd been waiting by the back door, and who said, "I've been thinking a lot about the relationship between the Israelis and the Palestinians. . . ."

His father was a tall man, also slender, like Virgil, with graying hair and round steel-rimmed spectacles. He'd played basketball at Luther College, down in Iowa, before going to the seminary. He

clutched in one hand the printout of his sermon; he'd been a pop-
ular man all of his life, and a kind of sneaky kingmaker in local
politics.

Virgil said, "Uh-oh."

"I immediately thought of Genesis 16:11 and 12, 'You shall
name him Ishmael . . .'"

Virgil continued it: "'. . . for the Lord has heard of your misery.
He will be a wild donkey of a man; his hand will be against everyone and everyone's hand against him. And he will live in hostility
toward all his brothers.'"

His father blinked and said, "I knew if I beat it into your head
long enough, it'd stick."

Virgil said, "Where's Mom? . . . And yeah, some of it did stick."

His father said, "In the kitchen. You know Ishmael is considered the father of the Arabs."

"I know that you'll be up to your holy ass in alligators if you
go telling people that the Arabs deserve what they're getting because the Bible says so," Virgil said.

His father followed him into the kitchen, saying, "That
wouldn't be the point, not at all. I'd never say that."

THEY SAT IN THE KITCHEN and ate pancakes and his father raved
and his mother chipped in with news of various high school
friends, and they both behaved as though they hadn't seen him for
years, when, in fact, he'd been there only a month earlier.

His mother inquired about any new wives, a friendly jab, and
he denied any new close acquaintances, and his father said, "But

you have to admit, it is passing strange that something that was written three thousand years ago seems to have such a relevance for today's world."

Watching them bustle around each other in the tight little kitchen, sixtyish and very comfortable, Virgil remembered the time when he was seventeen and the folks had a little dinner party, three other couples plus Virgil. One of the couples was Darrin and Marcia Wanger. Darrin was president of a local bank, a tall, broad-shouldered man with an engaging smile. Virgil remembered how he had caught his mother and Darrin Wanger touching each other with their eyes, and how he thought then, *My God, they're sleeping together.*

Old times in the rectory . . . And who knows, maybe he was wrong.

But even thinking about it now, he thought not. His mother said, "You put so little syrup on those pancakes that it got sucked right down inside. Take some more syrup."

THEN IT WAS the best part of an hour in church, Virgil sitting in the back; but twenty people, mostly older, stopped to say hello to him, and touch him on the shoulder. Good folks. His father did his rave, and it all seemed well-reasoned and kind.

At nine o'clock, he was on his way back to Shinder. Duke was just coming into town and Virgil turned in behind him and followed him down to the Welsh house. They got out of their trucks at the same time, and Duke nodded at Virgil and asked, "How was church?"

"Fine. My old man did his sermon from Genesis 11 and 12, and moved on to the Palestinians and the Israelis. . . ." Virgil gave him a one-minute version, and Duke, though an asshole, proved a good listener, and when Virgil finished, he said, "Sounds like your father is a smart man."

"He is," Virgil said. The crime-scene van was parked in the swale in front of the Welsh house, and Virgil asked, "You know what time they got here?"

"About three hours ago . . . around six o'clock," Duke said.

He and Virgil went inside, where Beatrice Sawyer was working over George Welsh's body. Sawyer was a middle-aged woman, more cheerful than she should be, given her job, and a little too heavy. She had bureaucrat-cut blond hair, went without makeup, and was wearing a lime-colored sweatshirt and blue jeans and boots. She saw Virgil and said, "Well, this one's dead."

"Thanks," Virgil said. "He was dead last night, too. Are you going to get anything off them?"

"Too early to tell, but I doubt that it'll be anything conclusive if it's a domestic. He was shot from eight to ten feet away, judging from the powder traces—there is some, but not much. The shooter was standing where you are, these two were standing where they fell. We'll recover both slugs, and they should be in reasonable shape—not hollow points, they look to be solids. We'll be able to identify the gun, if you come up with it. There were no shells around, and I won't know for sure until we pull the slugs, but it was probably a revolver."

"If you get DNA, why won't it be conclusive?" Duke asked.

"Because if it's a domestic, there's a lot of reasons for the shooter's DNA to be all over the place," Sawyer explained. "There doesn't appear to have been a struggle—no defensive or offensive marks on George's hands or arms, which means that the killer didn't close with him. Shot him from a distance."

"But you might get some DNA that would narrow it down," Duke said.

"Possibly," Sawyer said. "But juries don't usually convict on the outside chance that somebody committed a murder."

"They do if I tell them to," Duke said. He didn't smile.

Another man, wearing a surgeon's mask and yellow gloves, came in from the back and said, "Hey-ya, Virgie."

"Hey, Don." Don Baldwin was a tall, thin man with a sharp nose who wore heavy black-plastic fashion glasses because he played in a punk-revival band on his nights off. Like Sawyer, he was wearing a sweatshirt and blue jeans. "What're you doing back there?"

"Looked like somebody might have slept in the back bedroom. We're working it," he said.

Virgil said, "Um," and then, "You look at their car?"

"Yeah, we'll process it. . . . I won't say that I expect much from it."

"All right," Virgil said. He turned to Duke and said, "Let's run down the daughter. I need to talk to her friends."

"Darrell's got the names."

AS IT TURNED OUT, Rebecca Welsh didn't have many friends. The Bare County deputies had come up with three names from high school, and only two still lived in the county. Nobody, including her parents, knew exactly where the third one was, but one of the deputies said he'd been told she was hooking out in Williston, North Dakota, among the oil crews.

Of the other two, Virgil spoke first to Carly Redecke, a short, dark-haired, dark-eyed girl whom he found working at the same store where George Welsh had bought his last beer. Though she wasn't exactly working when he found her: she was in the back room, sitting on a couple of beer cases, smoking a cigarette.

"I haven't heard from her since last summer," Redecke said of Welsh. "She had a place somewhere up in the Cities and was doing night restocking at a Home Depot."

"Do you have a phone number for her?"

"Yes, but she doesn't have that number anymore," Redecke said. "I called it at Christmas, and I got one of those messages that the phone had been disconnected. But I still got it, if you want it."

Virgil made a note of the number, asked her if she knew anyone who might know better where Welsh would be.

"There's a bunch of old Shinder people up in the Cities—I was up there myself for a while, but it scared me, so I came back. I'm thinking of trying over in Sioux Falls. There's nothing here."

"Of the old Shinder people, was she hanging with anyone in particular?"

"Wooo . . . you might try calling Mickey Berenson. She keeps track of everybody. I got her number, I think it's still good."

Redecke didn't have much more, other than to say that Welsh was "the hottest girl ever to come out of this place. She could be like a movie star."

On his way over to see the second woman, he called Mickey
Berenson, who was sleeping when he called. He explained the situation, and said, ". . . so we're trying to get in touch with her."

"Oh, jeez, I haven't seen her in a long time. You know, she was
hanging out with Jimmy Sharp. He's from Shinder, too, he was
two grades ahead of us. I think they were getting serious."

She didn't have Sharp's number, either, but said Sharp's father
lived in Shinder, and might know where his son was, and maybe
Becky, too. Virgil thanked her, and went on to Caroline O'Meara's
house, and found her loading sacks of used clothing into the bed
of a Toyota Tacoma. She and her mother, O'Meara said, were on
their way to a flea market, and were already running late. "I talked
to Becky, mmm, last fall, I think, about Halloween. She was back
with Jimmy Sharp, they were cruising around town in Jimmy's
dorkmobile."

"And that would be . . ."

"A black Pontiac Firebird, about a hundred years old. Like he
was king shit, or something. My boyfriend said he'd be lucky to
get it back to the Cities before the tranny fell on the ground."

"You sound like you don't care for him," Virgil suggested.

"Well, he's an asshole. Ask anyone. He was the biggest bully
the whole time I was in school," she said.

"You know where he works?"

"No. I doubt that he works. Might sell a little pot or something. He had a job down at the Surprise for a while."

"I was just there."

"Yeah," she said. "You come to Shinder, you wind up at the
Surprise. If you live here, you wind up working there, sooner or

later. Jimmy got fired after he got in a fight with Larry Panero. Larry wouldn't hurt a fly, but Jimmy got on him and never quit."

"Huh. Where could I find Jimmy's father?"

SHARP'S FATHER LIVED in an old wind-burned farmhouse at the far northwest corner of town. O'Meara had told him to look for the only red-painted place at the end of January Street, with a dirt track leading up to the side of the house: "Mean old redneck, is what he is." A broken-down garage sat at the end of the track.

Virgil pulled into the dooryard and got out. There'd been a little breeze, early, but that had gone, and the place was dead silent—so silent that he paused, just to listen, and heard nothing at all. The nearest neighboring house was probably two hundred yards away, with an old car parked in front of it, but there was no movement there, either.

Virgil paid attention to the general vibe, then stepped back to the car, climbed inside, got his gun, and slipped it into his back waistband, under his jacket. Bad feeling. He went to the back stoop, knocked, got no response, knocked louder. Still no response. He backed off and looked toward the garage, with its antique side-folding doors. The doors were partly open, and after another look around, he went that way.

The car inside the garage was a newer Dodge Charger, with current Missouri plates. There was nobody around the garage, and he turned to walk away when he noticed the bumper stickers. One side featured an oval Thizz Hands sticker, and the other a sticker that said, "Free Li'l Boosie." Li'l Boosie, Virgil believed, was currently spending his days in the Louisiana State Pen for issues involving guns and drugs; and, judging from the house, he thought it exceedingly unlikely that Old Man Sharp—he didn't know the old man's first name—was a big gangsta rap fan.

Which made the car, in the eyes of a perceptive law enforcement official, something of an anomaly. Virgil noted the car's tag number, went back to his truck, called the number into the BCA duty officer, and told him to run it.

After a moment, the duty officer asked, "Uh, where are you, Virgil?"

"In Shinder. Minnesota. Out west," Virgil said.

"Where's this car?"

"Sitting in a garage out here," Virgil said. "I'm looking at it."

"You got your gun with you?"

"Yeah. What's up, Dave?"

"The thing is, people are looking all over for that car," the duty officer said. "A guy was apparently murdered for it in Bigham, night before last. The same people probably murdered a young girl just a couple blocks away from there, about five minutes before that. . . . I mean, you need some backup, man, or get the hell out of there."

Virgil got the details, and said, "I'll check with you later."

He looked at the house: still dead quiet. He thought about it, then called Davenport, who said, without first saying hello, "You're about to fuck up a perfectly good Sunday morning, aren't you?"

"You know those murders in Bigham Friday night?" Virgil asked.

"Just what I heard around the office, when Ralph came back. Why?"

"Apparently the killers stole a car from one of the victims," Virgil said. "So, I was out here looking at these two dead people, and tried to track down their daughter to see if she might know something. To cut the story short, I'm looking at that car. So now, we have four dead. We might have a spree."

"Ah, shit," Davenport said. "Who've you told?"

"You and Dave Jennings," Virgil said. "I gotta tell Duke, but, uh, you might want to talk to the patrol guys and get the early warning system going."

"All right. You talk to Duke, I'll start jackin' people up. Who're we looking for?"

"Right now, I'd like to talk to a Jimmy Sharp and a Rebecca Welsh, who were both living somewhere there in the Cities. That's about all the detail I've got, but I will get back to you with more."

"Do you think Sharp and Welsh . . . ?"

"I don't know, but it's a possibility."

"Quick as you can," Davenport said. "If it's a spree, we gotta move."

VIRGIL GOT ON THE PHONE to Duke, told him where he was, told him what had happened, and asked him to come over with some deputies. "There's nothing moving here now, but that could change," Virgil said.

Duke said, "I'm activating the SWAT. And me'n a couple other men'll be there in four minutes. You hang tight."

Not like he had some other goddamn pressing thing to do, Virgil thought, looking up at the weathered old house.

FOUR MINUTES IN THE CITIES and New York and Chicago and LA were different from four minutes in Shinder, where four minutes was quite literal: you could drive from one end of town to the other in four minutes, with a choice of routes, in a place where two cars in the same block was a traffic jam.

Fifteen seconds after Virgil got off the phone with Duke, the sirens started, rapidly got louder, and four minutes after they talked, a shoal of sheriff's cars piled into old man Sharp's farm-yard. Duke was alone in the lead car; he got out, walked around to the trunk, popped it open and took out an M16 and a magazine, and snapped the magazine into place.

He said to Virgil, "I'm good."

Fifteen seconds later, Virgil was surrounded by six deputies and Duke. He pointed toward the garage. "We've got two dead at the Welsh house, two dead in Bigham, and the stolen car here. I think that's enough to go into the house without a warrant—somebody could be dying inside. So. One of you guys come with me, and the rest of you post around the house in case we get a runner. Don't shoot unless it's in self-defense. We really need to talk to somebody."

Duke said, "I'll be going in with you, and John Largas, he'll come, too." He nodded at an older deputy. "The rest of you take the corners of the house."

Virgil looked around: there was a woodlot a hundred yards or so behind the house, and some scrubby lilacs along the drive, but no real cover other than the garage. He said, "Somebody can post up beside the garage, but you guys on the other side, stay close to the house. I mean, get your backs right against it. You don't want to be standing out in the middle of the yard where somebody could shoot you down before you know it. All these places got deer rifles and shotguns. Okay? Everybody understand?"

They all nodded, and the group broke up, the deputies pulling their pistols, and Virgil led Duke and Largas to the back door. Virgil pounded on it for fifteen seconds, shouting, "Police. Open up. Open up."

Duke said, "Kick it," but Virgil didn't. Instead, he reached out and turned the knob, and pushed the door open. They were looking at a mudroom, a half dozen ragged coats hanging from pegs, maybe fifteen ball caps moldering on a shelf, and four or five pairs of worn shoes and boots under a bench. Two beat-up umbrellas sagged in one corner, with an old single-shot .22 rifle with a rusty barrel. The place smelled like dirt and sweat.

Another closed door led into the kitchen; the door had a glass window in it, and Virgil looked through.

"Got a dead guy," he said. Duke looked through the glass, and Virgil said, "Through the far door. You can see a shoe with a foot in it. He's dead, unless he picked that spot to take a nap."

Duke said, "I'm afraid to touch the doorknob."

"Got to go in, in case he *isn't* quite dead." Virgil put his hand flat on the face of the knob, so he wouldn't touch the parts that would have fingerprints, and turned it, and the door popped open. They stepped through the kitchen in a straight line, Duke leading

with the M16; Virgil was not inclined to walk into a possible gun-
fight in front of a man with a machine gun. But the house was
quiet. From the far door, to the living room, they could see the
body—a middle-aged man with a five- or six-day beard, in a long-
sleeved woolen undershirt and jeans, lying flat on his back with a
bullet hole in his forehead.

Largas, behind Virgil, said, "That's five. Good God almighty."

4

THEY CLEARED THE HOUSE, then Virgil told Duke, "We need to round up everybody in town who knew Rebecca Welsh and James Sharp, get them in one place so we can brainstorm with them. We need to figure out where Welsh and Sharp are, right now."

Duke nodded, turned to a deputy, said, "Get those two girls we talked to, get them to name everybody who knows these people. We'll meet up at the elementary school. . . ." He looked at his watch. "At eleven o'clock sharp. Get Don Watson to open the place up."

The deputy left, and Duke asked Virgil, "What else?"

"The neighbor's house down the road has a car outside, but I didn't see anybody there. We ought to check all the neighbors, make sure folks are okay."

Duke said, "I'll get that going. What are *you* going to do?"

"I'll call the crime-scene people, get them over here, talk to the DMV and find out what James Sharp, the old man, drives, and get people looking at it." He thought for a second, then said, "Then

I'm going to call my boss. . . . And listen, I need everything you've got on those Friday murders in Bigham. Who's working that?"

"Ross Price, he's our investigator. I'll hook you up with him."

VIRGIL STARTED with the DMV—James Sharp Senior drove a ten-year-old, extended-cab, silver Chevy pickup—and then called Davenport. "Jimmy Sharp and Rebecca Welsh hung with a bunch of people in the Cities. I've got one name you could call to find out exactly who that might be . . . who else they know. I already spoke to her this morning, so she's familiar with the situation."

"You're sure it's Welsh and Sharp?" Davenport asked.

"It's better than fifty-fifty. Sharp's got a bad rep here in town as a bully who might sell a little dope. Welsh is his girlfriend. If you actually spot them up there, look to see if they might be driving his old man's Chevy truck. I think the killers have it, whoever they are. Welsh's folks' car is still in their garage."

"What's your next move?"

"We're having a séance over at the elementary school with everyone who knew Welsh and Sharp. If they're running, I need to know which way they're going."

"Good luck with that," Davenport said. "I'll get things going here. Stay in touch."

VIRGIL DOWNLOADED Jimmy Sharp's and Becky Welsh's driver's license photos to his cell phone, and spent a few minutes looking at them. Jimmy was a kid who a lot of people would have said was handsome—he had the cheekbones and the squared-off chin, but there was something about the cast of his features that wasn't quite right: he looked sneaky. Becky should have been pretty: blond, small nose, big eyes, but there was a disappointment about her face—a disappointment with life—that made her look sad, and a little too hard.

But then, he thought, maybe makeup could fix it.

THE GATHERING AT Gerald Ford Elementary School brought in about thirty townspeople, who were sitting on metal folding chairs, talking quietly among themselves, when Virgil arrived. Virgil had told Duke about the silver pickup, and Duke had called back to his office and had an alert broadcast through the local sheriffs' association, which covered eight counties in the western part of the state.

Virgil was wearing the black sport coat and collared shirt he'd worn to church, which passed for fairly sober wear in a country town. He smiled at the crowd when he came in, with Duke trailing behind, and picked up a folded chair, shook it open, and planted it in front of the group.

He introduced himself, and Duke, and said, "Y'all may have heard what's going on, here. We're trying to find Jimmy Sharp and Becky Welsh. I can tell you that Mr. and Mrs. Welsh and the senior Mr. Sharp were all found shot to death. We haven't been able to find Jimmy or Becky. We don't know whether they were involved in the shootings, or if they might be victims, or maybe they don't even know about them. Anyway, we need to find them, and since you all know one of them, or both of them, we were hoping you could throw out some ideas about where they might be, or might be going, or who we might contact to find that out."

A square-faced man with straw-colored hair raised a hand and asked, "Isn't it a little . . . abnormal . . . to be talking to everybody at once like this?"

Virgil said, "This is an abnormal situation. We were hoping that if you folks listen to each other, and mix it up a little, we'll spark off some ideas. We're brainstorming."

A woman off to one side muttered, "I don't know nothing about this."

Virgil said, "Look, what kind of a kid was Jim? When you knew him? Who knew him best?"

Everyone looked around, and eventually most of them focused on a young man who stirred nervously and then said, "We used to hang out, some. Not like we were good friends."

Virgil: "Was he a good kid, bad kid, middle-of-the-road?"

The young man said, "He was . . . okay . . . most of the time."

Somebody snorted, then an older man said, "Oh, horseshit."

That got them going.

JIMMY SHARP was a thin young man of average height, with long black hair and what one man said was "a joker's face, like the joker on a playing card." That seemed mostly to mean Sharp's smile, which often formed itself into a sneer, usually with a cigarette hanging from his bottom lip.

A man named Ralph, who identified himself as one of Sharp's teachers through sixth grade, said that he'd begun bullying other children in third or fourth grade, after he'd been held back the first time. "He was one of those kids who just started getting his hormones early, and probably got whacked around by his father, and he never got along with books, and that all turned him into a little punk. His mother, whose name was Jolene, if I'm not mistaken, took off from here about that time, and hasn't been back, as far as I know."

The crowd agreed that she hadn't been back, and that she was an O'Hara, and the whole family was gone now since Bernice died. None of them had ever come back, and Jimmy had no other relatives around.

"He used to hang out at the Surprise. Butch thinks he was stealing from there, but never caught him. He wasn't smart in school, but he could be clever when he wanted to be," Harvey said.

"What'd he steal?" Duke asked.

"Ask Butch."

"I hate to accuse somebody," said an old man in an old blue suit, with a thin, prairie-dried face.

"You Butch?" Virgil asked.

"Yeah. Kids would come in, you know, steal candy, try to steal cigarettes or comic books, or get me looking one way, and steal a *Penthouse* from under the counter. I'd catch them, and call up their parents, and that'd end that. But Jimmy . . . I never caught him because I think he was stealing *food*," Butch said. "He'd hang around outside until I went to get something for somebody, and then he'd slip into the store and stick something in his pants, then go on over and look at the magazines and comics. I wouldn't see him until he was right there, and I'd be watching him like a hawk, and he'd never take anything. But I think he was stealing. And I think he was stealing stuff like Dinty Moore stew. It seemed like I'd never sell that stuff, I'd never see it coming across the counter, but at the end of the month, it'd pretty much be gone."

"But you hired him to work there . . ."

"Yeah, against my better judgment. He got out of school and couldn't catch on with anybody—not even the army wanted him—so finally I gave him a job," Butch said. "He lasted about a month. He kept bumping heads with the other kids, and I had to let him go. I won't tell you what he called me when I gave him the news."

"You afraid of him?" Duke asked.

"No, not exactly. I never felt like he'd come after me, but I did think that there might have been a lot of reasons for him being like he was . . . but, when all was said and done, he was sort of a bad kid. Just a mean, bad kid, who liked to see other people get hurt. Like I said, he might have had his reasons."

"You know his old man?" Virgil asked.

"Of course. I know everybody in town. He was grown-up Jimmy Sharp."

A woman said, "An asshole."

Somebody else said, "That's right."

The crowd was getting into it now. "How about Becky?" Virgil asked.

"Wild kid," somebody said. "She was going to New York or somewhere, to be an actress."

"She was pretty," somebody else said. "Had a face like an angel, when she was in grade school here."

"She ever go to New York?"

"Nobody from here goes to New York," Butch said. "They all come back to the Surprise."

A WOMAN STOOD UP, jeans and a turquoise-colored blouse, with a piece of silver Indian jewelry at her neck. She'd been sitting next to a man with a long brown ponytail, and Virgil tagged them as the town liberals.

She said, "Jimmy and Becky are like a lot of kids from here—they've got no hope. There aren't any jobs here, they're not sophisticated enough or well-educated enough to move to the big city and work there, they see all these things on TV that they can never have. They give up. We don't give them hope. We don't even give them anything to work with."

A heavyset man in a jean jacket said, "Come on, Sue. Plenty of good kids come from here. They just aren't two of them."

"That's easy for you to say, Earl. Your boys are gonna get a farm that's worth, what, right now . . . three or four million dollars? All they have to do is drive a tractor long enough, and they'll be rich. But most people here don't have a farm to give to their kids. That's what I'm talking about."

Virgil jumped in: "That's all fine, but we really can't change the culture in the next couple of days. I need to know more about these kids—what they're like, where they're probably going."

"All they ever talked about was going to Los Angeles and working in the movies," a young girl said. "If I were you, I'd start looking around Sioux Falls or out by Mitchell. They're probably on their way."

"Not if they're driving Jim Sharp's Chevy," said a broad-shouldered man with oily blond hair. "The gol-darned tires on that thing won't get them past Marshall. Jim brought it in for gas last week, and the deepest tread was the tread-wear indicators. Tires are like paper and the transmission sounds like it's made out of rocks. Won't get them fifty miles, unless they find new tires."

"Becky worked for a while over at a McDonald's in Marshall—maybe they went there. At least she knows the city," a woman said.

THEY TALKED FOR a few more minutes, until the people began repeating themselves, and Virgil called it off. Out on the school porch, he said to Duke, "We've got a couple dead-enders with a gun. We've gotta find that pickup, Lewis. The problem is . . . we might find more dead folks when we find the pickup."

"I'll get onto Marshall, have them check the place street by street," Duke said. "And every other town for fifty miles around. We won't be able to keep it quiet. We'll start getting the media messing with us."

"That's not all bad," Virgil said. "The more people spotting for us, the better. We'll just have to put up with the bullshit that comes with it. Or really, you will—you'll be the face on this thing, until we get them or there's more shooting."

"So maybe instead of sneaking around until they find out, we oughta just go ahead and bring the media in right away. Make an appeal."

Virgil nodded. "Think about how you want to do that. We're

not even sure that these kids are involved . . . but we do need to find them."

"Let me think about it," Duke said. "What're you going to do?"

"Call people up on the telephone," Virgil said.

DAVENPORT, working the phones with a couple of other BCA agents, had tracked down Jimmy Sharp's last known address, a room in a postwar house on St. Paul's East Side. The owner, whose name was Ronald Deutch, had originally rented the room to another man from Shinder, named Tom McCall. McCall had let Jimmy and Becky sleep in his room for the week before Deutch kicked all three of them out for non-payment of rent.

"As far as we could tell, all three of them were effectively homeless," Davenport said. "Deutch was renting them the room for fifty dollars a week, and they were two weeks overdue and couldn't come up with even a night's rent. They left there two weeks ago, and the landlord hasn't seen them since."

"So there might be three of them, instead of two," Virgil said.

"Yeah. You gotta see what you can find on this McCall guy."

"I'll do that," Virgil said.

VIRGIL HAD BEEN WORKING the telephone from his truck, where he could keep the phone plugged into the charger. He'd just hung up from the Davenport call when a man stepped up beside the truck and knocked on the passenger-side window. He was a thin man who wore a cowboy hat, a tan, western-style canvas sport coat, and rimless eyeglasses. Virgil ran the window down and the man said, "I'm Ross Price. I'm the—"

"Investigator," Virgil said. "Hop in. We need to talk."

Price got in and said, "Five dead. These kids have gone crazy."

"If it's them," Virgil agreed. "I've talked to Duke about the murders Friday night, but I'd like to get the details."

"I've been writing up everything. I've got files on my computer I could send you."

"Do that. But just tell me what you've seen so far."

Price looked out the window, scratched his forehead, then said, "It seems simple, but it feels complicated. I've never been the lead investigator on a murder where we really needed investigation. I've done two murders, but we knew who did both of them the minute we walked in the door. One was a bar fight, the other one was a domestic. But this one . . ."

Virgil nodded: "I know what you mean. My first murder investigation, you know, a real investigation, I was so confused that I didn't know if I was coming or going. But, after a while, it smooths out. So just tell me what you saw, and what people told you."

THE MURDER VICTIM was named Agatha Murphy, shot in the head during what looked like a burglary gone bad. Or a robbery gone bad—Price wasn't sure which it was.

"They came in like burglars. We think three of them, but it

could have been two—the surviving witness wasn't sure about that. At least one was a woman. But two men and a woman, that fits with what you've got going here."

"Yes, it does," Virgil said. "What kind of neighborhood was it? Was the house picked by chance?"

"I can't say," Price said. "They passed a lot of houses that looked as good as the O'Leary house. That had me confused. But now that it seems like these kids are from here in Shinder, it makes more sense. Mrs. O'Leary was from here in Shinder, and I guess she was flashing some expensive diamonds. . . ."

Price repeated the story about O'Leary and her jewelry. He said one of the intruders apparently came in through a back window that had been left unlocked, and then opened a back door for the others. They'd crept through a sleeping house, eventually entering the front bedroom where two women, sisters, were sleeping. One of them, Agatha Murphy, was staying at her parents' house after separating from her husband some months earlier. The other, Mary O'Leary, was a senior in high school, six years younger than Agatha.

"They came in the bedroom, said they were there to do some robbing," Price said. "Ag Murphy—they call her Ag—got up in their face, and one of them knocked her down. That spooked them, and they ran for it. But before they went, the leader shot Agatha in the forehead and killed her. Medical examiner said death was instantaneous. Mary O'Leary says that Agatha was kneeling on the floor when she got shot, and was no threat to the killer. He shot her down in cold blood. Just . . . nuts."

Virgil: "Did they ask for money or jewelry?"

"Didn't ask for anything. The leader said he was there to do some robbing, but then, the girl got on him, and he hit her and then shot her. Then they ran."

"Can Mary identify them? Any way at all?"

Price shook his head. "The leader had a flashlight in their faces. Your crime-scene people couldn't come up with prints, and we haven't heard back about DNA but they weren't too confident about that, either. They did find some denim threads on the windowsill, and some brown cotton threads that might have come from gloves . . . so they were ready to do it."

"The back window . . . Did the O'Learys say why it was open?"

"They didn't think it was. Everything else was locked. And I'll tell you something—this is about the only bit of real detecting I've done: I saw that whoever opened that window pried it up with a knife, or maybe a screwdriver. A knife, I think. But I looked at all the other windows down that side of the house, and you know what? There's not another knife-dent to be found. They went right straight to the open window and pried it up. It's like they *knew*."

"Nice piece of work there," Virgil said. "Like the window had been spotted in advance."

"The thing is, the windows have locking levers on both sides. They fold down to lock, up to unlock, but you can't see what position they're in from outside. You either knew the window was open, or you had to try them all. Or, you got a giant coincidence."

"We got a saying about coincidences in the BCA," Virgil said.

Price bit. "Yeah? Like what?"

"Nothing's ever a coincidence, except when it is."

"Jeez, I'll write that down. That really helps," Price said.

. . .

THEY TALKED FOR a few more minutes, and then Virgil said, "What I'd like is for you to do two things for me—hunt around Bigham and find out if Jimmy Sharp, Becky Welsh, and Tom Mc-Call were staying there for the last week or so. They couldn't make the rent in the Cities, so they had to be staying somewhere cheap, or free. Maybe with some friends? I don't know. . . . But if you find them, have some backup."

"I'll put the word out. If they were there, we should know today," Price said. "What's the other thing?"

"Find out where Jimmy's car is. It's an old black Firebird, the DMV has the tags. They apparently drove here in the Charger and left here in the truck. So, where's the Firebird? We can't find his old man's truck, either, so they might have a new set of wheels . . . but maybe, maybe they went back to the Firebird. We really need to know how they're traveling."

"But if they had the Firebird when they hit the O'Learys' house, why did they have to hijack a car?"

"I don't know."

"I wonder . . ." Price scratched his forehead again.

"Yeah?"

"They go into the O'Leary house, planning to rob it . . . I wonder how they thought they were going to get away? They couldn't plan on finding a guy standing next to his car."

Virgil said, "Huh." They thought about that for a minute, then Virgil said, "Maybe they were planning to kill everybody in the house, and take a car. And panicked, instead."

"Jeez . . . you think? There were five people there."

"But then, they're nuts," Virgil said.

PRICE LEFT, and Virgil went back to the phones. He called the O'Leary house, now curious about the victims of the first crime, and found that Marsha O'Leary, Ag's mother, was in the hospital, suffering from exhaustion. Her husband was with her. He talked to Marsha's mother, Mary Hogan, who said that Marsha had been particularly friendly with two women from Shinder, classmates, Bernice Sawyer and Harriet Washburn, whom Marsha had known since before kindergarten.

"For Shinder things, they'd be the best ones to talk to," Hogan said. Her voice had an elderly scratch to it, but tough and dry, like a woman who'd seen some death.

"I'll do that," Virgil said.

VIRGIL TALKED TO SAWYER FIRST. She was a thin, friendly woman with a big country kitchen. Her parents owned the local grain elevator, and her husband worked there. "I couldn't believe it when I heard about Ag being murdered. I thought, my God, what are they doing up there?"

Sawyer had gone to the class reunion, and the dance, and remembered that Becky Welsh had been working the food service, serving desserts.

"Marsha was wearing her diamonds. I don't know how Becky could have missed them—the most diamonds anybody around here ever saw. Marsha did it on purpose. She had a couple of old rivals here, who wound up leading pretty modest lives, and she was . . ." Sawyer smiled. "Sticking it to them, I guess you'd say."

She'd never heard of a Tom McCall. "He doesn't live in Shinder, and I don't believe he's ever lived here, because I know everybody who lives here," she said.

When he was done with Sawyer, Virgil touched bases with Washburn, because he couldn't think of what else to do, and Washburn confirmed what Sawyer had said. Becky Welsh had almost certainly seen the diamonds. Washburn, who also claimed to know everybody who lived in Shinder, agreed that there was no Tom McCall, either in the present or in the immediate past.

Virgil left Washburn, went out and sat in his truck; then called Duke, learned that Duke had been in touch with the local media, and had been called by both KSTP and Channel Three television in the Cities.

"You ever heard of a kid named Tom McCall?" Virgil asked. "About the same age as Sharp and Welsh?"

"There are some McCalls in the county," Duke said. "I haven't specifically heard of a Tom."

"Get somebody to call around to the McCalls you know," Virgil said. "There may be a Tom McCall running with Sharp and Welsh." He told him what he'd gotten from Davenport.

"Got any more ideas?" Duke asked.

"I'm sitting here in my truck thinking some up," Virgil said. "I'll let you know as they come along."

"Do that."

Virgil called him back one minute later. "I just had an idea, though it's slightly disturbing."

"Go ahead."

"I think you should call up all the rich people in town, and make sure they're alive."

There was a moment of silence, then Duke said, "Mother of God."

"Yeah. These kids are flat broke, they don't even have gas money, probably. They need money. They gotta be looking for it."

5

JIMMY SHARP, Becky Welsh, and Tom McCall had driven to Shinder after the O'Leary and Williams murders.

Halfway back, Tom said, "I think we fucked up bad. The cops'll never stop until they figure it out."

"Fuck 'em," Jimmy said. "They got nothing to go on. And fuck those O'Leary assholes. Kill them again, if I could."

Becky patted his arm and said, "It just makes me so fuckin' hot."

Jimmy glanced at her. Made her so fuckin' hot: yeah, well, that was a problem he didn't want to talk about.

AND TOM DIDN'T WANT to think about it. He'd been hanging around the edges of the Becky-Jimmy relationship for a while, and he knew something wasn't quite right, but he didn't know what it was. What he knew for sure was, he'd been hot for Becky since he'd first laid eyes on her in the ninth grade. After he left school, he hadn't seen her for a while, but when he ran into the two of them in the Cities, it all came back.

Tom had never slept with a pretty woman. Those he'd gone with had been the leftovers, and he was the best they could do. Every time he'd touched Becky—taking her arm, touching her shoulder to direct her at something—she'd flinched away, as though he were diseased.

Why was that? Why did pretty women treat him like shit? Why did Becky look right through him as though he weren't there? The longer it had gone on, the more his fantasy/dream sex had become mixed up with violence. He'd show them who the strong one was; he'd show them Tom the Barbarian . . .

Tom didn't know what to think about the killing of Ag O'Leary or the black guy. He did know that he had nothing to do with it. He was just walking along and Jimmy suddenly went crazy and killed them. He was clean.

Would he stay clean if he hung around with Jimmy? If Jimmy went down for a couple of murders, where would that leave him and Becky? With Jimmy out of the picture . . .

After he got kicked out of the navy, Tom had gone to work for a desperate home security agency, which mostly meant he drove around dark suburban neighborhoods looking for false alarms. He never did find a house that had been broken into—in fact, he'd found a fairly small percentage of the houses he'd been sent to, because he got lost easily. That shortcoming got him fired—or laid off, as his supervisor put it.

When the unemployment ran out, he had a two-week job as a pizza delivery man, but had the same problem as he did with home security. When he got fired by the pizza joint, he landed a job as a door-puller for another security company. Door-pulling was exactly what it sounded like: he spent the evening driving around to suburban office complexes pulling on doors to make sure they were locked. He got fired from that one when a late-working accountant found him sitting on a step smoking a joint.

After that, things got tough. He tried sitting at an interstate off-ramp with a cardboard sign that said: "Homeless Navy Vet, Please Help," but on an average six-hour day, pulled in only twelve dollars. On the other hand, the work wasn't onerous, and he might have stuck with it, if he hadn't met Jimmy and Becky at a Taco Bell.

They knew each other from the countryside. Tom had been born on a farm five miles east of Bigham, and met Becky and Jimmy in high school. They'd run into each other again in the Twin Cities, where Jimmy and Becky had gone looking for work. Six weeks after their reunion in the Twin Cities, here they were, cutting cross-country in the dark, and Tom, in his own dim way, was thinking over the possibilities.

A COLD CLOUDY April night in the Minnesota countryside is darker than the inside of a coal sack. They sped along through the night, right on the edge of outrunning their headlights, missing a coon running down the road, the animal glancing back at them with amber eyes.

They got to Shinder in the middle of the night, pulled into the yard. The old man's truck was sitting there, and Jimmy pulled around it and said, "Tom, get out and open the garage doors. Let's get this thing out of sight."

Tom got out in the headlights and pulled open the garage doors; a snowblower was blocking the entrance, and he jacked it around until Jimmy could squeeze by. They were pulling the doors shut behind the Charger when the old man hollered down from an upstairs window, "Who the hell is that?"

Jimmy called back, "It's me."

"What the hell do you want?"

"Need to come in for a while. We could use some breakfast."

"Get the hell out of here, you little fart. I don't have anything for the likes of you. Now, scat."

"Scat, my ass," Jimmy shouted. He turned to the other two and said, "C'mon. Door's never locked."

"Get the fuck away from my house."

Jimmy went through the back door, Becky behind him, Tom holding back. In the kitchen, Jimmy flipped on the light, went to the refrigerator, pulled it open, took out a plastic bottle of milk, and said to Becky, "There should be some oatmeal there in the bottom cupboard, next to the sink."

She pulled open the cupboard door, and there was a cylindrical box of Quaker Oats on the shelf. She took it out and was holding it in her hands when the old man came storming down the stairs and into the kitchen.

"You fuckers get out of here," he said. He waved his hand at Jimmy, a dismissive gesture. "You got no rights here no more. Give me that oatmeal."

"Stay away from her," Jimmy said.

"Shut the fuck up."

"No, you shut the fuck up. I'm tired, and we got some trouble over in Bigham, and I'm not putting up with any shit anymore. We're gonna have breakfast and figure out—"

"I'm gonna throw your ass out," the old man said. He took two steps toward Jimmy, and Jimmy pulled out the gun and pointed it at his forehead. The old man stopped, and sneered at him and said, "You got a gun? You think that makes you a man?"

"Don't know about that, but I know that there're some dead folks who don't worry about that no more," Jimmy said.

"Dead folks, you ain't got the guts." Then a wrinkle appeared in the old man's forehead and he asked, "What the fuck you done?"

"Killed a white girl and this black dude over in Bigham," Jimmy said. "I hate your old ass and I got half a mind to kill you, too."

"Gimme that fuckin' gun," the old man said. He made the mistake of taking a step toward his son, and Jimmy shot him in the forehead.

Though the old man must've been dead instantly, his body apparently didn't know that, and he took four quick backward steps on his heels, then fell in the doorway to the living room. Becky looked at Jimmy and said, "Crazy old fuck."

Tom came in, looked at the body, and said, "Jeez, you killed your pa."

"And it felt pretty fuckin' good," Jimmy said. "Help me drag his ass into the living room. I want to eat some oatmeal, and I don't want to look at him while I'm doing it." To Becky he said, "Go on. Cook us up some oatmeal."

. . .

THE BODY DOWNSTAIRS did cause some unease, and Tom eventually got a blanket and went out and slept in the Charger. Jimmy and Becky went and slept in Jimmy's old bed, which smelled of mold, but neither was about to sleep in the old man's. Becky insisted on sex, whining until Jimmy gave in. They took a shower together, but Jimmy knew it wasn't going to work—it just didn't work for him—and they went in the bedroom and Becky went down on him, and it still didn't work.

Then he went down on her, after threatening to kill her if she told anyone, and she definitely believed that he would kill her, after what she'd seen that night, and with the body in the front room, but when she screamed down five or six or eight orgasms, she couldn't have cared less about the body.

Maybe nothing else worked, but Jimmy was good with his hands and mouth.

THEY GOT A RESTLESS couple hours of sleep, and wound up back in the kitchen, eating more oatmeal. Jimmy said, "We need to get rolling, if we're going to Hollywood. We get out there, we'll be okay."

"What about your pa?" Tom asked. He glanced nervously at the kitchen doorway, where he could see a leg below the knee, a shoe, and a dirty white sock.

"Fuck him. Who's gonna know? Everybody in town hates his

ass, nobody ever comes here," Jimmy said. "We'll take the Charger over to Marshall tonight and ditch it."

"No gas in the Charger," Tom said. "I tried to heat her up last night, when I was sleeping out there, and it ran for three minutes and died. No gas."

"You dumb shit," Jimmy said.

"Good thing I did it," Tom said. "If we'd tried to go anywhere, we would of got about a mile, and then we would've been walking, where everybody could see us. Don't got enough money between the three of us to buy a gallon of gas."

Jimmy said, "Well, we got a few bucks. When I shot that bitch last night, I saw a wad on the dresser and grabbed it."

Becky said, "Really? How much?"

"Quite a bit," Jimmy said. He dug in his pocket and pulled out a fold of cash. Becky reached out and said, "Let me see," but he pulled it back and stuck it in his pocket.

"None of your business," he said. "But we need more. We need a clean car that will get us where we're going, and we don't have enough to get one."

Tom said, "We could just get bus tickets—"

"Fuck a bunch of buses," Jimmy said. "Let me check the old man."

They walked through the kitchen to the body, couldn't look directly at him, but felt his pockets and came up empty. Jimmy said, "Must be upstairs." He went up to the old man's bedroom, came back down a minute later, and said, "Eighteen dollars and thirty cents. We got more off the black dude."

Becky said, "We might get a couple of bucks off my folks."

Jimmy said, "Good idea. We'll take the old man's truck."

. . .

BECKY'S FOLKS didn't have any money, but they had the same attitude that James Sharp Senior had, and they didn't like Jimmy at all. Old man Welsh was hungover, and not about to put up with any shit.

"Do I look like I'm made of money? When I was your age, I'd been working for five years."

"That's 'cause you could get a job way back then," Becky said. "You can't get one now, and I mean, *you* can't get one now. How long you been eatin' off Mom?"

"You little fuckin' brat, I raised you and fed you and now you come around with your peckerwood friends with your hands out—"

"You just call me a peckerhead?" Jimmy asked, his voice quiet.

"Peckerwood," the old man said. "I said peckerwood. But you want me to call you a peckerhead? Okay, you're a peckerhead."

Becky's mother snorted at that: funny stuff. She stopped smiling when Jimmy took out the .38.

"Now, we don't need that," Becky's father said.

"You think I'm a peckerhead now?" Jimmy asked. He pointed the gun at Welsh's chest. "Come on, say it."

"You're not one, you're not one," Ann Welsh said. She farted in fear, and the smell spread through the kitchen and Tom said, "Aw, Jesus . . ." and waved his hand in front of his face.

"Let's just calm down." Welsh lifted his hands, like cowboys used to do on TV when they were giving up.

"No. I want to hear you call me a peckerhead again," Jimmy said.

Becky said, "Yeah, call him a peckerhead."

Welsh was sweating furiously now, and he said, "I don't know what to do."

Jimmy said, "Easy. Just what I told you. Call me a peckerhead."

Welsh said, "Don't point the gun—"

"Call me a peckerhead, or goddamnit, I'll blow your fuckin' brains out," Jimmy said.

Welsh whimpered, and Jimmy smiled at the sound, and Welsh licked his lips and muttered, "Peckerhead."

Jimmy shot him in the heart, and Ann Welsh turned on a dime and made for the back door, got three steps and Jimmy, stepping along behind her, shot her in the back of the head. He looked at them on the floor and turned to Becky and asked, "You hate me now?"

Her eyes were steel gray and she shook her head once: "No. Fuck 'em. They ruined my life."

Tom said, "We better get out of here."

Becky said to Jimmy: "Let's go to Marshall. I know where we can get it all—car, money, everything."

6

VIRGIL SPENT A FRUITLESS Sunday morning sitting in his truck, calling people on the telephone—people turned up by Davenport in the Twin Cities, people in Shinder who knew Becky Welsh or Jimmy Sharp, or any of the dead people, scratching for any connection.

The most confounding thing, at least for the moment, was the disappearance of the elder Sharp's truck. They had it on some authority that it wouldn't make it fifty miles, but he couldn't find it anywhere in Minnesota, Iowa, or North or South Dakota, and at this point there were several hundred cops looking for it.

Duke asked, "Where do you think it is? Give me a guess."

"It's down in a creek bed somewhere, where it can't be seen from a road, and they're camping out with it, or it's in a garage or a barn and they've got new wheels."

At one o'clock, they had two nearly simultaneous breaks. Virgil had the crime-scene crew work over the Charger, and they'd found dozens of fingerprints, both in the front and back seats, and because of the extreme amount of plastic in the car, they got good ones. At one o'clock, they got a return on one set of them: Tom McCall, who had no criminal record, had been fingerprinted when he went into the navy, and his fingerprints were in the federal database.

A few minutes later, Duke called to say that he'd found McCall's mother, an elementary school teacher in Bigham. McCall's father had gone out for a loaf of bread a few years earlier and hadn't yet returned.

"I want to talk to her," Virgil said. "I'll be there in half an hour."

He called Davenport and said, "Tom McCall was in the car, in the backseat. So I think I can call it: James Sharp, Becky Welsh, Tom McCall. I don't know Sharp's or Welsh's status yet, but I'm assuming they're all in on it."

"Good bet," Davenport said. "You got a lot of media coming your way. It's gone viral."

"That's okay: it's a snake hunt now," Virgil said. "The more eyes, the better."

VIRGIL DROVE NORTHEAST TO BIGHAM, watching the tattered spring earth roll by. The land was creased by creeks and drainage ditches, broad fields showing the remnants of last year's corn and bean fields. Later in the spring, when the ground warmed up a bit more, and dried out, the farmers would get out and plow and plant and the fields would take on their customary neatness; but now, everything looked beat-up.

Still cold.

It wouldn't be easy to conceal a big silver truck, though—even out on the prairie, sparsely populated as it was, people got around, looked at their fields and down their creeks, and a truck would be hard to hide at this time of year. In August or September, they could put it in the middle of a cornfield and it might not be found until the harvest. Not in April.

He coasted into Bigham on that thought, and found the elementary school.

THE KEY THING about Virginia McCall, Virgil realized after talking to her for one minute, was that she never said her son didn't do it.

They spoke privately in the principal's office, Duke leaning against one wall, chewing on a kitchen match, while Virgil sat across from McCall, their knees nearly touching. She was a tall, vague woman, thin, small-boned, her brown hair worn long. She had a sprinkling of small dark moles on her right cheek.

"Nothing has ever worked right for him," she said, her hands flopping restlessly in her lap. "He . . . I don't know. He was never assertive. He's not stupid, not at all, but if somebody told him to jump off a roof, he'd do it. If you didn't tell him what to do, he wouldn't do anything. I don't know how that happened. His father went away . . ."

"So . . . what was his relationship with Jimmy Sharp?" Virgil asked.

"I don't know Jimmy very well. I know Becky better," McCall said. "They both went to high school here, but I'm in the elementary school. They hung out together. Jimmy and Becky are . . . you know . . . not very bright. Becky was quite attractive. Blond, with a figure. How she got out of school without getting pregnant, I don't know. The boys would cluster around her—I'm sure she was giving it up. Most people thought she'd be homecoming queen in her senior year, but the girls all voted against her. Everybody knew it, but she never quite understood what happened."

She said Tom had been discharged from the navy because he suffered from psoriasis, which had also kept him off sports teams in school. "We'd tell everybody that it's not contagious, but you know . . . who wants to take a chance?" After the navy, he'd worked in Bigham stocking a grocery store, and then had gone off to the Twin Cities, where he'd gotten a job as a security guard.

"I knew that he'd seen Becky," she said. "He's always been interested in her. He mentioned her, but he never mentioned Jim. I don't know if they're hanging out."

As far as she knew, he was still working as a security guard. She hadn't heard from him in months, and didn't know how to get in touch.

WHEN HE'D WRUNG HER OUT, Virgil walked over to the high school, where he talked with the assistant principal in charge of discipline, whose name was Robert Frett. All three had had some disciplinary problems; Jimmy Sharp had been close to expulsion a couple of times, suspected of providing marijuana to other students, but there'd been no proof. He'd also been in a few fights, but had been smart enough to keep them off school grounds.

Becky Welsh had a tendency to skip school; McCall hadn't skipped, but he could go weeks without doing mandatory homework.

"They were just pains-in-the-behind," Frett said, shaking his head. "I never suspected they'd get involved with anything like this. Never saw this coming. Though Jimmy was a mean kid."

WHEN VIRGIL WENT back to his truck, he had a better picture of the trio, but nothing that would help him locate them. The Bare County courthouse was six or seven blocks down Main Street from the elementary school, and he parked out back, at the law enforcement annex, went inside and found Duke.

"We got Jimmy Sharp's car. No doubt now—it was behind the apartment house where that colored boy got killed," Duke said. "They must've planned to rob the O'Learys and then run right down the hill to the car. I thought about that and it's what I would have done."

"So it's all coming down to the truck," Virgil said.

"We got some media on the way," Duke said. "We need to figure out who's going to talk."

"Not me," Virgil said. "We usually leave that to you elected guys."

Duke nodded. "Good enough. What are you going to do?"

"Just wait," Virgil said. "There's not much more to do. They'll pop up, sooner or later. Probably sooner. Tomorrow. I just pray to God they don't kill anyone else."

"What do you think about that?"

"I think there's a good chance that they will," Virgil said. "I think there's a good chance that they already have—they parked that truck in somebody's garage, and that somebody is already dead, and they're on their way to Los Angeles."

"Now what?"

Virgil said, "Well, I'm here. I think I'll go talk to a couple of O'Learys. The other guy who got killed . . . Emmett Williams? You know where I'd find his people?"

"His sister lives here, he was staying with her. I'll get her address if you want it, but that looked to us like a killing of opportunity. They were running and he just got in the way and got shot down. I don't think there's much in it, for you."

"Probably not," Virgil agreed. "But what else am I gonna do?"

VIRGIL GOT ADDRESSES for the O'Learys and Williams's sister, and got them spotted on a city map by the sheriff's secretary. The O'Learys lived out from the center of town, on a ridge overlooking the river; Williams's sister, whose name was LuAnne Rogers, lived in an apartment building on the edge of the downtown, a few blocks from the courthouse. Virgil drove over, parked in front of a hardware store, and walked back across the street. Rogers's apartment was over a bridal and prom dress shop. Virgil climbed the stairs and knocked on the door.

The door was opened by a small boy, maybe five. "Your mom home?" Virgil asked.

A woman called, "Just a minute," and Virgil heard dishes clattering, and then a lanky good-looking black woman came to the door, carrying a dish towel, and asked, "Can I help you?"

"I'm with the state Bureau of Criminal Apprehension," Virgil said. "I want to chat with you about your brother, if you're Miz Rogers."

"Yeah, I am. Come in."

Virgil stepped inside, and the woman said to the boy, "You go on and play your game. I'm putting you on the watch, one half hour."

The boy scuttled away, and the woman said, "He's got a Wii skateboard game."

Virgil said he was sorry about her brother, and asked if she knew, or if any of her friends might know, if there was any connection between Williams and Sharp, Welsh, or McCall.

"That's the first time I ever heard those names," she said. "You know who did it?"

Virgil said, "Maybe. We're looking for three young people, two men and a woman. You'll be hearing about it on TV."

"I don't allow much TV in here," she said. "And if I don't allow Brad to watch it, I can't watch myself. But I guess I'll make an exception."

She said again that she hadn't heard of any of the three. "Emmett was here for two weeks, and he was going back home next week. He really didn't have time to meet anybody up here."

"Where's home?"

"Kansas City. He'd been hassled around by his ex-wife down there, and he came up here to get away for a while. Then . . ." She teared up a bit, and wiped the tears away. "Emmett and I weren't real close. He was seven years younger than I am, and . . . we just weren't that close."

She said her husband, Bradley Senior, was a plant engineer

who installed computer-assisted wood-cutting machines and designed production lines, and was doing that at a local furniture factory. They'd been in town for six months and would be there for another three, and then would move on to the next job.

They talked about Emmett, and about growing up in Kansas City. Virgil decided after a few minutes that she had no real information. When he stood up to leave, she said, "I hate to ask you this, because this is all so terrible . . . but, our car?"

"I'll try to get it back to you quick as we can," Virgil said. "I just can't promise when that'll be. Do you have some other way to get around?"

"The company rented us a car, but we'd like to get our own back. It's pretty new."

"I'll see what I can do," Virgil promised.

ROGERS HAD BEEN straightforward about her distance from her brother, and though she was saddened and depressed by the killing, she was dealing with it. The O'Learys were a different matter.

Marsha O'Leary, Ag's mother, was still in the hospital, suffering from exhaustion. Her husband, John, was at home when Virgil arrived, taking a break from the hospital vigil, replaced by Marsha's mother. The surviving daughter, Mary, and four sons, Jack, James, Rob, and Frank, were scattered around a large living room and dining room. Jack was playing light jazz on an upright piano, sounding quite a bit like Harry Connick Jr. Virgil could imagine sitting on the front porch on a moonlit night, spooning with a young neighborhood lady, while Jack's piano tune trickled through the screen door. . . .

VIRGIL HAD CALLED AHEAD, and Mary had met him at the door. She was a square-shouldered young woman of medium height, probably not yet twenty, with dark hair and large, dark, direct eyes, wearing two sparkly diamond studs at her ears. She had dark circles at her eyes and her nose was red, from crying. She was wearing a green blouse and jeans.

John was sitting in an easy chair in the living room, and the four boys came in as Mary introduced Virgil to her father. All of them had curly dark hair, conservatively cut, with dark eyes and broad shoulders. They were a bunch of good-looking, athletic Irishmen in sweatshirts and jeans and moccasins, with an easy air of money about them; and an ugly bitter air of tragedy.

"Why did this happen?" John O'Leary asked. "We're the nicest goddamn people on the face of the earth."

Virgil shook his head. "I'd tell you that it happens all the time, except that it doesn't. It's pretty rare," Virgil said. "Random killings are just . . . incomprehensible. We've got an idea now who did it, two or three loser kids from Shinder. They apparently knew your name, knew you were well-off . . . they got desperate. That's what we think."

He told them what he knew about Sharp, Welsh, and McCall, and the oldest three of the boys knew of Sharp and Welsh, and vaguely remembered McCall. "Didn't really know them," said

Jack. "Jimmy Sharp was a year behind me and a year ahead of Jim, I think."

Jim nodded and said, "That's right. Becky was a year younger than me. Everybody said she was kind of a punchboard, but I never knew her well enough to know that. McCall was in there somewhere. He was one of those guys you don't remember very well . . . kind of joked around, but the jokes were always pretty lame. Maybe he was in the same grade as Becky? I don't know. You think they really did it?"

"It looks that way," Virgil said. "It's possible that it's McCall and two others, and they killed Mr. Sharp and Mr. and Mrs. Welsh because McCall knew them . . . but I think it's probably Sharp. And Becky Welsh."

The three older O'Leary boys were in college—Jack in medical school, the other two in pre-med, all at the University of Minnesota. Mary was a senior in high school, Frank a sophomore. Ag had been the oldest of them, and, they said, probably had not known any of the suspected killers.

Frank said, "If Ag had gone to med school instead of getting married, none of this would have happened. If she hadn't had that temper, if she'd just been quiet . . ." And he sobbed once, stuck a knuckle in his mouth and turned away, and his father patted him on the shoulder.

"It's not Dick's fault," John O'Leary said to Frank. Virgil hadn't known that Ag was married; he assumed that "Dick" was her husband.

Mary: "If he'd taken better care of her, she wouldn't have been here."

"And then maybe it would have been you that got killed," Jim snapped.

Virgil broke in: "Trying to backtrack a trail of what-if's . . . everybody does it, but it doesn't help. The trail gets too twisted up, and you wind up damaging people who really don't need it."

Rob said, "We know that. We've even said that."

Jim said, "But we keep doing it anyway." He glanced at his father, then said, "Excuse the language, but it's because Dick is such a . . . dick."

VIRGIL TALKED TO them a bit more about Sharp, Welsh, and Mc-Call, but none of them knew of any direct connection between themselves and the three suspects, except that their mother, Marsha, and Sharp and Welsh all came from Shinder. "But Mom left Shinder before they were even born."

Virgil nodded, but didn't mention the diamonds worn to the reunion; it would just be another cause for unwarranted backtracking, and sleepless nights.

Instead, he said, "So tell me about Dick."

Dick Murphy was a couple of years younger than Ag, but they'd both gone up to the University of Minnesota, where they'd dated, had become serious, and eventually, after Ag graduated, had married. Dick's father ran an independent insurance brokerage in town, and Dick quit school after three years to go to work as a salesman.

"They're pretty rich, Dick's whole family," Rob said. "Dick was a running back on the football team, pretty good, he was always bombing around in those Mini Cooper cars in high school, and then he got a BMW when he went to college. You know, he's a sales guy—he talks good and he looks good, but he's sort of a dick."

"He really loved her, I believe," John O'Leary said. "I wouldn't have let them get married if I didn't believe that."

"Dad . . ." Mary said. She seemed fondly exasperated.

"You don't think so?" John asked. His tone of voice suggested that he had his own doubts, Virgil thought.

"In his way, maybe," Mary said. "Ag was hot, and we're pretty rich, too, and Dick sees himself driving around in a convertible with a hot rich chick. But I think it could have been some other hot rich chick, and he would have been just as happy."

"I'd like to know more about how she lost the baby," Jack said.

"He didn't have anything to do with that," Mary said. "If you're thinking . . . He didn't."

"Didn't want it," Jack said. "He almost told me so. He had it all planned out. First they'd get a boat, then they'd get a cabin, then they'd get a time-share at Park City . . . then maybe they'd get a kid. Like when they were fifty."

"Ah, jeez," Mary said. "So he's a dick. But he still didn't have anything to do with the baby."

They all sat around and looked at each other for a minute or so, then John said to Virgil, "Dick didn't have anything to do with this. He's not a bad guy."

Jim: "Except that he's a dick."

"I'm perfectly willing to believe you, that he's not a bad guy,"

Virgil said to John. "But let me ask one last ugly question, and then I'll leave it alone."

"What you're going to ask," Jack said, "is, 'Did Dick, the dick, get anything out of her death?' And the answer is, 'Uh, yes.'"

John said, "Jack . . ."

Jack said, "The cop wants to know, Dad."

They reminded Virgil of his relationship with his own father: fond, but contentious. Virgil said, "So tell me about it."

Rob said to Virgil, "The day we're born, the old man sends a check to Fidelity Investments for the full exempt gift amount, for that year. Then he sends another check every birthday, every year. We were all told from the time we were old enough to understand it, that this money was to pay for our graduate school. It wasn't for cars, or dope, or women, or any of that. It was for grad school. Dad would pay for undergrad work, but this fund would pay for graduate study. Ag didn't do any graduate study. How much did she have in there, Dad?"

"She might have spent some of it," John O'Leary said.

Frank said, "Bull hockey. She probably had more than a half-million dollars—because I've got that much, and she's been collecting for a lot more years."

Turning directly to Virgil, he said, "Our old man is no dummy. He got our money out of the market before the dot-com crash, then got us back in until things started looking ugly again, a few years ago. He got us back out, and after *that* crash, got us back in. . . . I don't know exactly how much she had, but it was a lot."

Virgil said, "A number would be nice. Just to give me a solid idea."

John mumbled, "Last time we talked about it, she had seven-seventy."

"More than enough for a boat and a cabin and maybe even a time-share," Frank said. "Unless, of course, she walked out on him."

"She wasn't going to buy a boat and a cabin, she was going back to med school," Jack said. To Virgil: "After she lost her baby, she moved out of Dick's house and came back here."

Virgil said, "When I hear about that much money, you know, I get curious, because I can't help it. But I'll tell you something: I'm about ninety-five percent, and climbing, that it's Sharp, Welsh, and McCall."

John O'Leary nodded, and said, "Okay. Then catch them."

"I will," Virgil said. "I just hope to God I catch them before they do any more damage."

"You think you will?" Jack asked.

Virgil looked at them: tough and bright, the whole bunch. He said, "No."

THEY TALKED A LITTLE more about the circumstances of the night of the murder—James and Rob had been at the university, but Jack had come home for the weekend. He and Frank were sleeping in separate rooms down the hall from the room where Mary and Ag were.

They were both awakened by shouting, then a gunshot, and then people running, and they ran into the hallway where they encountered their father and mother, heard people running down below . . . but then they heard Mary screaming that Ag had been shot. Jack had started after the killers, but his father wrestled him back into the hallway, fearing that he'd also be shot.

Then John and Jack had gone to treat Ag, but knew immediately that she was dead. "Never any doubt," John said. "She was just . . . gone. I'm sure she never knew what happened. No pain, nothing."

Virgil asked about the kitchen window. "That's a mystery. I never looked at it. The lock. I talked to Marsha, she never looked at it, I talked to the housekeeper, she never looked at it. . . . It should have been locked. I guess it wasn't."

"Wonder when the last time . . . Dick . . . was in the kitchen," Frank asked.

John shook a finger at him: "That's enough. Shut up."

MARY TOOK VIRGIL to the door, while the males sat slumped in the living room, all looking as tired as men can look. Mary looked back at them and said, "Ag was the oldest. Because there were so many of us, she really wound up being a babysitter for most of us. She took care of us growing up."

"I'm so sorry," Virgil said, and he was. Then he asked, "When Ag lost her baby, you're sure Dick didn't have anything to do with it?"

She shook her head and said, "I'm sure as can be. She and a friend went shopping up in the Cities that day, and Dick was here. I saw him myself, and Ag was fine when she left. She called us from the hospital, told us that she'd lost the baby. She was only six weeks along, so it wasn't like a big awful thing. She just started bleeding, and they went to the emergency room, but the baby was gone. She was back here the next day."

"All right," Virgil said. "Like I said, I'm ninety-five percent that I know who did it, I just have to find them."

He took another step and said, "Just to cross all the t's and dot all the i's . . . what was the name of the friend who went to the Cities with Ag?"

Mary touched her neck, just at the collarbone, and said, "Why, Laura Deren. She's an old friend of ours. Ag's, especially. She lives here in town—she's an accountant."

"Thank you," Virgil said. He looked out at the town—the O'Leary house was just at the crest of a hill, looking out over it— and he said, "You've got a great view up here."

"It looks awful to me, right now," Mary said. "It looks cold and lonesome forever."

VIRGIL CALLED DUKE. "Heard anything?"

"Silent as a tomb. Can't figure out where that silver truck went. We've stopped every silver truck for five states around."

"Well. Keep looking," Virgil said. "The media on you yet?"

"Yes. They're setting up on the courthouse lawn. We'll have a press conference in a couple hours."

"I'm gonna stay clear," Virgil said. "If you need any information from me, give me a ring."

"I'll do that," Duke said. "I should be okay. I did a few of these during the hassle over the so-called concentration camp."

"I suppose you did," Virgil said. "I'm going back to Shinder, and then probably on to Marshall for the night. Nothing much to do except monitor the phones. Not until they pop up again."

THE CRIME-SCENE CREW was still working on the two sites in Shinder, but had nothing that was either new or relevant. Virgil made some calls about getting the stolen car back to the Rogers family, and was told that it would be a few more days. He called LuAnne Rogers and told her that.

If Sharp, Welsh, or McCall had had more friends, there would have been more talking to do; as it was, Virgil sat outside the Surprise, eating an ice cream sandwich, and tried to think of something that he needed to do, that would help, but he couldn't think of anything.

Eventually, he drove over to Marshall, called his parents and invited himself to dinner, then took a shower and a nap.

Thought, as he drifted away, that everything had gone too quiet, and smiled at the thought, remembering the old black-and-white films on late-night TV:

The drums . . . the drums have gone quiet. They always go quiet just before they attack.

7

WHEN VIRGIL ARRIVED FOR DINNER, there were three freshly painted chairs sitting in the mouth of his parents' two-car garage. His father collected old furniture from the congregation, repaired it, painted it, and passed it along to anyone who needed it, except the twenty or so people who populated the local Church of Scientology, which he loathed.

"If I go to hell, which would be very disappointing, I can tell you, after all my efforts, it'll be because I really . . . despise those people," he said. He was in the mudroom, scrubbing his hands with odorless mineral spirits. "I can't find it in my heart to forgive them," he said. "It's the biggest con job in the history of the United States. It makes what's-his-name look like a piker."

"Good old what's-his-name was a jerk, that's for sure," Virgil said.

"You know who I mean. That guy who stole all those billions of dollars. The Ponzi scheme."

"Madoff."

"Yeah. Him. They make him look like a piker," his old man said.

"That's interesting," Virgil said. "I don't think I've heard the word 'piker' and 'Madoff' in the same sentence before."

"So now you have," his father said.

Virgil followed him into the kitchen, and they chatted while the old man finished the scrub-up with soap and water, and his mother grilled some hamburger and sliced some large purple onions, and they all ate cheeseburgers together, with fries and beer, and they picked at him about the murder. Then Virgil said, "Yeah, I understand Becky worked over here for a while, at the McDonald's. None of them could get . . . What?"

His father had stopped chewing in mid-bite and was staring at Virgil. He said, "Don McClatchy wasn't in church this morning. Neither was his wife. They're almost always there."

Virgil said, "Don McClatchy?"

"Runs the McDonald's."

His mother had given Virgil a couple of folded paper towels to use as a napkin, and he popped the last piece of cheeseburger in his mouth and dabbed at his face with the towels, and said, "Come on. Let's go over there."

"We could call them in one minute," his father said. "I've got them on my computer."

Virgil shook his head. "I want to see them. These kids probably tried to rob the O'Learys because they thought the O'Learys were rich. They probably think her boss at McDonald's is rich."

"They *are* rich . . . at least for Marshall."

The McClatchys lived off Horizon Drive, a half mile or so from the Flowers place. They were there in two minutes, driving Virgil's truck; his father pointed it out: "Light's on."

"You stay here," Virgil said. He got his gun out from under the seat, checked the magazine, made sure it was seated, and put the gun and holster under his back beltline.

"Try to avoid getting shot," his father said.

"I will."

"Maybe I better come with you."

"Okay. Get your gun, so you'll have something to do if they're inside and start shooting," Virgil said.

"Virgil . . ."

"Stay here," Virgil said.

VIRGIL TOOK A LONG look at the house, then walked up the circular drive to the front door and looked through the window. He could hear music playing, but couldn't see anyone. After a few seconds, he reached out and pushed the doorbell, then stood back and put one hand on his pistol.

He heard footsteps, and a moment later a young woman opened the front door and looked out at him. She didn't open the storm door. He said, "I'm Virgil Flowers. I'm with the state Bureau of Criminal Apprehension. I'm looking for Mr. and Mrs. McClatchy."

She said, "They're not here."

She didn't seem to be under any particular duress, so Virgil let go of the gun and took his ID out of his jacket pocket and held it so she could see it. Then he asked, "Could you step out on the porch and tell me where they are?"

She hesitated, then said, "Sure," and stepped out on the porch. "Why do you want me out here?" and, "Are you related to Reverend Flowers, over at—"

"I'm his son," Virgil said. "Could you tell me where Mr. and Mrs. McClatchy are? And who you are?"

"They're in Naples." Virgil frowned and she said, "Florida. Until the twentieth. They go down there to play golf so they can get a jump on the season. I live down the street. I take care of the dogs. What happened?"

"I just . . . uh . . . Do you know where they're staying?" Virgil asked.

"Yes. I have an emergency number for them."

She got the emergency number, and by that time Virgil knew that she wasn't hiding any killers. He explained about the suspects in the murders. "I don't think you have a problem, but don't hurry to open the door. Check first. Feed the dogs and go home. Don't hang out."

She was wide-eyed. "I saw about the murders on TV. When are you going to catch them?"

"Soon—but don't take any chances," he said. "My dad's out in the car. Wave at him."

She stepped off the porch to look around a stunted cedar, and waved. Virgil could see the old man wave back.

"So we're good," he said. "But—be careful."

In the car, the old man said, "So we're good."

"Yeah, we're good. It was a long shot. But I'd like you to call the McClatchys."

His father did, and one of the McClatchys answered, and they had a brief gossipy chat, and then his father hung up and said, "Now we *are* good. And thank the good Lord for that."

VIRGIL DROPPED HIS FATHER off and went back to the motel, watched a movie on pay-per-view, got undressed, took a shower, then lay on his bed and thought about God, and eventually, almost drifted off to sleep. Almost.

Then he was wide awake, said to the ceiling, "Ah, bullshit." He lay there for a few more seconds, then looked at the telephone. Not that late; but then, his parents usually went to bed about nine o'clock.

He picked up the phone, pushed the "home" button, and ten seconds later his father asked, "Virgil?"

"There are two McDonald's in town. Do the McClatchys own both of them?"

"No, the one out on 23 is Rick Box. I don't know where they live . . . in town, though. Are you going over there?"

"Maybe. Rick Box."

"Yeah. Rick and Nina. Maybe Paul Berry would know, I think they belong there. You want me to come with you?"

Berry was a Catholic priest, and an old golfing pal of Virgil's father. "Thanks, but I'll be okay. I'll get back to you. Like, tomorrow."

"If anything happens, call me tonight."

Virgil didn't call the priest. Instead, he brought his laptop up and signed onto the DMV computers. Rick and Nina Box were both licensed drivers. Rick was thirty-six and overweight, and Nina was thirty-four, and they lived on Parkside, not far from the Mc-Clatchys.

Virgil got dressed, went out to his truck, and drove over; not *really* that late, still well before midnight, but the streets were empty. The Boxes lived in a brick-and-clapboard ranch house that was elbow-to-elbow with other ranch houses, and right next door to the parents of a guy, Randy Carew, with whom Virgil had played high school basketball seventeen or eighteen years earlier. Old man Carew always had a couple cases of beer in the garage, and Virgil had stolen more than a few bottles from him.

Virgil went on past the Boxes' place, past the Carews', to the next house, stopped, got out, and walked up the Carews' drive-way. There was no sign of a light, but there was no sign of a light in most of the houses on the street. He leaned on the doorbell. Nothing happened for a moment, and then he heard an impact, feet hitting a floor. A minute later, an older man came to the door, looked out through the glass panel, turned on the porch light, opened the door, and said, "Virgil?"

Virgil thought, *God bless you,* and said, quietly, because he couldn't remember Carew's first name, "Mr. Carew, I'm with the Minnesota Bureau of Criminal Apprehension now. I'm a cop."

"I knew that." Carew was wearing a pajama top and jeans, and was barefoot.

"I need to come inside and talk to you for a minute," Virgil said.

"You're not here for the rest of my Budweiser, are you?"

Made Virgil laugh, and he said, "Not at the moment, but maybe later. I need to take a second of your time."

"Sure, come on in," Carew said, holding open the door.

Virgil stepped across the threshold and Carew called, "Viv? It's Virgil Flowers."

"Virgil? What's he want? The rest of your beer?" She came out a minute later, a robust woman in a pink terrycloth bathrobe, and Virgil remembered that her name was Vivian. She said, "C'mere, you," and grabbed Virgil by the cheeks and bent him over so she could kiss him on the forehead.

Carew asked, "What's going on?"

"Probably nothing," Virgil said. "I'm trying to chase down some kids who've gotten themselves in a lot of trouble. . . . Killed some people over in Bigham and Shinder."

"We saw it on TV," Carew said. There was wonder in his voice. This didn't happen. Not here.

"The thing is, one of them worked at a McDonald's over here, and they're kinda dumb, and it's remotely possible . . . *remotely possible* . . . that they're targeting people that they think can give them money or a new ride. The McClatchys are fine, and I just want to make sure the Boxes are okay."

"Haven't seen them today," Vivian Carew said, her fingertips going to her mouth. "But it was kind of chilly. They might not have been out when we were."

"You haven't seen a silver pickup around . . ."

The Carews looked at each other, and then Carew said, "Virgil, there was a silver pickup in their driveway this morning. An old Chevy . . . kinda crappy-looking. Broke-down. It was there when I got up this morning. It was gone by lunchtime."

Virgil said, "Ah, man."

"What does that mean?" Vivian asked.

"It means I need more cops. A whole lot of cops," Virgil said.

MARSHALL DIDN'T HAVE a whole lot of cops, but more than enough—maybe eighteen or twenty city officers, and ten or twelve sheriff's deputies. Virgil walked back to his car, after warning the Carews to stay inside, called the law enforcement center, got the duty officer, and filled him in as he drove over.

When he got there, a city patrol car was pulling into the parking lot, just behind a sheriff's deputy's car. Virgil got out, said hello to the two cops, realized that he vaguely knew one of them, who said, "I've read about you in the newspapers, Virg. Goddamn, can I get a job like yours?"

"You'd have to fuck up first," Virgil said, and they all went inside, where they were joined by the duty officer, who said, "I called everybody. We'll have ten people here in a couple of minutes."

THE TEN MINUTES seemed to take forever, but in something like six or seven minutes, the sheriff walked in, and Virgil decided to start: they all gathered around a computer and Virgil pulled up Google Maps and got an aerial view of the Box house; all of the city cops and all but two of the sheriff's deputies knew the street pretty well. Virgil said, "We need to block it off."

As he detailed the blocking action on the computer monitor,

two more officers showed up; they were members of the drug task force, trained in SWAT-type entries, and the sheriff designated them to enter the house, with Virgil. Virgil didn't have full SWAT equipment, so he'd go in last.

Virgil finished and said, "We need more planning, but we just don't have the time. If they're in there, and they don't know we're around, they could kill the Boxes anytime."

"If they haven't already done it," the sheriff said.

"That's right," Virgil said. "We'll block the place, then we'll call. If they answer, I'll take it from there. If there's no answer, then we'll approach the front door, and if we still get nothing, we'll enter."

"Better not have messed with my cheeseburger man," one of the drug guys said, as he slapped the Velcros on his vest.

"You know him?" Virgil asked.

The drug guy said, "Sort of. By sight."

"Anybody know him well?" Virgil asked. "Anybody know any of their relatives?"

"I don't think they went to school here," somebody said. "When they opened the other McDonald's, I think I heard they came up from Worthington."

"All right . . . so we'll have to do it cold," Virgil said. He told the duty officer to hold any late arrivals at the law enforcement center. "We don't know how it's going to break. We might possibly need people with cars. So keep them loose."

Half the cars went to an elementary school south of the Box house, and the rest went to Horizon, north of Parkside. They coordinated with handsets and cell phones, crossing backyards in the dark, until they had the target house surrounded.

Virgil called from his cell phone. The Box phone rang four times, then kicked over to an answering machine—but they'd gotten lucky: an answering machine, and not the phone company answering service. He said, "Mr. Box, this is the Marshall Fire Department. We've got a major problem at the McDonald's. If you're there, could you pick up, please? We need to talk with you immediately. Please pick up."

No answer, no lights, no movement.

Virgil called on his handset, "Everybody stay in place, we're going to make an approach."

They came in from the garage corner, a blank windowless wall where they couldn't be seen. Virgil and the two drug cops stopped there, and Virgil whispered, "Give me a flashlight." One of the men handed him a Maglite, and he stepped around to the back of the garage, eased up to a back window. The inside of the garage was dark. He risked a peek, and could see almost nothing; he looked longer, couldn't see anything that looked like movement. He risked the flashlight, and found himself looking into an empty garage.

Had the Boxes gone somewhere as well? But the silver truck had been there in the morning. . . .

He crept back to the two drug cops. "Nothing in the garage. Maybe they're gone."

"So now what?" one of them whispered.

"I want to look at the front door." They moved to the front corner of the garage, then Virgil got on his hands and knees and crawled alone along the sidewalk, under a picture window and past a thawing flower bed, to the front door. He checked the door with the flash. No damage.

All right. One of the drug cops crawled up with what looked like a stethoscope, and put the sensor against the door. They sat for one minute, two minutes, then the cop said, "Nothing at all."

Virgil said, "So let's go in."

The first cop continued to listen while Virgil crawled back to the second cop, alerted everyone to the entry, and brought the second cop back to the porch. The first cop, still listening, shook his head. "I don't think there's anybody in there. Not alive, anyway."

Virgil eased the storm door open, tried the knob. Locked. Backed off. The second cop whispered, "Looks like a pretty good door. Metal." He meant, hard to take down.

Virgil nodded. "Let's take a look at the garage."

They crawled back down the sidewalk, updated everybody on what was happening, tried the garage overhead door, which was locked down, and the side door, which was also locked, but had a six-pane window. Virgil used the stock of his pistol to silently pressure-crack the glass in the lowest pane, then picked out the pieces and tossed them in the flower bed. When he could reach through without cutting himself, he did, and turned the doorknob and the three of them eased into the garage. The connecting door to the house was locked, but was a hollow-core door, much flimsier than the front door.

"We can get a hammer in here," one of the cops whispered.

"Let's do it," Virgil said.

The cop made a call, and two minutes later another cop snuck around the corner of the garage carrying a twelve-pound maul.

Virgil said to the maul-carrier, "I'll turn on the flash, you hit it." And to the two drug cops, "You get in line and go on in. There should be lights right next to the door. Go all the way to the back before you stop."

When everybody was on the same page, Virgil lifted the flash and said, "On three," and counted. On two, he switched the light on, and on three, the hammer smashed the door open. The first cop hit the lights with his hand, and stopped dead in the doorway.

Virgil said, "Go," and the cop said, "Can't."

Virgil looked around him at two bodies in the living room, both facedown on the carpet.

The lead cop said, "Boyoboyoboy . . ." and it flashed through Virgil's mind that the bodies looked like cows lying in a pasture. He said, urgently, "Go on to the back. Step around them, go on to the back, make sure there's nobody can get out in the hallway."

The cop did that, following the muzzle of his shotgun down a hallway toward what looked like a bedroom wing until Virgil said, "Okay, hold it there. Watch the doors."

He motioned the second drug cop to the kitchen, and the second cop cleared it and said, "There's a couch here. They've barricaded a door."

Virgil went that way and found a couch jammed end-wise between a hallway wall and a door that apparently led to the basement. "Why?"

Then a boy's voice called, "Mom? Mom? Dad?"

VIRGIL GOT FOUR MORE COPS in the house. He said, "Those are kids down there. I don't want them to see their parents. You guys make a barrier, and we'll take them straight to the front door so they never see them. Okay? Everybody."

Everybody nodded, then they lifted the couch away from the door. Virgil looked down the stairs at two children, a boy perhaps six, who was holding the hand of a girl who was maybe four. The sheriff was at his shoulder and he said, "Oh, no, no, no." He went down the stairs and said, "Kids, come on up here. Come on with me. Come on with me, honey."

He picked up the girl, and the boy took his hand, and Virgil said, "Out the front." The sheriff took the kids outside, carrying the girl, towing the boy with his hand; the boy looked back at Virgil, and Virgil saw the truth in his eyes: the kid knew, at some level.

One of the cops, a heavyset balding man in his fifties, watched the kids go and then started to snuffle, and Virgil said, "Okay, okay, everybody . . . We got a lot of work to do. Let's hold it all together."

One of the drug cops said, "What if they're coming back? Maybe we oughta get the kids out of here and set up an ambush."

"We can do that out a few blocks," Virgil said. "If that's the Boxes in there, we'll have to assume that they've got the Boxes' cars and they've still got the truck. We need tags for the Boxes' cars—there could be two of them. . . . Set up a watch . . ."

One of the cops, a sergeant, said, "I'll get that going," and he jogged away, and another cop came from the back and said, "Cars isn't all they got."

Virgil: "What?"

The cop said, "There's a gun safe back here. It's open, but there aren't any guns in it."

Virgil went to look. The gun safe was five feet tall, of a forest-green metal, had foam barrel slots for eight long guns, and five of the slots appeared to have been used. At the top of the safe were four foam-lined slots for handguns, and all four appeared used.

On the floor of the safe, a couple of ordinary plastic bags showed a flash of brass, and Virgil picked them up. Inside the first was a variety of empty shells: 9mm, which would be a handgun; a couple of dozen .44 Magnum, which could be either a handgun or a carbine, but most likely a handgun; a dozen or so .308 rifle shells, and as many in .223, and a bunch of little .22s. The other bag was full of empty 12- and 20-gauge shotgun shells.

"They got themselves an army," one of the cops said.

THE CHIEF OF POLICE, who'd been out with his wife at her sister's house, showed up, and he and Virgil and the sheriff got together in the driveway. Up and down the street, lights were going on, and Virgil sent a cop to tell people to turn them off. The chief, a burly man with heavy glasses, said, "We've got a perimeter set up. If they try to come back in, we'll nail 'em."

The cars' descriptions were going out to all agencies: a year-old Chevy Tahoe, a four-year-old Lexus RX 400h.

Virgil asked, "What about the kids?"

"Social Services lady has them—they heard the shots that killed their folks. They couldn't get out of the basement, no windows. They've got relatives down in Windom. We're looking for them."

The chief said, "Now what?"

Everybody looked at Virgil.

8

WHEN THEY LEFT the Welsh house, after killing Becky's parents, nobody said anything for a very long time—Jimmy smoked a ciga- rette and peered out the windshield like he expected Jesus Christ himself to pop out of the roadside weeds. Then Becky launched into a monologue about how her parents had never given her the things she needed to achieve her goals. Achieving goals had been the one constant refrain she'd taken out of high school, the one thing they drummed into you: about how if you didn't do this, that, or the other thing—pay attention and learn algebra— you'd never achieve your goals.

Like she was going to be a rocket scientist, or something.

You had to be seriously dumb, she said, to believe that rocket science shit. Being a small country high school, classes were less age-segregated than they might be in big-city schools. By the end of the year, most ninth-graders knew most of the upperclass- men and you knew what happened to them when they got out of school.

A few of the lucky ones, the rich ones, mostly teachers' kids, went to a state university somewhere. More went out to a two-year college, which was like going to another level of high school, where you learned auto mechanics or how to fix the big windmills that were sprouting all over the place. But most of the kids struggled around to get jobs and five years later they had two kids and the parents were working separate shifts at a Lowe's or a Home Depot somewhere, making just about enough to stay off food stamps.

Wasn't any of them going to become rocket scientists.

Algebra. Fuck algebra.

If she were going to avoid Home Depot, Becky had a pretty good idea of what she had to do, and none of it involved algebra. She was pretty, and had the tits and ass to go with it. Those were her assets; algebra wouldn't help.

But she had no tools. The tools just weren't available in Shinder, or in Bigham, either. You didn't get to the top, like the Kardashians, living out in the sticks. She begged her folks to take her to Los Angeles, or even the Cities, or even over to Marshall.

But they were afraid. They were small-town people—*small-time* people. They couldn't even imagine other possibilities. They sat stupidly on the couch and drank their beer and watched the bright life on cable and told her to get a job.

So they died, and she felt nothing for them.

All that came out of her in the thirty minutes it took to drive to the Boxes' house in Marshall. While she was talking, Tom, in the window seat, his thigh pressing against Becky's, peered out at the passing farm fields and thought about how crazy it all was. There'd been a logic to the death of the girl in Bigham, and then the black guy. The first was a robbery gone bad, which can happen when a gun is involved. The black guy had to die so they could make their getaway. He understood that.

But old man Sharp, the Welshes . . . Jimmy and Becky had gone over the edge. This was just nuts. Tom wasn't the brightest bulb in the marquee, but he was smart enough to know that he was in the darkest kind of trouble, and there wasn't going to be any Los Angeles, any Hollywood, not anymore.

The only reason he'd stuck with them, hadn't tried to walk away yet, was Becky. He could see her watch the violence, and eat it up. She liked it. And Tom found himself drawn to it, as well. He'd kill somebody, if it would get him Becky, with the provision that nobody would find out. He was not so much of a dead-ender that he didn't care about prison, or about getting shot to death by the cops. Jimmy could sneer at such things, but Tom couldn't. He would have walked away, if it hadn't been for Becky. He didn't want to protect her, he didn't want to romance, he just wanted her. Wanted to bang her brains loose. Wanted to show her just how strong he was . . .

Marshall turned out to be even crazier. They didn't even *know* the Boxes. Becky had worked for Box for a few months, had taken stuff to his house a few times, deliveries, knew that their names were Rick and Nina, and, she said, that they were assholes, but they didn't really *know* them.

When they arrived, the Boxes' garage door was going up, and when Jimmy pulled the beat-up old truck into the driveway, Rick Box had come out of the garage to see what was up.

Jimmy got out of the car with one hand behind himself, like he was hitching up his jeans, and when he got close enough, he pulled the gun and pressed it against Box's chest and said, "This is a stickup," and Box said, "What? What?"

Jimmy backed him into the garage, then through the door and into the kitchen. As they were walking him backward, he looked over Jimmy's shoulder at Becky and said, "I know you. You worked the counter."

Becky said, "No, you don't." She was no counter girl; she was a star.

Box's wife, Nina, was cleaning up the kitchen when they came through, and they could hear the kids yelling at each other, and Becky said to Jimmy, "I didn't know they had kids."

Nina saw the gun and said, "Don't hurt us, don't hurt us," and Jimmy said, "All we want is some money and a car. Get in there on the rug and sit down."

Becky said, "I'm gonna put the kids in the basement."

Jimmy said, "Do that," and Nina cried, "Don't hurt us," and Jimmy said, "Shut up," and to Becky, "Get the kids."

She got the kids, the little boy brave and solemn as he marched through the living room, the girl saying, "Daddy, Daddy," and crying, and Becky took them down the stairs. She was back a moment later and said, "No windows. No way out."

Jimmy said, "Maybe find a hammer and nail the door shut."

"We can just push a couch over there," Tom said. "Here." He pushed a short two-cushion couch out of the living room and between the basement door and a hallway wall, so the door couldn't be opened.

Nina Box said, "We'll give you anything you want."

She was a little heavy, but not bad-looking, and Jimmy asked Tom, "You want to fuck her?"

Rick Box said, "Hey," and started to get to his feet, and Jimmy shot him in the heart, and he fell down and curled himself like a snail.

Nina began screaming, and Jimmy said to Tom, "Well, you wanna?" When Tom said, "No, I guess not," Jimmy said, "Okay," and aimed the pistol at her head and pulled the trigger. The hammer fell on an empty cylinder, and Jimmy said, "Shit," and then he grinned at Tom and said, "Goddamn good thing that didn't happen with *him*. He would have kicked my ass."

Nina started to get up and Jimmy hit her in the face with the gun and she went down, and Jimmy said, "Let's look around. There'll be a gun around here somewhere."

They found the gun safe, in an extra-deep closet in the main bedroom; the key was hanging from a hook, and when they opened the safe, Jimmy found four handguns and some long guns, including a black rifle. He said, "Oh, boy, I always wanted me one of these."

But he left the rifle on the bed, loaded the nine-millimeter, figured out how it worked. Guns are wonderful machines: simple, precise, efficient. Anyone can use them—they don't discriminate between high and low, smart or stupid. To a gun, everybody's equal. Jimmy prodded Nina Box back into the living room, looked at her, then at Tom, and said, "You're sure?"

"Yeah."

Nina looked at her dead husband and began to shake with fear and regret and said, "Please don't," but Jimmy shot her in the head and she fell beside her husband and, like him, curled herself into a snail shape.

. . .

JIMMY, BECKY, and Tom spent the rest of the day eating, watching television, and ransacking the house. They got two hundred dollars in cash, which Jimmy added to the stash. Becky said, "Tell me how much we've got." Jimmy smiled, uncurled the sheath of bills, licked a finger, and counted it out: a little over twelve hundred dollars.

Tom said, "Holy shit. You must've took a thousand dollars off that girl."

"Not exactly," Jimmy said, but he wouldn't say anything more, even after Becky started picking at him. Finally, she asked, "Did you get that money for killing her?"

Jimmy said, "Shut up."

Tom thought, *Jeez. He did. He got the money for killing her.*

THEY WATCHED TELEVISION, but it was all cable stuff, and they didn't know that they were being hunted until late in the afternoon, a "Five dead in Minnesota" news flash.

The next thing they knew, they were looking at photos of themselves; and the sheriff—Duke, they all knew who he was—said that they were looking for a silver Chevy truck, and he said the numbers on the plate.

Tom rocked back and said, "We're cooked, goddamnit, I knew it, we're cooked."

Jimmy asked, "How could they know all that? How could they know it?"

Tom said, "Fingerprints. Witnesses. Somebody saw us, that's how. Everybody in town knew us."

"Gotta think, gotta think," Jimmy said.

"You don't gotta think at this very minute. What you gotta do is get that truck out of the driveway," Tom said.

THEY DIDN'T KNOW IT, because they weren't smart enough, but they were cruising purely on luck when Jimmy and Tom took the truck out of town, sticking to back streets, out into the countryside, with Becky driving the Boxes' Tahoe behind them.

Jimmy had figured out that as long as the cops were looking for the silver truck, they wouldn't be looking for anything else. He didn't know the land west of Marshall very well, but he knew what he was looking for, and he found it eight or ten miles out of town, a long snaky creek with a low bank. He drove the truck off the road and across the corner of a cornfield, then into the trees next to the creek, running over saplings and small stuff until he was stopped by a fallen log.

By that time, he was far enough back that the truck couldn't be seen from the road. The farmer would find it when he started plowing, but that'd be a while yet.

When they were all back in the Tahoe, Jimmy said, "Let's get back to the house. Sit and figure out what to do. We got to get out of here. Maybe . . . Florida. Or Alaska. We need a map."

At the Boxes', they ate Cheetos and watched more television, switching around local channels, and Becky found herself to be a star. The TV people had gotten her yearbook photo, which looked pretty damn good, she thought.

"You're famous now," Jimmy said.

At the end of the broadcast, the news channel put up two telephone numbers, one for the sheriff's office and one for the state Bureau of Criminal Apprehension, "Ask for Agent Virgil Flowers," and Jimmy laughed at Flowers's name and said, "If I was going to give myself up, it'd be to somebody named Flowers. I sure as shit wouldn't give up to that fuckin' Duke. He's crazier than we are."

THE PHONE NUMBERS got Tom thinking. When the other two were in the kitchen, he went through Rick Box's pockets and, sure enough, found a cell phone. Later, when he had a chance, he went through Nina Box's purse and found another one. He made sure they were turned off, and put them in his inside jacket pocket.

The next time Flowers's number came up, he wrote it in the palm of his hand. He went in the kitchen a minute later, wrote the number on a piece of notepaper, and put it in his back pocket, and scrubbed off his hand.

He was still in the kitchen, drinking a Pepsi, when Jimmy wandered in, looked at him. He said, "I think we got something. Got an idea."

Late that night, they went on a scouting trip to a town called Oxford, fifteen miles out of Marshall. They took both of the Boxes' vehicles, and left the Lexus at the Walmart Supercenter on

Highway 59, before they left town. If they needed to switch vehicles, it'd be there, Jimmy said.

So they scouted Oxford, but there wasn't much to see. When they came back, they couldn't get through to the house. There were cops all over the streets—they were clustering around the Boxes' place. Becky was driving, and took a left as soon as she saw them.

"Goddamn, that was close," Jimmy said, looking back. "Somebody must've seen that truck this morning."

"Now what?" Becky asked.

9

VIRGIL WORKED INTO THE NIGHT: called the crime-scene crew out of Bigham, where they'd checked into a local motel for the night. Virgil listened while the Lyon County sheriff and a social worker talked to the two kids, and then got Duke out of bed and told him about it.

"You think they're gone from my county?"

"I don't know where they are, Lewis. They might be running for the West Coast. But they might be coming back to you, since that's the country they know best. I just got no idea."

They learned that the Boxes had two cars, and that both were missing. Whether one might be in a shop somewhere, they didn't know, but the killers now had access to either two or three vehicles, and they put out stop orders on all three.

A BIT BEFORE three o'clock in the morning, Virgil got back to the motel, beat, and had just taken his boots off when he took a call from the BCA duty officer in St. Paul, who said, "We've got an incoming call from somebody who says it's an emergency, about those guys you're chasing. He wants your number."

"Did he say where he's calling from?"

"He said he's traveling, but he needs to call you right quick, or he's got to turn his phone off."

"Is there an ID on the phone?"

"Yeah, it's a guy calling, but it's a woman's phone. A Nina Box."

"Give him my number," Virgil said. "Jesus, give him my number. Then see if you can track the call, get all over the call . . . that's one of the guys we're chasing."

The duty officer went away, and fifteen seconds later Virgil's phone rang. He said, "Yeah. Virgil Flowers."

"This is Tom McCall."

"How do I know that?" Virgil asked. He needed to keep McCall talking.

"Jimmy shot the Boxes. He shot Mr. Box in the heart with one gun and then shot Mrs. Box in the head with another gun that he got out of the Boxes' gun safe in the bedroom. That good enough?"

"Tom, you've got to come see me," Virgil said. "You are in deep, big trouble, but if you're calling, I can probably help you out."

"Listen, I got nothing to do with this," McCall said. "I was hanging with Becky and Jimmy in Bigham—we *are* friends, I admit that, or anyway, we *were* friends. Jimmy and Becky said they were going over to a guy's house in Bigham because the guy owed Jimmy some money for dope, and they'd come back and pick me up. When they came back, they were driving this other car, and, man, I didn't know what they done until the next day when Jimmy shot his old man."

"It's all Jimmy?"

"It's all Jimmy . . . but Becky is his girlfriend, and they're gonna kill me. I can't get away from them. I know they're gonna kill me. I got the Box kids down the basement, I think they're all right, Jimmy wanted to kill them, too."

The Box kids remembered Becky pushing them down the stairs, so McCall was probably lying about that.

"Where are you?" Virgil asked.

"I don't know. Becky was driving when we left the Boxes', and they made me sit in the backseat. Becky's in a Shell station, we're getting gas and groceries. I'm sitting low in the seat, but Jimmy's out walking around, smoking. . . . They think I'm sleeping, but they don't know I got this phone. I'm scared to run. You gotta get me out, man. They're both crazier than bug shit. You gotta get me out."

"You're in a Shell station. Are they gonna hold it up?"

"No, no. I don't think so. We're in some town, but not Marshall. I don't know my way around so good. . . . But listen, I'm innocent. I didn't do any of this shit. I can tell you something that nobody knows. When we were in Bigham, we had NO money. NO money. So Jimmy went over to this girl's house in Bigham, and when he came back, he had a thousand dollars in cold cash. He didn't say so exactly, and I'm afraid to ask, but I think he was paid to kill her. He and Becky talk— I think Jimmy's coming back. Get me out, man, get me out."

Virgil shouted, "Call me back."

Maybe too late: McCall was gone.

VIRGIL PUNCHED UP the number of the BCA duty officer and at the same time brought up his computer; the duty officer said, "Sorry, Virgil, he was on AT&T and I still don't have anybody who can help me out. I got the phone number and your number and maybe we'll get something out of that."

Virgil told him to call anytime he had anything of substance, and then did a search for Shell stations in Minnesota. There was one at Springfield, probably fifty or sixty miles away, but there was no way that one would be open at four o'clock in the morning; the other one was at Luverne, just off I-90. That one was a possibility.

Another minute of digging on the 'net got him a phone number, and he called it, but there was no answer. Luverne didn't have a police department, but was covered by the Rock County sheriff. Virgil had that number in his database, called it. The duty officer said, "Tell you what—they aren't open. If he told you he was calling from the Shell station in Luverne, he was pulling your weenie."

"Could you send a car by?"

"I'll have one there in two minutes."

"If you see them, don't try to go one-on-one—for one thing, there are three of them, and they are killers. Get everybody you can find to help out."

Then Virgil sat on his bed and stared at his telephone. Ten minutes later, Rock County called back and the duty officer said,

"Virgil, there's nobody there. The station's closed. There's nothing moving downtown, nothing at all. If they were here, they're gone—but I got people looking anyway."

Virgil thanked him and hung up. He called the duty officer at the BCA and told him to get set on Nina Box's cell phone. "If he calls again, I want to know where he is, and I want to know *right now*. I want them all over that phone. If they want a warrant, get one. Call when you find out, and call me whatever time it is."

Then he called Springfield, wound up tracking down a police sergeant, who confirmed that the Shell station was closed and had been for hours. He told the cop why he was calling, and the cop said they'd keep their eyes open, "but they weren't buying any groceries here."

Virgil thought about that for a while, and wondered why McCall had specified a Shell station. Was it possible that he'd been at a Shell station earlier? If they were going to Los Angeles, they wouldn't be going out I-90. On the other hand, I-90 did go west, and everybody said Jimmy Sharp was a little dumb.

HE DIDN'T THINK he would sleep, but there wasn't much of an alternative—nothing to do but think—so he finished undressing, lay down, and opened his eyes at seven-thirty with a good solid four hours of sleep behind him; and felt not bad. He rolled out of bed and called Duke, and told him what had happened.

"Ah, jeez, you didn't have any way to run him down? You had nothin'?"

"I had nothin'," Virgil said. "I was pulling my hair out, trying to think of something. One thing for sure, we got the right people. And we got the highway patrol and every sheriff's deputy in four states looking for the pickup and the Boxes' cars . . . but what else is there?"

When Virgil got done with Duke, he called the BCA and found out that while Nina Box had an AT&T phone, the call had come in on a non-AT&T tower, through some kind of roaming arrangement, and they were still trying to sort out the wheres and whens.

"Let me know," he said.

VIRGIL NEEDED TO SCRATCH out some kind of plan, and he'd always found a good place to do that was a restaurant booth. He went over to a Perkins diner and got a booth and ordered the barn-buster breakfast, two eggs, hash browns, three buttermilk pancakes, with whole wheat toast, and lots of butter and syrup. He got his iPad and a stylus out and began doodling.

McCall had said that Jimmy Sharp had come back from the O'Leary house with a thousand dollars; that he'd been paid to kill Agatha. The O'Learys had said that if Ag died before the divorce, her husband would get three-quarters of a million dollars, or more. Virgil had known people to kill for three-quarters of a hundred dollars, so it wasn't hard to believe that somebody would kill for three-quarters of a million.

He'd have to talk to Duke about that, and then make another pass at the O'Learys. He liked seeing his folks, but maybe, he thought, he should find a motel over in Bigham.

. . .

"WELL, VIRGIL FLOWERS, as I live and breathe," a voice said, and he turned in the booth.

In his own defense, Virgil thought later, her breasts were right there, in a form-fitting sweater, practically in his ear. He did *not* goggle at them, but even if he had, it would hardly have been insulting, given their quality, and perhaps he did delay a microsecond before lifting his eyes to hers and saying, "Sally! Hey, jeez, I heard you moved to Omaha."

Sally Long. She was short and dark-complected, with black eyes and black hair, fifty percent Sioux, she'd told him, both of her grandfathers being full-bloods. She had been a high school junior when Virgil, a senior, had taken her to the junior prom. He'd spent the rest of the following summer plotting to get into her shorts, but never had. She said, "I did. With my husband. He's still there. With his second wife."

Virgil said, "Uh-oh." He pointed her to the seat on the other side, and she slid into it and smiled. She'd always been a happy sort.

She said, "Yeah," and shrugged, and said, "We had a few good years." There was a beat, and then she said, "Okay, a few good weeks. He was a fuckin' goat-roper right from the start."

"I'm sorry."

"No, you're not," she said. "I heard you're an important cop, and you've been in shoot-outs with spies, and that you've been married four times and divorced all four."

Virgil: "That's a lie. It's three."

They both laughed, and the food arrived, and she ordered a much smaller breakfast, but when it came, she used just as much syrup. The thing was, Virgil was really pleased to see her; happy right to the bottom of his toes. She seemed happy enough to see him, too.

"Your old man still got that tire place on 59?" he asked, as he worked through the pancakes.

"Yep. I'm the manager, now," she said. "You need your tire changed?"

Virgil's mind went blank for a moment, then he said, "Maybe," and the idea of a motel in Bigham slipped away.

THE NEXT TIME Virgil looked at his cell phone, he realized that they'd been talking for more than an hour. He'd told her about chasing the three killers, and the possibility that they were headed west. Now, he said, "Ah, man, I've got to go. I'm staying at the Ramada. There's a good chance I'll be back tonight, unless we run these kids down. You wanna go out for a salad and a beer?"

She would. He got her phone number and took off.

He tried to plan—he really did need one—but his mind kept skipping back to memories of Sally and that summer before he went to college. He'd been juggling three simultaneous romances, which was not easy to do in a small town; impossible, actually— he'd been caught out by all three of the women. Or girls. Or whatever they are when they're still in high school.

Crazy days. First time he'd ever smoked dope; remembered sitting up behind the Olson brothers' barn, by the old abandoned cattle pen, smoking ditch weed and fooling around with Carol Altenbrunner . . .

. . .

THE CRIME-SCENE CREW had shifted to the Box house in Marshall, working with the Marshall cops. Virgil stopped there first, wending through a line of TV trucks to get there. All the major Twin Cities stations were there, and local stations from all over western Minnesota and eastern South Dakota. A Twin Cities newspaper reporter named Ruffe Ignace saw him go through the line and put a hand to his cheek in a "call me" sign. Virgil nodded, held up a finger, meaning "It'll be a while," and went on through.

At the Box house, he learned from the crime-scene crew that the couple had been killed with two different guns, one an old-fashioned .38 revolver that shot one-hundred percent solid lead bullets, the other a 9mm shooting modern copper-jacketed hollow-points. They'd picked up the 9mm shell and could see a partial print on it, but hadn't determined who the print belonged to.

"Right now, I'm ninety-nine percent that the .38 was the same one used to kill the first several victims," said Sawyer, the crew leader. "I'm just eyeballing it, but it's the same kind of mungy old lead. I suspect he changed to the nine-millimeter because he'd run out of bullets for the .38. It's a six-shooter."

"I'll tell you what, Bea, you're right. We got it from another source," Virgil said, and he told her about talking with McCall.

Duke had come over to Marshall from Bigham, and Virgil took him aside and said, "What do you know about the Murphys there in Bigham? Ag O'Leary's husband—or Ag Murphy's?"

"Ag Murphy," Duke said. "What's up?"

Virgil told him about the conversation with McCall, and McCall's claim about the thousand dollars. Duke pinched his bottom lip as he listened, then said, "First time I ran for office, Stan Murphy—he's the old man—gave five hundred dollars to my opponent because my opponent was favored to win. The next time I ran, he gave five hundred dollars to me. We had an old-timey Episcopal church there in town, and Stan was a member. They had a big hoorah about women being priests and homosexuals and all that, and the congregation split in half. Stan didn't do anything until he saw which way a couple of the richest guys in town were going, and then he went with them."

"You're saying . . ."

"The old man's all about money. Nothing else. Just money," Duke said. "In fact, somebody told me that back in Butternut Falls, where he was originally from, he was a Catholic, and didn't join up with the Episcopals until he got here and saw which way the wind was blowing. Where the money was."

"Okay. But what about Dick?"

"I don't know the boy that well," Duke said. "He was a pretty good running back in high school, not good enough for college ball, but okay—he was honorable-mention all-conference, or something. But given his old man's attitude, I'd say some of that must've rubbed off."

"So if Ag's getting a divorce, and she dies before it gets done, the kid gets seven hundred and fifty thousand dollars," Virgil said. "Does that engage your interest?"

"It does," Duke said. "But if there's anything there, you'll have to find it. You've met my investigator. He's all right on some things, but this is out of his league."

"I may go over and talk to folks in Bigham," Virgil said. "I wanted you to know."

. . .

AFTER TALKING to the Marshall chief of police, and the sheriff, Virgil got back in his truck and called Davenport, and filled
him in.

"You made all the national talk shows," Davenport said, when
Virgil had finished. "They're saying *Bonnie and Clyde*. They're saying *Natural Born Killers*. You could probably sell an option on a
movie, if you move fast. Everybody in the world is headed your
way, and they're all hoping for a big bloody shoot-out."

"Most of them are already here," Virgil said. "I just saw Ruffe."

"That figures. He's still trying to get to the *Times*," Davenport
said. "You want me to send you any help? Jenkins and Shrake are
available."

"Lucas, it's mostly a hunt and everybody for a hundred miles
around is hunting for them. Jenkins and Shrake wouldn't add
much to that. I'm just hoping McCall gets back to me."

"All right. Well, anything I can do," Davenport said.

"I wish you *could* do something," Virgil said. "It's the most
frustrating thing. We know who's doing the killing, but how do
you find them? You gotta wait until they fuck up, and they could
kill any number of people before they do that."

VIRGIL CALLED RUFFE IGNACE. He'd worked with the reporter a
few times, in an "I'll scratch your back, if you scratch mine" arrangement that had usually worked out well for both of them.
Virgil regarded him as almost trustworthy. Ignace answered on

the first ring and asked, without preamble, "You working on any-thing else for the *Times*?"

"No, but just between you and me, I've almost got a story locked up with *Vanity Fair*. Just a matter of signing the contract."

There was a long silence, then Ignace said, "If you aren't lying, I'm going to kill myself."

"Use a lot of pills and alcohol, that's the best way," Virgil said. "Guns and ropes, you can get it wrong and wind up a vegetable."

"Aw . . . Jesus."

"So you wanted me to call?"

"Aw, Jesus." More silence, then, "I went to the press conference this morning. I need some details that nobody else got. I'll be just about exactly twenty-four hours behind the TV people."

"What do I get?" Virgil asked.

"I can't promise favorable mentions, because that would be unethical. But I can't help it if I feel favorably toward you."

"All right." Virgil gave him a few crime-scene details about the bodies, the murder scenes, about how he'd linked the car in James Sharp Senior's garage to the murders of Ag O'Leary Murphy and Emmett Williams.

"That's good, that's good stuff," Ignace said. "So—off the record, just between you and me . . . what are you doing for *Vanity Fair*?"

AFTER TALKING TO IGNACE, Virgil left Marshall and drove to Bigham, thinking about the O'Learys and the Murphys, and a little about Sally Long. Like this: *Gonna have to be careful with the Murphys and the O'Learys, I don't want to spark off a feud that'll get the kid lawyered up . . . talk to them, get the details, swear them to silence . . . What do I say to Dick? How do I get started . . . ? Boy, she really kept her figure over the years. . . . She looks better now than she did in high school. . . .*

He teased at the Murphy puzzle; if it was true that Dick Murphy paid for the killing of his wife, Virgil had three potential witnesses, all of them mass murderers. In Virgil's experience with mass murder, which was mostly through TV news, Sharp and his friends were likely to wind up dead before they ever got to a court.

As he was going past Shinder, he got the phone out again and called Davenport: "You said, and I quote, 'Anything I can do.'"

Davenport temporized: "Well, that was maybe a little hyperbole."

"I need to get into your database for Bigham," Virgil said.

After a few seconds' silence, Davenport said, "Okay. What are you looking for?"

"The baddest people in town. Not stupid, though," Virgil said. "I want somebody you might go to if you were thinking about hiring a killer."

"I won't have anybody like that," Davenport said. "The best I can do is, I might have somebody who could point you in the right direction."

"That'll work," Virgil said.

"Give me a couple hours," Davenport said.

. . .

DAVENPORT HAD SPENT the best part of two years building a database of people in Minnesota who would talk to the cops, and who also knew a lot of bad people. He had a theory that every town of any size would have bars, restaurants, biker shops, what he called "nodes" that would attract the local assholes.

He was trying to get two informants in every node, and did that by selling what he called "Cop Karma."

"Karma's just another word for payback," he told the more sophisticated of his recruits. "You stack up some good karma points with me, and the next time you drive into the ditch, if it's not too serious, you could get yourself some payback."

The network was paying dividends, but Davenport kept the whole thing close to his chest. "If you got some highway patrolman calling you up every ten minutes, trying to solve the local speeding crisis, it won't work," he said. "You only call on the heavy stuff."

GETTING DAVENPORT INVOLVED gave Virgil even more time to think about Sally, and as he turned the crest of a hill and dropped down the valley that led into Bigham and to the Minnesota River, he decided that he really had to put Sally aside.

A romance, hasty or otherwise, would divert his attention from the investigation, and Sharp, Welsh, and McCall had to be stopped; and Murphy, if he was involved, had to be tagged.

As he came up to the first stoplight in town, he took out the cell phone again and punched in Nina Box's number. As it had earlier in the day, it switched immediately to a recorded answering message. McCall had turned the phone off, but when he turned it on, the first thing he'd see would be five calls from Virgil.

He'd planned to go to the O'Learys' place and have a long talk with them about Dick Murphy. Instead, he went to the Pumpkin Cafe, got a BLT and fries, and a Diet Coke, and read the local newspaper, and waited.

He was on his third Diet Coke when Davenport called back. "I've got two names and phone numbers for you. You'll have to meet them somewhere private, because they don't want to be seen with you."

"Not a problem. Are they on their phones right now?"

"They are. Waiting for you to call," Davenport said. "Don't give them too much shit, and call me and tell me where you're gonna meet, in case something goes wrong."

"Are they gonna be a problem?"

"Shouldn't be. But . . . I don't know some of them as well as I should."

"Can they keep their mouths shut?" Virgil asked.

"If you use the right threats."

THE FIRST GUY was named Honor Roberts, and he said he'd meet Virgil at the Parker Bird Sanctuary where Bare County Road 6 crossed the Minnesota River. "There's a chain across the entrance, but if you look close you'll see that the lock is broke. You can lift it right off and come in. Be sure you put it back up when you come through."

The second source was a woman named Roseanne Bush, who'd meet him in the town's only tattoo parlor, which was called The Bush.

"We gonna be okay there?" Virgil asked.

"Yeah, we're not open till six. You can park in the back of the Goodwill store and walk down the alley. The door'll be unlocked, just come on through."

THE BIRD SANCTUARY was ten miles northwest of town, a piece of damp land with a lot of bare-branched cottonwoods in the loop of an oxbow of the Minnesota River. There was nobody else on the road when Virgil lifted the chain off the steel post, went through, and replaced the chain. A gravel road wandered back into the woods, and Virgil, though an outdoorsman, had to wonder what kind of birds were being preserved. Crows? Blackbirds? Starlings? He didn't know of any rare species going through there. Sandhill cranes, maybe? But didn't they usually hang out in cornfields?

Roberts was sitting on the tailgate of a Chevy pickup truck, smoking a brown cigarillo down to the end. He was a tall, thin man, with ragged hair and bright blue eyes, dressed quite a bit like Virgil, in jeans and barn coat. He was wearing brown cowboy boots, and stood with the boots crossed at the ankle. He said, "Well, you look like Flowers, from what Davenport told me."

"I am," Virgil said. "We wouldn't have called you up if it weren't pretty important."

"If it's about these people going around shooting everybody, I don't know much. I know Jimmy Sharp, but I never met either of the other two, far's I know."

"I'm not so concerned about Jimmy, unless you know where he is," Virgil said.

"If I knew that, I'd call somebody up. That boy is nuts," Roberts said.

"Okay. What I'm looking for is somebody you'd hire to do a killing for you. Who'd do it for money."

Roberts said, "Huh."

Virgil added: "Not a complete dumbass, who'd get caught and roll over on you."

Roberts uncrossed his boots and snapped the cigarillo butt down the road. "That's a tough one. Who do you think did the hiring?"

Virgil said, "What do you do for a living?"

"I buy and sell," Roberts said.

"A fence?"

"That'd be a goddamn uncharitable way to look at it," Roberts said.

"Okay, well, this is the way it is," Virgil said. "I'll tell you who I'm looking at, but if the word gets around town, and it goes back to you, I'll bust you, and I'll fix it so Davenport can't save your ass."

Roberts tipped his head and said, "I can keep quiet."

Virgil: "I've been told that Jimmy Sharp was hired to kill Ag O'Leary Murphy by Dick Murphy. Murphy stands to inherit three-quarters of a million."

Roberts whistled and said, distractedly, "No wonder."

"No wonder what?"

"I saw Dick shooting nine-ball down to Roseanne's Billiards last night, and he seemed pretty goddamned cheerful for some-body whose old lady just got killed."

"That right?"

"Pretty goddamned cheerful," Roberts said.

"This is not owned by Roseanne Bush, is it?" Virgil asked.

"Yeah, she owns pretty much every low-life place in town," Roberts said. "You know her?"

"No, but I heard about her. That a lot of bad people hook up around her."

"She might find a killer for you," Roberts said. His eyes nar-rowed in thought, and he asked, "If you think Dick hired Jimmy Sharp . . . why are you looking for another killer?"

"Because Sharp's kind of a dumbass, I'm told, and I'm not sure he'd be the first person you'd go to, if you were looking for some-body to do a good job on it."

Roberts said, "Huh. You're smarter than you look."

"Thanks."

"You know, if Dick was gonna sneak up on somebody and ask that question, 'Would you do a killing for me?' I bet the first per-son he'd ask would be Randy White. They played football together, and they hang out some. Randy was a linebacker and a mean little jerk. He'd try to hurt people. Everybody knew it, but the coach is just as mean as he was. A fuckin' rattlesnake. There was rumors he'd slip Randy ten bucks for every starter he'd take out of a game. I'm not sure I'd believe that—it's just too goddamned wrong."

"And White is still around town?"

"Oh, yeah. He works for the county road department," Roberts said. "Digging holes, filling them in. Runs a snowplow in the winter. He runs with a crowd that's too fast for him. Out to the Indian casinos and such. Needs money all the time."

"You ever done any business with him?"

Roberts showed a thin smile. "Maybe. County's always got some surplus equipment floating around."

WHITE WAS THE only name that Roberts really had. "I keep thinking of all your qualifications," he said. "There are two or three people around town who might kill for money, but every one of them's a bigger fool than Jimmy. I can't see Dick Murphy talking to them about it."

"What are the chances that Dick Murphy would do it himself?" Virgil asked

Roberts laughed, almost a bark, sharply cut off. "Zero," he said. "Dick's one of those smarmy little assholes who goes greasing around town, spreading trouble. If you want somebody to goad a couple drunks into fighting each other, Dick's your boy. He's a real friendly sort, when you first meet him, but the longer you know him, the less you like him. Just like his old man."

"Maybe I oughta be looking at his old man."

Roberts shook his head: "Naw. His old man wouldn't give five seconds to Jimmy Sharp. Or to Ag O'Leary's money, either. He doesn't need her money, and he sure as hell is too smart to try to kill her for it. Nope. It's Dicky you want."

Virgil left him in the bird sanctuary, peering up into the trees with a pair of binoculars. He wasn't, he said, looking for anything in particular, which seemed odd, but then Virgil didn't know much about watching birds. Instead of educating himself, he went back to town, to talk to Roseanne Bush.

BUSH WAS A RUGGED-LOOKING young woman; dark-eyed and dark-haired, her hair streaked with silver and red like tinsel; she'd never be called pretty, but might be called magnetic. Virgil found her sitting in her tattoo parlor throwing darts at a target face on the men's room door. Her shop smelled like patchouli oil and leather, and a smoker's haze stuck on the windows.

Virgil told her the same story he'd told Roberts, and she said, "I'm the same age as Ag was, two years older than Dick, and let me tell you something about little Dicky." She pulled at her bottom lip for a moment, as if pulling her head together, and then she said, "He didn't exactly rape me."

Virgil said, "Not exactly."

"Not exactly. We were a year out of high school, and we were drinking in my old man's bar after hours, and Dicky kept pouring it down me . . . hell, it was free . . . and he is a good-looking thing . . . and, he just did it to me," she said. "I kind of think I resisted, but I was no virgin, and I kind of think I led him on . . . but I think I tried to say no, and he did it anyway. The problem is, I'm not sure of any of that 'cause I was too damn drunk. But I'll tell you what: I haven't gotten drunk since then."

"So it might have been a rape, and even if it wasn't, he's an asshole."

"Yeah, that'd be fair," she said. "So's his old man. Anyway, he's got this friend, Randy White . . ."

White was the only name she had, though, like Roberts, she said there were a few more dumbasses who'd probably agree to do a killing, but nobody that anyone would trust.

"You think Murphy would have trusted Jimmy Sharp?"

"Oh . . . yeah. They knew each other. I saw them shooting pool a couple of times, but what passed between them, I don't know. Jimmy wasn't book-learning smart, but when he decided to do something, he'd get it done, somehow. You ever know a guy like that? He'd come up with one bad idea after another, and then he'd execute them?"

Virgil thought of a couple cops he knew, and said, "Yeah, unfortunately." Then, "But Dick would trust Jimmy."

"Jimmy would not squeal on Dick, if that's what you're asking. He's too proud to do that."

"So Jimmy would have been a possibility. Along with this White," Virgil said.

"I think Randy would have been the first choice, but yeah, Jimmy would have been a possibility."

When they finished talking, he asked her about her businesses, and she said she currently ran the tattoo parlor, a billiards parlor and bar, a motel, and a tavern. "My business plan calls for me to take the supermarket in three years—it's in trouble, but I think I could make a go of it. Then the bank. Once I got the bank . . ." She lifted a hand, then closed it into a fist. "I'll have the whole town right here."

"Jesus Christ, remind me not to move here," Virgil said.

She laughed and asked, "You want a tattoo? I could give you a nice little BCA, with a dagger through it, and some drips of blood running down your arm."

"But it'd hurt," Virgil said.

"Just a little bit."

"I try to avoid pain, in all its forms," Virgil said.

RANDY WHITE.

He asked Bush where White might be found, and she said, "Probably down at the county garage, out on County Road 2. He doesn't work real hard."

Virgil went down to the county garage, which turned out to be a Korean War–era Quonset hut, where he found a supervisor named Stan. Stan said that White was probably out on County 4, down past Stillsville, throwing roadkill into the ditch. "He's supposed to bury anything smaller than a deer, but it'd be a cold day in hell before you'd find him doing that. Just throw it in the weeds is good enough for him. That is, if he's not sitting in a beer joint somewhere, sneaking a beer. . . . Uh, you're not related, are you?"

"No, no, just want to talk to him."

"About Jim Sharp?"

"You know Jim?"

"Know who he is," Stan said. "Know he used to hang with Randy. Randy says this morning, when I asked him if he heard from his old friend Jimmy, he'd hit me upside the head with a shovel if I told anybody they was friends, which they were."

"You don't sound too worried about getting whacked," Virgil said.

Stan hitched up his Fire Hose work pants: "I'd kick the sonofa-bitch's ass, if he tried."

"You don't sound that close," Virgil ventured.

"I'm just tired of doing all my job and half of his," Stan said.

VIRGIL HEADED DOWN TO STILLSVILLE, most of which could have been built under an apple tree. There was a combination gas station and grocery store, with a pale-eyed Weimaraner guarding the place. Virgil went in and bought two cold Schlitz longnecks, since they didn't have any Leinies, put them in his truck cooler with a couple cold bottles of Diet Coke, got in the driver's seat, gave the dog the finger, and took off. He found White leaning on his shovel a couple miles south of town, his head on his hands, staring across a vacant field.

Virgil pulled up behind the orange county truck. White roused himself to look at Virgil, and asked, "Who're you?"

"Cop," Virgil said. "Bureau of Criminal Apprehension. I need to talk to you about your friend Jimmy Sharp."

"Stan tell you we were friends?" White asked. You could see the linebacker in him: the wide shoulders, the heavy hips. Virgil had some trouble with linebackers in high school, and wouldn't have wanted to run into White. But now White had the beginning of a beer belly hanging over his belt, and his nose was already going red with alcohol.

"I never talked to a Stan, but just about everybody else in town told me," Virgil said. "They said you were asshole buddies, you and Jimmy and Dick Murphy."

White's eyelids flickered, almost as if somebody had thrown a punch at him, and Virgil thought, *Uh-huh*. And he said, "So I brought along a couple of beers, and thought we could find a place to sit and talk."

A PLACE CALLED Shepard Creek was a few hundred yards down the road, and they went there, Virgil trailing along behind the orange truck. They parked on the gravel shoulder just north of the bridge, and Virgil got the cooler out of the truck and followed White down the bank.

The creek had decades earlier been dammed by local farmers to make a swimming hole. The swimming hole never quite worked out—it silted up over the years—but the remnant of the dam was still there, a pile of small gray granite boulders dug out of local farm fields. A few extra rocks had been left on the bank, to make seats around a fire hole.

Virgil handed White a beer and took a Coke for himself. They sat on a couple of the flatter rocks, and Virgil asked, "Any fish in here?"

"Bullheads, maybe," White said. "Snakes. It's about half mud."

"Smells like bullheads," Virgil said. They tipped up their bottles, and Virgil said, "So I've been told, on pretty good authority, that Dick Murphy paid Jimmy Sharp to kill Dick's wife. That there was no robbery up at the O'Leary place: Jimmy went up there to kill."

White shook his head. "I honest to God don't know anything about that. I don't want to go to prison, but I just don't know anything about it."

"I'll tell you what, Randy. I've sent a lot of people up to Still-water, but I never sent anybody that I didn't think deserved it," Virgil said. "And I did send up a lot of people who deserved it, but never thought I'd get them. Now: a number of people have told me that if Dick Murphy paid Jimmy Sharp to kill Ag Murphy, he probably would have asked you first."

"He didn't," White said, and Virgil watched him take a long pull at the bottle, drinking about half of it down, his Adam's apple bobbing like a yo-yo.

"But you know *something*," Virgil said. "I can see it in your face. There are lots of people dead right now, and it all started with Ag Murphy. If you cover up even the slightest little thing, and I find out about it, you'll go down as an accomplice to multiple murders. You'll do thirty years."

"Well, shit, man, I had nothing to do with Ag Murphy," White said.

"But you know something."

White tipped the bottle up and finished the beer, and threw the bottle into the creek. The bottle floated gently back past them, under the bridge and out of sight. Virgil said nothing at all, and after a minute, White asked, hoarsely, "You got another one of those?"

Virgil went up to the truck and got the second bottle of Schlitz, handed it to him. White said, "I was shooting pool with Dick, probably two weeks ago, and he says, 'You know what that bitch did?' He was talking about Ag. He said, 'Bitch went up to the Cities and killed my baby boy. She and her lesbo girlfriend went up there and got an abortion.'"

Another minute of silence, then Virgil asked, "Was that true?"

"I think it was," White said.

"But there was something else he asked," Virgil said.

White took a sip of the beer, then held the bottle between his knees, looking down at the dirt of the fire hole. "He said Ag had a bunch of money. A whole lot, and if something happened to her, he'd get it. He said she deserved whatever she got. 'Cause of the abortion."

"And what'd you say?"

White looked sideways at Virgil. "I said, 'I don't want to hear about it.' And I didn't. After a while, we were shooting pool, and Dick said, 'I didn't mean nothin' by it.' I said, 'Good,' and let it go. When I heard she'd been shot . . . I couldn't believe it."

"You should have gone to the sheriff," Virgil said.

"Duke?" White made a half-choking sound, something like a laugh. "If I'd gone to Duke, he'd of slapped my ass in jail so fast . . . and I'd still be there. The likes of me, I'd never get a break from the likes of him. The thing is . . . Dick never asked me. Never came up again."

"But you think he had Ag murdered. That's what you really think," Virgil said.

Another pull at the bottle. "Yeah. That's what I think. But he never said anything direct."

They sat looking at the creek for a minute, then Virgil stood up and dusted off the seat of his pants. "You take care," he said.

"That's it?" White asked. "Take care?"

"I might need you as a witness someday. If that happens, I'll expect you to tell the same story you told here. But maybe it won't happen. In that case . . ."

"He'll get away with it."

"Does that bother you?"

"Yeah, it does," White said. "A lot. I don't know why. I've always . . . kicked a little ass myself. Never ran from a fight. But Ag, she was a nice girl. She never needed no little cocksucker like Jimmy Sharp shooting her."

Virgil squatted down, said, "I do have another question for you. I was talking to a guy who said that when you were linebacking, the coach would give you ten dollars every time you took out a starter for the other team."

"Not true," White said, but he smiled into his beer bottle.

"Then what was it?"

He looked up at Virgil, and the smile might have been pained. "It was five dollars, and only for running backs, quarterbacks, and receivers."

"That's one of the evilest goddamn things I ever heard of," Virgil said. "In high school ball? It's a fuckin' game, man."

"Not in our conference, and not for our coach. If that sonofabitch ever loses a game to Redwood Falls, he's toast. He's outa there. He's gone. But you're right. It's evil, and I shouldn't never have done it. But, you know . . ."

"What?"

"I needed the money."

VIRGIL SIGHED and gave up on football. He said, "Listen, Randy. You're the only witness against Dick Murphy. Murphy may still be in touch with Jimmy. So you've got to take care. I'm serious. You stay away from Murphy, and might want to lock your doors at night—or maybe head out for a few days. We know Jimmy's got himself some hunting rifles."

White nodded, and said, "I got this supervisor. Stan. If you could fix it for me to get a couple days off, I could drive up to the Cities. I got a cousin there I can stay with."

Virgil said, "I can fix that. It'll be fixed when you get back."

"Okay. Okay."

"You have a little thing about Ag Murphy?" Virgil asked.

"No. Hardly even knew her. Didn't really know her until she married Dick. That's when I really got to know her," he said. He stopped, and Virgil waited, because he wasn't done. He said, "She was a nice girl. Friendly with everyone. I knew her in high school, and she was always nice to me, and then when, you know, she came back here with Dick, I'd see her around, and she'd always stop to talk. . . ."

"But there was really nothing there . . ."

White said, "Ah, Jesus," and it came out like a sob.

10

INTERESTING.

Randy had a thing about Ag Murphy, and Dick Murphy was apparently so ignorant of that fact that he'd tried to recruit Randy to murder her. That was one semi-solid piece. Only semi-solid because Murphy hadn't actually made the request; it had been *understood*, and juries wouldn't always buy that. But if Tom McCall had another piece . . .

As he drove away from White's truck, Virgil tried McCall's phone again, and again was shuffled off to Nina Box's voice mail.

Where the hell were they? What were they doing? They could be halfway to California, if nobody had been looking for them—but half the nation was looking for them, and there was no way they could have avoided that net.

Unless they'd killed somebody out on an isolated farmstead somewhere and were driving the victim's car out across the prairie toward Los Angeles, or down to the Mexican border. . . .

. . .

THEY WEREN'T DOING any of that; and McCall wasn't answering the phone because he was too busy.

Jimmy Sharp had a weird feeling about Tom. Like Tom wasn't with them anymore. His eyes just weren't right. He'd always been a little slippery about eye contact, but now he could hardly look at Jimmy at all.

They got into Oxford early in the afternoon, working the back roads into Bare County, dodging down side lanes when they saw other cars coming. Oxford was no bigger than Shinder, but because it was tucked away in the far southeast corner of Bare County, with no other towns close by, it had something that Shinder didn't: a branch of the Bare County Credit Union. Becky had once applied for a job there, but hadn't gotten it.

And they needed the money now: they were bandits, and they were famous, and they were going to jail if they were caught, but first they'd make a run for it. Jimmy had a vague idea that they might find a way to get to Cuba, or some other place far south.

Becky had her doubts, but she was in for the ride.

Tom . . .

JIMMY DECIDED THAT when they hit the credit union, he and Tom would go in together. Becky would drive and wait in the street outside. He didn't trust Tom to wait, and didn't want to come running out the door and see the getaway car disappearing over the horizon.

Though no place in Minnesota should be dusty in April, Oxford was. There hadn't been any recent rain, and half the streets in the town were still unpaved, with gravel-and-oil surfaces. Six or eight blocks in the center of town had tar roads, including the single-street business district, which consisted of a Marathon gas station and convenience store, a bar named Josie's, a barbeque restaurant with a cartoon pig cutout on the door, the credit union, and three empty buildings, one with a fading sign in the window that said: "Artist Lofts Available."

When they came into town, Becky said, "There's a chicken on the street."

A white hen was pecking at gravel on the side of the road, and Jimmy sped up a little, tried to clip the chicken with the passenger side tires, but missed, and the indignant pullet scuttled back into the yard she'd come out of.

Tom was in the backseat again, 9mm handgun in his lap. He said, "They'll have guns in the bank."

"No, they don't," Becky said. "I went out with a guy once, Bill Hagen, who worked in a bank, and I asked him if he'd shoot a robber and he said they weren't allowed to keep guns in the bank because the banks were afraid they'd shoot a customer and get sued. He said it was cheaper and safer to give up the money."

Tom said, "Bill Hagen is only like seventeen years older than you are."

"So what?" She added, "The thing is, they got money ready to give us—"

"Yeah, yeah, and it's going to explode on us, you already told us," Jimmy said. She'd seen it happen on one of the crime-scene shows. "So we're not taking that money."

Then Jimmy asked Tom, "Who's Hagen?"

"Asshole up in Bigham. He's gotta be like forty."

Jimmy asked Becky, "You fuck him?"

Tom snorted in the backseat, and Becky said, "Shut up," and to Jimmy, "What if I did?"

"Nothing. Just wondered."

Tom asked, "What were you? Fourteen?"

"I was a senior in high school."

"Everybody shut up," Jimmy said. "Everybody get ready. We're two blocks away. Get your hankies."

They had handkerchiefs to cover their faces, and ball caps to cover the tops of their heads and their eyes. Tom had the handgun, and Jimmy had the pump-action .30-06 with an extra magazine in his pocket. The gunstock was made of a black synthetic, and was big and frightening.

"I bet they have guns," Tom said.

"I told you, they don't," Becky said.

"We got no choice," Jimmy said. "The cops know about us. So we either get enough money to run, or we go to prison for life, if they don't shoot us down like a bunch of dirty dogs. If we take a hundred grand outa here, we're gone. We disappear like a fart in a cyclone. It's the only chance we got."

Tom thought, *No, it isn't.*

Jimmy said to Becky, "When I get out, you slide over and get ready to roll. We'll be inside one minute." And to Tom, "Get your mask up."

. . .

THEY'D GONE INTO THE BANK, the guns out front, screaming at the three women inside, about the time that a Bare County deputy sheriff named Dan Card, alone in his patrol car, was turning the corner onto Main Street, six blocks out. Everybody in the world was looking for the Boxes' Tahoe and Lexus, and as he rolled along the street, which he'd done probably three thousand times before, without ever having witnessed a single crime of any kind, he realized that one of the cars parked in front of the Oxford Credit Union looked right. It would only have been about the twentieth big SUV he'd looked at that day, but as he got closer, he realized it was the right color, and though he wasn't much interested in cars, he knew enough to know, when he was a block out, that it sorta looked like a Tahoe. He couldn't see the plates, but they looked like Minnesota plates, which was to be expected . . . but they were another point.

He picked up his microphone and said, "I have a Tahoe at the credit union in Oxford."

The dispatcher came back with, "You got the plates?"

"Not yet. I'm just coming up."

"Let us know," she said, sounding bored. Probably the two-hundredth Tahoe call she'd taken that day.

As he got closer, he could see that the plates weren't the ones he was looking for. He stopped, and said, "I got a plate for you. Could you run this?"

He read off the plate, and then got out of the patrol car. He could see somebody in the driver's seat, sitting there, but looking at him in her mirror. That was nothing new; everybody did that;

but the car's engine was running. That wasn't quite right, not when gas was $3.50 a gallon and rising.

Card left his door open so he could hear the dispatcher, and loosened the gun on his belt; the excited dispatcher came back, her voice urgent: "Dan, those plates go to a Ford F150 so there's something wrong there—"

And at that moment Jimmy and Tom, with the masks on their faces, burst through the front door of the bank and out into the street, carrying grocery bags in which they'd put the stolen currency.

THE FIRST PART of the robbery had gone just fine. They'd crashed through the front door, found three women inside, one behind the counter and two more in a side office, gossiping; there were no customers. Jimmy pulled down the women in the office while Tom pointed his gun around aimlessly and thought about shooting Jimmy in the back, but Jimmy was so on top of everything, so manic, that Tom chickened out and wound up waving his pistol at the mousy-looking woman behind the counter.

Jimmy shouted, "Get the money, get the money, get the money . . ."

They'd both brought paper grocery sacks inside with them, and Tom ran around behind the counter and started scooping money out of the cash drawers and into his sack, and Jimmy shouted at the boss woman in the office, "Open the safe, open the safe"—he pointed the rifle at the other woman's head—"or I'll shoot this woman right here, right now."

The boss woman scurried into a back room that had a two-foot-by-two-foot safe built into a concrete wall. She fumbled with the combination a couple of times, then got it. There were stacks of money on small shelves inside. Jimmy, though disappointed by the small size of the safe, scraped the money into his bag and then shouted at Tom, "Let's go. Let's go."

He didn't shoot anybody, because this was a robbery, not a killing. The two lines didn't cross in his mind. Jimmy held the gun on the women until Tom got to the lobby, and they both burst into the sunshine at the same instant.

The cop was a complete surprise.

THE COP WAS STANDING THERE, just down the street, and was pulling his pistol from his holster. Jimmy and Tom burst through the door and, when they saw him, came to a stumbling halt, and then Jimmy shouted at Tom, "Go," and he fired a shot at the cop, missing, and they both ran. The cop started shooting at them, missing three times, and then just as Jimmy got to the car, fired a fourth shot that hit Jimmy on the back of the thigh and knocked him down.

Tom went down at the same time, frightened by the gunfire, did a squirming turn on his stomach, and started pulling the trigger on his 9-millimeter. He was firing purely out of panic, hardly knowing where the cop was. Card had ducked behind his car door and, as luck would have it, raised his head behind the window glass just in time to catch one of Tom's panicky 9-millimeters.

The slug punched through the glass and then through the frontal bone of Card's forehead, through his brain, to the parietal bone at the back of his head. By the time it got to the parietal bone it had shed so much mass that instead of punching through, it deflected and spent a few hundredths of a second rattling around inside Card's brain, which Card didn't know because he was already dead.

He fell in the street, on his back, and in a last dead reflex motion, threw his arms out to his sides, so that he looked like a picture of a dead man.

Jimmy dragged himself to the car and crawled in, and bleated, "I'm hit bad. Man, I'm hit bad." He'd brought the guns and money with him.

Tom was in the back, with his bag of money, and he shouted, "Go, go," and Becky put her foot down and cried, "How bad are you? How bad?"

"It's pretty fuckin' bad," Jimmy cried. "Jesus, it hurts so bad."

JIMMY HAD PLANNED to go fourteen miles straight up County 9, then left on 99, a side trail, then up a jigsaw path of back roads to the house of an old man who'd once hired Jimmy's father to cut a bunch of dead trees and grind out the stumps. Jimmy had been made to go along and help, and he'd remembered two things: that the old man was an asshole, and that he was isolated. He lived alone in an old farmhouse with a garage on the side, farming a half-section, making just enough, in a good year, to keep himself in a decent truck and a winter vacation on the Gulf Coast.

Jimmy figured to kill the old man and take his truck. They'd lock the Boxes' car in the old man's garage, and since nobody liked the old fucker, it could be weeks before anybody went looking for him. Probably not until it became obvious that he wasn't doing his spring plowing. By that time, they'd be . . . somewhere else.

He hadn't told Tom where he was planning to go, because Tom . . .

He no longer trusted Tom. Truth to tell, Tom's days on earth were numbered, and truth to tell, that number was One.

BUT THEY DIDN'T go to the old man's place, not then. They wound up in a cornfield. Sometimes, the corn didn't get harvested before the snow fell, and wound up standing through the winter. Eight miles out of town, down a narrow side road, they saw a field like that, and Jimmy, screaming with the pain of the rough roads, pointed them down into a dry ditch, then sideways to the field. They didn't care about the car, and drove it right over the fence and into the cornfield. They could be seen from the air, but not from the road.

Jimmy was hurt bad, but not as bad as he might have been. The cop's bullet had blown open a wound along the outside of his thigh, almost like the flesh had been gouged out with an ice-cream scoop. There was blood everywhere. Becky got a blouse out of her bag and made a bandage and tied it tight around the wound, knotting the bandage with the arms of the blouse.

Blood began soaking through, but it didn't seem uncontrolled.

Becky said, "We gotta get some medicine. Some pain medicine."

"Where we gonna do that?" Jimmy groaned. His face was white as a dead man's, his teeth showing yellow against his white skin.

"They're gonna be all over this place," Becky said. "Tom shot that cop, and he wasn't moving. He might be dead. In an hour, we won't be able to move. Not until night."

"Well, what're we gonna do?" Tom asked. "He's hurt too bad."

"I'm getting better since we stopped," Jimmy said, but then he groaned again.

"We passed that little house, not more than a half mile back there," Becky said. "We could go back, see if they got any medicine."

Jimmy said, "You're just going to say, 'Can we borrow some medicine?'"

"I'll take a gun," Becky said.

"You think you can pull a trigger?"

"As good as you. I'll come back, fix your leg as good as we can, then we'll . . . go on."

Jimmy groaned and finally said, "I can't think of anything else."

"We'll leave you in the car. You can run it if you get cold," Becky said. "I don't think it's even a half mile back there, we'll be there in fifteen minutes. Back in a half hour."

Jimmy looked at Tom: "What do you think?"

"I think you need that medicine," Tom said. "If we're lucky, we could get something to kill the pain."

"Okay," Jimmy said, and after a minute, "Don't leave me. Becky, don't leave me."

. . .

NEITHER BECKY NOR TOM was in very good cardiovascular shape. They jogged and walked when they ran out of breath, then jogged some more; the house was actually only six hundred yards back down the road, and they were there in less than ten minutes. When they got close, they swerved off into a field so they could come up to the house on the far side of the detached garage. At the garage, they peeked in a window and saw a black Jeep; the other space was empty.

"Probably somebody home," Becky whispered.

She looked down at her handgun, a revolver, not yet used. Jimmy had loaded it for her, said, "There's no safety, so it's simple. Just pull the trigger."

"Don't shoot anybody if you don't have to," Tom said.

She nodded and said, "We gotta hurry. We'll try the back door. If it's locked, you gotta kick it in."

The door wasn't locked. They went through into the mud-room, and then into the kitchen, the floorboards creaking below their feet, and a woman called, "Will? Will?"

Becky was leading with the muzzle of the gun and she and the woman got to the door between the living room and the kitchen at the same time. The woman was maybe thirty-five and blond and thin, with her hair pulled back in a ponytail, and she was wear-ing a white blouse and blue jeans and soft slippers and every single detail of that crystallized in Tom's eye as the woman blurted, "Who are—"

Becky pushed the gun toward the woman's heart from two

feet and pulled the trigger. The trigger blast from the .44 Magnum was violent and deafening, and the woman toppled backward and died.

Becky said, "Jesus, I did it." And she said to Tom, "We gotta find the medicine and get out of here."

But then they both stopped and looked down at the dead woman's face, and Becky said, "She was pretty," and they both looked for a few more seconds, and the silence in the house was deep and pale, as though the sunshine were pulling back.

Becky was trembling, and her face was flushed; she was hot. Power of the pistol. Tom looked at her, and at the woman's body, then said, "Give me the gun."

Becky handed it to him, almost absentmindedly, still focused on the dead woman. Tom took the gun, then ventured, "Listen . . . you wanna do it?"

Becky was puzzled. "What?"

"We've got a little time. You want to go back in the bedroom?"

Her mouth dropped open, and the disbelief was right there on her face, quickly followed by scorn. "Are you crazy? You geek, I'd never . . . jeez, you sick fuck."

She started to turn away, and never saw Tom's hand coming.

Tom was tall and thin, but he had a bit of muscle and a little reach. The palm of his hand hit her square in the face, like a tennis racket hitting a ball, and Becky flew backward onto the kitchen floor. Tom put the gun on the kitchen counter and grabbed Becky by the neck and dragged her screaming and sputtering blood from her nose, back through the house to a bedroom, where he threw her on the bed. She rolled facedown and tried to crawl away from him, but he crawled on top of her and started pulling her clothes off.

She fought, but he raped her; and he enjoyed it. A lot. He enjoyed the sex, and he enjoyed the open-handed beating he gave her before and after. After he did it once, he had an impulse to apologize, but felt the sex coming back up, and remembered the way she'd whimpered, and sitting astride her hips, looking down at her, how wonderful she looked, all naked, and that got him going again, and he beat her again and raped her again, and finally he was done.

He pulled on his shirt and pants and said, "Don't tell nobody about this," and left her there. On his way out, he stepped over the dead woman's body, picked up the pistol, got the dead woman's purse off the cupboard, found her car keys, and went out to the Jeep.

BECKY HEARD HIM GO. Pushed herself up, staggered into the bathroom, looked at herself in the mirror. Her face was a mask of blood. She washed it off as well as she could, remembered to look in the medicine chest, got lucky, found a half-used bottle of Oxy-Contin prescribed by a dentist, took it, along with a tube of Mycitracin, took some clean sheets from a linen closet, thinking to make bandages, and was walking to the door when she heard the vehicle pulling into the driveway.

She looked out and saw a black Ford F-150 coming in.

Nearly panicked, she looked around, then ran into the bedroom, opened the bedroom closet, saw the 12-gauge pump shot-gun. She knew shotguns—most males out on the prairie, includ-ing her father, had one. A box of shells was right there on the floor, and she loaded two of them, fumbling a third onto the floor, jacked one into the chamber. When a tall man in a Twins ball cap pushed through from the mudroom, she was right there in the middle of the kitchen, still bleeding from cuts on her forehead and from her nose. He said, "What?" and she shot him.

Thirty seconds later she was in the truck, backing out of the driveway. A minute after that, she was pulling up next to the Tahoe in the cornfield.

Jimmy looked at her bloody face and said, "What?" and Becky said, "He raped me."

Jimmy said, "What?"

And she said, "C'mon, we gotta go. We gotta run." She began weeping, and she led Jimmy hobbling to the new truck, and pushed two OxyContins into his mouth and asked, "Where're we going, Jimmy? Where're we going?"

TOM HADN'T THOUGHT out all the necessary strategies for sur-render, but was pretty sure that he didn't want to let the Duke's deputies get their hands on him first. He wasn't entirely sure that he could blame the cop shooting on Jimmy, but there were no wit-nesses, and he thought he probably could. Still, the sheriff's depu-ties were bound to be pissed, and so he thought he'd better call Flowers first.

But even that frightened him. Should he keep on running? He

had forty dollars, which would get him halfway across South Dakota, and Becky and Jimmy sure as hell weren't going to be talking about this Jeep.

On the other hand, the woman's husband would be coming home, and they'd be looking for the Jeep anytime now. . . .

On balance, he thought, he'd be better off with Flowers. It took him a while to get his guts up—and he stopped once, at a turnout, to take a leak, and to throw the .44 into a culvert. Becky had scratched his back, which had kept him going at the time but now hurt like hell.

Becky.

He thought about it, and then felt himself smile. Whatever else that had been, it'd been worth it. If he lived through the rest of the day, his half hour with Becky would take care of his dreams for ten thousand nights. He'd never before just taken *anything*. But he'd taken her: she wouldn't soon forget Tom McCall.

But that was then.

He said to the sky, "Gonna take some shit now," but he finally pulled the cell phone out of his pocket and turned it on and punched up Flowers's return number. Flowers came right up and said, "Tom? Where are you?"

11

VIRGIL TALKED TO THE county administrator and fixed Randy White's paid leave, without giving up the exact reason. "We think that these killers might be a danger to him, and he's a witness on some relevant matters that I can't talk about, so we want to get him out of sight for everybody's good."

The county administrator, a short, stocky, gray-haired man with a buzz cut, who almost had to be a former Marine, said, "God bless you. Take him."

Randy, Virgil thought as he walked back to the truck, was not universally respected as a hard worker. He got Randy on his cell phone and said, "It's done. You'll be paid and it won't count against vacation. Get up to the Cities, but you stay in touch. I don't want to have to go looking for you."

He was thinking about getting another bite to eat when Duke called, screaming, "They hit the credit union in Oxford. There's a possibility that one of our deputies got shot, Dan Card maybe got shot, a guy's running him into Marshall in his truck. That's what we hear, we don't know anything."

Virgil found Oxford in his truck atlas. It was about as far away from him as it could be, and still be in Bare County. As he pulled out into the street, he saw two sheriff's cars bust a red light a couple of blocks away, and he hit his own flashers and took off after them, headed south out of town at high speed.

THE ROADS WERE CLEAR and dry and they were all running with lights and sirens. On the way, Virgil called Davenport and told him about it, and that there might be a cop down. Seven or eight minutes later, Davenport called back and said, "Card is dead. I just talked to Marshall. They had an ambulance run out to meet the guy bringing him in, but they say he's gone. You gotta get these guys, Virgil."

"You know the problem," Virgil said.

The problem was, they knew who the killers were, but they couldn't find them. If they'd fled Oxford an hour earlier, they could be anywhere in a circle maybe fifty miles in radius from Oxford. Using the formula $A = pi\ r$ squared, A being the area and r being the radius and pi being 3.14 (roughly), they could be almost anywhere in an area of 7,850 square miles, and the area was expanding rapidly, with every moment they went undiscovered.

"I know the problem, but this is crazy, this is out of control."

"Everybody in the state is looking for them," Virgil said. "What do you want me to do?"

A minute after he got off the phone with Davenport, Duke called and said, "Dan Card is dead, but he shot one of the gang. We've got blood in the street, but we don't know which one. The bank was robbed by two masked males, and one of them got hit."

Duke was going on when Tom McCall called.

Virgil's phone beeped with the incoming message, and he saw who it was, and he said to Duke, "I got McCall on the line. I'll call you back."

Duke said, "Hey—" but Virgil clicked through to McCall and said, "Tom? Where are you?"

MCCALL SAID, "Virgil, I'm running. Jimmy's been shot in the leg, Becky just killed some woman in some farmhouse, I'm on the highway, I stole a Jeep and ran away from Becky, I got no gun, but Jimmy shot a cop, I think, and those deputies are gonna kill me if they find me. I don't know what to do—"

"How bad is Jimmy?"

"He's hurting, he's bleeding bad, but they made a bandage out of a shirt. But fuck a bunch of Jimmy, man, I'm out here, I'm all fucked up—"

"I got you," Virgil said. "You tell me where to go, and I'll meet you there. Figure out the roads and an intersection, and I'll take you in."

"I don't know what road I'm on. I'm out in the sticks."

"Where's the woman who got shot? Are you sure she's dead? Where are they?"

"On County 9, right straight out of town . . . out of Oxford.

They pulled into a cornfield, an uncut cornfield. They're hiding in the corn, must be eight or ten miles out of town."

"North, south . . . ?"

"I don't . . . north, I guess. Up toward town, toward Bigham."

Eight or ten miles north of Oxford on 9. Not that far from where he was. Virgil switched the cell phone to speaker, said, "You hang on here, I need to look at my map."

He got the atlas off the passenger seat, found 9 out of Oxford, realized he had to jog east to catch it. He hated to cut McCall off, but he had no choice. "Tom, you need to call me back in five minutes, and I'll bring you in. But I gotta get an ambulance and some cops going to this woman you say got shot."

"You gotta help me, man. They had me held *prisoner*."

"Call me in five minutes," Virgil said. "I'll bring you in."

Virgil was still trailing the deputies' cars, all rolling at eighty miles an hour or so, where they could, where the roads weren't too bad, but they were coming up on an intersection that would take them over to 9 and the two sheriff's cars went straight through, and without any way to talk to them directly, Virgil took the turn and called Duke and told him McCall's story.

Duke said, "I'm coming into Oxford now, but some of it is lies for sure, because we're talking to the witness and he said one guy was shot, but it was the *other guy* who killed Dan. It was your boy McCall."

"He's calling me and I'm gonna bring him in, but we've gotta find this house where the woman is down."

"Okay, those boys who were ahead of you are the closest. I'll turn them around," Duke said. "You know where you're going? Exactly?"

"Over to 9 and then south toward Oxford. McCall thinks they're ditched in a cornfield, a standing cornfield about eight or ten miles north of town. There's not that much standing corn this year."

"You see them, you wait until we get there with the artillery," Duke said. "We don't need you dead and them running."

"If I spot it, I'll go on past to this farmhouse where McCall says the dead woman is. We can't take a chance on that."

"Call me. I'm heading that way. I'll get everybody heading that way, but you'll get there first. Call me."

Virgil threw the phone on the passenger seat and put his foot down harder, both hands on the wheel. It was two miles on gravel over to 9, which was a good blacktop road. As he came up to it, he could see a cloud of gravel dust straight ahead, on the other side of the intersection, and thought about going after it but didn't. The woman who'd been shot . . .

IF HE HAD GONE after it, he'd have caught Becky and Jimmy in the black Ford. Jimmy was feeling better, with the pain pills in him. The pain wasn't entirely gone, but it had eased, and his mind was clear, and he kept coming back to Tom McCall. Becky had told him about the rape, and she was still breaking down, weeping into her chest. "That sonofabitch, I should have shot him. He's fuckin' talking to the cops right now."

"He doesn't know where we're going."

"They'll be all over this county in half an hour," Jimmy said.

"Becky, you gotta go faster. Faster, c'mon, it's a good way yet, we gotta go faster, we got no time."

VIRGIL SAW THE STANDING corn from a half mile out, a patch of tan on the otherwise dark earth. He slowed to a normal pickup speed, fifty miles an hour, and cruised on by it, checking it out. No sign of a truck, but if they were in deep enough . . . Then he crossed a culvert and saw tracks in the dirt and thought, *Yes.*

A moment later, he came up on a farmhouse that sat a hundred feet off the highway; the mailbox outside said "Towne." The garage was open and empty, a nasty black rectangle like a missing tooth, and the openness of it caught him, and he said, "Oh, shit," and he pulled into the driveway and called Duke, who answered instantly.

"I'm three miles south of 10 on 9, pink house with a garage on the side standing open, no sign of a car, it's maybe a half mile south of some standing corn and there were some tracks going off there. I think it's them. I'm going in the house."

"You don't go in that house, you stay right there," Duke said. "That's an order, mister. We're not more than three or four minutes out."

"Fuck that," said Virgil, and he rang off, got out of the truck, took the shotgun out of the back, pushed in four double-ought shells, and let the gun's muzzle lead him down the driveway.

As he went, he heard his phone ring. McCall, probably. He let it go.

The back door was open and he stepped through, into the mudroom, saw a man's body lying on the floor and beyond him a woman, and then the man groaned and one arm twitched and Virgil jumped across his body, charged through a dining room and then the living room and back around through the kitchen, over the woman's body—her sightless eyes stared straight up at him, she was dead—and back to the man.

He'd been shot with a shotgun, but much of the blast had apparently gone between his biceps and his chest, knocking a bloody patch in his rib cage and a piece out of his arm. He was lying in a pool of blood, but Virgil had seen bigger pools, and he put down his gun and called Duke and shouted, "We got two down, one dead, but one's still alive. We need a medic here RIGHT NOW. Get somebody here RIGHT NOW."

Duke said, "Hold on," and then came back. "We've got an ambulance rolling, but it's gonna be a while. One of my guys got medical training, he's right behind me . . . he's got a medical kit . . . I'm coming up on you now."

Virgil looked down at the wounded man and couldn't think of what to do: he was not a medic, and was afraid that anything he did would be worse than nothing. The man was oozing blood, but not pumping it. Then he thought of the empty garage, and the two bodies, and he slipped the man's wallet from his pocket, opened it, found his driver's license, and ran back out to his truck.

As he was crossing the driveway, Duke swerved into it and came to a dusty screeching halt next to Virgil's truck. Another sheriff's car was right behind him, and Virgil shouted, "Inside."

Duke shouted back, "What're you doing?"

Virgil called, "I think they took their cars. I'm going to get an ID on their cars."

Duke ran up the driveway into the house, and a deputy from the second car unloaded a med pack from the trunk and ran toward the door, after Duke. Then two more sheriff's cars arrived, coming from the same direction as Virgil had, the cops piling out into the yard.

DUKE WAS BACK OUT fifteen seconds later, as Virgil was waiting for a reading on the victim's auto registrations. He had them thirty seconds later, writing the descriptions on a notepad: one black Jeep Cherokee, one black Ford F-150 pickup, registered to Clarence and Edie Towne. He got the tags for both of them, then climbed out of the truck and gave the note to Duke and said, "We're looking for these vehicles. McCall is in the Jeep, Sharp and Welsh probably have the pickup. It's possible they're still up in the cornfield."

Duke issued orders that sent deputies to the corners of the cornfield, where they could see anybody trying to get out, and designated two other deputies to accompany himself and Virgil off the shoulder of the road into the cornfield.

Virgil said, "I need as many of them alive as we can get. There's another thing going on here—we need them alive if we can get them without taking too big a risk."

"No risk," Duke said. "Alive if we can get them with no risk. I don't want anybody else shot. You all know about Dan. . . . All right. Let's go."

They took off, moving at speed, led by the deputies who would go past the cornfield and then post up on its corners. Virgil led the sheriff's own truck, and two more, ten seconds behind the first two.

As they went, he thought about the cloud of dust he'd seen disappearing down 10. Had that been them?

A minute after they left the farmhouse, Virgil took his truck off-road, down into the ditch, plowing along through dead grass, then onto a track that led down to a dry creek. He could see where somebody had busted up the other side of the creek bed, running over small saplings, and he stopped and got his shotgun out, and the other cops stopped behind him and he waved for them to spread out.

"Don't anybody shoot anybody else," he said. Every one of the deputies was carrying an M16, and they moved toward the corn in a skirmish line; and Virgil realized that with the limited visibility ahead, any hope of taking Sharp and Welsh alive was bound to be futile. There'd be no real chance of surrender, because they simply couldn't be seen well enough, and nobody would take a chance that they were surrendering when they might just as well be ready to open fire.

The best chance, he thought, was if they'd both been shot and were on the ground.

"Got a truck here, got a Tahoe here," one of the deputies screamed, and the line shifted in his direction, then stopped, then started forward again, collapsing on the target area. Virgil and Duke both jogged along the skirmish line, from opposite directions, and then Virgil saw the truck, but no sign of life around it.

They moved up slowly, cops leapfrogging past each other, always one or two focused on the truck while the others covered, and when they got close enough, Virgil called, "Don't shoot me," and jogged up to the truck, stopped, listened, then peeked in the back window. The truck was empty.

"Nobody," he called. "Watch the corn, watch the corn."

"Another track going out this way. There was another truck here," somebody called, and Virgil went that way and looked. The corn had been knocked down by another vehicle that had come in and stopped ten feet from where the first one was parked.

"Reversed in here and backed out," a deputy said. "They're in that Ford."

Virgil stepped back to the Tahoe and Duke, who'd been looking in the passenger-side door, said, "Somebody got hit hard. Lotta blood."

Virgil looked in; there was a lot of blood, but not as much as there would be for somebody who was bleeding to death. McCall had been telling the truth: Jimmy had been hit, but not incapacitated. They'd be looking for a place to hide, where they could give the wound some attention, which meant somebody in an isolated farmhouse could get killed in the next little while.

Virgil said all that to Duke, who had already put out a stop order on the Townes' Jeep and pickup.

"We're gonna need the National Guard in here. We need to shut down every intersection for fifty miles around," Duke said. "I'll call the governor." Then he asked, "What about McCall?"

Virgil nodded and went to his phone and punched in the callback number. McCall answered on the second ring and whined, "Where are you, man, where are you?"

"I need to bring you in, Tommy. Where're you at? You figured that out?"

"I'm on 79, going up toward town. Going, ah, north, I guess. I'm driving slow. Man, don't tell the Duke, those fuckers will kill me bigger'n shit."

"You pull over and wait. I'm coming," Virgil said. "Just wait. These folks down here are madder'n hornets about the cop that Jimmy shot, and you really do want to wait for me."

"I'll pull over, man."

"I'm coming," Virgil said.

THEY RANG OFF and Duke said, "We're coming with you."

"Behind me," Virgil said. "I need this kid."

Duke bristled. "This kid is the one that shot Dan. This Jimmy business is all lies."

Virgil said, "Okay, I'll buy that, but I don't want to scare him any worse than he is. He doesn't trust you, and I don't want him to run off and hide and maybe kill somebody else. So you stay back."

Duke seemed about to say something else, but then he nodded and said, "I'll give the order."

They rolled out of the ditch and onto the road, Virgil with Duke behind him, and another patrol car behind Duke, and Virgil thought it could be a close-run thing. Duke and his cops would kill McCall if they could get away with it; any excuse would do.

12

VIRGIL HADN'T TOLD Duke exactly where McCall was, so Duke had little choice but to follow. A second patrol car fell in behind Duke. With everybody in several counties looking for McCall, there was a fair chance that some other cop would get to him before Virgil did, which would not be good. Virgil put his foot down, determined to get there first, pushing eighty miles an hour, and then ninety, which was about as fast as he could go on gravel roads without killing himself: the 4Runner was a decent truck, but it wasn't a sports car.

None of which was made easier by the fact that he had to read his map book as he went. If McCall was on Highway 79, Virgil would have to make several zigzags up the road grid to get to him, and make them as soon as he could, since he didn't know exactly how far north McCall was.

So they did that, going as far east as he could on each zig, before it ran out, finally getting onto a road that was big enough to take him all the way to 79. All three vehicles made a screaming turn on 79, and ran hard for ten minutes, and then Virgil saw the black Jeep on the side of the road, maybe three-quarters of a mile ahead.

In his side mirror, Virgil saw the second patrol car pull out into the passing lane, and Virgil moved over until the center line was running down the middle of his hood. The deputy in the second car pushed him for a few seconds, then Virgil, his eyes flicking to the rearview mirror, saw Duke wave at the other cop, who backed off.

Virgil slowed sharply, and Duke nearly rear-ended him, then Virgil floored it again, leaving Duke momentarily behind. A hundred yards ahead of the other two cars, and twenty-five yards short of the Jeep, Virgil stomped on the brakes and slewed sideway across the highway, felt the inside wheels lift off the road for a second, then slam back down.

He jammed the truck into "Park," jumped out, carrying the shotgun, and jogged down toward the Jeep. McCall got out of the truck with his hands in the air. Virgil shouted, "Put your hands on the truck. Put your hands on the truck."

McCall turned and put his hands on the truck roof, in sight, and Virgil ran closer, stopping twenty-five or thirty feet away, and shouted, "I'm going to come in close. If you move your hands, I'll shoot you. If you move your hands—"

"I won't move, I won't move," McCall shouted back. He was looking over his shoulder, pale, frightened. Virgil took another step forward as a deputy caught up with him. The deputy had a handgun pointed at McCall and he screamed, "On your knees, on your knees—"

Virgil shouted at him, "Put your gun down. Put your gun down—"

The deputy was focused on McCall and shouted, "If you don't go down on your knees, I will shoot you—"

Virgil stepped next to the cop and pushed the handgun off line and said, "If you shoot him, I'll arrest you for murder."

The cop flinched then, and looked at Virgil in disbelief. "What are you doing? What are you doing?"

"Put the gun down," Virgil said. "If you shoot him, I'll send you to prison for murder. Put your gun down."

"He killed Dan—"

"He's quit. Put your fuckin' gun down," Virgil said.

The cop looked back at McCall, and for a second Virgil thought he might fire; but then he looked back at Virgil and said, "This is bullshit."

Duke came up. Virgil had seen him moving slowly out of his car, and faster only when he saw Virgil pushing on the deputy, but never quite in a jog. He'd expected the deputy to kill McCall, and didn't want to be right there. Now he called, "What's going on here?"

Virgil walked to McCall and said quietly, "I'm going to put some handcuffs on you. The safest thing you can do is cooperate, because these guys want to kill you. If you've got cuffs on, they can't do that. Now, face the truck and put your first hand behind your back."

McCall did that, and said, "Virgil, honest to God, I never hurt anybody. I was a hostage. They took me as a prisoner."

"Other hand," Virgil said.

McCall put his other hand behind him and said, "Jimmy shot that officer. I yelled for the officer to get down, but Jimmy—"

"You lying sack of shit," the deputy shouted. "We got witnesses." And to Virgil: "I ought to bust you for interfering with me. How would aggravated assault fill out your day?"

Virgil said quietly, "You were looking for an excuse to murder this man. You were interfering with an arrest while you were doing it. I'm going to talk to the attorney general about it. We may have to consider charges even now. We don't allow lynchings in Minnesota. And we don't allow convicted felons to be lawmen."

"Bullshit—"

Duke snapped at the deputy, "Watch your language." To Virgil: "You'd have a heck of a time making that argument with any jury around here."

"There wouldn't be a trial around here, it'd be up in the Cities," Virgil said. Then he backed off: "But if you keep this fellow off me, we'll just call it a bit of overenthusiasm, or excitement, and let it go at that."

Duke said, "You know he killed Dan."

"That's what I heard," Virgil said. "I'll be happy to slap him in Stillwater just as fast as you would. But we're gonna have a trial before we do that. We're not going to shoot him down in a ditch."

McCall said, "I never—"

Virgil said, "Shut up," and, "You have the right to remain silent. Anything you say can and will be used against you in a court of law. You have the right to an attorney. If you cannot afford an attorney, one will be provided to you. You got all that?"

McCall nodded dumbly, and just to be sure he understood it, Virgil said, "Listen, you don't have to talk to us if you don't want to, but if you do talk to us, it can be used against you when we get to a trial. We'll provide an attorney to represent you. You sure you got that?"

McCall said, "Yeah, I got it. But I didn't do anything, I was kidnapped—"

"We all just want to make sure you understand about the attorney," Virgil said.

"Okay."

Virgil said to Duke and the deputy, "You're witnesses to the Miranda. He's my prisoner. It'd be best for all of us if we put him in jail over in Marshall, because if anything happened to him in Bare County . . . Well, the trouble would be so deep it's unlikely that any of you would be working in law enforcement again. So I'm taking him."

The deputy looked at Duke and said, "Sheriff, you can't—"

Duke snapped, "Don't tell me what I can do." He nodded at Virgil. "Take him. But I want to know every word that comes out of his mouth."

"You'll get it," Virgil said. "Let's get the crime-scene people over here to take this Jeep apart. We don't want to miss a single thing. And don't let anybody touch it—we don't want any confusing DNA or fingerprints."

And Virgil asked McCall, "Where's your pistol? You were seen with one."

"I don't got no gun. They wouldn't let me have no gun with bullets in it, because they were afraid I'd shoot Jimmy. Becky's got the gun. She used it to shoot some woman back there, in the farmhouse. Did you find the farmhouse?"

"We found it," Virgil said. "Who shot the man?"

McCall looked confused. "Wasn't no man when I went running out of there. Becky shot this woman, and then there's some other stuff, and she went to look for medicine for Jimmy, and when she went up the stairs, I grabbed the woman's keys off the kitchen counter and ran out to the driveway and jumped in the Jeep. I didn't see no man anywhere."

Duke said, "This Clarence Towne is going to make it. Got word from the medics: he looks bad, but he's got one good lung and no arteries hit, so we'll find out if the boy is telling the truth on that. Not that it'll make a hell of a lot of difference."

Virgil said, "It could make some. . . . Tom's in a lot of trouble, but there are things that could count to his benefit, if we go to trial."

As he said it, he swiveled away from McCall so McCall couldn't see his face, and winked at Duke and the deputy. Duke showed a tiny nod, and said, "So take him. I don't want to look at him anymore."

"Crime Scene'll be here pretty quick," Virgil said. "Don't let anybody touch that truck."

VIRGIL GOT MCCALL into the front seat and locked his handcuffed wrists to an eyebolt under the seat, using a chain that let McCall sit upright but not move much.

"What happens if we roll the truck? I couldn't get out," McCall whined.

"I know. You'd probably burn to death," Virgil said. McCall blanched, and Virgil added, "Relax, Tom. You're still alive, and you wouldn't have been if anybody else had gotten to you first. And I'm not going to roll the truck. Probably."

Behind them, Duke had turned around, with the other patrol car behind him, and they headed back toward the farmhouse.

It was a fifty-mile run into Marshall, and Virgil started by telling McCall that he was in desperate trouble, and almost certainly going to prison forever. "You can only help yourself by cooperating. If you're convicted, maybe get early parole or something."

After ten minutes of bullshit, with McCall breaking down to weep, and to claim his status as a victim, not a killer, Virgil, feeling that he'd primed the pump, held up a small handheld digital recorder and said, "I want to make a record of our talk. You know, your lawyer can use it to prove you cooperated."

"I guess it's okay," McCall said.

Virgil turned the recorder on and said, "I just want to make sure that you remember that Miranda warning. Remember when I told you that you've got a right to remain silent . . ." He went through it again, and McCall said, "Yeah, yeah, I remember."

"Great," Virgil said. "Listen, tell me about Jim Sharp and Becky Welsh. We gotta find them before they kill anybody else. You know where they're at?"

"In a cornfield, I think," McCall said. He told Virgil about running out of Oxford, with Jimmy bleeding from the leg wound, about hiding in the cornfield, about walking back to the farmhouse to get medicine and a different car.

As he told the story, he slowed, and his eyes caught Virgil's, and Virgil realized that he was editing the story as he told it. Some of it, at least, was a lie. "We got down to this farmhouse, and there wasn't anybody home. The back door was locked, but Becky knew

how to get it open with a driver's license. We, uh, we got inside . . .
uh, we were going to look for medicine, but, uh . . ."

"Yeah? What about Becky?"

"She always wanted to fuck me. That's the God's truth. She'd
play footsie with me under the dinner table, like she was daring
Jimmy to catch us. Jimmy'd kill her if she did. But then, Jimmy
was hurt so we got to this empty house and she said she wanted to
fuck me and we went back into this bedroom and did it. She had
this big gun—"

"She had a big gun and made you take her back into the bedroom and f—" He remembered the recorder, and covered himself.
"—have sex with her?" Virgil's skepticism shone through.

"No, no, not exactly *that* way. . . . I could take it or leave it, you
know. She makes me nervous. She wants to be smacked around
a little, which is weird. Anyhow, we were back there, just finished up and getting dressed, when we heard this Jeep come into
the driveway. We didn't know it was a Jeep, but it was. Anyway, she
gets up with this gun, and this woman walks in through the
kitchen and Becky goes around through the dining room and gets
in behind her, and I hear the woman saying, like, 'Who the fuck
are you?' and *Boom.* Becky shoots her. I go running through the
dining room, and I say, 'What'd you do? Oh, no, not another one,'
and Becky said, 'Don't tell Jimmy what we done, about fuckin'
me,' just like the dead woman didn't count for nothing. Then she
said she was going to go upstairs and look for medicine, and I said
I'd watch the road. Soon as I heard her upstairs, I grabbed the keys
off the counter and ran out to the Jeep and took off."

"And you never saw a man . . ."

"No. Never did. I just took off and I didn't stop running until I got you on the phone and you told me to stop. I was cooperating."

THERE WAS SOMETHING screwed up about the story, Virgil thought, but he called Duke and told him about it. "Have somebody check that back bedroom, see if there might have been some sex going on there."

"I'm right outside. Just hang on," Duke said. Virgil heard a screen door slam, and Duke saying something to somebody else, then Duke came up and said, "Well, something happened here. There's some blood on a pillow. Not much. Like a cut or something. Looks like it's been used, the blankets are all over the place."

"Get Crime Scene on it," Virgil said. "Don't let anybody else in there."

When he got off the phone, McCall said, "You believe me now?"

Virgil said, "Maybe."

And after a minute, Virgil asked, "Tell me what happened at the O'Leary house."

"Okay. Okay. Jimmy didn't have any money. Never did. Didn't have a pot to piss in, nor a window to throw it out of. I had an apartment, up in the Cities, but lost my job, and was running out of rent, and Jimmy said if we could get to Bigham, he knew a guy who'd get us jobs. I had like eighteen dollars, for gas and some food. So we went there, in Jimmy's old car—we actually spent a night living in the car, and it was colder 'n shit. The car was a piece of shit, and kept breaking down, the starter didn't work, and the guy who was supposed to get us jobs didn't know where we could get one. So then Jimmy said he knew this O'Leary guy, and me and Becky should come along with him . . . and maybe get a loan. We started out late, and we didn't know exactly where it was, and the car was giving us trouble, so we left it in this parking lot and walked. It was pitch-dark when we got there. We went down the side of the house, and I sez, 'What the hell is this?' and Jimmy pulls out this gun and puts it up against my chest, and he sez, 'You're gonna open a window, big guy, or I'm gonna shoot you in the heart.' He's a short guy, and I'm not, so we went to this window, and I lifted it up, and he pointed the gun and said, 'Get in there,' so I went in there."

McCall said the three of them crept through the house, Mc-Call quaking in his shoes. Jimmy forced him to climb the stairs, then pointed him to the front of the house, where they woke up two girls in a bed. "One of the girls started screaming, and Jimmy shot her. And somebody started yelling from another part of the house, and I ran, and they all come behind me."

Out in the street, they ran down the hill to the car, but couldn't get it started. Jimmy completely freaked out, McCall said, but then they saw a man come out of the apartment house and walk over to his car. Jimmy jumped out of the car and ran over and shot him. "Just like that. Not even a howdy-do." A minute later, they were on the way to Shinder.

"They kept telling me, 'Tom, we're gonna kill you, you mother-fucker, if you make one noise or try to get away.'"

"But where did the money come in?" Virgil asked. "This money he had?"

"Well, we got to Shinder, and we were going to hide in Jimmy's house until things quieted down, but Jimmy, man, he was like, crazy, and he got in an argument with his old man and shot the old fucker down.

"Jimmy said we'd have to run, sooner or later, and the old man's truck was no good, we needed some money to get a better one, and I said, 'Shit, where'll we get any money?' and Jimmy said, right out of the blue, 'Well, I got a grand.' And Becky and I both said, 'What?' and he pulled this roll of brand-new twenties out of his pocket. He said he took it off that girl he shot, but that's bullshit. It was pitch-dark in there, and she was in bed. She had the money between her legs or something? I don't think so."

"So where do you think he got it?"

"That's the thing. Becky kept giving him shit about it, so he whips out this old pistol and blows across the barrel, and sez, 'Never thought you'd be fuckin' a hit man, huh?'"

"A hit man?"

"That's what he said. But that's all I know about it. That he called himself a hit man," McCall said.

"If somebody paid him to kill the girl, who would that have been?" Virgil asked.

McCall shrugged. "I got no idea."

"How long were you in Bigham?"

"Three days . . . well, we got there late one day, then overnight, then another day, then overnight, then another day, and that night was the, you know, thing at O'Leary's."

"Okay. When you lifted the window, did you have to force a lock?"

"Nope. Went right up. Zip. Like it was greased," McCall said.

"Did Jimmy pick it?"

"Yeah. He went right to it. It was pretty high up, it was over a kitchen counter, so it was a little too high for him. That's why he needed me. And I wasn't going to say no, with a pistol pointed at my heart."

Virgil thought it over, and then said, "Those nights when you were in Bigham . . . what'd you do?"

"Hung out, mostly. Didn't have the money to do much. Shot some pool. Jimmy thought he was a pool shark. But he's not. He looks like a pool shark, but he's really bad at it."

"Was Jimmy hanging with anybody in particular? Did he seem tight with anyone?"

McCall looked at Virgil for a long moment, then said, "You know, I got an answer to that, but I think I need to talk to a lawyer. Like you said, you'd get me a lawyer."

Virgil thought, *Ah, shit.* He'd been so close, but with the tape running, he had no choice. "All right. We'll stop right here, get you to Marshall, and hook you up with an attorney."

He turned off the tape and said, "You motherfucker, you killed that cop. I hope you rot in hell."

That put a further dent in the conversation. McCall cowered against the passenger-side door until they got to the law enforcement center in Marshall, and Virgil turned him over to the sheriff.

After spending a half hour on paperwork, he called Davenport and said, "One down. But somebody else is probably dead, unless Jim and Becky are out in another cornfield."

"They can't hide for long," Virgil said. "The governor just put the National Guard on the roads—they're deploying at every intersection out there. As soon as they're in, they'll organize teams of troops and cops and hit every house on the prairie."

"How long will that take?"

"Probably be in place by tomorrow morning, and the search'll start by tomorrow afternoon."

"That means that they'll probably kill them," Virgil said. "I need Jimmy alive long enough to get the guy who paid him to kill Ag Murphy."

"Who'd that be?" Davenport asked.

"Ag Murphy's husband."

"Really? Well—good luck with that."

13

VIRGIL FINISHED UP with the sheriff's department, copied the McCall interview to his laptop, and left the recorder in the LEC evidence room. He had a Diet Coke and a conversation with the sheriff and the Marshall police chief, then called Duke. Nobody had any idea where Sharp and Welsh had gone. Deputies were running all over Bare County, and the adjacent counties, looking for the Townes' truck, but nobody had seen it.

"I fear for what we're going to find when we catch up to them," Duke said.

"So do I," Virgil said. "I have no idea of whether they're north, south, east, or west. I wish I knew, because I'd like to be there when we do find them."

AFTER THAT, Virgil was at loose ends. Since he was there in Marshall, anyway, and because everybody had his cell phone number and would be in touch if anything broke, he called Sally Long. She answered on the third ring and said, "Virgil Flowers: you *did* call."

"If you're not real busy, we could get dinner," Virgil suggested. "Maybe go over to the Six and catch a movie."

"Or maybe just find someplace to talk about our feelings," she said. And, into the silence, "Just kiddin', there, cowboy."

"Jeez, you scared the heck out of me," Virgil said. "Every time I do that, I get divorced."

HE SPENT the next three hours at his hotel, much of it on the phone or the computer, keeping up. There was a long story about the murders, out of the *Star-Tribune* website, with profiles of the suspects; and more stories from Omaha, Kansas City, and Fargo. Chicago, New York, and St. Louis had picked up AP stories, which were rewrites of the *Star-Tribune*, but Los Angeles had a columnist on the ground. And television from everywhere.

Channel Three out of the Cities had video from a National Guard MP detachment showing soldiers loading up a bunch of Humvees, and the reporter said that most of the MPs had gotten back from Iraq that past fall, and had serious experience running checkpoints and roadblocks.

Virgil was mentioned in the *Star-Tribune* as a "top BCA agent and troubleshooter," which meant that Ignace was sucking up to him.

The last part of his motel time he spent making himself pretty and swell-smelling, buffing up his cowboy boots and shaving again. After a last check, he headed out the door, not feeling particularly guilty about it, either.

Sally was living in a small blue house not far from the university. A young blond woman, perhaps twenty years old, came to the door, crunching on a stalk of celery filled with orange pimento cheese spread. She said, "You must be Virgil. Sally'll be right out."

"Who're you?" Virgil asked, as he stepped inside. The house was neatly kept, and sparsely furnished, like a bachelor woman might do it.

"Barbara," the woman said. "I'm a student. I rent the garage loft from Sally."

SALLY TOOK ANOTHER five minutes and Virgil sat on the couch and watched Barbara munch through another two stalks of celery—Virgil turned down the offer of one, saying, "We're going out to dinner"—and found out that Barbara was studying studio arts. "The problem is, I don't have any talent," she said.

"That's a good thing to find out," Virgil said.

"The other problem is, I'm not interested in anything else. So, what do *you* think I should do?"

"Why'd you italicize the *you*?"

"Because I've asked everybody else, and they all give me bullshit answers. So see, I'm relying on you to give me a non-bullshit answer." She crossed her legs, and cocked her head, waiting for an answer.

"Well," Virgil said, after a minute, "I never wanted to be a cop, but I just kind of got there. I didn't plan it, but I found out that it's pretty interesting. So, if I were you, I'd look around for something that seems like it might be an important job, and just *pick it*. Even if you're not too interested in the general subject matter right now, if it's really important, you'll get interested in it later, when you start learning the details of it."

She peered at him as she gnawed down the second of the two celery stalks, then said, "That sounded less bullshitty than most answers. Not entirely un-bullshitty, but mostly."

"Well, good, then," Virgil said. "I passed."

"PASSED WHAT?" Sally asked, as she came into the room from the back of the house. "Are we talking kidney stones?"

Virgil stood up and thought, *Ooo,* and pecked her on the cheek. She was wearing a silky black blouse and tight black jeans, tucked into cowboy boots with turquoise cutouts that looked like they were right off the prairies of New York's Upper East Side.

"Talking about what Barbara should do in life," Virgil said. And, "Great boots. You got horses?"

"Two," she said. "The old man's got a ranch west of town."

THEY TALKED ABOUT Barbara on the way out to the Blue Moon, a steak house that wasn't terrible. And they talked about horses, which Virgil didn't know much about, except that they sometimes bite people, and that the French sometimes ate them with both red and white sauces. Then they talked about Barbara's problem.

"You know, when I was in high school, I was going to be a lawyer and do great things for the Indian people," Sally said. "When I got to college and started talking to people, I found out that there are more lawyers helping the Indian people than the Indian people can really use. So then I didn't know what to do, and when I got divorced, I called my dad, and he said, 'Come back here and run the business.' I couldn't think of anything better at the moment— I figured I'd do it for a couple of years and then go back to school— but now, I find out that running the business is pretty interesting. And I have fourteen employees who depend on me to do good, and I kinda like that. The responsibility. It's the first time I feel like I'm really doing something."

"You *are* doing something," Virgil said. "One of the problems with these kids I'm chasing is that they never did anything. I'm not sure how much of that is their fault, but if they'd had something to do, other than sit on their asses, or shoot pool . . . none of this would have happened. Maybe."

"Everybody needs something," she said. Then, "You know what? Everybody *deserves* something."

They got to the steak house, were seated in a U-shaped booth, and ate salads and pork chops, and gravitated together until their thighs were touching under the table, and Virgil began to feel really warm.

When the waiter took away the main-course plates, Virgil asked, "You want some dessert?"

She put her hand around his wrist and said, "Sure. I'd like a little Flowers."

. . .

HE GOT HER BACK to the motel, and on the bed, and pulled off her boots one at a time and dropped them on the floor, then pulled off the tight jeans, stopped when the waistline got down to her knees, and turned his head up and laughed, and when she asked, "What?" he started pulling again and said, "I've been waiting to do this since eleventh grade."

She surprised him and said, "So have I—been waiting for you to do it."

The jeans came off, and so did everything else, and they got busy, and an hour later, she muttered into his shoulder, "Well, that was better than pumpkin pie. With whipped cream, even."

"Far better?"

"Maybe not far better," she said.

"Then we just gotta try harder."

"I could do that."

A while later, he said, "We should have done this a long time ago."

She said, "I was too young. You weren't, but I was. You were like a big goddamn dangerous thing, you had hormones coming out of your ears. You scared the heck out of me. In a good way, kinda—you'd get me so hot—but it just didn't seem right. Then, of course, you jumped Linda Smith."

That sat there for a minute, then Virgil, cornered, said, "True."

"Was it worth it?"

He thought again, and then said, "Yes."

That made her laugh, and she asked, "Whatever happened to Linda?"

"She married a rich farmer guy from over by Chamberlain. I think she works part-time for some kind of social services agency over there."

"South Dakota?"

"Yeah. Jackie Bolt told me they've got a place that looks down on the Missouri. Supposed to be really pretty. I guess they spend their winters down in Panama. That's what I heard. They go big-game fishing. They've got a sailfish in their farmhouse living room. In South Dakota."

THEN, since it was impossible to screw *all* the time, he told her about chasing Sharp and Welsh and McCall, the details of the various killings, and the problem of finding Sharp and Welsh; at the same time, stroking her nipples and other good parts.

"See, we know everything—we'll convict them in one minute, when we get them to court. But we can't *find* them. This country is too big."

"But there are so many people looking for them."

Virgil pushed himself up on an elbow, trailed a finger down to her navel, and said, "I was on another case that involved a guy out in the countryside. The thing is, he sold a bunch of dope to a dealer down in Worthington, and the Worthington cops got there about two minutes late, and this guy took off and the cops were chasing him. They chased him about fifty miles or so, before they caught him, and then he dumped his car and started running through the cornfields. This was at night, and they lost him.

"He was a Canadian guy, and what we found out later was, he

decided to *walk* back to Canada. He broke into houses and a convenience store along the way, to get food. I got involved when he
was somewhere up in Yellow Medicine. So I figured out, sitting in
this motel, you could get about five hundred and eighty football
fields, between the goal lines, not including the end zones, in a
square mile. Yellow Medicine County, I happen to know, is about
seven hundred and sixty square miles, because I looked it up. So
that means you could have about thirty-five thousand football
fields in Yellow Medicine. Could you hide in a football-field-sized
patch of land out in farm country? Damn right you could. If the
guy lay down in a ditch, you could walk right past him. You can't
even figure out how to find somebody who's doing that. So we
can't find them. Becky and Jimmy. We don't think they're far away,
especially with Jimmy being shot. But where?"

"What happened to the Canadian guy?"

"He got away," Virgil said.

"Completely?"

"Completely. But he was a dope dealer, so he's probably gotten
to his use-by date."

"You mean, he's dead?" she asked.

"Or rich enough to have quit," Virgil said. "A few of them
manage to do that. You see them sitting on their yachts down in
the Caribbean."

"I don't think of Canadians as being drug dealers," she said.

"They are," Virgil said. "Generally, as a nation, they're pretty
depraved. At least, that's been my experience."

"See, that's another thing I didn't know."

Now she sat up and asked, "Why don't you cops have experts
on chasing people? I mean, you've got experts on everything else."

"Never thought of that," Virgil said, studying her parts in an academic way. They were very good. "I mean, how would they get to be experts? What would you study?"

"You know—how people think when they're running. Where they'd run to. How they'd think about it. That kind of thing. You know, psychologists."

"Well, maybe somebody should," he said.

Then they got involved again, and then they went to sleep—Virgil liked sleeping with women (the sleeping part), and so it wasn't until four o'clock in the morning that his eyelids popped open and he said, "Ah, man."

She twitched, and he groped around on the nightstand and knocked his wallet on the floor, and she woke up and rolled toward him and asked, "What are you doing?"

"Calling Stillwater penitentiary," he said. He found his cell phone.

"At four o'clock in the morning? What for?"

He told her, and she said, "I'm flattered, but if you're going to do that, you'll have to leave pretty soon."

"Pretty soon," he agreed.

"It's been a while since I've done this," she said. "You think . . . ?"

"I don't have to leave *immediately*," Virgil said.

STILLWATER WAS THE biggest penitentiary in Minnesota, and though it wasn't the only one, or the closest one, it was the one with most of the experts. Virgil talked to a skeptical duty officer who, in any case, said he'd pass along Virgil's request.

"Just get the warden to call me on my cell. He knows me. I'm going to assume that he'll cooperate, and start that way."

"I dunno . . ."

"Get him to call me," Virgil said.

AT FIVE O'CLOCK in the morning, feeling fairly light in his boots, he and Sally shared a kiss in the cool morning air on the motel room's doorstep, and he said, "I'll try to get back tonight, but I don't know how that's going to work out."

"Catch the kids. When you come back, I want your full attention," she said.

FROM MARSHALL, which was not all that far from South Dakota, to Stillwater, which was on the river that separated Minnesota from Wisconsin, was a three-and-a-half-hour drive, assuming no hang-ups in morning traffic. Virgil left Marshall at five o'clock, took six or seven phone calls from various prison officials, including the warden, over the next three hours, and finally the warden called at eight o'clock and said, "We're ready to go when you get here."

"I'm hung up in traffic on 494 headed toward the airport," Virgil said. "It could be a while."

"You got lights and a siren?"

"Yeah, but that'd get me there about one minute sooner, and the noise would drive me crazy. I'll just coast," Virgil said. "Hey— thanks for this. It's goofy, but it's all I got."

"I think it's kinda interesting," the warden said. "I read about what you did up in Butternut Falls. This is sort of like that."

STILLWATER PRISON SITS on a hill in Bayport, Minnesota, a few miles south of the town of Stillwater, and why it wasn't called Bayport prison, Virgil didn't know; nor was he curious enough to find out. The prison was not a particularly welcoming place, but neither was it particularly grim. Virgil had been inside perhaps a dozen times. He called ahead two minutes before he got there, parked across the street, locked up his guns, and walked over to the administration building.

An assistant warden named Ron Polgar was waiting for him and escorted him to the warden's office. The warden was a tall, thin, pink-faced man in his thirties, with steel-rimmed spectacles; a career correctional bureaucrat named James Benson, he could have been an accountant. He was notable for his adamant opposition to capital punishment, which Minnesota did not have, and would never have, if Benson had anything to do with it.

"Virgil," he said, standing up as Virgil came into the office. Virgil said, "How you doing, Jim?" and they shook hands.

"You must be pretty much in a rush . . ."

"Unless the Guard finds them this morning, which could happen," Virgil said. "You got my guys together?"

The warden nodded. "We're herding them into a classroom right now. We've got the projector and screen set up with a laptop. I hope you know Windows."

"Yeah, I should be okay," Virgil said. "How'd you pick the guys?"

"Talked to everybody," the warden said. "Your requirements were peculiar—people from out in the rural areas, shitkickers, I think you said, willing to cooperate, fairly bright. And that's what we got. Bright, but not exactly geniuses. We've got what, a dozen of them?"

"Eighteen now," Polgar said.

"I didn't want them to be really dumb, that's all," Virgil said. "I don't need geniuses for this."

"Got you covered," Benson said. "They're just run-of-the-mill . . . shitkickers."

"Excellent," Virgil said. "Let's go."

"Let me know what happens," Benson said.

VIRGIL AND POLGAR processed through several locked gates into the secure area and walked over to a classroom, where the inmates were waiting under the eyes of two guards. They were an odd assemblage for the prison: for one thing, they were all white, which was unusual, even for Minnesota. They were dressed in a variety of street clothes, jeans and sweatshirts for the most part.

They all wore the same skeptical look on their faces.

Polgar nodded at the two guards and went to the front of the room and said, "Okay. Everybody pay attention. You've got an idea of why you're here, and you know that there may be some pretty good benefits for taking part. If you change your mind and don't want to take part, let us know, and we'll take you back to your unit. Raise your hand if you've changed your mind."

He held up his hand as an example, and the group stirred, but nobody else raised a hand. Polgar said, "Good. I'm going to turn you over to Virgil, here, and he's going to tell you what we need, and then we'll turn the projector on for a little show."

Virgil stepped up and said, "Most of you come from out in the countryside, just like I do, which is where I got the idea to ask for your help. I'm sure you've been watching television and know our problem—we've got a couple of kids running around killing people, and we need to stop the killing."

"You gonna kill them when you catch them?" one of the inmates asked.

Virgil wanted to be as honest as he could be, since he needed them to work with him. He said, "You know what happens in these situations. We'd like to take them alive, because we'd like to talk to them. But this is not robbery or burglary or car theft—these kids are crazy and they're killers. This kind of thing usually doesn't end well. A lot of the time, these people kill themselves rather than give up. Or they decide to go down shooting. I can't tell you any different. We will do whatever we have to, to stop them."

There was another stir through the crowd, a rustle of grunts and two- and three-word exchanges, and a few nods.

"So what I'm going to do is tell you the story, what happened, and then we're going to the computer," Virgil said.

He told the group everything he knew, from the murder of Ag

Murphy to discovery of the Welshes and old man Sharp, and all of the rest of it, right up to the credit union robbery. He described the shoot-out in the street.

"Jimmy Sharp was hit in the leg. From the description we got, the slug didn't break any bones, but messed up the outside of his thigh. It won't kill him, at least not right away. They couldn't go to a hospital, of course, so they went to an isolated farmhouse to look for medicine. . . ."

He described the scene at the Towne house, and McCall's description of sex on the bed, and the murder of Edie Towne.

"So then McCall took off with the Jeep," Virgil said. "He called me on a cell phone and gave himself up. I arrested him, and he told us about the cornfield where he thought Sharp and Welsh might be hiding. Like I said, we'd already found that, but it made me think he might be telling the truth about the rest of it. But that's all we know. What I'd like to do is for you all to think about that, and between us, we'll try to work out where Sharp and Becky Welsh might have run to."

"How would we know that?" one of the inmates asked.

"You can't know, for sure," Virgil said. "But I believe there's a good possibility that if we all think what *we* would have done, we might come pretty close to what they've done."

THEY TALKED IT over for a while, and then Polgar fired up the computer and the projector, called up Google Maps, and threw up an aerial photo of Oxford, in which you could clearly see the roof of the bank. Virgil tapped the picture: "Here's the bank. Here's

where the cop was. They came running out this way, to the waiting Tahoe—Becky Welsh was driving. After the shoot-out, they
ran north."

Virgil traced the killers' route out of town, to the cornfield
where they hid, and touched the Townes' farmhouse. "From here,
McCall ran further north, then east, and then north again, and
then east, and then north."

Polgar reduced the scale on the map, to include the entire
route.

"I picked McCall up right here," Virgil said, tapping the map.
"Now, Becky Welsh kills Edie Towne and shoots Clarence, and she
drives back up the road to the cornfield where Sharp is waiting.
They know that McCall has run off. They don't know why, but
they must know that there's a chance he'll turn them in, so they
can't go anyplace that he might know about. They've got to go to
someplace new. They've just got to invent this place."

The problem had captured them.

A short thin man in the back row called, "They can't go back
toward town, or any place in a circle around the town, because
there's gonna be cops coming in from all directions. Did you know
what kind of truck they stole from this guy?"

"Yeah, pretty quick," Virgil said. "It hasn't been seen since
then."

Somebody else said, "So they got off the road. They couldn't
go north, toward Bigham, because they'd figure that's where all
the sheriffs would be coming from."

They all agreed that Sharp and Welsh would go sideways—
east or west—out of the cornfield, probably turning at the first
available road.

Virgil asked, "If it were you, would you go back toward Marshall? Remember, they've always been talking about going west, toward Los Angeles, but they killed two people in Marshall."

"Didn't you say that the ambulances and everybody were going to Marshall?"

"I did say that," Virgil said.

"Wouldn't they hear them?" the same guy asked.

Virgil looked at the map and considered. "You know, they might. It's quite a ways, but it was pretty quiet out there."

Somebody else said, "Nah. I had some cops coming after me one time, sirens and everything, and I never heard them until I saw the lights behind me."

"Yeah, but, they gotta know that Marshall was going to be a hornet's nest."

After some more discussion, the inmates voted unanimously that Sharp and Welsh had gone east, toward the only country where they hadn't yet done anything, or stirred anybody up. Since McCall might have betrayed them, they would have gotten off the big highway as soon as they could, and would have stayed off them: back roads only.

"Remember, the cops know what car they're driving and it's on television everywhere. They can't go through any towns where people might see them. . . . Jimmy's in pain and maybe bleeding still. He might not be able to go too far. They come from around there, and they do know the countryside."

"So they go east, and never would jog north," said a hulking blond in the front row. "They jog south."

"Why is that?" Virgil asked.

"Look at the map. The Minnesota River comes slanting down

across there, and they'd get pinned against the river. You can only cross it on main highways, and you said that they needed to stay away from where people could see them. Back roads only."

They all looked at the map, and then somebody said, "Bob's right."

Somebody else said, "But they could be thinking of hiding out in the woods. Lots of woods around the river, all the rest is farmland."

"They need to eat, they need maybe to see some TV, see what the cops are doing," said the blond man. "No. I believe they'd jog south, and keep jogging south to get past those little towns around there."

A very tall man with overgrown eyebrows said, "They gotta get off the road. I can feel that in my gut. Gotta get off the roads. Cops got helicopters, they're looking everywhere. You could run for a while, but the longer you run, the more scared you'd get. Could you guys run for an hour? I don't think I would."

They all thought about it, and Virgil said, "I want to hear everybody on that. Think about what this guy just said. How long could you stand to run?" He pointed at a road, and traced it going east. "From here to here is one minute. From here to here is four or five minutes. These are sections, so each one is about a mile."

The argument started and flowed around the group, and they started voting with shows of hands, at each intersection. But at each intersection, the possibilities multiplied, and it became apparent that there was no one solution—but there were other solutions that seemed, to the inmates, impossible. "You just can't go there," one of them said about a particular route. "You just run into too many people."

They asked questions about Sharp, Welsh, and McCall, to get an idea of what kind of people they were, and one man said, "I was kind of like them, up to the time I got caught. I'll tell you what, they won't go too far from home. They won't get down into no strange country, where they don't know how things work. They might try to go up to the Cities, since they been there, but too many people would see them. . . . I'd say, they might go over into the next county, but not too much farther."

"I bet they go someplace down around I-90, thinking that maybe if things quiet down, they could make a break for it some night. Get a long way down the road, east or west."

A couple of other inmates, who'd been silent up to that point, chipped in to disagree: people like Sharp and Welsh, they thought, might talk about LA, but they'd never go there, not when push came to shove. They might go to Worthington, or Windom, but it'd be unlikely that they'd go much farther than that, especially since Sharp had been wounded.

Eventually, after two hours, Virgil had three relatively small circles on the map of south-central Minnesota. Most of the inmates—there were always a few holdouts—thought they'd be in one or the other, and most thought that the middle one, one that bent to the southeast, would be the most likely.

The circle took in the southeastern corner of Bare County.

"I think we're done," Virgil said, looking at the map. "I appreciate the help, and I'll tell the warden that, and anybody else who'll listen."

They all seemed pleased with that, and then the hulking blond man raised his hand and Virgil nodded at him.

"I'll tell you something. Jimmy and Becky were partners, and

Jimmy got shot. Tom McCall said they went to this house to get medicine, and she fucked him on the bed there. He's lying. She wouldn't fuck him like that. A woman wouldn't do that. They'll put out almost anytime, but they wouldn't if somebody got shot in a bank robbery. That kind of thing don't get women hot. It pushes some other button."

"There is some evidence that they had a sexual encounter on the bed in the back," Virgil said.

"I didn't say they didn't fuck, I said she didn't fuck him," the blond man said. "What happened was, he raped her. The thing is, a bank robbery, and a bunch of shooting, could get a guy all hot. Wouldn't get a woman hot, not if somebody was hurt. Not if it was a friend."

Half the crowd looked skeptical, and half looked like they might agree. The blond said, "Think it over. You're McCall, you're hot for this chick, but you've never been able to get to her. Here's your last chance, 'cause you're going to turn them in. What have you got to lose? They're already gonna get you for a bunch of murders, what's a little rape, even if they believe her? So, you fuck her. But she's still trying to get away—get medicine, get back to Jimmy. She's gonna take out fifteen minutes to fuck somebody after they just killed this farm lady, and somebody else might come at any minute? I don't believe it. I believe McCall fucked her, but I think it was a straight-out rape."

Again, the crowd was divided, but Virgil said to the man, "I know Tom McCall just a little bit, from having talked to him. I believe you might be right. He's a fuckin' weasel."

"I am right," he said.

"And I'll follow it up," Virgil said. To the rest of the group: "I want to thank everybody for your help. I'll do whatever I can to see you get credit for it. And keep an eye on the TV. You'll see how the story comes out, and whether or not you were right."

VIRGIL, back on the street, called Davenport and told him that he was coming through St. Paul before heading back west. "Meet you at Cecil's," Davenport said. "I'll buy you lunch and you can tell me about it."

14

BECKY WELSH HAD SPENT a lot of time around rough guys, and had slept with a few, but had never before experienced anything like a rape. After loading Jimmy into the truck, and they got back on the road, Becky began to weep again. Jimmy's pain had diminished, but he was confused, partly by shock and partly by the drugs, and he asked, "What the fuck's wrong with you, anyway?"

She looked over at him and said, "I told you. Tom raped me."

"What the fuck?"

"He raped me," Becky said. "He pushed me down on the bed and raped me and beat me up. Then he did it again and then he took off. Then the guy came and I shot him and I'm just, I'm just, I'm just . . ."

Jimmy seemed to think about that for a while, or maybe his mind just wandered, but finally he said, "I'll kill the motherfucker. Where is he?"

"He took off. I don't know where he went," Becky said. She looked over at Jimmy. "You gotta promise me."

"What?"

"If we catch him, I get to kill him. I'm gonna cut his balls off, and then I'm gonna shoot him in the stomach and watch him die."

"Deal," Jimmy said. And, "Where'd you get this truck?"

BECKY TOLD HIM the whole story, from the time they left him in the cornfield until she loaded him into the truck; he remembered everything after that. "We gotta get your leg bandaged up better and I got some stuff we can put on it."

"We need to get as far away as we can," Jimmy said. "They'll be tearing up the countryside. Did Tom get all our money?"

"No, no, we got the money, it's behind the seat," Becky said.

"See if you can reach it," Tom said.

Becky fished around behind the seats and got the handles of the two grocery bags and pulled them over the seat and put them in Jimmy's lap. She said, "You know what I think? I think he's gonna turn himself in and blame everything on us."

Jimmy nodded, but didn't seem to be tracking very well; his eyes were bright, either because he was reviving, or because he was feverish. She reached out and put her hand on his forehead and thought he felt warm. Not real warm, but pretty warm.

"You might be getting an infection," she said. "We need to get some medicine on there."

"Need some pills, penicillin or something," Jimmy said.

Becky sobbed again, then wiped the tears out of her eyes, steadied her voice, and said, "You're sounding a lot better, honey."

"Feeling better," he said. Then, "We better cut on south. We don't want to meet any more cars than we have to. Stay on the gravel. If you see any gravel dust, try to find a place to turn off."

They went south, and she said, "What are we going to do? Everybody in the world is looking for us."

Jimmy said, "We need to get down south of Arcadia. There's this old guy down there, he lives alone, off the road. You can hardly see his house. My old man and I ground up his stumps one year. Mean old motherfucker, wouldn't let me in the house to take a shit. I had to go out in the field."

"What's his name?"

"Joe something. I don't know. But I'll remember the house. He's got an army tank out behind the house. All fuckin' rusty, but it's a real tank." He was quiet for a moment, then added, "I'll remember the turnoff. We'll get the truck out of sight and lay up there for a day or two, until I'm better." He weighed the two bags, bouncing one in his left hand, one in his right, chose the heavier of the two and counted the money.

"Thirteen thousand," he said, when he finished.

"Oh my God," Becky said.

He counted the other bag and said, "Nine thousand. Holy shit, we got twenty-two thousand dollars. We can go anywhere we want."

"If we don't get caught first," Becky said. "How far is this old man's house?"

"Twenty minutes, half hour. I'm not exactly sure. But I know how to get there from here."

And he did, but it was more like forty minutes, snaking around on back roads every time Jimmy got a bad feeling about the road they were on. By the time they got there, he was fighting to stay awake. "Fuckin' dope's all over me," he said. "But we're close. See them silos?"

A big farm on the north side of the road showed five huge blue metal silos, standing shoulder to shoulder, in three different heights, like brothers.

"Is that it?"

"No, but he's down this road. Maybe a mile." A minute later he said, "There. Up that hill."

Becky looked up a long, low hill, under some power lines that had small black birds sitting on them, looking down at her. She could see the roof of a house, but nothing else, set behind a wood-lot of winter-gray trees. A dirt track went up the hill from a mailbox on the road.

She turned past the mailbox and started up the hill. A line of barren apple trees edged the driveway on the left, and a patch of dirt with the remnants of last year's vegetable garden trailed away on the right, at a flat spot halfway up the hill. The track was rutted in places, and Becky steered around the ruts, and when they came to the crest of the hill they saw an old man in overalls standing next to an older red Ford pickup, about to get into it.

"Pull up there next to him, like we want to ask a question. Run my window down and put your fingers in your ears," Jimmy said. He had the pistol in his hand, between his legs.

Becky did what he said, pushed the button to roll the window down, and stopped next to the mean-faced old man, who asked, "Who are you?"

"Just us," Jimmy said, and he stuck the gun out the window

and shot the old man in the chest. The man reeled backward, then fell on his hands and knees, and then, improbably, got to his feet and staggered toward the house.

Jimmy got out of the truck, but his leg gave way and he fell down. He used the running board and then the fender to pull himself back up, and then hobbled after the old man, feeling not much pain but weak and unsteady, limping so hard that he could barely lift his hand up.

He chased the old man that way, the two of them barely making headway, the old man looking fearfully over his shoulder while holding his hand over the hole in his chest. Jimmy fired another shot and missed, and then another one, and missed again, but hit the house. Then Becky was there and said, "Give me the gun."

The old man was almost to the side door of the house, and she ran after him and she aimed the gun at the old man's back and pulled the trigger and the old man went down again, but was still alive, groaning, and Becky saw that she'd shot him in the shoulder.

"Go ahead and kill me, bitch, you got me," the old man said, rolling over and trying to stand again. He had blood on his mouth. Becky pointed the gun at his face and pulled the trigger, but nothing happened, and she saw it was locked open: out of ammo.

"Fuck this," Jimmy said. He limped back to the truck and the old man tried again to get into the house, and Becky kicked his legs out from under him, and he went down, flat, and she saw the big growing patch of blood below the straps on the overalls. She stepped to the door and pulled it open, and saw what he was going after. An old pump .22 was standing in the corner of the mudroom. She picked it up and stepped back outside.

Jimmy was digging in the truck for another gun, but Becky was figuring out the safety on the .22, clicked it off, pointed the gun at the old man, who moaned, "I give up."

She shot him in the head, and he shook, and tried to push himself up again, so she pumped the gun and shot him again, and he shuddered, and this time got to his hands and knees, and she pumped again, and the third time shot him behind the ear and he went down hard.

Jimmy called, "He dead?"

"I think so," she said. She prodded the old man's face with the muzzle of the gun, and he didn't flinch or move or tremble.

Jimmy came limping back with a pistol and pointed it at the old man's temple and fired. The old man's head bumped up, and this time, there wasn't any doubt.

"Okay. Let's get him out of sight," Jimmy said.

Becky dragged the body away from the house, toward a tumbledown wooden shed that stowed a couple of rusty pieces of farm equipment, a grain drill, and an ancient disk. The old man was amazingly light, and she had no trouble at all: she hid the body behind the shed door.

When she turned around, she saw the tank. No question about what it was, a real tank, but the front end had sunk deep into the turf, and its barrel seemed to slump with age, like it needed some kind of military Viagra to get it going again.

She shook her head, puzzled by it, then turned back to the house. There were two scuff lines in the dirt of the driveway that looked exactly like the heels of somebody who'd been dragged to the shed. She thought about kicking some dirt over the scuff marks, and over a couple patches of blood, but then thought, if the cops get that close, they were done anyway. She followed Jimmy inside.

ABOUT HALF THE LIGHTS in the house worked; and it smelled like a hundred years of chicken noodle soup, *Life* magazines, and *National Geographics*, and cigarettes. But there was a big flat-screen television in the front room, with a La-Z-Boy and a couch and a satellite connection, and a DVD player, and a stereo system with hundreds of CDs.

"I'll check the bathroom and the bedroom and see if the old fuck had some medicine," Becky said.

The old fuck did. The medicine cabinet was a gold mine. He'd apparently had tooth problems, and had yellow plastic tubes half-filled with more OxyContin and a couple of dozen penicillin tabs. Some of them were outdated, but they'd be better than nothing, she thought. She also found a plastic box with a red cross on it, and a label that said: "Farm Family First Aid Kit."

She took them downstairs and found Jimmy figuring out the TV. "I looked at the CDs, just a bunch of shit," Jimmy said.

She picked one of them up and it said: *Goldberg Variations*. She'd seen some stuff in *Cosmo* about variations, but that didn't seem like this. She tossed it on the floor and said, "Lay back on the couch. I need to look at your leg."

"Let me get the TV on," he said. His eyelids were drooping again.

He got the TV on, to a replay of *Dancing with the Stars*, and lay back and closed his eyes. Becky decided not to try to get his pants off, so she got a knife from the kitchen and cut through the denim. There was an entry wound at the back, and then a blown-out channel in the flesh along the outside of Jimmy's thigh. Another two inches to the left, and the bullet would have missed completely. On the other hand, two inches to the right, and it would have blown the bone out of his leg.

It looked bad, she thought, but not *that* bad.

She said to Jimmy, "I can fix this."

"That's good," he said, distantly, and then apparently went to sleep. She got to work, cut off the pant leg and pulled it down, went into the kitchen and got some paper towels, wiped off the wound with hot water. When it was clean, it looked worse, like raw meat. She sprayed it with some Band-Aid disinfectant, then covered it with two four-by-four-inch sterile bandages from the first aid kit, one for the entry wound, the other for the exit.

When everything was covered and looking neat, she woke up Jimmy and made him eat four of the penicillin tabs. "You're gonna be okay," she said.

"That's good," he said, and he went back to sleep. She covered him with a blanket from the bedroom, then went back to the bathroom, stripped off her clothes, and stood in the shower and washed away every bit of Tom McCall.

That done, she went back out to the living room, wrapped in a towel, and found Jimmy snoring on the couch. She left him there, went back to the bedroom, and fell on the bed. In two minutes, she was asleep.

Five hours later, she woke up and heard music. Strange music, like something from a nightclub. What *was* that?

Holding the bed blanket over her shoulders, she went back to the living room and found Jimmy watching television. She looked at the screen, which showed a half dozen men having sex with one another in an improbable oral-anal chain. Jimmy cackled and said, "The old fuck was queer as a three-dollar bill. He's got, like, a hundred of these things."

She looked at the screen and said, "Jeez. That's nasty."

"Look at that guy," Jimmy said. "He's got a cock like a fuckin' horse."

Jimmy, Becky thought, looked wide-awake; more than this, he looked *excited*.

And she looked at the screen again and back to Jimmy, and suddenly understood a lot. She thought, *Oh, no.*

15

VIRGIL AND DAVENPORT hooked up at a restaurant across from St. Kate's, a Catholic girls' college where Virgil had done some of his best work in chasing women, when he was a student at the University of Minnesota. The thing about Catholic girls was, they had a deep feeling for sin, which made catching them a lot more satisfying than it might have been otherwise.

Davenport was waiting in a back booth, chatting with a woman sitting at an adjacent table; he was wearing one of his two-million-dollar suits, but was tie-less.

Virgil nodded at the woman, who looked mildly put-out by his arrival, and slid into the booth opposite Davenport. He said, "How y' doin'?"

"Only fair," Davenport said. "The governor says that if we don't catch these kids in the next couple of days, it'll knock two points off his popularity. He cut funding for the highway patrol, and the union's been looking for something to stick up his ass."

"He didn't actually cut funding, he cut the funding request," Virgil said. "The actual funding went up."

"A technicality," Davenport said. "Also, you're starting to sound like a Republican."

"Sorry."

"So . . ."

"Can't go much longer," Virgil said.

"But they could kill a lot more people."

"I know, everybody knows. It's a goddamn disaster, Lucas."

THEY ATE REUBENS, and Davenport said, "We're getting a lot of credit for you arresting McCall, so anything you want . . ."

"I'm heading back down as soon as I get out of here," Virgil said. "I've got a few places to look now. If you could send me a couple guys, and we find them . . ."

"What about the Murphy thing?"

"That's why I want to find them. Because of the Murphy thing. I'm buying the idea that Murphy paid to have Ag murdered. I'd like to keep either Jimmy or Becky alive—both of them, if it's possible—and get them to talk about Murphy."

"Might not be possible," Davenport said. "A couple of deputies down there more or less told the TV people that it's a duck hunt. It's shoot on sight."

"They were going to kill McCall, too, but I got to him first," Virgil said. "But if they get to Jimmy and Becky, it could be that Murphy walks on a murder."

"I'll send you Jenkins and Shrake. I'll have them on the road in an hour, in separate vehicles. You need to turn over every rock you can find. Then, when it comes to *our* funding . . ."

"See, that's what we *really* needed," Virgil said. "A good reason to catch them. Like funding."

"You know what your problem is?" Davenport asked, jabbing a french fry at Virgil.

"I'm sure you're about to tell me."

"Yeah. You only think of one thing at a time. See, a smart guy, like myself, we know it's important that we catch these kids, but we also know funding is important. There's no conflict there."

"I feel chastened," Virgil said.

VIRGIL GOT OUT of the Cities, heading straight west, then cutting southwest. Davenport called as he was clearing 494 and said that Jenkins and Shrake would take a couple hours longer than he'd thought, but would definitely be in Bigham that night.

On the way west, it occurred to Virgil that if Sharp and Welsh were hiding in a farmhouse somewhere, they were probably watching television—and that he might be able to communicate with them.

He was working through that idea when he ran into his first National Guard patrol, twenty miles north of Bigham. Traffic was jammed for a half mile back from the checkpoint, and he used his lights to jump the line, driving along the shoulder. Two Humvees were working the checkpoint, with an M16-armed MP behind each vehicle, as a third MP checked the cars and waved them through.

When Virgil came up, the first MP stopped him, checked the truck, and then waved him through.

And this, he thought, was well out of the search area.

He was stopped three more times before he got to Bigham. At the last stop, he showed the MP his identification and asked, "Are you guys set up here permanently? Or are you roaming around?"

"We move around. Headquarters is set up in Bigham, and they move us."

"Good."

Virgil got to Bigham a few minutes after three o'clock in the afternoon. The Guard was working out of a field tent set up in the parking lot of the law enforcement center, and Virgil checked in with a red-faced major who was running the operation. The major, who was a lawyer from Moorhead in civilian life, showed him a map of the covered area, which included Bare and all the adjacent counties, with a bias to the west, to take in Marshall.

In addition, there were either Guard or sheriff's deputies on the north side of every exit onto I-90, which was well to the south, to prevent Sharp and Welsh from crossing the highway and heading south into Iowa. There were also patrols at every bridge over the Minnesota River, which would keep them from going north. Mutual aid agreements had brought in other sheriffs' deputies, highway patrolmen, and even town cops to patrol east- and west-bound roads out of the area.

The prison focus group had suggested a bias to the southeast. Virgil told the major about the group, but the major said they didn't have enough patrols to extend very far to the southeast, unless they broke off patrols to the west. "I'd like to cover you, but we've got certain realities to deal with."

Those realities, the major suggested, included the fact that two people had been executed in Marshall, and that the Guard needed to cover the areas where the politicians were screaming the loudest.

The major added, "The way we're set up, they'll hit some kind of patrol if they try to move, unless they've already gotten outside the interdiction area. Then, you know, all bets are off."

VIRGIL STOPPED AND SAW DUKE, who had nothing much to say except that everybody was working, and it was killing his overtime budget. When he walked out of the office he glanced across the street where a number of television trucks were parked, and at that moment, Daisy Jones came around the back of the truck, saw him, did a double take, and raised a hand. Virgil went that way.

Jones was thin, blond, and fortyish, or maybe forty-five-ish, and to Virgil's knowledge had a fondness for little white truck-driver pills, which she bought from little white truck drivers. She was also one of the smarter on-camera people he'd met; a fairly good reporter, all told.

She met Virgil in the middle of the street and took his hand and said, "Have I mentioned recently just how attractive you are?"

"No, and I can use all of the flattery you've got. I'm feeling pretty ragged," Virgil said.

"I might have a few teeny, tiny questions about this murder rampage, as well," she said. "For the Twin Cities' most important news outlet."

"And I might have a few teeny, tiny answers for you, if you're willing to deal."

"If you want to meet back at your motel, I'm sure we can work something out."

"I'm not strong enough for that," Virgil said. "I was thinking more in terms of you putting up the BCA phone number when I tell you how Tom McCall and Becky Welsh had sex after killing one of their victims."

"Oh, Jesus, that's a deal," she said. "As long as you don't lie too much."

"I'll lie hardly at all," Virgil said. "The other thing is, you have to make it look like you spontaneously caught me in the street."

"Not a problem," she said. "You go back in the sheriff's office and look out the window, and when you see me doing a stand-up, you walk out and I'll run over and grab you."

"Two minutes," Virgil said.

"Make it five minutes," she said. "I've got to powder my nose and fix my lipstick—we're also shooting for network."

VIRGIL WENT BACK across the street to the LEC, down in the basement canteen where he spent a few minutes in the men's room sprucing himself up, then got a Rice Krispies marshmallow bar from a vending machine, and a Diet Coke. He went back upstairs and ate the marshmallow bar and watched as Jones set up in the street, and started doing the stand-up. Virgil took a swig of the Coke, ran his tongue over his teeth to make sure no marshmallow was stuck between them, and walked outside.

Jones was looking at the camera, then half-turned to gesture toward the LEC, did another double take when she saw Virgil walking down the sidewalk, and called, "Virgil Flowers, Virgil Flowers." She led the cameraman over, at the same time saying into the microphone, "This is Virgil Flowers, the unconventional Bureau of Criminal Apprehension agent who brought in Thomas McCall yesterday. Virgil, could you answer a question for our audience?"

"The, uh, media relationship is being handled through Sheriff Duke's office."

"Just one question," Daisy urged. "There is a very strong rumor going around that Becky Welsh and Tom McCall may have had a sexual encounter in the bed of one of their victims, moments after shooting that victim. Is that true? Can you tell us if that's true?"

Virgil seemed to consider for a moment, then said, "Uh, I had a conversation with Mr. McCall as we were driving to the Marshall law enforcement center yesterday, and he indicated that Becky Welsh had initiated a sexual encounter with him at one of the victims' houses, shortly after shooting the victim. We do have some physical evidence for such an encounter, but I, uh, well, that's all I'd prefer to say at the moment."

"So you confirm that."

"I'll just stick with what I said. Nice to see you, Daisy."

"Nice to see you, Virg."

VIRGIL WALKED AWAY and heard her pumping excitement into her voice as she recapped the interview. He was back in his truck, getting ready to pull out, when she rattled up next to the driver's-side window in her high heels and said, "Thanks. I owe you. And thanks for using my name."

"Remember to put the BCA phone number up," Virgil said.

"Would you tell me why you're doing that?"

"No."

"You're trying to get Becky to call you, aren't you?" she said. "You're trying to get her to call, because . . . because you can track the cell phone tower, and then . . . Oh, my God! You're so . . . manipulative."

"If you put that on the air, I'll strangle you and throw your body in the Minnesota River," Virgil said.

"I won't say a word, until you catch her," Jones said. "Then I'll say a lot of words."

THE DAYS WERE GROWING longer as they moved deeper into April, but it was late enough in the afternoon that Virgil wasn't inclined to start the road search he'd plotted out with the prison inmates. With Jenkins and Shrake running late, it'd be nearly dark before they arrived.

And then, since every farmer within two hundred miles was now guarding his property with a shotgun in his hand, approaching lonely houses in the dark did not seem like a good idea. And if you weren't killed by a farmer, you just might find Sharp and Welsh, who'd light you up before you knew what was happening.

Virgil called Jenkins and told him to call Shrake, and that both of them should check into a motel somewhere close by. "Call me tonight and let me know where you are. We'll head out on the road early tomorrow."

"How early?"

"Right after it gets light."

Virgil looked at his phone for a minute, then dialed. He got John O'Leary on the second ring. "This is Virgil Flowers, with the BCA."

"You got the rest of 'em?"

"Not yet. I'm glad I caught you. I need to talk to you."

"Come on over. We're all here—the funeral's tomorrow morning."

"I don't want to intrude."

"Come on over, Virgil. I wanted to thank you anyway, for catching the first one of those little vermin."

ON HIS WAY OVER, he called the Lyon County sheriff, in Marshall, and asked if McCall had gotten representation.

"Yeah, he's signed up with one of our public defenders, Mickey Burden. You need to talk to her?"

"Yeah, and maybe the county attorney. Got the numbers?"

He called the county attorney first, a Josh Meadows. "I talked to Mickey an hour ago. She's a little pissed about that interview you did with Channel Three, and about the questioning of Mc-Call, when you were driving him in."

"It was all aboveboard," Virgil said.

"That's one of the things she's pissed about. It's all right there on the tape," Meadows said.

"You gave her the tape?"

"No, but we described it to her, as a courtesy. We're going to have to give it up pretty quick, though. She's going for a court order right now."

"As a personal favor to me, and since she's going to get it any-way, could you give her a copy now? Or let her listen to it?" Virgil asked.

"I could, if you tell me why," Meadows said.

"Because I want her to hear that McCall was holding out a critical piece of information—and that if I don't get it, that's an-other strike against him. I've got another thing going here, which I will tell you about when I see you, but it's complicated. I need McCall to talk to me."

"All right. I'll talk to her, see what she says," Meadows said.

"I'm going to call her and make an appeal. Maybe it'll help," Virgil said.

"Fine. Tell her to call me, then."

HE CALLED BURDEN as he pulled up outside the O'Leary house, and sat in the street and talked to her.

"You poisoned the whole jury pool when you said they'd had a sexual encounter," Burden said, when she came up on the phone.

Virgil said, "No I didn't. He was bragging to me about it. What can I tell you?"

"You should have kept your mouth shut," she said.

"I've got reasons for doing what I did, and if I were to tell you about them, which I won't, I think you might approve," Virgil said. "Anyhow, I've called to tell you that I asked Josh Meadows to release the interview tape to you, and he agreed. You can get it right now."

There was a moment of silence, and then she said, "I wonder why I'm so suspicious?"

"Because I want something," Virgil said.

"Ah," she said. "That's why."

"When you listen to the end of the tape, you'll see I stop the interview when McCall asks for an attorney. He was about to give me some critical information, but then decided to withhold it, thinking maybe he could use it to get a deal. I need the information, but it has a very short shelf life. Short, and getting shorter by the minute. If he wants to get anything out of it, he better talk to me tonight. Tomorrow morning might be too late."

"That's outrageous."

"Maybe, but it's not my doing. It's his, and Becky Welsh's and Jim Sharp's. If Welsh and Sharp shoot it out tomorrow, and get killed, then McCall's value goes to zero."

More silence, then, "I'll talk to my client."

Virgil said, "Do that. And let me give you my phone number."

THE O'LEARY MEN were waiting for him in the living room again. Ag Murphy's mother and her sister were at the funeral home. Marsha O'Leary refused to leave her daughter's body until it was safely in the ground, John O'Leary said. Her children were taking turns sitting with her.

"I hope you all do well," Virgil said, looking for the right words. "I know this has to hurt, but I hope you don't let it do any more damage than it has to. You seem like a pretty great group."

"We are a pretty great group," said Jack, the oldest son. "We won't get over it, but we'll get on."

"I hope so," Virgil said.

After a moment, John O'Leary said, "So . . . you have something specific you wanted to talk about?"

Virgil said, "Yes." Then, after a moment, "When was the last time Dick Murphy was in the house, before the shooting?"

"Couple days before," John O'Leary said. He looked around at his kids, who nodded. "Yeah. Two days before."

"Was he in the kitchen?"

"I suppose. He was around the house. You think he had something to do with it? Is that where we're going?"

"I'm trying to cover all the bases," Virgil said.

"No, you're not," said Frank, the youngest kid. "You know something."

Virgil knew they were smart; ducking away from the fact of the matter wouldn't fool them, not for long.

"Look," he said, "I don't want this getting out of the house. Maybe not even to your wife or daughter, either, just because . . . they're a little emotionally tender, and I don't want them giving away my case by confronting Dick Murphy before I've got it nailed down. And anyway, I could be wrong. Okay?"

They all nodded.

"I'm ninety-nine percent sure your daughter was shot and killed by Jimmy Sharp," Virgil said. "Sharp, the night before, had so little money in his pocket that he was sleeping in his car. After shooting Ag, he had a thousand dollars in his pocket, and he told Tom McCall that he'd taken it from Ag's bag."

"That's not right," Rob O'Leary said. "Ag borrowed twenty bucks from me to go see a movie, because time was short and she didn't want to run by the ATM. And when she went to the ATM, she never took out more than a couple hundred. She used credit cards for almost everything."

"Tom thinks Sharp was paid to kill Ag," Virgil said. "He said that Sharp referred to himself as a hit man."

"That motherfuckin' Murphy," said James O'Leary.

John O'Leary stood up and walked around behind the easy chair he'd been sitting on and leaned on it: "What's his motive? The money? I don't know if you're aware of it, but his old man's one of the richest guys in town. He's got more money than we do."

"But he doesn't give much of it to Dick," said Frank. "He gave him a car, and maybe picks up the payments on that house, but other than that, he's got him working a salesman's job and getting salesman's pay."

"Money would be a factor," Virgil said. "The other thing is . . . Murphy apparently thinks that Ag went to a clinic and aborted their child. At least, that's what he supposedly told one of my sources."

That rattled them: John O'Leary shook his head and said, "That's not possible. She'd never do that."

Rob and Jack agreed, but James was more reticent: he said, when the others had quieted, "I don't think it's out of the question."

His father said, "What?"

James said, "I don't think it's out of the question."

"Why?" John O'Leary asked. "Explain that."

James said, "That's just what I think." But Virgil thought he might know something; because of the anger flickering through the others, he didn't press it, and John O'Leary bent the conversation away when he asked, "When are you going to pick him up?"

"I got this Murphy stuff from a guy who's for sure a cop killer, and possibly a rapist, who's looking for a way to make a deal. He's not a reliable source. A jury won't trust him," Virgil said.

"But you suspect him," said Jack O'Leary. "Maybe a little more than that."

"I talked to a guy here in town who Dick Murphy sort of brushed by with a suggestion that Ag was a big problem for him. But he never got explicit about what he wanted. The guy *thinks* he knows what Murphy wanted, but who knows if we could ever get that into court," Virgil said. "I can get that guy's testimony. I can also show that Dick Murphy and Jimmy Sharp were shooting pool the night before the killing—not that night, but twenty-four hours earlier. I might be able to get some bank records that show Dick Murphy took a thousand bucks out of the bank, if he did that. Even so, I don't know if that's enough. It'd be strongly suggestive. . . ."

"This other guy, it's Randy White, isn't it?" Rob O'Leary asked.

Virgil shrugged and said, "I don't want to get into that."

Rob said to his father and brothers, "It is." He nodded at Virgil. "You can see it in his eyes."

And Virgil thought they probably could. "I don't want you talking to anybody about this. Not Murphy, not Randy White. What I need for you is, any further information you can provide about motive, specifics about Murphy going back into your kitchen, alone—and I don't want you to make up any bullshit. That never works."

"You need more circumstantial stuff," said John O'Leary.

"That's right. Anything you've got that would help build a case."

"We'll have to bring Mom and Mary into it," James O'Leary said to his father and brothers. "We'll have to tell them to man-up, suck it up. They can do it. They were the ones who were here the whole time Murphy was over that night."

John O'Leary nodded. "But not tonight. Let's wait until tomorrow. Until Ag's gone."

Virgil was an only child, and while his parents were loving, he'd never been part of the complex web of a large family. He was struck by the tribal vibe he got from the O'Learys, the all-for-one, one-for-all thing. Because the family was so big, the older kids had taken care of the younger ones, and Ag, as the oldest, had almost been a surrogate mother for them. Their bitterness was all-encompassing, and fed on itself as they talked about her.

Before he left, Virgil said, "Listen, I don't want you guys checking around on Murphy on your own. Stay away from him. He'll be at the funeral—I don't want you hassling him. He doesn't know I'm coming yet, and I want to keep it that way as long as I can."

They all agreed they'd do that. "I'll be okay, as long as I don't have to talk to the sonofabitch," Frank said.

"Try to avoid any open hostility," Virgil said. "It'd scare him, and I don't want him covering anything up, if there's anything to cover."

. . .

VIRGIL WAS THINKING about the gun that Sharp had used to kill Ag Murphy. It was possible that Sharp had the gun all along, but if they were sleeping in a car . . . a gun was money, if you knew where to sell it, and Sharp almost certainly did. On the other hand, it might have been the kind of asset that he couldn't have let go of. Still, if it came off the street here in Bigham, it'd be nice to know who the previous owner was.

Back in the truck, Virgil called the public defender in Marshall, but was switched to her voice mail; he hung up without leaving a message.

He thought again about the gun, and about Honor Roberts, the fence he'd talked to at the bird sanctuary. He called him and asked, "You didn't sell Jimmy Sharp a gun, did you?"

"Hell, no. I don't deal in guns. That's nothing but trouble."

"If you needed a gun in Bigham, where'd you go?" Virgil asked.

"You know . . . there isn't anyplace, in particular," Roberts said. "You might just ask around, or you'd hear somebody had a gun for sale. It's not like in the Cities, where somebody makes a business out of handgun sales."

"So the only way to get one here would be . . . hanging out."

"That's about it," Roberts said. "On the other hand, most people have a gun or two. If they didn't buy it themselves, they inherited it. You could get one at an estate sale."

"Well . . . poop."

The gun was still a possibility, if Murphy supplied it to Sharp, but not one that he could work through quietly. Once Sharp was taken down, he could have the sheriff make a public appeal for information, and maybe something would shake loose.

He decided to head over to Marshall, forty miles away by road, a half hour or so if you had police flashers. He did, but still got hung up on a half dozen Guard checkpoints. He had just cleared one of them when the public defender, Mickey Burden, called and said, "I see a missed call from you."

"I was wondering if you'd heard the tape and had a chance to talk to McCall."

"I did. And I talked to Josh Meadows, and he said that there's not much of a deal available. He'd be willing to tell the judge that my client cooperated, but wouldn't recommend any change in sentence in return for the cooperation."

"I don't think you can hope for much that way," Virgil said. "I think the most you could really hope for is to create some doubt about what Tom actually did, and then point out that he cooperated when given a chance."

"Oh, shit," she said, suddenly sounding tired. "You know . . . if you want to come talk to Tom, you can. I told him you'd be coming, and I recommended that he speak to you. To cooperate."

"I'll be there soon as I can be," Virgil said.

JOSH MEADOWS, the county attorney, turned out to be an affable guy who looked like he spent a lot of time on a golf course; he had short red hair, was wearing a polo golf shirt and white socks—

no shoes—when he and a sheriff's deputy and a court reporter met Virgil at Meadows's office at seven o'clock. Meadows said, "You're cutting into my dinnertime."

"Mine, too," Virgil said. "Had to be done."

Burden arrived a couple minutes later. She was a short brown-haired woman in her forties, who carried a briefcase the size of a steamer trunk.

The pre-interview meeting was short. Meadows told Burden that he was not prepared to offer McCall any consideration whatever, but if Virgil wanted to take the stand as a defense witness and say that McCall had cooperated, he would make no effort to challenge that. "You have to consider, though, that I probably won't be the prosecutor. We don't know who the prosecutor will be. I would imagine that whoever is McCall's final representative will try to get the trial moved out of Bare and Lyon counties because of the media attention."

"For sure," Burden said. "There really is no proof that McCall shot anybody—"

"Except that an eyewitness says he did, and it's hard to think how anybody else might have done it," Meadows said. "But it's up to you, Mickey. It's Virgil or nothing."

"All right," she said. To Virgil: "I'm going to place a limitation on the questioning: you can ask about James Sharp but you can't ask about the shooting in Oxford, or about what part Tom McCall might have had in the robbery and shooting in Bigham."

"That might be a little tough, but I think I can skate around it," Virgil said. "Stop me if I step on your toes."

"I will," she said.

. . .

WHEN THEY'D AGREED on the rules, the deputy left, and came back five minutes later with another deputy and, between them, Tom McCall, who was wearing handcuffs and leg chains that allowed him only to shuffle along, rather than stride. Running would be out of the question.

The deputies sat him down, and Burden took him through the deal, although she'd already done that when she talked to him before the meeting. He nodded that he understood, and then said, aloud, "I got it, I got it," though Virgil didn't think he quite understood how little he was getting.

After a little more talk, Virgil said, "Okay. Tom, on the way back here—"

"You said you wanted me to rot in hell," McCall said.

"Yeah, I sorta do," Virgil said. "But that has nothing to do with the question. The question I have is, who was Jimmy Sharp hanging out with in Bigham? Anybody in particular?"

"We were only there for two nights. During the daytime, we went around to see if anybody had a job, and at night we'd go over to this pool hall. Bar and pool hall. Because they had free peanuts that we could eat if we all bought a beer. I ate about a pound of those fuckers."

"So you were at the pool hall. Would this be Roseanne's Billiards in Bigham?"

"Yeah, something like that. Yeah. Roseanne's pool parlor."

"And was Jim hanging with anyone in particular?" Virgil asked.

"Not the first night, but sometime on the second day we was

there, he met up with this guy, Murph. He thought Murph might be able to get us a job because his old man was some kind of big deal in town. Well, that didn't work out, but the second night, they were shooting pool for a long time."

"This wasn't the night when Ag Murphy got shot. This was the night before that?"

"Careful," Burden said.

"Everybody knows when Ag Murphy got shot," Virgil said. "I'm just asking about the date, not about the shooting."

"Not that it makes any difference," Meadows drawled. "We already got him on tape as admitting he was at the house."

"That tape may be challenged, as would be your last comment," Burden snapped.

Virgil made a time-out signal with his hands and said, "No lawyer stuff right now, okay? I'll avoid the actual shooting . . . unless Tom wants to talk about it."

"He doesn't," Burden said.

"Okay," Virgil said. Back to McCall: "So starting the second night in town, he was hanging out with Murph. Would you recognize Murph?"

McCall nodded. "Sure. I shot about six games of nine-ball with him."

"Did you win?"

"No. He's a pretty good nine-ball player. He was some kind of athlete at the high school."

Good detail, Virgil thought. "Did Jimmy beat him at nine-ball?"

"Oh, shit no. Jimmy is terrible at pool. Any kind of pool."

"So . . . you say that the next night Jimmy had a thousand dollars. But he couldn't have won that from Murph, shooting pool?"

"No fuckin' way, man," McCall said.

"So when would Jimmy have gotten the money?" Virgil asked.

"He didn't have no money that night," McCall said. "Didn't have any the next day, until he borrowed ten bucks off some guy so we could get some breakfast. We went down to the IGA and bought a loaf of bread and jar of peanut butter and one of jelly, and we ate that, and then Jimmy and Becky went off some-wheres, and I met up with them that afternoon, and they still didn't have any money. Then Jimmy left Becky with me, and when he came back, late that night, we were in the car, he had this gun and he said we were going to do some robbing—"

"Stop," Burden told him.

Virgil asked, "He didn't have the gun before?"

"Nope. That was the first time I ever seen it."

Virgil leaned back in his chair and said to Meadows, "I've got nothing more to ask at the moment. Mickey won't let me get closer to the robbery, but I already know what happened there, anyway."

"Okay," Meadows said. "So let's bring this—"

"Wait," Virgil said. And to Tom: "You think he got the money from Murphy?"

Tom said, "Can't think of no place else it could have come from. That money popped up like a gopher out of a gopher hole."

"And you told me they were brand-new twenties. Is that right?"

"Yep. Brand-new and shiny. You could smell the money ink on them, when Jimmy flipped through them."

Virgil spread his hands and said, "I'm done."

16

VIRGIL CALLED UP SALLY on her cell phone and said, "Shoot, I was driving into town on 68 and you know what happened?"

"You got a flat tire?"

They met at the Perkins, and when Virgil slid into the booth, Sally said, "My reputation is going to be shredded. Changing the same guy's tire two nights in a row."

"Promise me you won't put it on Facebook," Virgil said.

"Facebook, the curse of the auto-tire repair business," she said. Then, "You didn't get them. I was watching on TV all day."

"No, we didn't. I think . . . tomorrow. We could get them tomorrow. We likely will. But I'm afraid there are going to be more dead people. Unless they went someplace, parked, and killed themselves."

"You think that's possible?"

"Five percent," Virgil said.

. . .

VIRGIL AND SALLY were just coming up for air, at the motel, when Becky Welsh, who'd been clicking around channels, found the interview with Virgil on Channel Three. She watched it, growing increasingly angry, then said to Jimmy, who was lying on the floor with his head propped up on a pillow, "They said we had a sex encounter. What the fuck? Tom raped me, wasn't no sex encounter."

"He's telling his side of the story," Sharp said.

His head was clear now, and the fever had mostly disappeared. The wound didn't look so good, but they were still spraying the Band-Aid stuff on it, and they'd convinced themselves that it was better.

Becky was freaking out, and wouldn't change channels, and wouldn't put any more pornos into the DVD player. Jimmy said he liked them because they were funny, but she didn't believe him.

Anyway, it was two hours before the regular news came up, and she saw the interview again. This time she was ready, and she said to Jimmy, "I'm going out. I'm taking the gun."

Now he rolled toward her. "Don't leave me."

"I'm not leaving you. I'm gonna drive into the gas station in Arcadia and I'm gonna get me a cell phone."

"From who?"

"From whoever. Fuck this shit. Wasn't no sex encounter." She started to cry again.

Jimmy looked at her and said, "Go on. Don't bring the cops back."

. . .

ARCADIA WAS A SMALL TOWN sixteen miles away, back in Bare County. Becky knew it because there was a park outside of town, with a small lake, a loop off the Mad River, and she and some kids from the high school had gone there on hot summer nights, with the cicadas going in the elm trees, and the fireflies out over the fields, to skinny-dip.

She got a ball cap before she left the house, swept her hair up under it, to give herself a different look. Outside, checked the gas in the old man's truck—it was more than half full—and took off, rolling carefully out the driveway, then turning west at the bottom of the hill. She stayed strictly on gravel roads, hunched over the steering wheel. Nobody was looking for that truck, but she knew about the National Guard roadblocks and didn't want to run into one.

And in fact, she saw one—a bundle of lights at a crossing a mile or so ahead of her, something you just didn't see out on this part of the prairie, at eleven o'clock at night. When she dropped into a dip in the road, she turned off her headlights, and when she came to a side track, took it, weaving her way toward Arcadia in the starlight.

When she got there, nothing was stirring. The only thing open was the gas station, with a single car parked by the pumps. She could see a man standing at the counter, chatting with the clerk, and waited across the street, impatient, until he wandered outside, got in the car, and drove off.

Nothing else on the street. She got her guts up, did a U-turn into the station. Still nothing moving. She sat there for another minute, then got out with the pistol in her hand.

The only sound was a faraway truck on the highway north of town. She walked past a flickering neon Bud Light beer sign to the front door, walked in with her head down, the bill of the ball cap covering her face. The counterman said, "Nice night."

She brought the gun up and pointed it at his chest, and she said, "Maybe not. Give me your cell phone."

He said, "You're—"

"That's right. I'll blow a hole clean through you if you look like you're going for a gun or do anything I don't tell you to do. Give me your cell phone."

The clerk was a tall thin boy with a prominent nose and a prominent Adam's apple that bobbed up and down in fear. He said, "Don't shoot me. Please don't shoot me."

"Cell phone."

He dipped in his pocket and pulled out a cell phone. She handed him the slip of paper with the state cop's number on it and said, "Call that number and tell them that you have to talk to Virgil Flowers. No, wait . . . first, get them grocery bags and fill them up with what I tell you."

She walked him through the store and got two plastic grocery bags full of candy bars and ice cream and Pepsi and corn chips and tortilla chips and salsa and dip and Hershey's bars and Snickers and a carton of Marlboros.

She had him put the sacks by the door and then waved the pistol at him and said, "Back to the counter. Call that number. Tell them your real name and tell them it's an emergency and that you have to talk to Virgil Flowers. Got that? Virgil Flowers. Don't tell them where you're at, or I'll blow your fuckin' brains out."

The kid was shaking like an aspen leaf, could barely punch in the numbers, but when it was answered, he said, "I gotta talk to Virgil Flowers. It's an emergency."

Becky couldn't hear the answer, but he looked at her and then blurted, "It's an emergency. My name is Dale Jones, and I gotta talk to Virgil Flowers. . . . I can't tell you that. No, I can't tell you that. Listen, I gotta talk—"

Becky lost her patience and said, "Give me the fuckin' phone."

He handed her the phone and she snarled into it, "This is Becky Welsh. If you don't put Virgil Flowers on this phone in fifteen seconds, I'm gonna kill this man."

The voice on the other end said, "I'm . . . Don't do that, please don't do that. I'm patching you through."

AT THAT VERY MOMENT, Virgil was licking Sally's nipples, and she was laughing at him because he was doing it, but he wasn't inclined to stop, though he couldn't have told anybody why. He'd been nursed by his mother when he was a child, so he probably wasn't suffering from a lack of breast contact; but nevertheless, here he was, lapping like a yellow Lab, when the phone rang.

He looked at the face of it, said, "Goddamnit, the most inconvenient . . . I gotta answer it."

He picked up the phone and the BCA duty officer said with a rush, "I'm patching through a woman who says she's Becky

Welsh and she says she's going to kill a man if you don't talk to her."

And he was gone and Virgil said, "Becky?"

BECKY SAID, "You sonofabitch, you said there was a sex encounter with Tom McCall, but there was no sex encounter—that mother-fucker raped me." She started crying again, and the muzzle of the gun was shaking, and the clerk backed up against the cigarette rack, his mouth hanging loose in white-faced fear.

"Becky, Becky . . . I gotta know it's really you and not a trick," Virgil said. "Where'd he rape you? Where in the house?"

"It was in that back room, down the hall to the left . . . no, to the right. It had a table with a big stack of magazines on it, and they had these pink shades on the bedside lamps."

She was exact. Virgil said, "Becky, don't hurt anybody else. Tell me where you are and I'll bring you and Jimmy in. The other cops around here, they want to kill you, because that police officer got killed in Oxford. They'll do it, too: they'll shoot you down like a couple of dogs, but I'll bring you in, like I brought in Tom McCall."

"Fuck that, you're gonna kill us anyway, one way or another," she said. "But I want it straightened out, on TV. I didn't have no sex encounter, he raped me . . . and I'll tell you what, I'm so pissed off I might just kill this man here to prove to you how pissed I am—"

"No, no, no, don't do that. . . . Becky, I talked to some peo-ple who told me they thought you'd probably been raped. That a woman wouldn't have voluntary sex under . . . those circumstances."

"That's right, no way I was going to have a voluntary sex encounter," Becky said.

"This guy you've got, let him go, and I'll fix you up to talk directly to the TV woman, so you can straighten her out," Virgil said.

"*You* straighten her out," Becky said. "But I'll tell you what, I'm going to kill somebody every day until this gets straightened out or you kill me. I'm gonna be watching."

"The man you're with . . . what does he do?" Virgil asked. He could feel the desperation clutching at his throat. "What does he do?"

"Runs a gas station store—"

"Ah, for cryin' out loud, Becky, you guys were trying to find jobs. Right? Weren't you? Tom McCall said you were looking everywhere, this poor guy is just like you. Got a horseshit job and just trying to pull it together. Don't shoot him, I'm beggin' you."

"I'll think about it," she said. "But I will kill somebody every day until this sex encounter gets straightened out. Just pull up next to them in the truck and shoot them in the head."

"Becky . . . I'll fix it. I'll fix it."

SHE WAS GONE. Virgil held on to the phone, said, "Becky? Becky? Becky?" and then a man said, "She's gone, Virgil. I got the number. It's a Verizon phone, and I got Verizon looking for the location, but it'll be a few minutes—"

Sally, at his shoulder, said, "Oh my God . . ."

Virgil said to the duty officer, "Get it get it get it . . . see if they can track the phone with the GPS."

BECKY TOLD THE CLERK to lie down on the floor, and said, "I'm parked right outside, and I'll shoot you big-time if you move. You better be goddamn certain, when you move, that I'm gone or I'll put a bullet right through your forehead."

She walked out to the truck carrying the grocery bags, threw them in the back, and took off. She was watching the counter where the clerk was, and saw no movement. She turned in the street and headed north, rolled out to the end of town, to a curl in the Mad River, and threw the cell out the window, into a ditch full of cattails. Then she reversed, went around the single block, away from the store, and turned south. A moment later she was heading out of town, and thirty seconds after that, she turned off on a side track and killed her lights again, to drive on in the dark.

THREE MINUTES AFTER Becky hung up, Virgil was pulling on his jeans, with the phone pressed to his ear, and the duty man said, "I got a call from the Bare County sheriff, says a gas station clerk just called them from the town of Arcadia, says he was held up by Becky Welsh. They're rolling."

It took Verizon nine minutes before they found the cell where the phone call came in. Their phone did have GPS enabled, and a

Verizon technician said that it wasn't moving. It was near the bridge over the Mad River, north of Arcadia.

Virgil punched off and called Duke, who snapped, "What?"

"You're headed down to Arcadia?" Virgil asked.

"Fast as we can get there."

"Becky called me on a cell phone she took off that clerk, and the phone has a GPS," Virgil said. "The GPS shows it as being near a bridge on the Mad River, north of town. Right on the north edge."

"Bet they're hiding there in the weeds, just like they did in that cornfield."

"Don't kill them if you don't have to," Virgil said.

"You coming?"

"Fast as I can."

VIRGIL RAN OUT to his truck, Sally chanting, "Go, go," as he went out the door. Lights and siren all the way: and he punched up the number for Daisy Jones at Channel Three. It was nearly midnight, but she answered on the second ring and said, "Virgil."

"Off the record."

"Okay."

"Becky Welsh just called me," he said. "The call came from a small town—"

"So it worked."

"Yeah, but she says if we don't retract that story about a sex encounter, she'll kill somebody else every day," Virgil said. "We need you to go on, with her claim: she says that Tom McCall raped her. I believe her. I'm afraid that we won't get to her in time, and she'll kill somebody tomorrow morning if you don't do this story."

"I can do it," Jones said. "I'll call the station now. We'll put it on every half hour."

"Good. Thank you."

"You know where she's calling from?" Jones asked.

"We know where she was a half hour ago. We know where the cell phone is. But I honest to God can't believe that she's that dumb. This isn't quite right."

"What town?"

"Arcadia," Virgil said.

"I'm coming as soon as I file. I'll likely see you there."

"Don't talk to me—talk to the sheriff."

FOR A CERTAIN TYPE of personality, found mostly on the plains, in the South and the Southwest, there is a great sense of pleasure in going out on the rural roads at night and driving as far and fast as you can. When you come up to a high spot on an overcast night, you can see domes of light scattered around the landscape, reflected off the clouds, marking the towns, almost like illuminated chessmen scattered around a vast chessboard.

Virgil was that kind of personality.

When he was a teenager too young to drive, he'd occasionally hitchhike somewhere ridiculous, like up to the Twin Cities or over to Sioux Falls, to do something ridiculous, like buy an ice-cream cone, and scare the brains out of his parents. When he was old enough to have a car, he roamed hundreds of miles out across the prairie, listening to the FM stations come and go, with all the newest pop and rock, dodging oncoming lights that might be cop cars, seeing how long he could keep the speedometer needle over the eighty-miles-an-hour mark. He'd see how lost he could get.

Part of it might even be genetic, he thought. One of his earliest memories, of men and cars, had been driving at night with his preacher father, riding shotgun in the old man's bottle-green Pontiac Tempest, the car smelling of nicotine and oil, listening to the radio, to the Pentecostals and the psychics and, best of all, Wolfman Jack on that border blaster signal out of Rosarito Beach, Mexico. Sometimes Wolfman would play one of his father's favorites, like the Stones singing "Faraway Eyes," and the old man would sing along with it, nothing like the man who climbed that pulpit every Sunday morning. . . .

The run to Arcadia held some of that, even as urgent as it was: running at high speed with lights, scaring himself when the wheels broke free at bridges and at unseen curves. He encountered four checkpoints; the word about Arcadia had gotten around, the MPs waved him through in a hurry, calling out encouragement as he barreled past the parked Humvees, in words he didn't have time to understand.

As fast as he moved, it took forty minutes to get to Arcadia, and when he got there, coming in from the south, he saw the sheriff's truck sitting at the gas station, and swerved over to the station, parked, and hopped out.

Duke was talking to a couple of his deputies, but turned to Virgil and said, "I been talking to your duty officer. He says the phone company says the GPS is right there by the river. There's nothing there but a dry cattail swamp and a ditch. I think she threw the phone out the window as she was going out of town."

"Your guys didn't run into anybody when they were coming down?"

Duke shook his head. "And I had them spread out as they were coming down, taking the roads that didn't have checkpoints. They didn't see anybody moving. Which means, if she went north, she didn't go north more than about, mmm, fifteen minutes, or we would have seen her. Probably—there were a few roads we couldn't cover."

"The clerk is sure she went north?"

"He's sure. As soon as he heard her truck start, he peeked out the window and saw her go, and when she was gone, he stuck his head out and saw her heading fast down the street. Then he called us. Going north, there's only one road, until you get a half mile out, then we start running into the farm-to-markets. I got the Guard and my guys setting up a perimeter. Starting tomorrow, we're going to squeeze them."

Virgil talked to the clerk, as Duke listened, making sure that the woman was, in fact, Becky Welsh. He'd never doubted it, after talking to her on the phone, and the clerk said, "It was her. Man, she looks like a killer. She's got those eyes. And somebody beat her up—her face had bruises up around her eyes, and her lip was cut."

"She was raped," Virgil told Duke. "Another little gift from our friend McCall."

"Should have killed him in that ditch," Duke said.

"No, we shouldn't have," Virgil said.

. . .

DUKE LAID OUT the arrangement of his forces, including the Guard and the highway patrol. "We were mostly north of here—we didn't think they'd be as far south as this. But we got here quick. They're in the net."

Virgil went back to his truck and got out his Minnesota atlas, and spent a half hour looking at the maps.

The Channel Three truck showed up a few minutes later, and Daisy Jones walked over and talked to the sheriff. Virgil went back to the maps.

Duke might think that Welsh and Sharp were in the net, and while Arcadia was pretty far south of Bigham, it was actually on the northeast edge of where Virgil's prison focus group thought they'd be. The heart of the search area, the focus group thought, should be south of Arcadia.

VIRGIL WATCHED as Daisy did a stand-up with the sheriff, and when she'd finished, he went over and said to Duke, "I'm going to get some sleep, but I'll be out here tomorrow morning. Where're you going to set up?"

"Right here," Duke said. "Don't sleep late. You might not be in on the . . . capture."

17

VIRGIL DROVE ALL THE WAY back to Marshall, still with the lights, running fast. Sally was gone, so he set the alarm on his phone, put it on the end table next to his ear, and was asleep when his head hit the pillow.

Sunrise was right around six-thirty, and at seven o'clock, Virgil was back out the door, carrying his duffel bag. The search area would be moving east, he thought, and Sally aside, Marshall was just too far away.

Jenkins and Shrake agreed to meet him at the Bigham Burger King, and from there, they'd head south toward the focus area; they said that a highway patrolman named Cletus Boykin was coming with them. "We can work in two-man teams that way," Jenkins said. "Boykin's an old friend of Shrake's, and Shrake says he's okay."

"What does that mean? He'll kill on command?"

"That, at least," Jenkins said. "He'll probably eat the dead, if you tell him to. See you in a half hour."

. . .

IN A COLD DRY SPRING, before the trees bud out, the morning sun seems to shine white like a silver dime on the horizon, and the clear air over the still-fallow ground gives the prairie a particular bleakness, if your mood is already bleak.

Virgil had a feeling that there'd be shooting before the end of the day, that people who were alive and even feeling good right then, maybe asleep in their beds, would be bleeding into the dirt before the sun went down.

Or maybe already: he called the Bare County sheriff's department and was told nothing had happened yet, but that Duke's forces were moving into position. Sometime in the middle of the night, the cell phone used by Becky Welsh had been found, and bagged, in case further proof was needed that she'd made the phone call.

Forty minutes after he left Marshall, running hard again, Virgil arrived at the Burger King and found Jenkins, Shrake, and Boykin drinking coffee among the remains of a nasty breakfast. Boykin was a thin, athletic man with white hair and sun wrinkles; he was wearing his highway patrol uniform. Virgil left his Minnesota atlas with them, and since he suspected that he might not eat again, and since the place offered the full menu twenty-four hours a day, he ordered a Double Whopper with cheese, large fries, and a Diet Coke; the bloat alone would carry him through to the evening.

When he was back at the booth, working on the Whopper and fries, Shrake, who had his face in a nutrition menu, said, "That's sixteen hundred and fifty calories, right there, most of it grease."

"Tastes really fuckin' good, though," Virgil said. He dabbed at his face with a napkin, wiped his fingers, and opened the atlas. "Okay. Here's the situation. The Bare County people think they've got Sharp and Welsh in a net that's roughly like this." He traced a circle on the map with a pencil. "My focus group thinks they'll be a little further south of that—south of Arcadia—and a bit west. The feeling was that they'd drop out of Bare County around here, after robbing that bank and Sharp getting shot."

They talked about the search pattern and tactics, and Virgil made sure they'd all be wearing their vests, which Jenkins and Shrake didn't like to do, and that the two teams would stay close, in case one of them needed support.

"If you don't wear the vests, I'll shoot you myself, just to make the point," Virgil said. Shrake would go with his friend Boykin, and Virgil would go with Jenkins. Shrake referred to Boykin as "Mad Dog" and "Pit Bull" and Virgil said, "You can call him anything you want, but I'm not gonna ask you why."

"Jesus, you've gotten pretty touchy," Shrake said.

"Lot of dead people," Virgil muttered.

"There are always a lot of dead people," Shrake said. "You can see them on TV all day. Little children fucked and chopped to pieces by freaks. Every day, sure as the sun rises, somewhere in the world, a little child—"

"Shut up," Virgil said.

"—will be slaughtered, and the TV people will find it and put it on your breakfast table. I've managed to handle that fact by deciding that I no longer give a shit."

Jenkins said to Virgil, "Don't encourage him. He's been on this rant for two weeks now."

"It's not a rant. It's my new meme," Shrake said. "I'm passing it to others."

He pronounced it "mem," and Jenkins said, "How many times do I have to tell you—"

"Meem," Shrake said. "It's my new meem. Hey, and I'm thinking about going on a vegan diet—"

"Ah, for Christ sakes, let me ride with Virgil," Boykin said.

"Let's go," Virgil said.

OUTSIDE, Shrake said to Virgil, "You have a tendency to try to do the right thing. If you have a chance, you'll try to save these kids' asses, and you could get shot doing that. Don't be too softhearted. If you run into them, let the kids call the cards."

"You—wear your vest," Virgil said.

THEY STARTED OUT in the middle of the focus area and spiraled outward. The farmhouses were generally a quarter to a half mile apart, usually not too far off the road, although some were set well back. They'd approach with the flashing lights, stop in the farmyard, and wait for somebody to come out of the house; occasionally, they'd find somebody already out working. The two teams leapfrogged each other, instead of going in opposite directions, so help would always be only a minute or two away.

At the first house they came to, Virgil stayed in the truck while Jenkins got out on the side opposite the farmhouse. It couldn't be seen from inside the house, but he was carrying an M14A1, a modified, fully automatic M14 military rifle that had been taken from a Canadian drug dealer a couple of years before. The rifle fired .308 rounds with better penetrating power than M16-based weapons, and would be useful for blowing holes through farm-house walls.

A minute after they showed up, a mixed-breed dog that looked like it might be mostly Aussie came running around from behind the barn and started barking at them, but stood off ten yards as it barked. Virgil decided he would not want to mess with it. A few seconds later, a farmer edged nervously out of the house, his hands in the air, and yelled, "Hey, Bob. Sit down. Sit down." The dog sat down. Virgil shouted, "Sir, could you come all the way over here? We're with the state Bureau of Criminal Apprehension."

When the farmer had come right up to him, Virgil confirmed in a low voice that he and his family were okay—"If your family is being held, we'll go away, and we'll be back with reinforcements and get you out."

"We're okay. I've got my twelve-gauge handy, and if they show up here, they won't be walking away."

"You take care," Virgil said. "They might not come driving up and knock on the door—they might come sneaking out of a field and jump you when you're walking out to the car. They're killers."

"We're all locked up tight and my cousin's coming up from Worthington in a couple hours with his guns. And we've got the dog out in the yard. Not much gets by him."

"Don't shoot each other," Virgil said. "Or the dog."

Before they left, Virgil asked if the farmer had seen any un-usual activity, or lack of activity, at local houses. He hadn't, and said his neighbors were staying in touch, even people who didn't like each other.

SHRAKE CALLED from down the road and said they'd cleared their first farmhouse.

IT WENT LIKE that all morning. In only two cases was there nobody home. In each case, they were able to locate the owners by phone and confirm that the house should be empty.

In one case, a farm couple emerged from the house wearing gun belts with leg tie-downs. They competed in Western shooting competitions, they said, and were not too worried.

At one o'clock in the afternoon, Duke called and said they had a possibility, and were setting up around the farmhouse. They knew there were people inside, because they'd been seen: but nobody had come out, and they'd ignored orders to come out.

Virgil's group broke off and drove north through Arcadia to join Duke's people. When they got there, they found fifty cops around the farmhouse, and out on the lawn, which was dotted with metal windmills and whirligigs. A couple of horses watched from an adjacent pasture, where an Owens cabin cruiser sat on fifty-five-gallon drums, a long way from any water big enough to float it.

"Can't get an answer out of them," Duke said.

The media showed up, but were kept way back, except for a

helicopter that buzzed over a couple of times. Duke went off to brief the TV people, who were getting impatient, pushing toward five o'clock deadlines. Another TV helicopter showed. Virgil saw a curtain moving in the front room window a couple of times, and once thought he saw the flash of a face.

The scene began to take on the aspect of a carnival, as more and more cops and soldiers came in, but then, around four o'clock, a frightened farm couple showed up and said that the people inside were almost certainly their four foster children, all teenagers, and all of whom were mentally challenged.

The farmer's name was Arnie Schmidt, who told Duke, "They're okay on their own, good with chores and so on, and wouldn't hurt a flea, really good kids, but they're probably scared to death. We told them today not to go out and not to let anybody in, because of these crazies. . . . I'm going to walk up there on the lawn and see if they'll come out to me."

Schmidt had been at a co-op and heard about the ruckus from a neighbor, picked up his wife from her job at the phone company, and had driven out as quickly as they could.

Duke told them he couldn't be responsible if they got hurt, and told them to stay well back down the lawn until they determined that there was nobody in the house but the children.

Schmidt immediately violated that, walking straight up to the front porch, while one of Duke's deputies yelled at him not to go so far; Duke said, "All that media's gonna be laughing at us, if all we've got is a house full of retards."

Virgil said, "You know what Ronald Reagan said about that."

Duke: "What's that?"

"Fuck 'em."

Duke disapproved. "I don't allow my men to use that kind of language."

"Good thing I'm not one of your men," Virgil said. "Look at that: they're coming out."

Four kids came out of the house, all boys, maybe ten to fourteen, the two tallest ones trying to explain to Schmidt what they'd done, the smaller ones crying as they looked at the circle of cars and trucks around them. Schmidt and his wife tried to calm them down, and the carnival packed up and in a half hour had gone away.

Shrake, sitting on the fender of Boykin's patrol car, said, "Well, that was enlightening."

"Another day on the job," Virgil said. "Let's get going."

They stopped in Arcadia to pick up Cokes and went back to work; they quit at six o'clock, having cleared an area of about five miles by five. If they'd worked another couple of hours, they would have found Welsh and Sharp, huddled in the old dead man's house at the top of the hill.

But then, working in the dark, they might have gotten themselves killed.

BECKY AND JIMMY were still hiding in the farmhouse, working their way through the bags of junk food that Becky had brought back from the convenience store. The night had been rough, with Jimmy's leg pulsing with pain. Becky rationed the pain pills, hoping to keep the pain at least bearable until they could get out of the area.

Jimmy said he couldn't move yet, and when he woke in the morning, and she washed his leg down, it seemed to her that the wound was starting to smell funny; and not in a ha-ha way. Some blood was still seeping into the bandage, but there was now a massive clot in place, and she was careful not to disturb it as she washed around the edges of it. The edges were yellow and puffy, but when she tentatively pried at them, she got blood instead of pus. She sprayed on a lot of the Band-Aid antiseptic, and re-bandaged it.

Jimmy said, "You know, you would have made a good nurse."

She said, "Thanks," and she really appreciated the thought.

THEY SPENT THE DAY in front of the television, watching the search. The TV people kept them up to date on the area where the hunt was going on, and while it wasn't far away, it wasn't close enough that they felt threatened. They had no hint of Virgil and his crew, who were much closer.

They talked about what they were going to do. Jimmy thought when they got better, they'd get in the old man's truck and head south. He'd once been to Missouri with his old man, and there was some rough country down there, where they might get lost for a while. He'd grow a beard and get some overalls so he'd look like a farmer, and when things had quieted down, they'd head farther south.

He'd decided they wouldn't go to Cuba or South America because the people there spoke Spanish. They'd go to Australia, he decided, because they spoke English there, and clicking around the TV channels, they came on a National Geographic special about Australia that made the whole place seem so neat that Becky got all excited and cried at the prospect. "Maybe I *could* be a nurse, in Australia," she said.

Jimmy hadn't looked at any more of the pornos, maybe because of the pain, or maybe because he was embarrassed by them, and when Becky steered the conversation around to their future relationship, he seemed happy enough to talk about it.

Becky asked, "You like me, right?"

"Sure. I always liked you," Jimmy said.

"It's just that, you know . . . we've only done it a couple times, and you always seemed to like that other thing better."

"All men like the other thing better," Jimmy said. "But you know, doing it, we just haven't had a lot of time. There didn't seem to be a good place, either."

"That's the only way you can have kids, though," she observed.

He was silent for a while after that, and finally she asked, "Don't you want to have kids?"

He said, "Don't know. Maybe." After a while, he said, "Tell you one thing, if we ever have kids, we won't treat them like we was. I mean, we'd be strict, but no hitting in the head, or anything like that."

Another long silence, then she said, "Did your old man do that?"

Jimmy showed some teeth in a grin and said, "One time, when I was about ten years old, I was sitting in the dinner chair and I said, 'I really hate these peas, they're all runny,' and he whacked me with his hand right on the side of the head, and I flew into the wall, I think, and it was like an hour later when I woke up on the floor. My goddamn head hurt for, like, two weeks. Dizzy, throwing up. When I got better, I thought about sneaking into his bedroom at night and killing the old sonofabitch. I'm glad I got to do that, finally. Got to do it before I die."

"We aren't gonna die," Becky said.

Jimmy said, "Yeah, well," and gestured at the TV, which was showing an aerial shot of a cluster of cop cars and army Humvees at an intersection, and a long line of cars stopped behind them.

"We're going to Australia," Becky said, trying to show some confidence.

THEY WATCHED FOR A WHILE, clicking around channels, and Jimmy said, "That beer sure was good. That hit the spot."

She helped him get into the bathroom and get his pants down so he could pee, and caught sight of herself in the bathroom mirror, and when he'd finished, and zipped up, she asked, "You think I'm pretty?"

"You're the prettiest girl I've ever talked to," he said. The truth was shining from his eyes, and she thought, it'd all been worth it, just to hear that.

LATER IN THE DAY, as the sun was going down, she made some Campbell's Cream of Tomato soup, but Jimmy had trouble hanging on to the spoon, so she fed him, and then he went to sleep on the couch. He was sleeping soundly when she started to get sleepy herself, so she put a blanket on him, and wrapped herself in a couple more blankets and a couple of sheets, and went to sleep on the floor next to the couch.

At two o'clock in the morning, Jimmy moaned, a long, low, blood-curdling moan that sounded right up next to death.

18

VIRGIL GOT ONE of the last rooms at the Minnesota Valley Lodge, where it seemed that half the cops in Minnesota were camped out, many of whom he knew. Whatever else had happened with this rampage, it was good for the local motel and diner business, he thought.

He ate with a couple of sheriffs and a couple of their deputies who'd come in on a mutual aid arrangement, talking about the state of the search, about the craziness of kids, about salaries and budgets and retirement plans, and one of the deputies wondered if there was any action in Bigham, and his boss said, "If you find any action, I'll tell your wife."

"What's the point in going out of town . . . ?"

The sheriff said, "Doug, the fact is, if you found any action, you wouldn't know what to do with it. I'd know what to do with it. Virgil would know what to do with it. You wouldn't know.

You'd just call up your old lady and say, 'Marge, I found some action. What should I do with it?'"

Doug said, "Well. You got me there. Maybe I'll just have another beer."

"Attaboy," said the sheriff.

AFTER DINNER, Virgil walked downtown to The Bush, where a
half dozen younger guys were shooting pool while a couple of
wives or girlfriends watched, everybody armed with bottles of
beer; and some older guys watched from the bar or sat elbows-on-
the-bar and talked. Roseanne Bush was working as the bartender
and, when she came down to him, asked, "What can I do you for?"

"You got a Leinie's?"

"Does a chicken have lips?" He didn't know the answer to
that, but she went down to a cooler and brought back a bottle of
Leinenkugel's, and popped the top off for him. He deliberately
chose a stool at the end of the bar, away from the others, and he
asked quietly, "Any of Jimmy Sharp's friends in here? Guys he shot
pool with?"

She said, just as quietly, and with a friendly grin, "What the
fuck are you doing coming in here and asking me that? I'm not
supposed to know you."

Virgil, "Any of them?"

She stopped in mid-sentence, then said, "The big guy in the
turquoise T-shirt with the orange thing on it. Donny Morton. He's
the only one. And he wasn't friends, they just shot pool together.
Now, don't ask me any more questions. Just git."

. . .

VIRGIL NURSED THE BEER for a while, then looked around, picked out the guy in the turquoise shirt with the orange thing on it. He had no idea what the orange thing was, but it looked like some kind of Indian symbol. Morton was no Indian: he was maybe six-seven, with long blond hair and a chubby pink face. Under thirty, Virgil thought, and maybe a biker; he had a wallet connected to his belt with a brass chain, wore heavy motorcycle boots, and put out a vibration.

He looked sort of mean, but in a hygienic, Minnesota way.

Virgil didn't want to give Roseanne away, and since Morton hadn't paid any attention to him, he finished the beer, laid five dollars on the bar, and headed for the door.

Outside, under the entrance light, he took out his pocket notebook, a Moleskine, and paged through some brief notes, until he found the name "Laura Deren." He'd been told by one of the O'Learys that Deren was the woman who'd accompanied Ag O'Leary to the Cities, where she'd either miscarried or had an abortion.

Once he had her name, he checked her driver's license at the DMV and got an address and ran the address through the smartphone's map program, and found that Deren was a half mile away.

With no traffic lights, wide streets, or even much traffic, Virgil walked to Deren's place in nine minutes by his watch and found that it was a smaller, older apartment building, of brown brick, built in a residential area. The front door was locked, but he found Deren's name on a doorbell and rang it. He got no answer, leaned on the bell for a while, still got no answer. As he turned to leave, a

Toyota Camry pulled into the parking area on the side of the building. A line of single-car garages was built along the length of the parking area, and the car waited while the door to one of them rolled up. The DMV had listed Deren as the owner of a Camry, and when the car had parked, a woman stepped out of the garage, aimed a key-ring remote at it, and the door rolled down.

Virgil stepped up and asked, "Miz Deren?"

She was wearing high heels and a suit, and he startled her, speaking from the dark, and she said, "Uh . . ."

Virgil said quickly, "I'm a police officer, with the Bureau of Criminal Apprehension. I'm investigating the death of Ag O'Leary."

Still tentative, she asked, "You have identification?"

"Sure." He took his ID out of his jacket and handed it to her.

There was still a light on above the garage, and she stepped back and scanned it, frowned, said, "Okay," and, "How did you find me?"

"I got your name from the O'Learys, and your address from the Department of Motor Vehicles," Virgil said.

More confident now: "Okay. What can I do for you?"

They went up to her apartment, and she offered Virgil a glass of wine, which he declined; she poured one for herself and sat in an easy chair, while Virgil perched on a couch. "This is a confidential conversation. I'd ask that you not speak to anyone about it, unless you feel that you need to talk to an attorney."

"Why would I need to do that?"

"I don't know. I couldn't object to your talking to an attorney, that's all. I don't suspect you of doing anything wrong. But I have some sensitive questions."

She gazed at him for a moment—she was a pretty young

woman with shoulder-length brown hair and brown eyes; her dress was a muted green chosen to fit well with her modest gold necklace. She'd kicked off her high heels when she sat down. "Sensitive questions . . . about Ag?"

"About Ag's relationship with her husband."

"Interesting," she said. "Will this conversation be made public?"

"Only as part of a court hearing, and if we get as far as that, there'd be more important issues than your privacy."

She nodded and said, "So ask a question."

"When you went to the Twin Cities with Ag, did she miscarry? Or did she have an abortion?"

She flinched at the word, and her eyes went flat, and Virgil had the answer.

She saw him react and realized that she'd given it away, so she told the truth. "We went to Planned Parenthood in St. Paul," Deren said. "We had an appointment, and the pregnancy was terminated. Her parents don't know that. They're all good Catholics."

"Does Dick Murphy know that?"

"I don't know. I haven't seen him since the day we went to the clinic. I did see Ag quite a bit, and she hadn't told him three days . . . I think it was three days . . . before she died. We'd put that miscarriage story out there, and her parents . . . whether she told him the truth or not, I don't know."

"Had she asked him for a divorce?"

"No. We don't ask for divorces anymore, Officer Flowers. We simply tell them. She'd told him."

"I knew that . . . about the telling," Virgil said. "I've been told myself."

"Well, there you go," Deren said. She smiled for the first time.

"The reason I asked about it," Virgil said, "was that Dick was apparently visiting her at her parents' house."

"He did. Ag was going through the fiction that they were separated, and they might get back together. That was so she could spare her parents' feelings—like I said, they're all Catholic over there—until she could get set up with an apartment in the Cities, and buy some furniture and so on. We were going to start doing that this week. Ag planned to work for a year, while she waited to see what happened with her med school applications. She was planning to go back to school."

"Did Dick ever get physical with her?"

"Yes. He raped her, but she wouldn't call it that. He knew better than to hit her. He'd twist her and squeeze her . . . he had a way of squeezing her that was agonizing, but didn't show much of a sign of anything. He'd put his arms around her from the back, with his knuckles turned into her breast bone, and he'd squeeze her really hard. She told me she thought she was dying when he did that."

"She didn't tell anybody else about it?"

"No. For one thing, it didn't leave a mark, like I said, so it'd be hard to prove," Deren said. "But what really worried her was, one of her brothers, or a bunch of her brothers, would go pound on Dick. An assault conviction doesn't help your med school application, and the whole bunch of them plan to be doctors."

"So she . . ."

"She had it all planned out. She was in her parents' house, and wouldn't be alone with him. And then, she was going to disappear," Deren said. "Go up to the Cities. Her family would know where she was, but Dick wouldn't. She'd only come down here for the divorce proceedings, which would be fast."

Virgil mulled that over for a minute, until she asked, "What's this about? Dick wasn't involved in her death. . . . I mean, I thought everybody knew what happened."

"We're pretty sure we know who pulled the trigger," Virgil said. "It was Jim Sharp. Murphy and Sharp were shooting pool the night before the night Ag was murdered. Jim didn't have a pistol, and was so broke that the morning of the shooting he spent the last of his money, the last of Becky Welsh's money and the last of Tom McCall's, on a loaf of bread and some peanut butter. That night, he had a gun and a thousand dollars."

She gazed at him for a moment, then whispered, "You think Dick paid to have Ag murdered?"

"That's the aspect that I'm investigating," Virgil said. "If she aborted his baby—"

"Oh, bull," she said. "Dick probably didn't want the baby any more than she did. Dick wants stuff—cars and cabins and boats, and he'd like to go to Vegas at Christmas. To get that, he needed to get at her trust fund. If you don't get him, he'll have it, too."

"I'm not sure what the status of that is," Virgil said.

Deren shook her head. "Ag didn't have a will. She was a young woman, she was in perfect health. Why would she have a will? What could go wrong? So . . . he gets it."

"Why did she ever marry him?"

"Well . . . he's good-looking. He's athletic. He's somewhat intelligent, and he pursued her. And maybe . . . Ag was a little socially awkward. She wasn't one of the social kids in high school, or college, either one. You know, a firstborn, with all the firstborn traits: bossy, pushy, privileged," Deren said. "And then, Dick wasn't an O'Leary. They are very good people, to a fault. Ag felt like she was on a railroad train to medical school. Had to be the hardest worker in high school to get the grades to get the best slots in college. Had to be the hardest worker in college to get the grades to get into medical school. Dick was like, 'Hey, chill out. Have a couple beers. Let's get in the car and run down to Vegas and roll the dice and go to the shows and get drunk and make love. . . .' So, they wound up getting married, and after a while, guess what?"

"What?"

She smiled ruefully. "She found out she was an O'Leary."

"He couldn't be too bright if he paid Jimmy Sharp to kill her," Virgil said.

"Unless he planned to kill Jimmy Sharp afterward," she said. When Virgil's eyes went up, she hastily added, "I don't know anything. I'm just saying . . . you know. And he could do it. And who'd ever see that connection?"

Virgil asked, "What do you do, Miz Deren?"

"I'm a bookkeeper, right now. I'm almost finished with my degree in accounting. I'm going to be a CPA."

"Can you keep this conversation quiet?" Virgil asked.

"I can. But you have to get him. Dick, I mean."

"We'll see. Right now, this is mostly conjecture."

"When you said he was playing pool with Jim Sharp the day before? That's when it added up for me. He did it. Paid Jim Sharp."

.   .   .

HER OPINION ABOUT that was interesting, but it'd be useless in court, Virgil thought, as he ambled back toward town. He looked in the doorway at Roseanne's, saw that Morton was still there, leaning against a wall, his pool cue grounded while two other guys worked through a game.

Virgil backed out, walked down to the motel, said hello to a few people, then went to his room, changed into dark slacks, a sport coat, and a collared shirt with a necktie. He saw Jenkins as he was walking toward the door, and Jenkins said, "Don't tell me you've got a date."

"I'm talking to a guy. I was watching him a little, a couple hours ago, in a beer joint, but he wasn't looking at me. I don't want him to remember that I was there."

Jenkins nodded and said, "You need somebody to watch your back?"

"Naw. I'm good."

He walked back to The Bush, still not in a hurry. When he stepped inside, the talk immediately dropped off: his dress had given him away as unusual, which he'd expected. He looked around, saw Morton looking at him, nodded at him, went that way. "Are you Don Morton?"

Morton nodded, and unconsciously chalked his cue tip. "Yeah. Who're you?"

"I'm Virgil Flowers. I'm an agent with the state Bureau of Criminal Apprehension. I need to talk to you for a moment."

A woman on a stool next to a bowling machine said, "He is. I seen him on TV."

Morton asked, "What'd I do?"

"Nothing, I hope," Virgil said. "We've been talking to a lot of people, and one of them told us you were playing some pool with Jimmy Sharp down here, before all the shooting started. We're just wondering what he had to say—what might have set him off."

"I don't know nothing," Morton said.

"So come and answer my questions," Virgil said. "We can just go sit in the front booth, where it's a little quieter."

Morton shrugged, a nervous assent, and followed Virgil back to the front booth. The woman who'd seen Virgil on TV asked, "Can I listen?"

Virgil grinned at her and said, "No. But I'll talk to you next, if you want. Did you see Jimmy down here?"

"Yup, I did," she said.

"Then sit right there," Virgil said.

HE AND MORTON sat in the booth and Virgil said, "I'll buy you another beer, if you want," and Morton showed some broken teeth and said, "I couldn't turn that down."

Virgil waved over the only waitress, and Morton ordered a Bud, and Virgil asked him, "You got anything at all that might be interesting? About Jimmy Sharp? What'd he talk about?"

"Well, he wanted to shoot for dollars, which is pretty low-rent, but he got some games, and . . . mostly talked about being up in the Cities. 'Bout the assholes up there. Had a really good-looking chick with him, this Becky, and this other guy, the one that got caught." He frowned, then flicked a finger at Virgil: "Wait a minute. Was that you?"

Virgil nodded. "Yeah."

"Surprised you just didn't put him down, right on the spot," Morton said, and he took a swig of beer.

"I don't do that," Virgil said.

Morton shook his head and said, "If I was a cop . . . Anyway, I shot some with Jim, and took a couple dollars off him, and that was about it."

"Did you see him shooting with Dick Murphy?" Virgil asked.

"Dick? Uh, yeah. They were shooting, some, but I don't know what they talked about. You'd have to ask Dick."

"Is he here?"

"Not tonight," Morton said. "The visitation for his wife is tonight. . . . He was here last night."

"Did he seem pretty broken up by her murder?"

Morton peered at him for a long moment, then said, "Look, I don't want to get Dick in trouble. He's not a bad guy."

Virgil said, "Really? He's not a bad guy?"

Morton's eyes shifted. A second later they came back, and he said, "You're not going to tell anybody what we're talking about here?"

"Not unless we get into court," Virgil said.

"I gotta live here," Morton said.

"I was born in Marshall, and I still live in a small town," Virgil said. "I know how it is."

Morton licked his lower lip. "Dick and Ag wasn't getting along. They were going to get divorced."

"Was Dick unhappy about that?"

"He started calling her 'the bitch.' The bitch did this and the bitch did that. So yeah . . ."

"He ever mention her money?"

"Money? No, not that I ever heard. I guess she had some, her being an O'Leary."

Morton didn't have much more, but when Virgil finished, he asked, "You think Dick got Jimmy to kill her?"

"I don't think anything in particular," Virgil said. "I just go around and ask questions that I think should be asked. Sometimes, interesting facts come popping out of the ground, like mushrooms."

"You got a pretty fuckin' good job," Morton said. "I wouldn't mind being a cop."

"Well, come on up to the Cities, go to school, get a job," Virgil said. "That's what I did. And you're right. It's a pretty good job."

"I don't think that'd work," Morton said.

"Why not?"

"I once defenestrated a guy. The cops got all pissed off at me. I was drunk, but they said that was no excuse."

"Ah, well," Virgil said. Then, "The guy hurt bad?"

"Cracked his hip. Landed on a Prius. Really fucked up the Prius, too."

"I can tell you, just now is the only time in my life I ever heard 'defenestration' used in a sentence," Virgil said.

"It's a word you learn, after you done it," Morton said. "Yup. The New Prague AmericInn, 2009."

Virgil was amazed. "Really? The defenestration of New Prague?"

. . .

THE WOMAN WHO WANTED to talk to Virgil was named Marjorie Kay, and when Morton went back to the pool table, she slid eagerly into the booth and said, "Fire away."

"Don't have anything to fire," he told her. "I'm just asking about who said what to whom, when Jimmy Sharp was here."

"Poop. I didn't talk to him," she said. Then brightened. "But I heard him talking to people. And I talked to his girlfriend, that Becky girl. And George Petersen, he told her, Becky, that he'd give her fifty dollars to go out to his truck with him. She got all mad, but Jimmy just laughed."

"George Petersen."

"He's an over-the-road trucker. He's on the road. He hauls chickens out of New Age Poultry."

"Was Dick Murphy here that night?"

"Dick? Oh, yeah."

"Did he talk to Jimmy?"

She looked at him for a moment, her eyes like pigeon eyes, curious but oddly cold and shiny and slightly protrusive, and then she whispered, "You think he was in on it? Ag's murder?"

Virgil repeated his line about not thinking anything in particular, but she wasn't buying it: "Bull-hockey, you think he did it. So do I. I told my sister that, right after Ag got killed. I said, 'That's really pretty convenient for Dicky, isn't it?' Everybody knows she had money."

"What do people in the bar think?"

She looked over her shoulder at the people around the table, and then came back and said, "They think the same thing as I do. It's pretty convenient. Dick doesn't get on with his old man. Surprised *he* wasn't murdered. The old man, I mean."

They talked for a few more minutes, and when Virgil wouldn't give her any inside information on the case, she went back to the pool table. Virgil paid for Morton's beer, walked back to the motel. An informal strategy meeting was going on in the breakfast area, a bunch of cops arguing about the best way to run down Sharp and Welsh. The wrangling was only semi-serious, fueled with alcohol. Virgil sat with Jenkins and Shrake, filled them in on his ideas about Dick Murphy, and told them about his conversation with Morton the defenestrator. They agreed to meet the next morning at eight o'clock.

Duke had been sitting with a bunch of deputies, looking tired, and before he left he came over and said, "We've got a bunch of guys laying back in the weeds, to see if they try to sneak out of the search area."

"Let me know . . . and get some sleep."

"You, too."

VIRGIL LEFT JENKINS and Shrake and went back to his room. He was sitting on the bed, setting the alarm, when a call came in from the BCA duty officer. "We got a call from somebody who says her name is Marjorie, and she says you've got to go back to Roseanne's. She says she's got a guy there who knows about Dick Murphy and Jim Sharp."

Something uncurled in Virgil's stomach, a warm sense of satisfaction: in most cases, there was a moment when things started to work for him, when things started to get done. He'd taken his boots off, and he put them back on and went out and walked back to Roseanne's.

The upside: if the guy really knew about Murphy and Sharp, he might have enough, with his other evidence, to bust Murphy. Especially, he thought, if they could get that thousand dollars off Sharp, and find out where it came from.

The downside: Marjorie . . . Kay? . . . that seemed right; Marjorie Kay was obviously blabbing about Virgil's ideas about Murphy. That wasn't all bad, but meant that he'd lost control of the rumor mill. Word would get back to Murphy, and he'd hunker down.

WHEN VIRGIL GOT back to Roseanne's, there were two guys leaning on the front of a pickup right at the door, drinking out of beer bottles, their backs to him. One of them heard him coming, and they both dropped their hands out of sight. Virgil grinned: they were breaking the law, just as he had, a few nights before, drinking outside the Rooster Coop back in Mankato.

He was going to say something as he went past, and was looking at the back of the closest one, and had just opened his mouth when the man turned and Virgil got a glimpse of a bandanna pulled over his face, like an old-timey bank robber, and behind that image was the image of an incoming fist and Virgil never had time to get a hand or anything else in the way, but he barely had the time to flinch away, and instead of connecting with the middle of his face, the fist connected with the side of his forehead and

knocked him down in the dirt and a half second later he was rolling away, his hands up around his head, unable to get far enough
away from them to get to his feet, as they kicked at his legs and
ribs and face. . . .

The gravel in the parking lot was cutting at him as he scrambled and went down, scrambled and went down, and he could feel
the palms of his hands and his shoulders getting cut, but all he was
thinking about was his head and his kidneys, protecting them
from the boots.

He never had the leisure to take a good look at them, but they
were wearing boots and jeans and leather jackets and ball caps and
the masks, and they weren't yelling or really making any noise at
all except occasional curses, and "Get him, get out of the way, get
out of my way . . ."

Whether they'd done this before, or not, he had no way of
knowing, but they weren't well coordinated. Virgil kept trying to
move in ways that kept one of them eclipsed behind the other, as
much as he could, and was succeeding at least some of the time,
and managed to get partway to his feet before he stumbled and he
called out, "Police officer. I'm . . ."

They kept coming and Virgil figured they must already know
that. They'd come for *him*, not for a fight. They'd either badly beat
him, put him in the hospital for sure, or maybe kill him, because
he just couldn't get away from them, but then a truck pulled into
the parking lot, splashing headlights across the three of them, and
Virgil kept moving and he saw more figures spilling out of the
truck, and he didn't know if he was further screwed, or saved,
when one of the new people called, "Hey! Hey, what the hell . . ."

Virgil shouted, "Police officer! Help me . . ."

One of the new people yelled, "He's a cop, let's get them. . . ." There was some running and scuffling, and then the two men who'd jumped him ran, down toward the end of the bar and around behind it and out of sight.

His rescuers didn't go after them. Instead, they squatted around him, four young men, two in sport coats, two in casual jackets, and one of them asked, "You all right?"

"I'm pretty scuffed up," Virgil managed. He pushed himself into a sitting position, but every time he moved, something hurt. "I think maybe . . . I ought to go to an emergency room."

One of the men said to another, "Go on in the bar and call the cops. And an ambulance."

Virgil said, "Thanks."

One of the men, whose faces he couldn't see very clearly, said, "Man, you are bleeding to beat the band."

Virgil said, "Artery?"

"No, I don't think so. You look like you fell off your Harley. Like seriously bad road rash. You really a cop?"

Virgil said, "Yeah." He still couldn't see them clearly, and began to suspect that one of the kicks had connected with his head; things weren't quite right. He asked, "Who are you guys?"

One of them, exactly who was unclear, said, "Pi Kappa Alpha."

Virgil thought he'd misheard. "What?"

"We're fraternity brothers . . . from the U . . . down here with a friend on spring break."

"Ah . . ."

The guy who'd gone inside came running back out and said, "I called nine-one-one. Everybody's coming."

More people came out of the bar to look, and Virgil tried to get to his feet, got halfway up with one of the frat boys holding his arm, and then fell back on his butt. The kid said, "Just wait. Somebody'll be here in a minute."

Virgil did not feel good.

THE COPS GOT THERE FIRST, and one of them looked at Virgil and said, "Criminy! It's the state cop, Flowers."

Virgil said, "Hi."

The cop said, "Set right there," and to somebody else, "You better call Duke."

A minute later, an ambulance arrived, and when Virgil couldn't make it to his feet, they locked up his neck and head, put him on a gurney, and loaded him aboard. His eyes still weren't quite focusing; he said to the ambulance attendant, "I'm a cop, and I've got to call somebody. Get my cell phone out of my pocket, will you?"

"We're not supposed to—"

"Just do it," Virgil said.

A minute later, Davenport came up and said, "Yo. You get them?"

"Not exactly," Virgil said. "I'm in an ambulance headed for the hospital. I just got the shit beat out of me."

VIRGIL WENT INTO the emergency room, where a nurse helped him take his clothes off, and a doc came and looked at him, and did some simple focusing tests, and recall tests, then said, "You've got a concussion. And you look pretty roughed up. We'll do some X-rays."

"The guys at the bar said I'm bleeding."

"Not enough blood to worry about. It's what's going on inside that worries me," the doc said.

He used his hands to probe at Virgil's chest and kidneys, while questioning him, and Virgil couldn't remember any particularly hard blows to the body. "I was trying to keep them on my arms and legs. . . . I was on my back most of the time."

The hospital staff drew what seemed like a lot of blood, and wheeled him around for the X-rays, and at some point Shrake and Jenkins showed up, and Virgil told them what happened, and realized that he could now focus on their faces. But he was very tired, and began to shake.

The doc, called by Shrake, came back and said that he might be suffering some post-combat shock, that the adrenaline overload was catching up to him, and that it should wear off fairly quickly. When Virgil told him he could focus, the doc said, "Excellent, that's a very positive sign," and went away again.

Shrake and Jenkins had disappeared, probably shooed away by the nurse, Virgil thought. He was alone for a while and may have slept, then the doc came back and said, "Good news: there's no sign of a skull fracture or any spinal problems. As far as I can tell, you don't have any broken bones. You may have some pulled muscles or some other soft tissue injuries. We won't know for sure until tomorrow. But you are seriously bruised up and you are going to hurt for a week. And you're still concussed. We're going to keep you for a while—overnight, anyway—to make sure that the concussion isn't too bad. We'll give you something to help you sleep."

. . .

THEY DID THAT.

When Virgil woke in the morning, Davenport was sitting next to the bed, tapping on an iPad, looking grim. Virgil cleared his throat, and Davenport looked up and said, "Well, you're still alive."

"That's the good part," Virgil said. "But I need a drink, and I've got to pee."

"I can get you some water, but you'll have to pee on your own," Davenport said. "I'll call the nurse."

With the nurse helping, Virgil got out of bed and walked to the bathroom, hurting every step of the way, peed—happy to see no blood—and when he came back out, Davenport handed him a glass of water and Virgil said to the nurse, "I'm okay. I'll use the chair."

He sat down—and it hurt to sit down—and Davenport said, "Tell me."

Virgil told him, and Davenport said, "We'll talk to this Marjorie, but five'll get you ten that whoever called Richards saw her talking to you, and used that to pull you back to the bar." Richards was the BCA duty officer who'd called Virgil the night before.

"That sounds right," Virgil said. "I really had my head up my ass: I bit on it like a hungry trout."

"Gotta rework your metaphors," Davenport said. And, "Duke was here. He said he'd see you this afternoon, but they're out running the search again."

"Wrong spot, I think," Virgil said.

Davenport continued, "Jenkins and Shrake are out tearing up

the countryside, looking for the two guys who jumped you. Those frat boys showed up at the right time, but they didn't get a license plate, and we can't find anybody at the bar who knows who they are. But we'll find them."

"Couple of assholes, not important," Virgil said. "They weren't very good at it, either. Probably friends of Dick Murphy. Maybe even Dick Murphy, for all I know. But: I think I worried Murphy enough for him to do this. That's the only reason I can think of that somebody'd jump me. If I could find those guys . . . maybe they'd talk."

"What do you have on Murphy?"

Virgil laid it out, and when he was finished, Davenport said, "I agree with you that he probably paid Sharp. We need Sharp to say so. Or Welsh to say that Sharp told her that."

"So we need to keep at least one of them alive," Virgil said.

Davenport stood up and said, "You take it easy. I think they're going to let you out this afternoon, but I already told the doc that if he thinks you ought to stay, that they ought to make you stay. Not to take any bullshit from you."

"All right. But I really do need to get out of here. This whole thing is probably going to end today."

"Can't go much longer," Davenport agreed. He stepped toward the door, then said, "You notice I didn't say a single fuckin' thing about you going up to that bar without a gun."

"I appreciate that," Virgil said.

"But if you had a gun with you, like you should have, as soon as you were hit, you could have rolled and come up with the weapon and just squeezed off a couple of rounds . . . even if you didn't hit anything, that would have ended it. They'd have run, and you wouldn't be in here. And if you'd hit one of them, we could talk to the guy about Murphy."

"No. That's what would have happened if *you* had a gun," Virgil said. "You can do that, because that's the way you think. If I'd had a gun, and even remembered it, I probably would have dropped it trying to get it out. Then I'd have really been up shit creek, with a gun floating around. I'm just no damn good with pistols, Lucas."

Davenport looked at him for a moment, then shook his head and said, "Take it easy, man. We'll find these guys. And I wouldn't be surprised if they resist arrest."

Virgil said, "Take care," and Davenport was gone.

HE STILL HAD a residual headache, but he'd had worse; and he'd hurt worse, like the time he got thrown off an ex–rodeo horse and pulled a groin muscle. He remembered the wrangler looking down at him and saying, "You take good dirt."

Maybe he did, he thought as he hobbled around the hospital room, because even though he hurt all over, he would have given a hundred American dollars to get five minutes alone with either of the guys who'd jumped him. "But not both at the same time," he said aloud, grinning at himself in the bathroom mirror. He had a bad scrape on the left side of his forehead, on his left cheek, and below that, on the left side of his jaw. He had a bruise the size of a Kennedy half-dollar on the right side of his forehead, and he could feel dried blood in his hair, right at the crown of his head.

He was wearing a hospital gown. He pulled the bathroom

door closed, peeled off the gown, and took a look at himself. He had a half dozen big boot-shaped bruises on each arm, more on his butt and thighs, and one on his shin. He was scraped mostly on his forearms and hands, where skin had been exposed to gravel, and on his knees.

He put the gown back on, went out and checked his clothes. The jeans were ripped at the knees, and would have to be tossed, and his jacket was a wreck. He thought about getting dressed, but instead, turned around, got on the bed, and went back to sleep.

THE NURSE WOKE him at ten o'clock, said that Dr. Rogers was about to look at him. Rogers, who was not the same doc he'd talked to the night before, took a long look at him and said, "All right. I'll give you a couple things that'll make you feel better . . . or hurt less . . . but I want you to stay away from aspirin and alcohol."

After telling Virgil what he could and couldn't do, he said that another doc, named Wu, would be in to see him in a few minutes, and if Wu signed off, he could leave: "But take it easy for a few days."

The next doc to show up wasn't Wu, but John O'Leary, who was wearing a short white staff doctor's coat. "I just heard what happened. Does this have something to do with Dick Murphy?"

"Maybe," Virgil said. "Maybe. Probably. I can't think of anyone else who'd want to put me in the hospital for a while."

"I don't get that," O'Leary said. "I'd think the last thing he'd want to do is get your dander up."

"I've been thinking about it," Virgil said. "The people around here, they've had a lot of people killed by Sharp and Welsh. Your daughter and Emmett Williams here in Bigham, three people in Shinder, two in Marshall, two more out in the country, and a cop . . . that we know of."

"You think there are more?"

"We'll find out when we locate them," Virgil said. "Anyway, the feeling here is that the local folks are going to kill them when they find them. It's absolutely turned into a duck hunt. But, when I got the chance to take in McCall, I got him to Marshall alive. I don't think Murphy would want me to get Jim or Becky to jail alive. Jimmy could turn on them."

"And you need their testimony."

"That's about it. . . . Uh, I thought you'd be at the funeral."

"I will be, but I have patients," O'Leary said. "Anyway, good luck with getting Sharp and Welsh. Truth is, I believe you're right about what's going to happen. I haven't talked to a single person here who thinks they'll be taken alive. Their best chance would be to drive down to Iowa and turn themselves in to the Des Moines cops. Some big-city police station, someplace far away from here."

"They're not smart enough," Virgil said. "Anyway, as soon as this Wu gets here, I'm gone."

An Asian man stuck his head around the corner of the open door. "Wu you looking for?"

WU TURNED OUT to have a good sense of humor and strong hands, and he only hurt Virgil a little. An hour later, Virgil was back on the street, still feeling creaky. He called what he suspected was the town's only cab, was told that in fact there were two, and rode back to the motel. Moving around helped; either that, or it was the pills that Rogers had prescribed, of which he had taken three.

Shrake and Jenkins were walking out as Virgil walked in, and Shrake said, "We've got a few names. We're going to go talk to them now. You think you scuffed them up at all?"

"Only their legs," Virgil said. "I was on the ground with the first punch, and after that, I was just trying to stay alive. I kicked one guy in the shins a few times, but that's about it. He'll have some bruises."

"One of those frat boys, a big guy, said he caught one of the guys a pretty good lick in an eye, and the side of a nose. Says the guy'll have a shiner."

"These names . . . are they tied to Murphy?" Virgil asked.

"A couple of them," Jenkins said. "The rest are from Davenport's network—local guys who might do something like this."

"Well, take it easy," Virgil said. "I need these guys scared and willing to talk to me. I don't need them all beat up and pissed off."

Jenkins patted him on the shoulder. "You're a fuckin' saint, Virgil," he said. "But I gotta tell you—I can't guarantee these guys'll be in pristine condition. I *can* guarantee that they'll be scared."

19

VIRGIL HAD A CHEESEBURGER and fries with catsup in the lodge's restaurant, feeling a little guilty about it—shouldn't you eat something healthy after checking out of a hospital? Lettuce, or something? He chewed carefully, because his jaw hurt, and then, though his headache had eased, he decided to go take a nap: he was still feeling a little shaky. Just a couple of hours, he thought, which would have him back on his feet by early afternoon. If Shrake and Jenkins were back by then, they could resume the search south of Arcadia.

He was sound asleep when his subconscious gave him a prod, and he opened his eyes. What? Somebody at the door. Just feet? Then, tentatively, a knock. He had the "Do Not Disturb" sign hung on the doorknob, so it wasn't the motel staff.

He rolled out of bed, jolted by a half dozen minor lightning bolts of pain in his arms, ribs, butt, and legs, called, "Just a minute," reached into his duffel and pulled out his 9-millimeter, and eased up to the peephole.

From a foot back, and a bit off to the side, he could see no-body; he put his eye to the peephole and then jerked back, and thought about what he hadn't seen. He hadn't seen anybody.

He called, "Who is it?"

A woman's voice, deliberately quiet: "Me. Roseanne."

A woman had called the duty officer the night before, to pull him up to the bar . . . but then, this did sound like Roseanne Bush. He said, "Stand back from the door. So I can see you."

She said, "Okay."

He risked another quick peep, thinking about the possibility of a whole bunch of slugs ripping through the door, and saw Bush backed against the far wall. He undid the chain, turned the knob, and pointed the gun at the space where somebody might come through. Nobody came through. He opened the door, and found Bush standing by herself in the hallway.

She said, "Don't shoot me."

Virgil said, "Come on in," and when she was inside, relocked and chained the door, and put the pistol away.

"God, I'm freaked out about last night," she said. "I'm so sorry."

"Not your fault. I was talking to people about Dick Murphy. I'm thinking the word got back to him." Virgil eased back on the bed, and Roseanne sat in the corner chair.

"Lucas called me last night, and gave me a hard time about who it might have been," Roseanne said. "I'll tell you what: you would not want to go up against him, on some dark night. Lucas, I mean."

"No, you wouldn't," Virgil agreed. They sat for a minute in silence, then Virgil asked, "So what's up?"

"Everybody is talking about the fight last night. Then a guy told me that Dick Murphy is getting out of town after the funeral. That he's going to Vegas." She looked at her watch. "The funeral's going on right now."

"Goddamnit," Virgil said. "Well: thanks for telling me. I'll head over to the church."

"You got a few minutes—it just started," she said. She got up to leave and said again, "I'm so sorry."

ALL SAINTS was a yellow brick church built at the edge of the hill overlooking the river, bigger than most small-town Catholic churches, probably because the town was half-Irish, and had been for a hundred years. Virgil was of the opinion that Catholic services were weird, but never told anybody that. He limped into the back of the church at twenty minutes to two; the place was jammed, which was fine with him, as it allowed him to stand inconspicuously in the back.

The interior was elaborately decorated in gold and yellow paint; it was built in the traditional cruciform style, and Ag O'Leary's coffin was sitting at the far side of the crossing, covered with a white-and-gold cloth. The O'Learys were all in the front row of pews on the right side of the church; there was a youngish man in the first seat of the first pew on the left side, in a dark suit, and Virgil suspected that he was Dick Murphy.

Virgil was standing between a thin, earnest-looking woman in a black coat that smelled of mothballs, her hair covered with a black hanky; and an older bald man in a green wool coat, with the

reddened face of a longtime drinker and the white hair and eyebrows of Santa Claus. They'd been standing, watching for a couple
of minutes when the old man leaned toward him and asked, with
beer-scented breath, "You're the state agent, right?"

Virgil nodded. "Yup."

"Heard you got kicked pretty bad last night."

Virgil: "Yeah."

The old man went back to watching the service, then Virgil
leaned toward him and asked, "That guy in the front pew, on the
left, in the suit . . . Is that Dick Murphy?"

"Yup." Then, after a few seconds, "The little prick."

Virgil watched for a few more minutes, then retreated to the
front steps and called Davenport. "The word is, Dick Murphy
is leaving town after the funeral. It occurred to me that we
might have enough to bust him as a material witness. Then again,
maybe not."

Davenport thought it over for a few seconds, then said, "Be
better if you could tell him what you're thinking: that you might
need to talk to him. Tell him you want him to stay in town. If he
can't do that, you want to know where he's going. And if you call
him back, and he doesn't come, then you'll bust him. Tell him if
he's busted, it might take a while to get him back here, and in the
meantime, he could spend quite a bit of time in some unpleasant
lockups."

Virgil said, "Good. I could have figured that out myself, if I
weren't so fucked up."

"You still hurt?"

"Yeah."

"You okay?" Davenport asked.

"Yeah. I just hurt."

"Getting old, man," Davenport said.

"But, fortunately, not as old as you," Virgil said.

VIRGIL WAITED OUTSIDE THE CHURCH, sitting in his truck, and when the funeral Mass ended, he climbed out and walked across the street. The ushers brought the O'Learys and Murphy out first. There was an older man with Murphy, probably fifty or so, and they looked enough alike that Virgil thought he must be Dick Murphy's father. Whoever he was, he left quickly, leaving Murphy on one side of the church steps, and the O'Learys on the other side, where they shook hands with people leaving the Mass.

Murphy looked like an athlete prematurely going to seed—still in his early twenties, good-looking with dark hair and broad shoulders, he was already showing a bit of a gut. He was a little wider than Virgil, but a little shorter. He wore a black suit that was too sharp for a Midwestern small town, like perhaps he got it at the young man's shop at the Las Vegas Barneys.

When the stream of funeral-goers had slowed to a trickle, Murphy stepped toward John O'Leary and said something, and O'Leary snapped something back. Virgil could see his teeth, and one of the O'Leary boys stepped in front of his father, as if to protect him. Murphy may have thought the O'Leary kid was about to attack him, because he shoved the kid's fist—was it Frank? Virgil wasn't sure—and the kid threw a punch. Not a bad one, either, Virgil thought, as he started running.

But the fight exploded across the church steps, three or four of the O'Leary boys going after Murphy as John and Mary O'Leary, along with the priest, tried to pull them off. Virgil got there perhaps ten seconds after the fight had begun, and began pushing people apart, roughing them, yelling, "Enough, enough . . ." James O'Leary had gotten ahold of Murphy's left hand and was trying to wrench off a thick gold wedding band, and was screaming, "Give me that fuckin' ring, you sonofabitch," and Murphy tried to wrench his hand away but James hung on, and got flung down the steps for his trouble, and then Virgil wrapped up Murphy and hustled him backward away from the O'Leary crowd.

James was hurt, a sprained wrist, and torn pants, and Murphy was bleeding from his lower lip and a mouse was swelling up on his cheekbone.

When they were thoroughly separated, the priest standing between Murphy and the O'Learys with his hands stretched out to them, like Moses parting the Red Sea, Virgil let go of Murphy and said, "Easy, now."

Murphy yelled past him, "The whole fuckin' bunch of you can bite me."

Jack O'Leary started across the steps, but John O'Leary and the priest grabbed him, and he subsided. The fight was done.

Virgil said to Murphy, "I'm Virgil Flowers, an agent with the Bureau of Criminal Apprehension."

"I know who you are," Murphy said. He spat a little blood off to one side and rubbed his lip. "You're the guy going around telling people I had something to do with Ag's murder."

"I'm going around asking people about your relationship with Ag," Virgil said, "because we have one witness who says he thinks you paid Jimmy Sharp to kill her."

Murphy reddened and poked a finger at Virgil's chest: "I swear to God, you tell people that, and I will sue you. I'll sue you right down to your shorts, and when they take your badge away from you, I'll come kick your ass."

"Last night wasn't good enough?" Virgil asked.

Murphy's eyes ticked away from Virgil's, like a second hand going to the next hash mark, and then came back, and he said, "I don't know anything about that. I heard about it, but it has nothing to do with me. It probably has to do with you going into a bar and asking questions. Especially that bar. They don't like people like you, going around smearing their friends for no good reason."

"I hear you're going to Las Vegas," Virgil said.

Murphy turned sullen. "No law against it. And I gotta get out of town, get away from these fuckin' holier-than-thou O'Learys, treating me like dog shit."

Virgil said, "I'll tell you something, Dick. I've got almost enough to arrest you. And I'll have enough, when I nail down a couple more things. I've been talking to my boss about whether to arrest you as a material witness, or let you go on to Las Vegas. We decided to let you go, but if I call you back here, you best get on the first plane back. Because if you don't, we'll issue a warrant for you. If that happens, you could spend three weeks or a month in various goddamned unpleasant lockups before you make it back here, where you can talk to a lawyer."

"I did not have anything to do with Ag's murder," Murphy said. "That's all I've got to say to you. I can prove where I was when she was killed, and it wasn't anywhere around there. So get off my fuckin' back."

Virgil said, "Good luck in Vegas, Dick. And you come back when I call or you'll regret it."

VIRGIL TURNED AWAY and walked across the steps to the O'Learys, who were talking with the priest. He hadn't met Marsha O'Leary, and when John O'Leary introduced them, she said, "Killing Jimmy Sharp and Becky Welsh won't bring Ag back, Mr. Flowers. Despite what my children might have told you."

Virgil nodded, but didn't have a reply, other than, "I feel really bad for you. This is a dreadful thing." He'd said the same thing at twenty other funerals over the years, and always felt a bit hypocritical saying it.

"On the other hand, if Dick had anything to do with it, I'd be very pleased to see him spend the rest of his life in prison," she said.

"Me, too," Virgil said.

"Are you coming to the cemetery?" John O'Leary asked.

"I wasn't planning to. I will if you think I might be needed to . . . keep order."

"Murphy's not coming out there," Jack O'Leary said. "At heart, he's a chickenshit."

Marsha O'Leary said, "That's not the kind of talk I'd expect from a doctor."

John O'Leary clapped his son on the shoulder and said, "You gave him a pretty good shot."

"Not good enough," Jack said. "He's still walking."

John said to Virgil, "We've got to go. We've got to swing by the emergency room and see if the dummy here broke his wrist." He had James by the arm and roughed his hair and said, "Basically, as a surgeon, you don't want to break your suturing arm."

Then they went off, the whole bunch, to the hospital, and then the cemetery.

The priest said to Virgil, "That Murphy can take a shot. When Frank hit him, I thought he'd go down." After a fifteen-second analysis of the pugilism, he said, "Say, you're not related to Reverend Flowers over in Marshall?"

Virgil said, "Yeah, I'm his kid."

"Really? He's quite the golfer. He was up here in Bigham with Paul Berry. You know Paul? The priest at Saint Mary's?—so we were down at the club here, and your old man is on the wrong side of the dogleg-right number two, and he takes out his four rescue club . . ."

And so on.

VIRGIL GOT BACK to the truck and called Jenkins, who said, "I was just about to call you. We're heading back to the Burger King for a snack. You want to keep looking at those farmhouses?"

"Yeah. You still got Boykin with you?"

"He's out running a roadblock, but he's available. You want me to call him?"

"I can't think of anything else to do right now," Virgil said. "Let's get back at it. I'll meet you at the Burger King."

At the Burger King, Shrake and Jenkins told Virgil that they thought they knew who beat him up: two guys named Royce Atkins and Duane McGuire. "We got a tip through one of Davenport's spies," Jenkins said. "We found Atkins, but we're not going anywhere with him. He's a mean sonofabitch, just the kind of guy you'd go looking for, to do this. We've got him nervous, but he won't talk unless we get something to squeeze him with."

"What's he do?"

"He's a roofer, out of work for now. He says when spring gets going, he'll get his crew back together. Right now, he sits on his ass."

"What about McGuire?" Virgil asked.

"McGuire might talk, but he took off before we got there," Shrake said. "We talked to his girlfriend. She said he was going on a road trip. We asked her if he helped beat you up, and she didn't say no. She said, 'I wouldn't know anything about that.' Which means yes."

"But you don't know where he went?"

"Not yet. But not far. His girlfriend knows where he is, but she's not scared enough to tell us yet. She will be, though. When we get him, we'll whip the dilemma on their young asses. One of them'll crack."

The "prisoner's dilemma" came out of game theory, but cops only used part of it. When they had two or more suspects, they'd make a simultaneous offer to all of them: talk first and you get a reduced charge on a plea bargain. Hold out, and you carry the full load. With your ex-buddy testifying against you, you could kiss your ass good-bye.

"I need them to do that—I need one of them, or both of them, to testify that Dick Murphy paid them," Virgil said. "If we can keep Jimmy or Becky alive, it won't be so critical."

"We better plan on it being critical," Shrake said.

THEY DROVE THROUGH Arcadia on the way south; Boykin said that the search was being run out of the filling station there. He'd be parked across the street.

When Virgil, Shrake, and Jenkins arrived, they found what amounted to a media village—three news helicopters sitting in a hay field just north of town, at least a dozen satellite trucks lining the main street, along with a dozen cop cars from various jurisdictions, and a half dozen Humvees. The Guard had set up a bunch of big olive-drab field tents, which smelled like telephone poles, and one of them was working as a cafeteria, passing out ham and egg-salad sandwiches, and bottles of water. They parked behind Boykin's patrol car and got out.

Boykin came over, carrying an egg-salad sandwich, and said, "The Ferris wheel ain't here yet," and Jenkins shook his head: "Dumb shits probably got lost somewhere."

Shrake: "That egg salad was made for the invasion of Iraq. I hope you got a case of toilet paper in the car."

"It's actually quite tasty," Boykin said. "I talked to the young woman who made it, who is also quite tasty." He added, "You're just in time. Duke is going to make a statement. He is in a bad mood, and when he makes a statement to the TV people, in a bad mood, like he was with that concentration camp thing, it is usually something to see. He does put on a show."

"Ah, man," Virgil said, and, "Excuse me for a minute." He walked across the street and got a Diet Coke at the gas station, and then with the other three, walked down to a Guard tent that was being lit up by the TV cameramen. He saw Duke a couple of tents down, and went that way.

"Sorry I couldn't wait for you to wake up this morning," Duke said, as Virgil came up. "But I heard it wasn't that bad. Though, I see you're limping."

"Got my ass kicked, is what happened," Virgil said. He said, "Lewis, we've got to talk. It's not going to help you to go out there and throw a fit."

"I know what I'm doing," Duke said. "I learned my lesson. I'm going up there, and I'm going to be polite, and tell them what's going on, and that we're following all the rules and regulations."

"They might start ragging on you."

"I've had that done before," Duke said.

"Just don't shoot anybody," Virgil said.

For the first time since Virgil met him in Shinder, to look at the Welshes' bodies, Duke cracked what might have been a smile; but not a pleasant one. He seemed to be fantasizing about the possibility of blowing up the media. "I can't make no rash promises," he said.

"Ah, man," Virgil said.

ONE OF THE GUARD people had created a large dry-erase schematic map of southwest Minnesota, and she put it up on the stage, with a red dry-erase pen. Duke climbed on the stage a moment later, along with a National Guard lieutenant colonel whom Virgil didn't know. With the media people pressing into the tent, Duke introduced the colonel, who pissed everybody off by citing his authority going back to Abraham, by giving the Guard credit for providing vehicles, sandwiches, and water, and by concluding with a confession that nobody had seen anything.

Duke then described the ongoing search of local farmhouses, using the red pen and the map to locate the tightening search— information that everybody already had.

A reporter called, "Bottom line—you haven't found anything, and as far as you know, they could be in Quartzsite, Arizona."

"Not at all," Duke said. "We've got very good reason to believe that they're contained."

"Then how come the state agents are looking for them way down south of here? Who's stupid?"

"Nobody's stupid. The state officers are working with a different set of parameters."

"How many more will die before they're caught? I'm not asking for an exact number, but how about an estimate?"

Shrake turned to Virgil and said, "Uh-oh."

The question was followed by laughter, which irritated Duke more than the question had, and he said, "I'm glad somebody can laugh at this tragedy. I assume you'll be showing that on your news shows tonight."

Somebody said, "Fuck you," just loud enough to be heard, but not loud enough for anybody to identify the source; Virgil thought it might be one of the cameramen. Duke said, "What was that?" and a senior reporter for one of the more dignified news channels said, "That was disgraceful," and there was a muffled "Suck-up," followed by more laughter, and then a man whom Virgil recognized as the second-string anchor for Channel Three stood and raised a hand, and Duke poked a finger at him.

"Sheriff Duke, everybody here has heard rumors that James Sharp and Becky Welsh won't be given a chance to surrender— that you've put out a shoot-to-kill order on them, a shoot-on-sight. Is that correct? Are you going to kill them? Or are you going to give them a chance to give themselves up?"

"I'll take them any way I can get them," Duke said. "If they turn themselves in, they'll be protected."

"I was told by a very reliable source in your department that one of your men would have shot Tom McCall except for the intervention of a state agent."

"I know that's a lie because my people don't talk out of school," Duke said.

Virgil put his hands over his ears as the anchor said, "You're calling me a liar? Wait a minute—did you just call me a liar?"

"I'm saying that none of my men—"

"Well, one of them did."

Another reporter: "I talked to the same guy, and he told me the same thing."

"Well, if you'd give me that man's name—"

"You'd fire him."

Duke's mouth flapped a few times, and then he said, "Damn right I would. There's nothing more important in law enforcement than loyalty, and you can't have every Tom, Dick, and Harry shooting off their mouths to a bunch of media whores who don't want to do nothing more than splash blood all over their TV screens."

Almost everybody—almost *everybody*—was delighted. Virgil turned to Shrake, Jenkins, and Boykin and said, "Let's go. Let's get out of here."

As Virgil and Jenkins got in Virgil's truck, Virgil could hear Duke screaming into the microphone.

Something about . . . "pissants."

20

BECKY WAS WORRIED about Jimmy. He was getting hotter all the time, his face red, his eyes glazed. He'd stopped complaining about the pain in his leg, and about most everything else.

They were still holed up in the old dead man's house, had eaten their way through a good part of the old man's food supply—bacon and eggs and bread and oatmeal—and most of their own junk food. The beer was gone.

Becky tried to keep Jimmy awake because she was terribly afraid that if he went to sleep, he'd die. She didn't know why she thought that, but she did.

Early in the afternoon, she helped him into the bathroom, and then back to the couch; she almost lost him on the way back, when he lost his balance, and they began to reel out of control. She managed to steer him onto the couch, and he screamed when his leg hit the leather.

Ten minutes later, despite her chatter, he went to sleep. She sat with him, watching his breathing, like a new mother with her first baby; and she kept one eye on the television, where she saw Duke's temper tantrum. From that, she took away one thing: if Duke's men caught them, they'd be killed.

She tried to wake Jimmy, gently rocking his shoulder, to tell him about it. He barely responded, cracking his eyes open, and then he was gone again.

She didn't know what Becky Welsh would do, so she thought about what a nurse would do, and on the basis of more than twenty years' sitting in front of TVs, she decided to look at the wound.

Jimmy was wearing nothing but his undershorts, and was asleep on his back, which made it easier to do. He was still wearing the big first-aid bandage, which was white on the outside, but as soon as you looked deeper, she could see that it had soaked up quite a bit of blood.

When she decided to look at the wound, she first went to the old man's linen closet and found his cleanest sheet. Pretty sure that wasn't good enough, she hand-washed it with a lot of dish soap, then tossed it in the clothes dryer and went and watched more TV while it dried.

And when it was dry, she made a new bandage pad by folding over the biggest part of it, and made ties by ripping off the ends. All, she thought, pretty professional.

Jimmy was deep in sleep. She tried to gently wake him, but this time he didn't open his eyes. Just as well, she thought. She used a pair of scissors to cut off the ties on the first-aid bandage, and then carefully peeled it off. The wound looked like a really bad, overcooked personal pizza, the kind with too much tomato sauce and islands of runny yellow cheese; the surface at the center was damp with blood, but it dried out toward the edges. The edge of the wound, where the leg was trying to heal itself, looked a bit like pizza crust, as well.

She didn't know it, but the deputy that McCall had shot had been using police hollow points on a .40-caliber handgun, and the bullet had done its work. The entrance wound was no bigger than Becky's little finger, but the exit wound was half the size of a dollar bill.

She still had some small bandages from the first aid kit, and she smeared some antiseptic ointment on one of them and brushed it across the top of the wound. Jimmy made a low throat sound, not quite a moan, and she stopped, and then started again. She was almost done, working from the middle to an outside edge, when she pushed too hard. The scab at the edge of the wound broke open, and a thumb-sized curl of yellow pus squirted out, almost like shaving cream from a can.

And it smelled, something of the stink of an animal dead on a hot summer highway.

She said, aloud, "Oh, no," and ran to the bathroom and got some toilet paper and came back and mopped it up, but then, feeling that the corruption should be removed, pushed on the wound, and more pus came out, and finally, some purple blood.

She looked at the wound for a moment, then went into the kitchen and got a fork from the silverware drawer, brought it back, smeared it with antiseptic, and used one of the tangs to pick and press another edge of the wound. And when it cracked, more pus bled out. She was ready for it this time, and the smell, and she worked methodically around the wound, picking at the parts that looked yellow or swollen. When she was done, she'd taken out enough pus to fill a small jelly jar.

A lot of pus.

When all she got was blood, she went back to work with the antiseptic, wiping the wound again, then binding it with the clean sheets. She threw all the dirty bandages and toilet paper in the trash, and came back and looked at Jimmy.

He was still sleeping, but the sleep looked easier, somehow.

A HALF HOUR LATER she was clicking through the relevant TV channels and found a helicopter shot; the shot was following a truck as it climbed a hill toward a farmhouse, part of the search. She was shocked when the camera pulled back a bit, to include the farmhouse in the shot, and she saw the line of distinctive blue silos they'd passed at a farmhouse down the road, a mile or so away. From left to right, there was a short one, then two very tall ones, then another short one, and one that was middle-sized.

The cops were on the other side of the silos, but were coming their way.

She said, "Jimmy. Jimmy, you gotta wake up."

Jimmy opened his eyes and groaned and said, "Man, I hurt."

"You're better, though. You passed out for a while, and I cleaned up your leg. Cleaned it out. I think you're healing up now."

"Jesus, it hurts," he said. "How many pills we got left?"

She crawled across the living room floor to the pill bottles, looked at the OxyContin bottle, and said, "Three."

"Gimme two."

"I think one would be better."

"Need two," he said. "Gotta find someplace . . ." His tongue flicked out, skittering over his dry lips. ". . . find someplace to get more."

She gave him two with a glass of water and said, "Jimmy, they're searching everywhere, and there was a helicopter, and, shit, Jimmy, they're right next door. They're gonna find us. We gotta go."

He looked at her for a moment, and she thought he didn't understand, then he said, simply, "Okay."

She took all the food and some blankets and a water jug out to the old man's truck, which was an old red Dodge. She put the passenger seat down as far as it would go, then helped Jimmy pull on a pair of the old man's pants, and helped him out the door. The stairs down through the mudroom were the worst part, but once he was outside, he hopped along fairly well.

"You're looking a lot better, honey," Becky said.

"Hurt like a motherfucker, though," Jimmy said. His face was so pale it was nearly green.

She had to help him into the truck, and when he was inside, asked, "Should I take anything else?"

He thought for a minute, then said, "Move the other truck into the barn and lock it up. Maybe, if they come up here, they'll decide he ain't home, and they won't come looking for this truck."

She nodded and ran to the Townes' black truck and drove it to the barn, hopped out, pulled open the barn door, and drove the truck inside. She closed the door, and ran back to the old man's truck.

"What do you think?" she asked. "Go for it? Head south? Hide?"

"Hide until tonight. Find a place, then we get the fuck out of here. You bring the money?"

"Yeah, I got all the money."

.   .   .

SHE TURNED THE TRUCK around and they rattled back down the hill. Off to the northwest, she could see a helicopter circling over the countryside. Hoped it wouldn't come after them . . .

She drove away from the farmhouse with the silos, staying on the smallest roads and the narrowest tracks. Every time she hit a bump, Jimmy groaned, and she said, "Sorry," and he said, "Keep going."

They'd gone maybe three miles when, as they were crossing the crest of a hill, Becky saw the remnants of an old farm on the hillside, the house burned to its foundations, and the outbuildings caved in. The driveway was covered with grass.

But the thing was, the woodlot was still standing on the north side of the house. She said, "I think I found a place."

Jimmy, who'd been slumping in the seat, pushed himself up and asked, "Where?"

"Go back through here, and hide in the back of the woods. Unless you go back and look, you'd never see us."

"Only got to last a few hours," Jimmy said. "Let's do it. I can't take much more of this fuckin' road, until the pills kick in better."

She turned into the driveway, threaded past the remnants of the ruined buildings, down an alleylike depression that led to the woodlot, and then found an even deeper hole in the woodlot itself. She drove carefully into it, and there, couldn't see out. She worried about getting stuck, but what was done, was done. She killed the engine and said, "I think we're okay."

Jimmy didn't respond for a moment, then said, "Fuckin' helicopter can see us."

"Not very well."

. . .

BUT SHE WORRIED ABOUT IT, and when Jimmy seemed to have dozed off again, she covered him with a blanket, got out of the truck, and looked around the abandoned farmstead.

Anything of value had been stripped off the place, but behind one of the outbuildings she found three old rolls of tar paper, the kind you put under shingles. The stuff was so old that it broke more easily than it unrolled, but eventually, with patience, she pulled off several long strips of it and draped it over the pickup.

When she was finished, the truck looked like a lump of raw dirt; from the air, she thought comfortably, it should be invisible.

She climbed back in the truck; Jimmy was snoring.

She sat and tried to think, but nothing came to her.

Wished she had the old man's television. That had been pretty nice.

A while later, it got dark.

And cold.

AN HOUR AFTER Welsh and Sharp had fled, Shrake and Boykin drove up the long hill toward the old man's house. Boykin, who was at the wheel, said, "If I was hiding, I'd take this place."

"You said that back at the Jenks' place."

"Well, that one, too," Boykin said. They came over the top of the hill into the farmyard and Boykin said, "Really looks deserted."

"This is David S. Gates," Shrake said, reading from his list. He picked up his phone, which had been in a cup holder, and poked in Gates's phone number. He was kicked over to the answering service.

"Give him a couple of honks," Shrake said. Boykin leaned on the horn for a minute, and they waited a minute, then tried the horn again.

"Nobody home," Boykin said.

"We'll come back. We got three more places," Shrake said.

Boykin did half a U-turn in the dirt driveway, then had to back up to make the rest of it, and Shrake said, "Pull over. Let me out."

"Why?" Boykin pulled over as he asked.

"Because I'm a detective, and you're not," Shrake said. "Get your rifle out of the back, get back behind the car, and cover the windows."

Boykin did as he was told, but after he was braced up behind the car, watching the windows in the house, he asked, "What?"

Shrake had his pistol out. "Look right there, those scuffs . . . what does that look like?"

Boykin looked; the driveway was a mixture of rock and dirt, and not far from the side door, he could see a scuff line that led toward a shed. "Like somebody dragged something, something like a body," Boykin said. He lifted the M16 toward the windows and clicked it over to full-auto. "You gonna look?"

"Don't let them shoot me," Shrake said. "And keep one eye on the barn."

"Shrake? Don't be an asshole. Call Virgil—at least get him leaning this way."

Shrake paused, then nodded and called Virgil. Virgil said, "We were just turning into the Roses' place. We'll be there in two minutes."

"Might be nothing," Shrake said.

"But it might not be nothing."

Shrake put the phone away and walked slowly sideways, watching the house, then the barn, looking for any sign of movement—but the place felt dead to him, and that particular feeling had never let him down. If somebody was breathing inside a building, he could usually feel it—a lot of cops could.

Boykin called, "Man, take it easy . . ."

Shrake had gotten past the house and was now halfway to the shed. A new line of windows, on the back of the house, now opened to him, and he called, "Watch the barn," and he watched the house windows as he followed the scuff line into the shed.

Where he found the body of David S. Gates.

Gates's hand was frozen in a tight position that Shrake recognized as late-stage rigor mortis, with the body starting to relax. So he'd been dead for a while.

From the car, Boykin shouted, "What?"

Shrake called back, "Got a body."

Then he saw the tank and yelled, "And we got a tank."

"What?"

WHEN VIRGIL ARRIVED, Shrake was still in the shed, and Boykin had moved from the car to a large oak tree in the front yard, from which he could see the front and far side of the house, while Shrake watched the back and near side. Virgil was on the phone and Shrake said, "All the windows are closed. No runners. No sign of life at all."

"Okay. Jenkins and I are going through the side door. Stay with us."

They went in with shotguns. The side door was unlocked. Jenkins led the way; just inside, they found one stairway going up four steps into the house, and another going down to a basement. Virgil stepped down to a lower landing, looked at the dark, cluttered cellar; he could smell old coal, dirt, and potatoes.

"What do you think?" Virgil asked.

"I can hold the stairway if you want to clear the basement."

Virgil dropped down the stairs, carefully, leading with the muzzle of his shotgun. At the foot of the stairs, he found a bare lightbulb operated with a pull string; he pulled on the string and got some light. The basement had a workbench against one wall, with a disorderly pile of tools and boxes of nails and screws and bolts; the other walls were lined with shelves filled with all manner of junk—broken hoes and rakes, snow shovels, gas cans. One set of shelves was filled with old Ball jars, all empty.

There was a closed door off to his right, and he pushed it open with a foot, still leading with the muzzle of the gun, and found more junk, including some antiques that his mother would have liked—crocks and creamers, an old chicken-watering can, a couple of battered-looking hoses, coils of outdoor extension cords. No living thing, other than a lot of insects and arachnids.

A mousetrap, snapped shut, was visible under a shelf.

He called, "Clear."

. . .

THEY SPENT TEN MINUTES clearing the rest of the house, then Virgil called Duke, who asked without preamble, "Find anything?"

"Yeah, we did," Virgil said.

BOYKIN STAYED OUTSIDE, to direct traffic, while Jenkins, Shrake, and Virgil looked at the living room. They found bandages soaked with blood and pus, a couple of empty pill bottles, a lot of beer bottles, wrappers from various kinds of junk food, and a pile of gay porn movies. The television was still on, and showed an aerial shot of a line of police and military vehicles churning down a gravel road, throwing up a cloud of dust. An excited reporter was saying, ". . . hasn't been confirmed but we've been told that it's possible that state agents have cornered Welsh and Sharp in a house south of the tiny town of Arcadia."

Virgil said, "Ah, man."

While they waited for the carnival to arrive, Virgil checked the barn, where he found the Townes' pickup.

"They've got Gates's truck. And they've had a lot of time," Virgil said.

TEN MINUTES LATER, Duke and the Guard lieutenant colonel looked at the body in the shed, and then the living room—everybody else was kept outside—and then the colonel asked Virgil, "Using very short words, and speaking slowly, tell me what it all means."

"Shrake has more experience with this than I have, and he says that it appears that Mr. Gates's body is in a later stage of rigor mortis," Virgil said. "Rigor sets in three or four hours after death and can last two days, or a bit more, especially if it's cold, and the body has apparently been outside since Mr. Gates was killed. If he's in the later stages, then he was probably killed right after they killed the Townes and left the cornfield. They probably came right here."

Duke looked around, puzzled, and then, "But . . . that doesn't help. The question is, when did they leave? If he's been dead ever since they killed the Townes . . . they could be in Mexico."

"I don't think so," Virgil said. "These bandages . . . Jimmy was hit pretty hard. There's a lot of blood and he's got a bad infection. I think they're not long gone—maybe chased out when they saw the search going on. I think Jimmy is in big trouble."

"Good," Duke snorted. Then, "What the hell is all this?" He picked up a DVD box entitled *The Isle of Men*.

Virgil chewed back a grin and asked, "What does it look like?"

"It looks like some kind of . . . homosexual . . . awful . . . Good grief."

"Yeah, there's a bunch of it here. Probably a hundred of them in the TV cabinet," Virgil said.

"You mean . . . ?"

"It's Mr. Gates's."

Duke said, "Huh," and dropped the DVD. "Well, you learn something every day."

The colonel said, "If they were here overnight, then they've been gone for more than twenty-four hours, and that means they probably got through the net, and they might be anywhere. But if they were here both nights, then they're probably still right around here. We've got people crawling all over the place, stopping every vehicle they see."

Virgil: "What I'm afraid of is, they're holed up again. That they took off last night, drove ten miles, and then"—he gestured around the room—"did it again."

"Oh, fuck me with a fence pole," the colonel said.

Duke: "Hey. Language."

The colonel ignored him. "Isn't there any way your crime-scene people could figure out how old the blood is? How long it's been drying? I mean . . ."

Virgil explained that it didn't actually work quite the way it did on TV, and that lab tests would take some time, and be mostly irrelevant by the time the tests came back.

The colonel asked, "Why couldn't they just stick their thumb into one of the bandages. If it comes back bloody . . ."

Virgil shrugged: "I don't know. Maybe they could do that. They'll be here pretty quick."

OUTSIDE, THE CIRCUS HAD RESUMED. Two helicopters were orbiting the house, and a line of TV trucks was stacked up on the road at the bottom of the hill.

Virgil asked Duke, "You want me to tell them?"

Duke said, "Virgil, I know you don't like me, that you think I'm an asshole, like all you city people do. And I gotta admit, I don't care for you that much, so I gotta tell you, given all of that, I appreciate the offer, because I know it has to hurt. But yes. I'd like you to tell them."

21

SO VIRGIL DROVE down to the end of the driveway and stopped at the edge of the road. Before he got out of the truck, he took his cell phone out of his pocket, pulled up a calculator, did a quick calculation, and wrote the number in the palm of his hand. The media guys were watching everybody coming down the hill, so when Virgil got out of the truck, walked to the middle of the road, and raised his hands in a "Come to Jesus" gesture, they stampeded over, not unlike a herd of hungry wildebeest.

He kept it simple: that state agents doing a systematic survey of remote farmsteads in conjunction with the Bare County sheriff's office and the Minnesota National Guard had discovered the body of a male shooting victim. They'd also found signs that the house had been used as a hideout by the fugitives who robbed the Oxford credit union; the signs included blood-soaked bandages, which led investigators to believe that one of the robbers had been seriously wounded.

"When you say 'fugitives,' you mean Becky Welsh and James Sharp, correct?" one of the TV reporters asked.

"We would certainly like to talk to them about any involvement that they may or may not have had in these events," Virgil said. He added that the victim had not yet been identified, and when he was, his name would not be released until next of kin were notified. That was routine cop-speak and drew no objections.

Ruffe Ignace, one of a half dozen newspaper reporters in the crowd, asked, "Virgil, do you have any idea when Sharp and Welsh left the farm—how far they may have gotten?"

"Can't tell exactly, but we think they probably spent the night before last at the farm, maybe the day yesterday, and then left sometime between last night and this afternoon," Virgil said.

A TV reporter said, "So you're saying it was Welsh and Sharp."

"No. I was replying to the substance of Mr. Ignace's question, of when the fugitives left," Virgil said.

Ignace said to the TV reporter, "Yeah, dumbass. And keep your mouth shut while I'm talking."

The reporter said, "Hey, we're live."

Ignace said, "So am I." To Virgil: "You cops are crawling all over the place, and if they went far . . . somebody would have stopped them, or there would have been some shooting. So that means they're close by."

Virgil said, "Ruffe, that's not exactly a question, but I'll pretend that it was, and I'd love to be able to answer it. We don't think they've been gone *very* long, but if they snuck out last night, at four in the morning, and killed the lights on the vehicle, and drove very cautiously at twenty miles an hour until it got light . . . well, that's forty miles or so. You know the formula: pi times the radius squared. If the radius is forty miles, square that, you get sixteen hundred, and you multiply that by pi . . ." Virgil put his hand to his forehead and rolled his eyes up, as if making the calculation. "About five thousand twenty-six point, uh, point fifty-four square miles. That's a lot of territory, which is our problem. Our biggest fear, of course, is that they've moved to another hideout, with the same kind of situation as we've got here."

"You mean more dead people," Ignace said.

"That's our greatest fear," Virgil said.

There were a few more questions, which Virgil answered or batted down, and then they went through the ritual of allowing each TV on-camera reporter to ask a question, mostly repetitive, so that cameramen could get a shot of them asking and Virgil answering.

That done, Virgil said, "We're finished," and walked back to his truck, where Jenkins had been waiting. Halfway back, Ignace cut him off and said, "I've got an exceptionally reliable source at Stillwater who said you did a focus group there, about where Sharp and Welsh might have gone from the robbery. Lo and behold, you and three other guys found this place, while two hundred people were looking elsewhere, and didn't come up with jack shit. That's a pretty interesting story, Virgil."

"I really can't talk about that right now," Virgil said.

"Well, I've got all the information I need, and I'm going to write about it tomorrow morning, unless you say you'll talk to me later," Ignace said. "If you talk to me later, I'll hold off until then."

"You write what you want," Virgil said, "but if you write that tomorrow morning, and it pisses off the people I've got to work with, then I will talk about it later . . . but not to you. I'll talk to Channel Three and the *Pioneer Press*."

"It's a shame you're taking that attitude, because that means that I've got to leave the decision in the hands of the production-crazed morons on the city desk," Ignace said. "If it were just you and me making a deal . . ."

Virgil said, "Tell you what—you hold off, and I'll talk to you later if I can clear it with my bosses. If I can't, then you write what you've got, without me. But I'll try to talk."

Ignace thought about that for a moment, and then said, "Deal," and walked away.

BACK IN THE TRUCK, Jenkins said, "Sweaty work," and Virgil said, "Yeah," and dug a Diet Coke out of the cooler in the back.

Jenkins said, "Davenport called and asked what you were up to. I told him to turn on the TV. Anyway, he wants a call back, when you can."

Virgil called, and Davenport said, "Pretty good job on the press conference. Sincere yet uninformative."

"Thanks."

"I told Shrake he was in for a commendation, for the way he spotted that body at the Gates place."

"Okay. And listen, it's been nice talking to you. I'll get in touch again later."

"Virgil: that guy who beat you up, Duane McGuire. He's hiding in his mother's junk shop in Sleepy Eye."

"Sleepy Eye? I'm twenty minutes away. Give me the address."

Davenport said the information about McGuire came from one of his network of informants who saw McGuire leaving a Sleepy Eye convenience store with a bag of beer, heading back to his mother's place.

THEY LEFT BOYKIN with his patrol car, and Shrake jammed himself in the backseat of Virgil's 4Runner. Shrake said, "We've still got nothing to work with."

"I know," Virgil said. "If Duane's home, we'll have to put on a little skit."

THEY WORKED ON THE SKIT on the way over; came into town from the north, cut Highway 14 and took it down Main Street, spotted Martha's Flea Market Creations, a small shabby shop with some lamps in the front window. They drove around the block, turned into a half-ass dirt alley that threaded behind the stores, and spotted the back entrance.

"Probably come running out of there," Virgil said.

Jenkins said, "I'll take it."

"Don't get hurt," Virgil said.

Sleepy Eye was a fairly prosperous place, a railroad town, three or four thousand people, Virgil thought. Not much moving on a cold April day. Shrake and Virgil went around to the front of Martha's, and parked and got out.

Always nervous going through a door . . . but they went through, a bell ringing overhead as Virgil pushed the door open. Martha was sitting there, leaning on a glass-topped counter, reading a tabloid newspaper of some sort. McGuire was just coming into the room from the back, carrying a plate that held a piece of what looked like corn bread. His eyes met Virgil's, and he dropped the plate and ran. Virgil shouted, "Stop," and Martha shrieked, "Oh my God. Police, call the police," and Virgil went through the inside door, with Shrake three steps behind him.

Virgil could see light coming through an open back screen door and, when he got through it, found McGuire sitting in the dirt, holding his hands to his face, Jenkins standing over him. Jenkins said, "He resisted."

McGuire said, "Mmmpph."

Virgil squatted next to him, looked up at Jenkins and said, "Put the cuffs on him." To McGuire he said, "You're under arrest for accessory to first degree murder, aggravated assault on a police officer, and so on."

McGuire took his hands down and said, "What?" He was bleeding heavily from the nose, and at that moment, Martha came running out, carrying what appeared to be a very old .22-caliber revolver with a long thin barrel. She waved it awkwardly and said, "All—"

Shrake hit her in the forehead and knocked her down, then stood on the gun until Jenkins rolled her over and put another pair of cuffs on her.

"And Mom's under arrest for aggravated assault on a police officer," Virgil said to McGuire.

Martha groaned and then screamed, "Police."

Shrake knelt next to her and said, "We are the police. We're arresting your son for all these murders and shit you see on TV."

"What?"

McGuire started babbling. "I had nothing to do with any murder, for Christ sakes. Did Royce tell you that? All we did was rough you up a little—hell, it was just a fight."

Martha started crying and said, "My head, my head."

"Probably ought to get her to the hospital," Shrake said. "I didn't have time to hit her easy."

Virgil said, "Okay, ma'am, just take it easy, sit there . . ."

A Sleepy Eye patrol car rolled into the alley, and a cop got out, a hand on his pistol, and Jenkins said, "Shit," and took out his ID and shouted, "BCA, BCA . . ."

McGuire said, "My mom's hurt."

Virgil: "I can't feel too sorry about that. I'm still hurting from you trying to kick me to death."

"We weren't gonna kill you, man. Just supposed to smack you around a little."

"I heard that Murphy wanted me dead," Virgil said.

"No, no, nobody wanted you dead."

Jenkins said, quietly, "Cop."

Virgil said to McGuire, "You're under arrest for assault. You have a right to an attorney. . . ."

The cop was talking to Shrake when Virgil finished, and he went over and said, "Sorry we didn't have time to call you, but we were afraid he was running. We just heard where he was a few minutes ago. We were over in Bare County with the search."

The cop was a hefty man, with little hair on his head; he looked down at McGuire and said, "Duane, were you hooked up with all that?"

"No, man, I just . . . Ah, shit."

"He and a pal beat me up, over in Bigham," Virgil said. "He admitted it before we could Mirandize him, just blurted it out. So . . . we're going to take him over to Bare County, drop him in jail."

"What'd Martha do?" the cop asked.

"She saw us chasing her son and came running out with a gun. Probably . . . misunderstood what was going on."

"She under arrest?" the cop asked.

"For now . . . we'll get her over to the medical center. What we do after that depends a little on Duane, here. And, of course, what Martha has to say for herself."

THERE'S A KIND of arrest that's simply tedious, with paperwork to be done and forms to be filled out, and care taken, and the arrest of the McGuires was all of that. A doctor at the medical center determined that Martha was not badly injured, and Virgil cut her loose after she signed a piece of paper that said she would not hold the state liable for any damage done to her, or her shop, during the arrest. A lawyer might later argue that the paper was signed under duress, but only if he was dumb: she'd come through the door with a gun, and might have been shot.

McGuire was cleaned up at the medical center, and got his nose taped and splinted, and they loaded him into the 4Runner and hauled his complaining ass back to the Bare County jail.

He'd never said, or even hinted, that he wanted a lawyer, and Virgil had Mirandized him, and he said he understood all of that, and that he'd been Mirandized before. So Virgil was in the clear when he asked, "How much did Murphy give you to beat me up?"

"Shit, I don't know," McGuire said. "He didn't give it to me, he gave it to Royce. I just went along for the fun of it."

"I can understand that," Shrake said. "Just a good-ol'-boy thing."

"That's right."

"So you didn't get anything?" Virgil asked.

"Royce give me a hundred bucks afterward. I think he got more."

By the time they got him to the jail, they had the whole story: Virgil, as he'd intended, had attracted Murphy's attention when he started interviewing people in the bar, and asked about Murphy. He'd gotten more of an answer than he expected, but more than good enough.

At the jail, they did more paperwork, and then McGuire was taken back to a cell, the jail guard greeting McGuire with, "Hey, Duane, what you been up to?"

"Same ol' shit," McGuire said. "Listen, I don't have no drugs stuffed up my asshole. Do you think . . . ?"

"Oh, I don't think so," the guard said.

"Aw, man . . ."

Outside, Shrake asked, "What's next?"

Virgil said, "Got to pick up Royce Atkins, and we've still got to find Sharp and Becky Welsh. That's the main thing. Murphy, we'll just leave him on the shelf for a few days."

By the time they got McGuire stashed, it was late in the day. Duke was still out on the hunt, and Virgil talked with the chief deputy, who said there had been no more hints that they might be on the fugitives' trail. "The sheriff just reoriented everybody around that farm you found, and people are working out from that. We're assuming that since they ditched the Townes' truck, they're running around in Gates's truck. Old red Dodge. We've got two choppers running a search pattern around the house, trying to see if they can spot it. Nothing so far, and with dark coming on . . . probably not going to find it tonight."

A HELICOPTER FLEW over Gates's truck and the abandoned farmstead just after full dark. A searchlight poked through the woods, then spent a moment probing the old sheds, then moved on down the road. Becky held her breath as she heard it coming in, and let it out when it moved on.

The beating blades woke Jimmy, who groaned and said, "This fuckin' leg is killing me," and, "What the fuck is going on?"

He sounded clear-minded, and Becky said, "A helicopter. Jeez, Jimmy, they're using everything. It's going away now."

"Didn't see us?"

"No, I put some old tar paper over the truck. We look like a pile of dirt."

"Good. We got any more pills?"

"One."

Jimmy took the pill and a long drink of water, and then asked, "What time is it?"

She said, "After seven. We've been sitting here a long time."

"Gotta move before it gets light," he said. "Get way south, toward . . . Ohio or . . . whatever."

"Iowa," she said.

"Farther than that. Ohio or . . . Kansas. Those helicopters . . . didn't think they'd get no helicopters to chase us."

"Got searchlights on them, just like in the Cities."

"If we could get to the Cities, we could get lost," he said.

"I don't think we'd get that far," Becky said. "That'd be running toward them. We've got to run away."

"Okay."

She was a little surprised by his acquiescence; he usually wanted to be the boss. She asked, "You want a cigarette?"

"Hell, yes."

She found a pack of Marlboros, shook one out for him, lit it with a paper match. The smoke smelled good, though she didn't smoke herself.

"I think I'm feeling better—my leg is better," Jimmy said after a while. She thought he might be lying, but she nodded. He said, "All we need is one good break. Get out in the open country and run. Some of that country down there, it's almost empty. That's what my old man said. He drove down to Texas once, and he said it's mostly empty. That's what we need."

"Okay," she said.

"We'll be set for life, starting with that money," Jimmy said.

"We might have to cross the border, you know, until this all blows over. Don't think we could come back here."

"I don't want to come back here," she said. The bitterness of the place almost choked her. "Nothing ever good has happened here. If we get down south . . . get a place to live. You know, you could grow a beard, I could do up my hair different."

"You're not gonna be able to make yourself less pretty," Jimmy said.

He startled her with that. She didn't say anything right away, but then said, fishing for a little more, "Oh, I'm not really that pretty."

"Yeah, you are," he said.

They sat and he smoked and she eventually said, "I'd like a daughter. I mean, I'd like a couple of boys, for sure, but I'd like a daughter. I know a lot of shit that I could teach her. You could teach the boys."

"I'd do that. Teach them to hunt," Jimmy said.

"I could teach the girls how to take care of the house," Becky said. "And cook. We could get some cookbooks. My mom, she couldn't cook, and didn't care. I ate so much macaroni and cheese it makes me sick when I smell it. And fish sticks. Man, I hate fish sticks."

Jimmy giggled, and after a moment, said, "I know where you're coming from. Macaroni and cheese. You know what makes me sick? Those little fuckin' slippery shells with tomato sauce and mushrooms. I must've ate about fifty gallons of those things. My old man could eat that shit morning, noon, and night. Christ, you go into my house, that's all you could smell. Those little fuckin' shells."

· · ·

THEY TALKED ABOUT food for a while, and then Becky found a couple of Snickers candy bars and they shared them, and then Jimmy asked, "You think we oughta get married?"

She stopped chewing for a moment, startled again, then swallowed. "You askin' me?"

"Well, yeah. I guess."

"Well, okay. Yeah, I'd marry you." And she laughed, and then clapped her hands. "I thought maybe nobody would ever ask me."

"You're so pretty, somebody was going to ask you. For sure. Lots of guys."

"Jimmy . . ." She moved closer to him and kissed him on the lips, and tried not to think about the porno films back at the old man's house. He kissed her back—and tried not to think about the porno films.

"I SHOULDN'T HAVE took that job, killing Ag Murphy," Jimmy said. "That kinda fucked me up in the head for a while, you know? It felt . . . pretty good. First time I ever felt that good, and then, you know, shooting that Negro. Just felt it right down to my balls. It was like I couldn't stop. . . . But if I didn't take that job, we wouldn't be here."

"You did all right," Becky said. "We wouldn't be here—we'd still be on the street, and starving to death. There wasn't anybody going to save us from that."

"Yeah, that might be right," he said. "You got another cigarette?"

She said, "When we get married, I don't think we should do it in a church. I don't think we should make any big deal out of it, you know? Maybe we should just go to some guy down in Texas, or Mexico, you know, and just dress in regular clothes, and do it. If you do it in a church, they put your pictures in the newspaper."

"We'll have to think about that," Jimmy said.

HE WAS SMOKING the second cigarette when she heard the sound of somebody sneaking up on them. She whispered, "You hear that?"

He listened, heard the rustling in the brush. "Yeah. You got the gun?"

"Got three of them now," she said. She found the pistol under the seat, then whispered, "Where are they?"

"Sounds like they're in front of us," he whispered back.

"What do you think?"

"If it's the cops, then they know we're here," he said.

"How?"

"Maybe the helicopter?"

She listened, then whispered, "Right in front of us."

There was a metallic scratching sound, and she said, "I gotta look," and hit the headlight switch. A twenty-pound raccoon was sitting on the hood of the truck, caught flat-footed, looked at them for a second or two, then dove over the side, the big striped tail bushed out like a chimney broom. She switched the lights off, and they both started giggling.

Becky laughed until tears came, and she said, "That was so funny. I was so scared, I almost wet my pants."

That started them laughing again.

THE TRUCK GOT COLD. Jimmy slipped back to sleep when they stopped talking, and she made sure he was completely wrapped with blankets, then wrapped herself in the remaining blanket and tried to go to sleep. It was not easy, sitting mostly upright, but the night was quiet, and she dozed.

When she woke, she was freezing, blanket or no blanket. Jimmy was still asleep. She was so cold that she decided to turn the engine on and use the heater; she did it, and ten minutes later, the truck was warm again.

She slept off and on for the rest of the night, sat up when she realized that she could see tree trunks. Dawn. Jimmy had said that they should leave while it was still dark, but it was too late for that. She wasn't sure she could take another day in the truck—they had water, but not much in the way of food.

She turned to Jimmy, and shook his shoulder: "Jimmy. Wake up. We gotta talk."

Jimmy didn't wake up. She shook him harder, and his shoulders rolled back and forth, but he didn't wake up. She cried, "Jimmy. Jimmy. Wake up, Jimmy."

When he still didn't wake, she peeled the blanket off him and looked at the bandage on his leg. The bandage was dry, but long, fiery-red tendrils of infection snaked out from under the bandage and up and down his leg, which was swollen to half-again its normal size.

She said, "Jimmy? Jimmy? Oh my God, Jimmy, are you dead or alive?"

22

VIRGIL WENT TO BED EARLY, because he could. He hadn't gotten a full night's sleep for a while, and was starting to feel stupid. He slept like a dead man for the first part of the night, but at five o'clock his eyes popped open, and he was wide awake.

He didn't want to be—a couple more hours of sleep wouldn't hurt at all, but his mind was moving and he couldn't get back. He tried a couple of sexual fantasies about Sally, but they didn't catch fire, so he spent some time thinking about God, and why he made people like Jimmy Sharp and Becky Welsh.

What part could they have in God's plan? Were they simply put here to kill people at random, because, for some people, people needed to be killed at random?

A mystery. He remembered a bumper sticker he'd seen in St. Paul that said: "Remember: Half the People Are Below Average." That, he thought, was probably the key to Jimmy Sharp and Becky Welsh.

They were below average, and God had made them that way. There was no way that they were ever going to be anything but that; they could watch all the above-average people they wanted, on television, driving around in big cars and making enormous amounts of money out of nothing . . . or just working at the post office, or going to trade school to be plumbers or carpenters. They'd never be able to do that. They were condemned from birth to a life of hard times and trouble.

If people were to tell the truth about Becky, her only route to a condition even resembling prosperity would be to sell herself for sex. That was all she had. The problem with that, morality aside, was that she probably wasn't bright enough to make the most of selling herself.

As for Jimmy—Jimmy had no chance at all. Abused as a child, neglected in school, he probably couldn't drive a nail. Or generate the ambition to do it.

Virgil rolled around for a while, thinking about it, blessed his parents for their genes. He was almost back to sleep when the phone rang, its screen popping to life, a brilliant white rectangle in the dark.

THE DUTY OFFICER was stressed: "Got Becky Welsh for you, calling on a cell phone that's registered to David Gates. We're trying to track it."

Virgil sat up, dropped his feet to the floor, so he could think: "Put her on."

Becky came up. "Hello? Is anybody there? Hello . . ."

"Becky, this is Virgil. Are you okay?"

She was crying. "Aw, God, I think Jimmy is dying. He's got big red streaks coming out of his leg."

"You gotta come in. He needs a hospital, really quick. If he's got red streaks, he could lose his leg . . . or die. Where are you?"

"I don't know, exactly. In a woods. I want to quit. I want to come in, and make people stop chasing us. I gotta get Jimmy in . . ."

"Do you know about where you are?" Virgil asked.

She said, "I know where that town is . . . the town with the gas station I was at. I'm down where you were looking yesterday, not too far, but kinda far, from that old man's house."

Virgil: "If you can get to Arcadia, I can meet you at the gas station. I can get an ambulance. We might have to take him to the Cities in a helicopter."

"Okay . . . okay. Don't shoot us," Becky said.

"We won't. I will be in Arcadia in a half hour. Can you get there by then?"

"I have to take a bunch of shit off the truck. . . . We have a bunch of shit on the truck so the helicopters can't see us."

"This is Mr. Gates's truck? A red Dodge?" Virgil asked.

"I think so . . . yeah, it's the old man's truck. The last one we took," she said.

"Becky: you've got to carry through with this. Meet me in a half hour at the gas station. It's the only way you can save Jimmy's life."

She started weeping again, and said, "Oh, God . . ." and then she was gone.

The duty officer came back and Virgil asked, "Did we get her?"

"I doubt we can get close to her. The GPS needs tracking satellites, and that takes a few minutes. We can see what phone tower she's closest to, but out there in the countryside, that's not going to give us much."

"All right, but see what you can get," Virgil said. "I'm going. I'm going."

"Take care."

VIRGIL GOT INTO his jeans and boots, pulled on a shirt and his jean jacket, got his gun, and went out the door, ran down the hall, and pounded on Shrake's door. Shrake came to the door wearing a T-shirt and boxer shorts, and asked, "Where are they?"

"Arcadia. Becky's meeting me there in half an hour. Get Jenkins and get moving."

"You gonna call Duke? Might be sort of a diplomatic problem if you don't."

"Yeah, I'll call him. . . . Fast as you can."

Virgil hurried on, punched up Duke's cell phone, and was instantly kicked over to an answering service. Phone was turned off. He called the Bare County sheriff's office on the way to his truck, nearly running into a light pole as he jogged along looking at the cell phone, dodged it at the last minute, and when a deputy came up, he identified himself: "I need Duke's home phone, *right now.*"

He got the number as he fired up his truck. He punched the number in, and a moment later a groggy-sounding woman answered the phone: "Hello?"

"Miz Duke?" Virgil realized he was shouting and tried to tone it down. "This is Virgil Flowers. I gotta talk to your husband."

Duke took the phone: "You got 'em?"

"I talked to Becky four or five minutes ago. She says Jimmy's dying of infection from the gunshot wound. She's going to bring him into the gas station at Arcadia. She was down south of there, somewhere around the Gates place. I'm meeting her in twenty-five minutes or so. I could use some backup."

Duke said, "Oh, man, oh, man. You got it."

"No sirens, no lights, let's not scare her."

"Got it. See you there." He was gone, and so was Virgil. He turned on his flashers, figuring they'd be okay for the first fifteen miles or so, and might keep him from clipping some farm lady out early, walking the dog. The sun was not yet up, and judging from the eastern sky, it probably wouldn't be for ten or fifteen minutes.

They were done, he thought. Best of all, nobody else was dead, if Becky and Jimmy were really hiding out in a woods, and he believed her when she said they were.

A flock of Canada geese flew overhead, not high above the road, in a pretty V; if he'd been walking, he could have heard their wings, and their informational honking.

Damn, he thought. *Damn: not a bad day to be alive.*

SHRAKE CALLED: "We're coming. We're . . . seven minutes be-hind you."

Then Duke: "We've got the roaming patrols headed into Arcadia. Not the Guard, just deputies. They'll see you at the gas station. I'm on my way. I'm leaving the house now."

BECKY SAT FOR what seemed like a long time before she could make herself move. Jimmy was dying. If he didn't die, they'd put him in prison for sure. And probably her, too, unless maybe Jimmy took the blame. But if that goddamn McCall gave himself up, he probably told them that she killed that woman at the rape house. But two could play that game—she'd tell them that Tom did it, and then raped her. They *knew* he raped her . . . and they knew he shot the cop. He was the killer—not her.

Goddamn him. She chewed on a thumbnail. Nothing was going to work—they weren't going to make it to Mexico, they weren't going to get married and have kids, it was all over. They wouldn't be able to keep the money . . . though maybe if she gave the money back, they'd go easier on her.

She tried talking to Jimmy again, but he was so deep that she knew it was impossible: he might never hear her again.

After a while, she got out and pulled the tar paper off the truck, threw it on the ground. She got back in and said, "Here we go," but then, just as she started the truck, she had another idea.

She considered the possibilities, then climbed out of the truck, got the bags of money out of the back, looked around, walked over to a collapsed shed, picked up a piece of siding, and used it to scrape a hole in the soft earth. She put the money in it, then scuffed dirt back over the hole and put the siding back on top of it.

She thought, *There.* If they wanted their money back, they'd have to make a deal with her. And money talked. The one thing she'd ever learned from her father that was probably right: money talked.

She got back in the truck, touched Jimmy on the forehead, then pushed his head back and kissed him on the lips. A minute later she'd threaded her way back through the trees and out to the road. The sun was still below the horizon, but was close—she could see the sparkle that comes just before the rim lifts itself above the earth.

Going to be a nice day, she thought.

She looked both ways at the road, which was empty, and turned the red truck left toward Arcadia.

VIRGIL WAS MOVING FAST, but somebody was moving faster, and a few minutes out of Arcadia, a sheriff's car caught up with him, then fell in behind, and they ran the last few miles together. The sun was up now, a shiny silver half-dime on the horizon, too white to look at, throwing long shadows across the road and kicking up dew-sparkles on the grassy shoulders.

They crossed the Mad River bridge going into town, slowed down, then slowed more as they came into the gas station. The station was closed, but that didn't matter: they weren't there for the doughnuts.

Virgil got out of the truck and noticed for the first time that the morning was cold and a little damp. A deputy got out of the car behind him and said, "The sheriff is on his way. He'll be here in seven or eight minutes."

Virgil nodded and said, "I want you around behind that house over there . . . in that side street where they won't see you until they're past it. I don't want you lurching out at them, but when they go by—you know it's a red Dodge pickup?—I want you ready to come in behind them, if necessary. Don't crowd them."

The deputy's eyes shifted away as he nodded and said, "Okay."

Then his eyes came creeping back and Virgil caught them and said, "And don't go shooting them. You just let them through. I know everybody's pissed, but Jimmy's apparently unconscious, so there won't be any resistance. And I need them. I need their testimony."

The deputy asked, "Does the sheriff know that?"

"Yeah. He knows."

Another car showed at the north end of the street, with headlights, and then the headlights died, and Shrake and Jenkins pulled in, in Jenkins's Crown Vic. Virgil said to the deputy, "If they're coming, they'll be here soon. So you go on, like I told you."

The deputy got in his car and pulled around the corner. Another patrol car came in from the north, as Jenkins and Shrake parked. Virgil said, "I want you guys with me, sitting on the cars, looking casual. Not too casual, but not like Airborne Rangers, either."

They got that, and he went to the second car and told them he wanted them on the north end of town, out of sight, so when the truck came in, he could block off the street that way. The deputy nodded, did a U-turn, and went that way.

A moment later, Shrake looked down the empty street and

said, "It's like that cowboy movie *High Noon*. Everybody waiting
for the shit to hit the fan."

The town was very still, Virgil thought.

BECKY WELSH'S HEART was pounding like a mill. Like going to
the dentist, but a thousand times worse, she thought. You were in
your car and nothing hurt and the sun was shining, but you knew
you were heading for something that was going to be bad, that
was going to be painful; but instead of getting a tooth pulled, they
were going to chain you up and treat you like an animal. . . . She'd
seen it all on TV, the orange suits, the women who looked like
witches—they didn't even give them their makeup, she thought—
and she started to cry.

For a moment, as she came over a hump in the road and saw
the intersection ahead, the intersection where she'd turn toward
Arcadia, and set everything going . . . she thought about leaving
Jimmy somewhere, on somebody's doorstep, and calling the cops
and then running back to the hole she'd just left. She fantasized
about that for a moment: a good-looking woman wearing expensive sunglasses, walking down a beach somewhere, like she'd seen
on TV, like Kim Kardashian or somebody, these colored waiters
watching her strut . . . No, erase that, some hot Mexican guys with
loose white shirts.

She thought about it, but in her heart she knew she couldn't
do it. She'd never been outside of Minnesota, except those few
times when she and some friends went to Hudson, Wisconsin, to
drink and hang out.

That was so far away now, all those times.

She looked over at Jimmy as she pulled up to the intersection. Left or right? Left to drop him somewhere, left to run, or right into Arcadia, and chains and jail. Jail maybe forever.

But hell, she thought, it couldn't be any worse than Shinder, could it?

She leaned across and kissed Jimmy again, but he made no sign that he even knew she was there. She turned right, for Arcadia.

DUKE ARRIVED, coming fast into town; he slowed, then stopped and backed up when he saw the patrol car parked on the side street. He didn't get out, and Virgil could see him talking into his radio. After a few seconds, he came on. Virgil didn't want the obvious cop car, with the lights, visible, and he gestured for him to pull in behind the gas pumps.

Duke did, and climbed out and said, "No sign of them yet. It's been forty minutes. Didn't she say thirty minutes?"

"She's got my phone number, and she hasn't called again," Virgil said. "She didn't know exactly where she was at, either. . . . And if she doesn't come in, we should be able to get some idea about where she's at from the cell towers . . . if there's more than one."

"Probably only one out here. If he's got a GPS chip, though, I think those go through satellites." Duke stepped out to the street, looked south for a moment, then said, "I gotta listen in . . ."

He went around and got into his car, and Virgil thought, *Listen to what?*

Jenkins said, "I thought there'd be more people here . . . more cars. There were all kinds of cars running around all night."

Then Duke called, through an open window, "They're coming in."

Virgil looked at him, frowned, looked down the street. Nothing moving. He called back, "How do you know that?"

Duke looked away for a moment, then said, "I thought it'd be best to have a couple cars down by the south bridge . . . just in case."

Virgil looked south again: nothing. He said, "You sonofabitch, that better not be an ambush. I need those two alive."

Duke said, "That might be . . . I'm not sure it's possible."

Virgil screamed, "You fuck . . ."

He jumped in his truck, and Jenkins clawed open the passenger door, and Shrake the back door, and they were all in and Virgil took off, and Jenkins said, "What do you think? Are they going to kill them?"

"Unless we get there first," Virgil said. "Ah, Jesus, these sons-ofabitches . . ."

BECKY SAW THE Mad River bridge straight ahead, and steeled herself. Once across the bridge, in town, it was done. What should she say to the cop?

She was thinking about that when she saw the wink of a windshield reflection by the bridge. They were supposed to meet by the gas station. What was this? She slowed down, and saw a quick motion by the bridge, like somebody ducking out of sight.

Then, straight ahead, but a quarter mile away, she saw a truck coming toward her, moving fast, no red lights, didn't look like a cop car, then another car behind that.

She slowed more, looked to her left . . . saw a hat, then another hat, then a man down in the ditch, and he was pointing a gun at her.

She shouted at the window glass, "We give up . . . we give up," and fumbled for the window buttons, the truck coasting closer and closer to the bridge.

She never felt the bullets: the first ones shattered her skull and she was gone; Jimmy was with her an instant later.

VIRGIL WAS NO MORE than a hundred yards away when he saw a deputy step into the road at the bridge, lift an automatic weapon to his shoulder, and open up on the truck. The truck was jumping and shaking, and he saw another man moving in the ditch to the left, and then a third, and they were firing and the truck was shaking and coasting and sliding off to the left. . . .

Virgil was pounding on the steering wheel and screaming, "No . . ."

The red pickup rolled off the road, lurched crazily down through the weeds and brush, and stopped with its front wheels in the Mad River.

Becky and Jimmy didn't know any of that; they'd been killed with the first volley, their bodies punctured forty and fifty times by the unending stream of .223 slugs.

. . .

VIRGIL JUMPED OUT of his truck and ran down the riverbank and looked in. The two lumps inside were a mass of blood and bone, hardly looked human; hardly even looked like remnants of humans.

Shrake and Jenkins were with him, and he turned and climbed back up the bank and brushed by Duke, who put up a hand to say something, but Virgil ignored him, and said to Jenkins and Shrake, "Get in the truck."

Jenkins asked, "You okay?"

Virgil said, "I've never seen that. I've never seen a cold-blooded murder, firsthand."

Duke said, "Hey, now."

Virgil said, "Fuck you."

23

VIRGIL WAS SO GODDAMNED mad he couldn't spit. He called Davenport and launched into a tirade and when he finally slowed down, Davenport interrupted and said, "The circumstances here—"

"The circumstances are cold-blooded murder, planned out ahead of time. There was no call to surrender. The truck was slowing down, almost stopped when they opened up. I looked at the bodies. They must've been shot a hundred times."

"Well, not a hundred times," Lucas said, trying to be reasonable.

Virgil: "I'm not exaggerating. There were four guys with M16s and thirty-shot mags. I think every one of them emptied their mags into the truck. That'd be what, a hundred and twenty rounds?"

"Jesus Christ," Lucas said.

"Yeah. I don't know what we do here. Do we charge Duke? Do we go after the shooters first . . . what?"

"Whoa, whoa, whoa. Slow down. We don't go after anybody,"

Davenport said. "If we do anything, we get the attorney general in there, let him send down a couple of his harder-nosed assistants. They already hate Duke. Get the bodies up here for autopsy, build some kind of a case. . . . But I'll tell you, I think it's futile, Virgil. They killed two people that everybody in Minnesota wanted dead. It's politically impossible."

"And Murphy walks. The guy who hired all this done, walks because of that fuckin' Duke."

"Not necessarily. You've still got a case on Murphy," Davenport said.

"Ah, it's weak, Lucas. If he gets a decent attorney, they'll shred us. I got a multiple murderer and a moron as witnesses."

"What about the money that Sharp supposedly got? Where's that?"

"Probably shot to shit, if it was in his pocket," Virgil said. "He looks like a slab of hamburger."

"So you recover that money, check Murphy's bank account . . . that'd help."

"We don't even know that he took it out of the bank. He's a gambler, he might have had it in cash."

"So investigate, Virgil."

After a long silence, Virgil said, "Lucas, I gotta warn you, because you're a friend. Not just my boss. But I'm going on TV here, and I'm gonna say what I think."

"Ah, Jesus, Virgil, it's never a good idea to say what you think, on television." Virgil could hear Davenport exhale, and then he said, "All right. Do it. Fuck him. But don't do it cold. Don't sound like an attorney. Get mad and let it show—you'll get it out there, and then, if we really gotta cover your ass, we'll say you were pissed . . . you were traumatized, you lost your case. We can cover you."

Virgil thought about that for a few seconds, then said, "I won't have any trouble letting it show. But I'll tell you what, man . . ."

"What?"

"I think you've been hanging around the capitol too much, that kind of thinking."

VIRGIL GOT OFF the phone and walked back toward the truck and saw Shrake and Jenkins coming up out of the ditch. They walked over and Shrake shook his head and said, "There could be some trouble. No gun in the truck."

"They deserve all the trouble they get," Virgil said.

Shrake said, "Yeah, but Duke's boys had their heads together, and I'm afraid they're gonna, you know . . ."

"Throw one down? I don't think so. Where's Duke?"

Virgil looked around, spotted Duke sitting in his truck talking on the radio. He marched over, Shrake and Jenkins trailing nervously behind, and when Duke looked up from the radio, he said, "No gun in the truck. If one of your assistant assholes throws one down, I'll bust him and put him on trial up in the Cities. It'd be about four felonies at this point. So you tell them to keep their hands off my crime scene."

"It's not your—"

"Fuck you," Virgil said. He turned and headed back toward the death truck. On the way, he said to Jenkins and Shrake, "I want one of you sitting on this truck until the crime-scene people get here."

"What're we getting into here, Virg?" Shrake asked.

"I just don't want anybody messing with the scene," Virgil said. "This was murder. I suspect they'll get away with it, the way the politics run, but I'm not going to make it any easier than I have to."

"It's not like Welsh and Sharp didn't have it coming—"

"That's not for Duke to decide," Virgil said. "And they murdered my case against Murphy, right along with Jimmy and Becky. Goddamn them. Goddamn them."

So they sat on the truck for an hour and a half, the Bare County deputies tiptoeing around them; every lawman and soldier in Minnesota wanted to look at the bodies, and Virgil chased them all off, until the crime-scene people showed up. Virgil briefed them on the possibility that somebody might try to mess with the scene; they said that wouldn't happen.

Virgil, Shrake, and Jenkins walked past a line of sheriff's cars on the way back to Virgil's truck, and when they passed Duke, who was standing with a Guard officer and a couple of deputies, Duke said, "You're starting to seriously piss me off."

Virgil said, "You think so? Wait about an hour." And he continued down the road.

Duke called after him, "What're you going to do?"

Virgil called back, "Fuck you."

BY THE TIME the crime-scene crew arrived, the town was full of cop cars, but no media trucks, because the media had been blocked out, not allowed across the Mad River bridge at the north end of town, and kept a half mile back from the road leading in from the south.

When it became clear that the cops weren't going to allow them in—at least not right away—they'd gathered by the north bridge, and that's where Virgil went, with Shrake and Jenkins trailing behind in Jenkins's car. The bridge was blocked by a deputy in a Bare County sheriff's car, and Virgil waved him out of the road. He backed up, and Virgil and Jenkins went on through, to the cluster of media vans and cars that backed up down the road.

Virgil pulled over and got out, and reporters hurried down toward him, and Shrake stepped close and said, "Bad idea, dude."

Virgil said, "I know. I'm gonna do it anyway."

The first reporters came up and Virgil said, "I've got a statement. I've got a statement as soon as you guys are ready."

A newspaper guy yelled, "What happened down there?"

Virgil: "Wait for the cameras."

They were all set up and spaced out in five minutes, and Virgil said, "Okay," and stepped out in the middle of the road, and he said, "This is going to be a very short statement, and doesn't represent any state authority at all. It's just me."

Everything had gone absolutely quiet, except for a couple of whirring machine sounds coming from a truck. Virgil went on.

"Becky Welsh and Jimmy Sharp were just ambushed and killed by Bare County sheriff's deputies, at the Mad River bridge on the south end of Arcadia. Welsh had contacted me by phone and offered to surrender. I called Sheriff Lewis Duke for backup, and arranged to meet Welsh and Jimmy Sharp at the convenience store in Arcadia, along with sheriff's deputies. This was the store that Becky Welsh held up a couple days ago.

"While we were waiting there, Sheriff Duke, without informing me or the other state agents, set up an ambush at the Mad River bridge on the south end of town. When Welsh and Sharp appeared, sheriff's deputies opened fire with automatic weapons and killed both of them, without warning. We have not at this point found any guns in the truck, nor did Welsh or Sharp offer any sign of resistance: I was there to see it. It's possible, from what Welsh told me on the telephone, that Sharp was unconscious when he was killed. Sheriff's deputies fired what I believe to have been at least a hundred rounds through the truck. Welsh and Sharp were torn to bits by the heavy volume of gunfire.

"In my opinion, this was a carefully planned execution that was tantamount to murder. If it were up to me, I would arrest Sheriff Duke and his deputies for murder, but that won't be up to me. I also believe that there was another person involved in all these killings over the last few days, and Welsh and Sharp would have been critical witnesses to that. Because of Duke's actions, a cold-blooded killer here in Bare County may very well go untouched by the law."

He stopped talking for a moment, and was met by total silence.

Then he said, "That's all I've got to say," and the screaming started.

WITH THE REPORTERS screaming at him, and as Virgil turned away, he thought the noise was probably audible all the way to the other end of town, where Duke sat in his car, looking down at the death truck.

Virgil walked back to his 4Runner. Jenkins was leaning against the door, grinned at him, and said, "Good show. But better you than me."

Shrake said, "You got some balls, buddy."

Virgil said, "Let's go get a cheeseburger. I'm gonna need my strength."

24

THE SATELLITE UPLINKS put the news of the shooting into the Cities within ten minutes, and every station in the state broke into their early-morning broadcasts to relay it. The video of Virgil was right behind that, and further video of Duke was ten minutes behind that.

Duke was uncharacteristically somber at the beginning of the press conference, and he lied like a motherfucker: "Gave us no alternatives . . . turned the truck at deputies on the side of the road, accelerated toward them . . . we weren't planning to ambush them. We wanted to make sure we closed the gate behind them, so whatever happened in town, they wouldn't get away to kill more people. . . . We'll cooperate with any investigation . . . proud of my men and what they accomplished today."

Ruffe Ignace yelled, "What'd they accomplish? The state agents arrested McCall, and they would have arrested Sharp and Welsh if you hadn't killed them."

Duke raised his voice to say, "Unless they opened up on the people waiting in town . . ."

"With what? They didn't have any guns."

"We didn't know that," Duke said. "They sure had enough guns during the last week. What were we supposed to do, wait until they opened fire on my men? Get some more people killed?"

It went rapidly downhill from there. Virgil, Shrake, and Jenkins watched reruns on the television in the motel lobby, along with a bunch of other guests who'd gathered around the television.

"You know what bothers me?" Shrake asked.

"Nothing," Virgil said.

"That's not true. I'm a very sensitive individual. What bothers me is, you could see the TV people pulling for a shoot-out. If you'd just arrested them and slapped them in jail . . . what fun is that? They were a hundred percent in favor of a shoot-out. So then they got it, exactly what they wanted, and then they turn on the sheriff like a bunch of wolves. Now they're like, 'Oh, we're all protecty about, you know, the right to a trial and innocent until proved guilty, blah blah blah.'"

"The sheriff deserves a bunch of wolves," Virgil said.

"We're gonna have to agree to disagree about that," Shrake said. "I think those kids got pretty much what they deserved."

"It's not about the kids," Virgil said. "It's about us."

"Aw," Shrake said. "Poor little kids."

Virgil said, "So you would have gunned them down."

"They give me any excuse, damn right I would," Shrake said.

"But that's the point—they didn't give them an excuse," Virgil said. "They threw away the guns, called ahead, and were coming in to surrender. So you would have stood in the ditch and blown them up with a machine gun?"

Shrake sighed and said, "No, I guess not. Any excuse, though . . ."

Virgil said, "Attaboy."

But then a thin, gray-faced old man in a tan button-front farmer shirt and green Sears work pants stepped over to Virgil, poked a finger at his chest, and said, "I saw you on TV. You're an asshole."

"Thank you for your support," Virgil said.

DAVENPORT CALLED AND SAID, "Henry—I mean, they're gonna have to send in an environmental clean-up team to hose out his office." Henry Sands was the BCA director, a recent political appointee. "And Rose Marie is madder than a hornet. You're gonna take some shit."

"And where are you in all of this?" Virgil asked.

"I'm behind you," Davenport said. "Like, way behind you."

"Yeah . . ."

"But you're okay," Davenport said.

"I'm okay?"

"Yeah. The governor called, and told me he didn't want to call you directly in case anybody ever asked, but . . . he likes it. As far as he's concerned, you can be Queen of the May. And with Henry and Rose Marie being like they are, they will pay very close attention to what the governor has to say."

"I don't even see how they can hear him," Virgil said. "You know, with their lips stuck so firmly to his ass."

"Hey, hey . . . let's not have any of that kind of talk. Let's be a little modest and self-deprecating. At least for a couple weeks."

"Lucas, I wouldn't turn down his help," Virgil said. "I've got old men telling me I'm an asshole."

"Yeah, well, you got the right old man behind you. He's gonna call Rose Marie and chill her out. You'll probably still take some shit, but you know . . . the attorney general is already drafting a statement about investigating the circumstances of the shooting. How can you lose, in Minnesota, when the liberal do-gooders love your ass?"

THEY TALKED A FEW more minutes about managing the publicity, and then Virgil asked, "What do you think about Murphy? What do I do?"

"Investigate him," Davenport said. "You've got some stuff: track it down. And tell Jenkins and Shrake to get back up here: vacation's over."

Virgil sent Jenkins and Shrake home, then went back to his room and stared at the ceiling for a while. Eventually, he got on the phone to Beatrice Sawyer, the crime-scene crew leader, and asked whether they'd recovered any money from the bodies.

"Yes. We got one thousand and six dollars from Sharp's wallet," she said.

"Twenties?" Virgil asked.

"Yes."

"Might have come from an ATM?"

She said, "Could have, I guess. But this feels like it came out in one chunk, and most people have limits that are lower than that."

There were three banks in town, a Wells Fargo, a Bigham First State Bank, and the Bare County Credit Union. Virgil made some calls and determined that Dick Murphy had three accounts at Wells Fargo. He called the BCA attorney and got a subpoena going.

"You gonna need it right away?" the lawyer asked.

"Tomorrow will be okay," Virgil said.

"We'll serve it up here, this afternoon, and you should be good to go, first thing tomorrow," the attorney said.

Virgil made a list:

1. Sharp was seen shooting pool and talking with Dick Murphy the night before the night of the shooting.
2. Sharp had neither money nor gun as late as the afternoon before he murdered Agatha O'Leary.
3. By that evening, he had a gun and $1,000 in cash.
4. Sharp flashed the money at Welsh and McCall and bragged about being a hit man.
5. Randy White felt that Murphy had solicited him to kill Ag O'Leary, but he declined.
6. Ag told Murphy she wanted a divorce. Murphy believed he would inherit the best part of a million dollars if Ag died before the divorce.

He had to investigate it all, but just wasn't up to it right at that moment. He lay on the bed, his brain churning through it. Eventually, he sat up and made a call.

"You got them," Sally said.

"Not me," Virgil said. "Listen, I gotta tell you. I got four flat tires and no way to get them patched here in Bigham."

"Sounds like an emergency," she said. "Have I told you about our emergency roadside service?"

THEY MET IN MARSHALL and walked along Main Street, looking in the store windows, bought Cokes at the drugstore and Virgil bought her a yellow rose at the flower shop, considered the pressure washers in the window of the hardware store, which would be useful for cleaning the hull of his boat, stopped to watch a funeral cortege go by, walked past the post office, and around and around, and Virgil told her about the ambush and the killings.

Sally said, "They shouldn't have done that."

"I don't think so—but not a lot of people agree with me," Virgil said.

"Maybe you ought to talk to your father."

"I don't really need the good Christian view. He's a great guy but he sees both sides of everything, and mostly just confuses me," Virgil said.

"Do you think you'll get Dick Murphy?"

Virgil considered, then said, "No. Not unless something weird happens. If I could find the guy who gave or sold the gun to Murphy, then I'd have a better chance. If I find that Murphy took the money out of the bank, one thousand dollars the day that Ag O'Leary was murdered, that'd help. If I got both of those things, and the right jury, then . . . maybe. But I don't think I'll get both of those things. I might not get either one. When Murphy made the pass at Randy White, he backed off instantly. So he's not *real* stupid."

"You have to be a little stupid to pay somebody to kill your wife," she said.

"Yeah."

They walked along and Sally said, "So when Larry and I were breaking up, and I found out about his little fling, I lay in bed for a couple nights and thought about killing him. I never would have done it, of course, but I thought about it, because it made me feel better. I came up with some general rules for killing your spouse. Number one: do it yourself."

Virgil was interested: "Really."

"Well, when you were getting all your divorces, didn't you want to kill somebody?"

"Mmm, no. I just mostly wanted to avoid alimony. The longest I was married was a year. There weren't any kids, no houses . . . I couldn't see why I ought to be on the hook forever."

"Are you?"

"No. They were nice enough women, in their own way. They mostly just wanted a do-over," Virgil said. "But I worried about it. One of them, we were married about ten days when I knew it wasn't gonna last, and I kept obsessing about it: on the hook forever? For ten days? I could see myself supporting the next husband. I saw him as a big fat unshaven unemployed guy in a wife-beater T-shirt who sat around on a sagging couch and yelled at the kids—oh, yeah, eight ratty kids with drug habits. . . . I never felt like killing anybody, though."

Sally laughed and said, "Well, did she do that? Marry a guy like that?"

"No, she married a small-business guy. He runs a grinder company, he has trucks that go around and pick up documents from big companies, that they're getting rid of, and he grinds them up. He does all right."

"Sounds fascinating."

"That's what I thought," Virgil said, with the first smile of the day. Nothing like having the ex-wife marry somebody more boring than yourself.

They sat in the park for a while, and then went and got something to eat, and as they were finishing, Sally said, "I'm going back to the store. You, you have to go back to Bigham and get started."

"That's not really what I want to do," Virgil said.

"I *know* what you want to do, but I'm not up for a nooner with a guy going through a depressive fit," she said.

"Nooner," Virgil said. "I haven't heard that word since I left Marshall. Makes me laugh."

"So . . ."

He sighed and said, "Yeah. I'm going back."

25

SO VIRGIL WENT BACK to Bigham, and the first thing he did was stop by the *Bigham Gazette* and talk to the editor, Bud Wright, who was also the lead reporter and photographer. "I have the information that would make a decent sidebar—is that right, sidebar?—okay, sidebar, and I'm willing to give it to you exclusively if you'll give me a break and run it big," Virgil told him.

The editor/reporter said, "I can guarantee it."

"I am looking for somebody who can tell me where Jimmy Sharp's pistol came from. It's called a Smith & Wesson .38-caliber Hand Ejector, Military & Police. It has a six-inch barrel—"

Wright said, "Slow down, slow down . . . A .38-caliber . . ."

Virgil told him that there was reason to believe that Jimmy Sharp had acquired the gun in Bigham, so, "Somebody's seen it. That doesn't mean they're in trouble—there's no law against selling a gun—but I'd really like to know how it made its way to Jimmy."

They talked for ten minutes, and Wright said the paper would be on the street the next morning, the first "extra" in the history of the newspaper. When he finished the interview, he got Virgil to stand in front of a piece of seamless paper and took his picture.

"If you find the gun, are you going to give us the first word on it?" Wright asked.

"I don't know," Virgil said. "Everything depends on the circumstances. But I sure would like to know where it came from."

He left Wright working on the story and walked down the street to the Burger King, got a package of fries, sat at a booth, and called Roseanne Bush and Honor Roberts and asked them to list all the people they knew who hung around with, or were friendly with, Dick Murphy.

He spoke to Roberts last, and when he got off the phone, he had seven names.

THEN THE INVESTIGATION slowed down. During the hunt for Becky Welsh and Jimmy Sharp, he'd been working twenty-hour days, and something happened every single day. It was like being in a war.

When he started investigating Murphy, it was like walking through waist-deep molasses.

He worked the seven names all day and most of the first evening, and got more names from the people he spoke to, and worked those names the next day. Several people said that Murphy was unhappy with Ag. Two said that he'd mentioned her money— but not in a way that suggested he was anxious to get it for himself. The references, they said, had been joking: "If I were as rich as my old lady . . ."

Virgil thought, *Murphy was thinking about it.*

LATER ON THE SECOND DAY, he got a call from the BCA attorney and was told that he could stop by the Wells Fargo and look at Murphy's account history. He did, and found that Murphy had withdrawn not one thousand dollars, but fifteen hundred dollars two days before Ag was killed.

With the help of the branch manager, he tracked the transaction to a young teller named George, who actually remembered it. "I gave him a thousand in twenties, and five hundred in fifties. I remember because we're supposed to chat with customers and make them feel like we're friendly, so I said, 'Going on vacation?' He said he was going to Vegas. I said, 'Man, wish I was going with you.' It was colder'n heck that day, and Vegas sounded pretty good."

The newspaper extra came out in the afternoon, with an end-of-the-world story about the killings of Welsh and Sharp. Virgil's sidebar ran big, with a BCA phone number for information.

Nobody called it.

Davenport said, "That was a long shot—I don't know what else you could have done, but who wants to be known as the guy who supplied the gun to Jimmy Sharp?"

"I was hoping he supplied it to Murphy," Virgil said.

"Same thing, since everybody in town knows you're looking for Murphy."

. . .

MURPHY RETURNED FROM VEGAS after a week and went back to work at his father's insurance agency. John O'Leary said Murphy hadn't done anything with the will—if he had, the O'Learys would know about it, since they were all in it.

THE CASE AGAINST Duane McGuire and Royce Atkins—and implicitly, against Murphy—was handled by two special prosecutors appointed by the state attorney general. They also investigated the shooting of Becky Welsh and Jimmy Sharp.

The attorneys, Sandy Hunstad and Brett Thomas, eventually found that they had no case against the deputies who killed Welsh and Sharp. While they were critical of the sheriff's command and control, they said publicly that problem was one of management, and was not a criminal affair.

Duke issued a defiant statement, supporting the actions of his deputies, but everyone was left with a sour taste. A half dozen people took the time to tell Virgil that he should be ashamed of himself for his criticism of Duke, who was only trying to defend the citizens against a couple of crazies. Only one told him that he thought Virgil was right, and Virgil suspected that guy was nuts.

The case against McGuire and Atkins was clearer, but the level of the charge was not. Since they'd used only fists and boots, and no other weapons, and Virgil was not seriously injured, Hunstad said that it was unlikely they could sustain a charge of Assault in

the First Degree, and would probably have to drop to Assault/
Three.

They could, however, file the Assault/One, because there were
special provisions for an assault on a police officer. Because the
prison penalty was much stronger—up to twenty years—they
would have more to work with in trying to convince Atkins to
give up Murphy. In other words, to extort a confession . . .

But Atkins wouldn't talk. The only thing they had that pointed
directly at Murphy was McGuire's belief that Atkins was paid by
Murphy.

THEY WERE WORKING through those possibilities when one of
Duke's deputies—one of the men who shot up Welsh and Sharp—
encountered Virgil on the street, pulled him aside, and said,
"You're an asshole for what you're saying about us, but that's neither here nor there. What you need to know is, I saw Dick Murphy's car over at Royce Atkins's girlfriend's house on Wednesday
night. On Thursday morning, first thing, she was at the jail talking
to Royce, and then to Duane. . . . They're cooking something up."

Virgil said, "Thank you."

The next day, McGuire began tap-dancing: he was no longer
exactly sure that anybody got paid to beat up Virgil. It might have
been, he said, a misunderstanding on his part.

Virgil talked to the attorneys, and Thomas said, "Look, Virgil,
we're with you on this thing. We can put these guys in jail for As-
sault/Three, I think, but the way things are, they'll get less than

five years. Murphy can talk to the girlfriend all he wants, and she can talk to Atkins and McGuire. Those are the rules. If we could prove that Murphy is paying them to give false testimony, that'd be different. You don't have anything like that."

"So they're going to walk?" Virgil asked.

"No. They're going to jail—but at this point, all we've got against Murphy is a fairly weak circumstantial case that I don't think we can convict on. We need Atkins to talk. If we can get him to talk, we can draw a better picture. We could show Murphy paying to hurt you. We can bring in Randy White's testimony, which suggests that he wanted Ag O'Leary killed. We can bring in the money found in Sharp's pocket. That might be enough. But you've got to get Atkins."

Atkins wouldn't budge, and finally his attorney told Virgil to stop coming around.

APRIL DRAGGED INTO MAY, and the weather finally started getting warmer, if not much wetter, and people in southwest Minnesota began using the dreaded "D" word, for "drought." On a very fine and dry May afternoon, a woman named May Lawson took a heavily weighted, chrome yellow Momentus golf club and beat her estranged husband to death with it, having caught him asleep on the couch in his new bachelor apartment. She then went back to the school where she taught fifth grade and pretended that nothing had happened.

Her husband, Rolf, had been conducting an affair with another woman who worked at the DMV. Virgil took about two days to figure all that out, and the tests came back with May's deoxyribo-nucleic acid all over the body—she'd apparently spit at him while beating him to death—and the school's maintenance technician found the Momentus golf club in a dumpster behind the school. May had wiped it, but hastily, and hadn't gotten all the prints, or all the blood, either.

That took two weeks, including the arrest and paperwork, and when Virgil got back to Bigham, the case against Murphy felt colder than ever.

Finally, Thomas and Hunstad sat him down and said, "Virgil, we talked to the big guy, and he said we should take a run at it. We're dead in the water right now. What we think is, if we take a run at it, and put the evidence out there, we'll probably lose. But if we do lose, and if the O'Learys sue Murphy for wrongful death, there's a chance they can keep him from inheriting that money. And make him a killer in the eyes of the community, just like with O.J."

"If that's all we got, I'll take it," Virgil said.

HE ARRESTED MURPHY that afternoon. Murphy was astonished and humiliated when Virgil marched him out of his old man's office building and dropped him into the Bare County jail on a charge of murder.

Duke came out to watch it, and said, as Virgil was leaving, "I don't think you got him, unless there's something I don't know."

"We'll see," Virgil said.

The next day, the local district court judge denied bail.

. - . .

THE O'LEARYS WERE EXULTANT . . . for about two days. Virgil met them at the courthouse, and led the whole bunch to a conference room, for an interview with Hunstad and Thomas. When the attorneys finished, they told the O'Learys the truth: that a conviction was unlikely.

"You mean he's going to get away with it?" John O'Leary asked.

"We'll ruin him in the community, and the charge will follow him for the rest of his life. Then there's the possibility of a wrongful death lawsuit, but that would be up to you."

"Wrongful death, my ass," Jack O'Leary exploded. "He's responsible for the murder of Ag. And he's going to walk away from it? I don't give a shit about the money, I want him in Stillwater."

"So do we," said Hunstad. "I'm just telling you, it's a tough case. If we had Welsh or Sharp . . . but we don't. We've got hearsay and suggestions and some money they found on Jimmy Sharp. We've got a confirmed cop-killer as one witness, and a guy who used to hurt high school football players for money, as our second witness. It's just tough."

Frank O'Leary said, "That fuckin' Duke."

Then Marsha O'Leary started sobbing, and the whole family began to shake.

VIRGIL TIDIED UP what he could, and then was called to look at a situation in which a young woman, the daughter of a Rochester doctor, had gone missing. That ate up most of a week, until he established that she was living in Illinois with her rock guitarist boyfriend.

The next week, he was in Owatonna, where some high school dopers had broken into the veterinary medicine chest at the Fleet Farm store and run off with some serious shit: horse dope that would blow their hearts through their chest walls. Another week was gone.

But that same week, Tom McCall, on the advice of his attorney, pleaded guilty to one count of murder of the deputy sheriff Daniel Card, and was sentenced to life in prison. He was, however, because of past cooperation and the promise of further cooperation if it were needed, allowed the possibility of parole. He would be in his mid-fifties when he got out of Stillwater. Virgil's only involvement had been written depositions, taken during sessions with McCall's court-appointed attorney, describing McCall's phone calls, his arrest, and the interview with Virgil in Virgil's truck. They hardly mattered, given two eyewitness accounts of the shooting outside the bank. News reports said McCall showed no emotion at his sentencing.

A WEEK AFTER THAT, he was lying in bed, late at night, at home in Mankato, when Thomas, the special prosecutor, called.

"Randy White is gone," Thomas said.

"What?"

"He's gone. He was supposed to show up for a deposition today. We don't know where. He didn't show up at work either yesterday or today."

"Ah, man."

"We talked to Davenport," Thomas said. "He says you should get over here and find him for us."

SO THEN HE was back in Bigham.

White's disappearance had the look and feel of something really bleak. He was gone, and his car was gone, but his apartment seemed lived-in—clothes in the closets, underwear on the floor. There wasn't much food in the refrigerator, but it hadn't been cleaned out, either.

Virgil had another talk with the newspaper editor, and got everybody in the county looking for White and his car.

The O'Learys asked Virgil, "What is this?"

Virgil couldn't answer. He couldn't even look full-time, because there was nothing to go on. There was no point in driving up and down the roads of Bare County, looking out the windows. . . .

May disappeared, and June came up.

And one day, Hunstad and Thomas said, "We can't hold Murphy. It's unethical. We don't have a case. We're going to drop the charges."

Virgil said, "Give me a week."

Thomas said, "Do you have anything more to work with than you did last week?"

Virgil shook his head. "No."

"Then we're going to call the O'Learys in and give them the news. If we can find White, we can refile."

"What if Murphy had him killed?"

"You think you could prove that? You can't even find his car, much less a body."

"Goddamnit," Virgil said.

Hunstad, who was kind of cute, gave him a hug. "Next time you're in the Cities, call me and we'll have a cup of coffee," she said.

THE NEXT DAY, she went to court and told the judge that with their main witness gone, the state had decided that they could not sustain the case, and so the charges were being dropped. "We reserve the right to refile, if we find Mr. White," she said.

Virgil was sitting across the street when Murphy walked out of the jail with his attorney. They talked for a minute or two, then the attorney clapped him on the shoulder and headed for the courthouse parking lot. Murphy jaywalked across the street into a newsstand, and a minute later reappeared with a fresh pack of cigarettes, stuck one in his face, lit it, looked around, and then walked away.

Virgil said a short prayer that he'd get lung cancer.

The newspaper later that week hinted that White might have been killed; the paper didn't say by whom, but everybody knew.

ON THE TWENTY-SEVENTH of June, Virgil was sound asleep in his boat on a quiet backwater of Pool 4 of the Mississippi River, off Alma, Wisconsin, while his pal Johnson Johnson beat the water with an aging Eddie Bait. Virgil's phone rang, and Johnson Johnson said, "I *told* you to turn it off."

"A young woman may be calling me," Virgil said, digging for the phone. "If she got out of Marshall early enough, we're gonna meet in Minneapolis."

"You're going to celebrate life?"

"That's right," Virgil said. He looked at the face of the phone and the call was, indeed, coming from the Marshall area code— but from an unknown number.

"Virgil Flowers."

"Virgil, this is Bud Wright, at the *Bigham Gazette*."

"Hey, Bud."

"Have you heard?"

Virgil sat up. "That fuckin' White. That fuckin' White is back, right?"

"No, no. No. Dick Murphy didn't make it home last night, or come to work this morning. One of Duke's boys found his car down in Riverside Park."

"I know it."

"There was blood on the seat," Wright said.

Virgil closed his eyes. Then, "Shit. I'm on my way."

"Do you have any comment?"

"Yeah: 'Shit, I'm on my way.'"

26

WHEN VIRGIL GOT TO BIGHAM, Murphy's car had been taken to the sheriff's impound area. Virgil went by Duke's office and was told that Duke was out. The chill in the office was still deep, and a deputy named Jim Clark only reluctantly showed Virgil the car.

The car was a BMW 328i. The small blood spot was just below the headrest; Virgil could see no sign of a bullet hole. He had the deputy open all four doors, and without touching anything inside, he looked at the back of the headrest and then the backseat. There was no sign of a bullet exit hole on the back of the headrest, or an entrance hole on the backseat.

"What are you doing about the blood?" Virgil asked.

"Our crime-scene specialist is driving samples up to the BCA," Clark said.

"Is Ross Price around?" Virgil asked. Price was the sheriff's investigator.

"Somewhere," the deputy said.

"I need to talk with him," Virgil said.

The deputy closed the car and locked it, and led Virgil back inside. The dispatcher got ahold of Price, who said that he'd be back in ten minutes or so. Virgil went down in the basement, got a Diet Coke and a Nut Goodie, then waited on the steps outside the law enforcement center.

Price was prompt: just about ten minutes after he talked to the dispatcher, he rolled into the sheriff's parking lot, and Virgil went over to talk to him.

"So how did all this come up?" Virgil asked. "Who figured out he was gone?"

Price said that late on Monday evening, Murphy had been seen at a local self-serve car wash, detailing his BMW. "We talked to a guy who saw him there, Lance Barber."

"Friend of Murphy's?"

"No. Lance is a baker, he works at Bare Bakers. He's an older guy, must be close to seventy. He went through the fast wash, and saw Murphy down there. As far as we know, he was the last one to see him," Price said. "He said he saw Murphy shining up his head-lights with a rag when he went into the automatic wash, and he was just going through the drier when Murphy drove out the exit lane."

That was that. Murphy didn't go to work the next day, and didn't answer his landline phone or his cell phone, either one. His father went around to his apartment and let himself in, and there was no sign of him.

"Then, we found his car parked down at Riverside Park," Price said. "It was unlocked, and we found that blood on the seat. Our crime-scene guy, Bob Drake, took a blood sample, just to make sure it was Murphy's, along with some hair and what looked like semen samples from Murphy's bed for comparison. Then we locked up the car so your guys could really get into it, if it turns out to be Murphy's blood, as I expect it'll be."

Virgil nodded, and then said, "And nothing since?"

"He hasn't charged anything on any credit cards, hasn't used an ATM, left two hundred dollars in cash in the top drawer of his chest of drawers. Hasn't used his cell phone. Doesn't have another car that we know of."

"You think he might have faked it?"

Price hesitated, then said, "I'm not smart enough to figure out what happened. It's all weird."

"Just asking what you think," Virgil said.

"What I *think* is, there's some chance he faked his own death, and his old pal Randy White set up a hideout and picked him up. Then I asked myself, 'Why would he do that?' As long as Randy is gone, Dick's not going to go to trial for murder. And then, there's Ag's money. He still hasn't gone to probate with the will. . . . Everybody's been waiting for that, because they're talking about the O'Learys suing for wrongful death. Anyway, he'd be leaving that money behind, at least for now, and that's not the Dick Murphy we know and love. So, *that* would make me think he didn't fake it."

Virgil nodded. "I could buy that. Unless, maybe, he knew that Randy was coming back."

"But why would he leave the money in the chest of drawers? Why wouldn't he have done a better job of getting out of town?"

"I don't know," Virgil admitted. "Unless Randy called and said he was coming back the next day, and he had to throw something together."

"But . . . would he be throwing something together, and then go out and wash his car so he could ditch it an hour later?"

Virgil said, "Hmm."

"But here's something that's sort of in favor of it being a fake: I can't figure out what kind of a killing wound would put that blood on the car seat, where it is. If somebody pointed a gun in the window and shot him, why wouldn't we find some evidence of a gunshot? If he was stabbed, why would he bleed backward into the seat back? Why wouldn't there be blood anywhere else? What it looks like, tell the truth, is like he cut his arm, and smeared some blood on the seat. We won't know for sure until your crime-scene people start taking the seat apart."

They walked over to Murphy's car and looked in the window, but nothing really came to Virgil. Would the O'Learys have taken the situation into their own hands? Had Ag O'Leary had some other relationship that Virgil didn't know about, and Murphy was killed by some unknown actor, in revenge? Could Randy White have been that relationship?

They looked at the spot of blood on the seat, and Virgil did not get the feeling that it was obviously a fake. What it was, was odd.

Virgil asked Price, "Am I still stinking up the place in the Bare County sheriff's office?"

Price grinned and said, "Barack Obama would run about forty points ahead of you, if there was an election."

"And Barack is not exactly in deep favor around here."

"Not exactly," Price said. "But there are a few guys who've been willing to say, privately, when the sheriff wasn't around, that the thing wasn't handled right. The Becky Welsh/Jimmy Sharp thing. I think one of them might take the sheriff on, in two years."

"Does the sheriff know that?"

"Oh, hell no," Price said. "Maybe it won't happen at all. We'll see."

"Does Duke know you're talking to me? Or do I have to be careful about mentioning it?"

"Oh, he knows," Price said. "When you asked the dispatcher to call me, he called Duke first. Duke told him to call me in . . . but he doesn't want to talk to you himself."

They thought about that for a moment, then Price asked, "Are you gonna take this over? The Murphy thing?"

"What can I do?" Virgil asked. "You've done everything I'd do. Maybe Crime Scene will turn up some DNA, and that'll take us somewhere. Maybe we'll find a body and that'll tell us something. Or maybe he'll show up."

Price sighed and said, "You know, if Jimmy hadn't gone up there with that gun . . ."

"If Murphy hadn't paid him to . . ."

"Yeah. Well, hell. Stay in touch," Price said.

VIRGIL STAYED IN TOUCH for two weeks, until the DNA came back on the blood: it was almost certainly Murphy's, because it matched hair, blood, and semen samples from Murphy's bed. Murphy had taken no money from his bank account, never used his cell phone or credit cards in that time. Then more DNA samples came back, on the car, and they were all Murphy.

A crime-scene tech who'd taken apart the car seat said, "I don't know how he was killed, if he was killed, but there was more blood there than it looked like. It wasn't just a spot. He bled through the spot for a while, and it ran down the inside of the fabric. Not a whole lot, but it wasn't just a wipe, or a smear."

"So what killed him?" Virgil asked.

"I'm thinking aliens."

"You mean like, Canadians?"

THEN, a day after the second set of DNA samples came back, Davenport called.

"You're not on the TSA's no-fly list, are you?"

"I hope not," Virgil said. "Where am I flying to?"

"Houston. By God, Texas."

"Why is that?"

"I thought you'd want to talk to Randy White, who was picked up yesterday afternoon after a DUI stop."

"Sonofagun," Virgil said.

VIRGIL FLEW INTO George Bush Intercontinental Airport the next morning, and two hours later was interviewing Randy White at the Harris County Jail.

When a guard brought White to the interview room, Virgil asked, "Randy, what the hell happened to you?"

White sat in the chair on the other side of the interview desk and said, "I couldn't deal with it anymore. You gonna take me back?"

Virgil said, "I don't know."

"I got a decent job down here."

"You know about Dick Murphy?" Virgil asked.

"Yeah . . . I feel bad about it, but I just couldn't handle it," White said. "Everybody's telling me that it's my information that'll send him up, but you know what? I really don't know if he wanted to kill Ag. I'd be the one to send him up, but I don't *know*. So I took off."

Virgil looked at him for a moment, but saw no guile in his eyes. He asked, "You really don't know about Dick?"

"Well, yeah: he got out," White said.

"That's not what I meant," Virgil said. "What I meant was, he's disappeared."

"What?"

Virgil peered at him. White's reaction was a little too dramatic. Off-key. "Goddamnit, Randy, if you're lying to me, I'll put you in Stillwater as an accessory to murder."

"Virgil—when I took off, Dick was in jail, and I never been back," White said. "I don't know what happened up there. I don't read the newspapers, I don't have a TV yet. I just don't know."

"Did Murphy pay you to leave?" Virgil asked.

"No, no. I just couldn't deal with it."

"I'm gonna want to look at your bank account."

Randy laughed: "And you'll see that the most I've had in it is about a hundred dollars."

"Murphy paid Jimmy Sharp in cash. He paid some guys to beat me up, in cash. So he'd give you cash."

"But he didn't," White said. He brushed hair out of his eyes and said, "I'll tell you, Virgil—I liked Ag. More than I should have, since she was my buddy's wife. I never would have lifted a finger to hurt her, for no amount of money. If I really thought that Dick done it, I'd hang him myself."

Virgil looked at him, and then asked, quietly, "You didn't do that, did you?"

White said, "No! No. I been here since I ran away. Virgil, I been here every day. You can ask. I'm working on a roof-tile crew."

But again, a little flat, a little off-key.

Virgil stared at him, and White stared back; they were locked up, and White never flinched. *Something going on here,* Virgil thought. *He denies everything, but he's defiant.* Had he arranged for Murphy to disappear? But White wasn't smart enough to engineer that. He wasn't smart enough to get Murphy out of jail, and then kill him. Not nearly smart enough.

Virgil said, "I'll tell you what, Randy. I'm gonna call my boss and see what he wants to do. So, I'm going to ask the folks down here to hold on to you for a while. Give you some time to think about it. We're talking murder here, and you're involved in this somehow. If you're hiding Murphy . . ."

White shook his head and looked at the guard and said, "Let's go. I'm tired of talking to him."

He stood up and Virgil said, "You gotta think about it hard, Randy. This is a life-altering decision. If you really liked Ag that much . . ."

Virgil trailed off, and turned his head to face the concrete-block wall. A thought prowling there.

The guard touched White on the shoulder, and they stepped toward the door that would take him back to a cell. As the guard opened the door, Virgil turned and called, "Randy!"

White turned to look at him, and Virgil said, "It was the fuckin'

O'Learys who paid you, didn't they? It was the fuckin' O'Learys who shipped you out of town so Murphy'd get out of jail. And then they killed him."

White opened his mouth to say something, but nothing came out for a moment, and there was panic in his eyes. Then he said, "No," and "Fuck you," and to the guard, "Let's go. This guy is a crazy man."

VIRGIL CALLED DAVENPORT and told him what he thought. Davenport said, "You don't have one inch of proof, Virgil. You saw it in his eyes? Give me a break: You don't even know that Murphy is dead. If he is, and an O'Leary did it, it could have been any one of . . . How many? Four or five? Who are you going to hang it on?"

"Goddamnit, Lucas, I *know*."

"Yeah. Well, both you and I know the biggest organized crime guy in Minnesota. We've both had long chats with him, and we've never touched him. Why is that?"

"No proof," Virgil said.

"Exactly. Tell you what: get back up here. It'll take a couple days to process the paper on White, and then I'll send a couple guys down there to get him, if you still want him. You go talk to the O'Learys, see if you can shake anything loose."

VIRGIL GOT A LATE FLIGHT out to Minneapolis and was home in Mankato by midnight. The next morning, he called John O'Leary and said that he wanted to talk with him and his children. O'Leary asked, "About what?" and Virgil said, "Dick Murphy."

O'Leary said he, Marsha, Mary, and Frank could be there, but that the older three boys were all in the Cities. Virgil said he'd talk to the boys later.

"What's going on?" John O'Leary asked. "Talk to them later? You think we had something to do with Murphy . . . disappearing?"

"I found Randy White," Virgil said.

"Yeah? So what? Does he know where Murphy is?" He asked the question with a hard edge in his voice. A real question, Virgil thought. If Murphy had been murdered, John O'Leary didn't know about it.

"I'll talk to you about that when I see you," Virgil said. "Anyway, what's a good time?"

After a moment of silence, O'Leary said, "Make it seven o'clock. I'm going to get the boys down from school. If you want to talk to us, you can talk to us all at once."

BIGHAM WAS A LITTLE more than two hours away, straight up the Minnesota River Valley, so Virgil had the best part of a day to kill. He caught up with his bills, filed expense reports, did some laundry, and caught up with a muskie forum on the 'net. When he was current with the world, he got the power washer out of the garage and power-washed the boat. It had last been in the Mississippi, and the Mississippi was now full of all kinds of weird flora and fauna, some of which hitched rides to other lakes and rivers in the scuppers of boats.

He'd just finished doing that, and was coiling the hose, when Davenport nosed into the driveway in his 911. "Out for a ride," he said. A lame excuse. He looked at the boat and said, "You ought to call that *The Governator*, because of the way you got it."

"Easy," Virgil said. "I'm a little sensitive about that. So, you down here to give me a talking-to?"

"No, but I thought we might have lunch somewhere," Davenport said. He was wearing a dark blue suit and a red-and-blue-checkered tie, the blue not coincidentally matching the color of his eyes. Virgil suspected the clocks on his socks would also match. "You can drive the Porsche, if you want," Davenport said. "There may be women watching."

"Mankato women don't fall over for something as crass as a Porsche," Virgil said.

Davenport shrugged. "That's not my experience. Anyway . . . you want to drive, or you want me to?"

Virgil took the keys: "On the off-chance you're right."

"What about your little sweetie in Marshall?"

"My little sweetie was too busy with work to go out last weekend. I have a feeling that we may be cooling off," Virgil said.

"But you'll still be friends."

"Sure."

"Good work," Davenport said. "Keep them as friends, and there's always a chance you'll pick up a piece of charity ass sometime in the future when you need it."

"If Weather heard you talking like that, she'd slap the shit out of you," Virgil said.

"True, but Weather isn't here," Davenport said. "Listen, are we going to stand here and bullshit, or are we gonna get lunch?"

· · ·

THEY WENT TO A DINER, and got the usual, for Minnesota, which was the New England equivalent of a Thanksgiving dinner, both of them going with Diet Cokes. "The thing about Diet Coke," Davenport said, "is that nice chemical edge to it. It's like drinking plastic."

"And it's non-fattening," Virgil said.

DAVENPORT: "You're not going to get the O'Learys, Virgil. They're probably as smart as you are, or nearly so. If they took out Murphy, they did it right. They're the kind of people who know all about DNA, and fingerprints, and all of that. They took their time to plan it. If what you're telling me about them is true, you can bet your life they won't turn on each other."

"Maybe I can turn White . . ."

"If you turn White, and he says they paid him to disappear, you'd have to prove they knew that would end the case against Murphy, and that Murphy would make bail, and they did that explicitly to give themselves an opportunity to murder Murphy. Their side of the story would be, they realized that Murphy was probably innocent, and they thought they might as well end the agony for the husband of their late, much-loved daughter."

"They couldn't say that with straight faces."

"But a lawyer could," Davenport said. "The other thing is, you're about to take on a clan of doctors. You know how hard it is to get doctors to practice in a place like Bigham? I bet that if you got a jury down there, even if they thought some O'Leary did it, they wouldn't convict. They just wouldn't do it."

"Lucas . . . you're saying they're going to get away with murder."

"They will, if they did it. I'm not sure that they did it, and neither are you. You know your case against Murphy? That was ten times stronger than anything you're likely to get against the O'Learys. You don't even have a body. A jury won't be sure, not given all the circumstances. You have one chance: that somebody confesses. What do you think the chance of that is?"

Virgil rubbed his forehead and admitted, "Slim and none."

"And Slim is out of town," Davenport said.

THEY ATE FOR A WHILE, and then Virgil said, "So you came down here to tell me to ditch the whole thing."

"Nope. You have the best clearance record that anybody ever heard of, and I'd never tell you to stop," Davenport said. "I just came down to tell you how it is. You won't get them."

Virgil: "Forget it, Jake. It's Chinatown."

Davenport looked around the café with its red leatherette counter stools, big men in coveralls, waitresses with beehive hairdos, then down at his plate of sliced turkey, mashed potatoes, dressing, and cranberry sauce, all covered with cream of mushroom gravy, and said, "No. It's sure as shit not Chinatown, Virgil. It's just life."

They thought about that for a bit, then Davenport asked, "What's going on with the guys who beat you up?"

Virgil shrugged. "Nobody's wanted to go to trial. The state

guys don't want to resolve anything until we figure out what happened to Murphy, and McGuire and Atkins apparently think that the more confused things get, the more likely they are to get a better deal. So . . . it's still out there."

"So everything's settled except the O'Learys . . . as much as it's going to be, anyway," Davenport said.

"Yeah."

They ate some more, then Virgil said, "I'm going to Bigham tonight. I'm going to take a shot at them. Just see if anything falls out."

"God bless you, man," Davenport said.

Davenport dropped Virgil at his house and said, "Watch the weather service. There's some bad shit coming in from Nebraska." Then he was gone, moving fast in the 911.

DAVENPORT WAS RIGHT. Bad shit coming down.

Virgil saw it on his computer, the weather radars all across the northern plains. A line of thunderstorms showed up in a crimson streak from western Kansas to eastern North Dakota, and the fattest part of the bowed-out line of supercells was aimed right at southwest Minnesota.

He called his father to tell him to keep an eye on it. "We've been watching it coming since yesterday," his father said. "This is a nasty one."

Virgil packed his Musto sailing suit in the back of the truck, just in case, and at three o'clock took off. Fifty miles east of Bigham, the sky turned cloudy, with the downward bumps of mammatus

clouds; never a good sign. The wind picked up, and the clouds overhead were churning like whipped cream in a blender, but there
was no rain. That would come, Virgil thought, but not yet.

He was dry all the way to Bigham. Beyond Bigham, though,
the sky was a dark wall of cloud, and the cottonwood trees in City
Park were whipping and twisting in the wind.

VIRGIL WAS EARLY. He checked into the same hotel where he'd
spent his time during the hunt for Sharp and Welsh, went up to his
room, and turned on the television. The Sioux Falls weather radar
showed the storm plowing toward Bigham: the leading edge of
the heaviest band was ten miles to the west and the weatherman
was screaming about wall clouds and the hook signature.

There'd been two confirmed tornadoes out of the system, and
a third one was suspected. Virgil called his father: "What's happening there?"

"It's something else," his father shouted into the phone. "It's a
hurricane out there, and a light show. No damage, though. We'll
be out of it in twenty minutes. There's supposedly a tornado down
south of us."

"Call me if you have a problem. I'm in Bigham."

"Bigham? Virgil, this baby is coming right at you."

VIRGIL GOT OFF the phone and went and looked out the window.
He couldn't see much, but the window was rattling in its frame

from the wind; then the rain came, a violent, pounding downpour that would last less than an hour, but might dump two or three inches of rain.

Virgil looked at his watch: six o'clock. He'd meet the O'Learys in an hour, but if there was a tornado out there . . .

THERE WAS.

With the weatherman focusing on the hook at the southern trailing edge of the supercell, he watched it as it skimmed a few miles south of Bigham and continued to the northeast.

A tornado's hard to track; an exact track usually can't be done until the next day, when the tornado guys look down at the track from the air. But looking at the weather radar, the small oval area of the supposed tornado appeared to run right over the town of Victoria Plains, which was eight miles south of Bigham.

Virgil watched the radar, listened to the rain, heard an ambulance scream by, and then another, and then a couple of cop cars. The weatherman had no specific information, so Virgil called the Bare County sheriff's office, identified himself, and asked the dispatcher if there was a problem.

"There is," she said. "VP took a direct hit, and it's a big storm. They're saying the whole town is torn apart."

"I've got lights, siren, and a 4Runner. You think I should get up there?"

"You probably should," she said. "We're calling everybody for help. There's some farms got hit, too, but we don't have any direct reports yet. Throw everything out of the truck except the first aid kit. You might be needed to transport people back to the hospital."

VIRGIL WAS ON HIS WAY in five minutes; he'd taken thirty seconds to pull on the Musto pants and jacket, and another two minutes to haul his gear out of the truck and up to the hotel room.

He couldn't see it, but the sun was low in the sky, and it should have still been broad daylight. As it was, it looked like three o'clock on a cloudy winter day, not quite dark, but not quite light, either; the rain was coming so hard that in places, the water ran over the curbs of the street and down the sidewalks. The truck shuddered with the impact. There were trees down in City Park, and a power company truck headed fast to somewhere—no lights on the north side of town—and then Virgil cleared the town and headed south, following the nav system through the pounding rain.

Victoria Plains—VP—was an ordinary farm town of a thousand people or so, implement dealers and grain silos on the outskirts, with a compact little business district, now half emptied by the two big-box stores in Bigham. There were rows of small prairie houses spreading in uneven blocks out from the central district, with an orange-brick elementary school just off Main Street.

Quite ordinary an hour earlier; now it looked as though a giant had stepped on it.

Virgil passed an ambulance coming out of town, running with lights and siren. A few minutes later, another went by.

The first houses Virgil saw were half-wrecked, and he realized, looking out in the dimming light, that all around them were foundations from houses that simply were no longer there. A man was running down the street through the rain, waving his arms. When Virgil stopped, the man looked at Virgil and said, "You're not an ambulance."

"You need one?"

"Yeah—if you can get . . . You gotta go around . . ."

"Get in," Virgil said.

The man wasn't wearing rain gear; he was wearing an athletic jacket and jeans and running shoes, and sputtering with the rain he'd absorbed. He said, "Go that way," and Virgil went that way. The man said, "There's a house down. They think a kid is still inside. I don't know, he's probably dead."

Virgil didn't have anything to say to that, and the man said, "We saw it coming. Thank God, we saw it coming. I think most people made it down the basement."

They traveled in a jigsaw route along back streets and down an alley, ran over electric wires a couple of times, dodged downed trees, and then the man pointed at a crowd of people working around what must have been an old Victorian house. The man got out in the rain and said, "Let's go," and he darted off toward the downed house.

Virgil zipped up the rain jacket and got out, pulled the hood up against the rain, and ran over to the house. A line of men were prying away pieces of siding and structural lumber and beams, and throwing them aside. When Virgil asked what they were doing, the man ahead of him said, "We can hear the kid. Four-year-old."

They threw lumber for ten minutes, then a big fat man suddenly disappeared into the hole they were making, and a couple of people yelled, "Take it easy, Bill, take it easy . . ."

Another man near the hole said, "He's got him. He's got him. He's alive."

A minute later, the fat man popped out of the hole, holding a kid like a rag doll. Then he bundled the kid in his arms and said, "Where's the ambulance? Where's the fuckin' ambulance."

Virgil yelled, "We'll take my truck. We'll take my truck."

The men carried the kid down to Virgil's truck and laid him in the back, and another man crawled inside with him, and the fat man yelled, "Down to Ericksons, everybody who can make it. Down to Ericksons."

Virgil turned the truck, hit the lights and siren, and took off.

VP was eight miles south of Bigham and the Bigham Medical Center, which Virgil knew well. He made it in seven minutes, the truck rocking in the wind and the rain, while the man in back shouted, "You gotta hurry, you gotta hurry."

At the medical center, two people ran out into the rain with a gurney and lifted the kid aboard. One of the two was Frank O'Leary, the youngest of the boys. He apparently didn't recognize Virgil, wrapped in the Musto suit, and the two of them pushed the boy off into the emergency room.

The guy who rode with Virgil shouted, "We gotta go back."

VIRGIL MADE THREE TRIPS, the two ambulances seven or eight more. On his last trip, Virgil took a woman who might have had a broken hip, in the back, while an elderly man, who'd ripped his hand on a nail, rode in the passenger seat.

VP was still a mess, and people still roamed the town looking for dead, injured, and missing, but mutual-aid cops and ambulances were flooding in, and a disaster headquarters was operating, and Virgil wouldn't be needed again.

The old man told Virgil he'd gotten hurt dragging broken lumber off a downed house, where they were looking for another old man who lived alone. They hadn't found him. The old man with the ripped hand said, "That sonofabitch is trying to get out of our golf game," and then he started to cry.

THE RAIN HAD STOPPED as suddenly as it had come, and the wind was gone; Virgil could see stars down toward the horizon.

When they got to town, Frank O'Leary came out with the gurney to get the woman with the hip, and Virgil realized that the woman helping him was his sister, Mary. Virgil led the old man inside, attracted the attention of a nurse, who looked at the old man's hand and took him away.

Before she went, she said, "There's coffee and cookies just down the hall."

Virgil went that way, and got a cup of coffee, and because there were plenty of cookies, took six. Then he went back in the hallway, toward the entrance, then stopped to watch the emergency reception area.

There were several gurneys and beds with people on them, and he saw Jack O'Leary, the med student, taking notes from a woman who lay propped up on a wheeled bed. He was nodding as he took notes, and then he stood up, said something to her, patted her on the arm, and moved on to another bed.

A moment later, John O'Leary came out of the back part of the ER, what must've been an operating room. He was wearing an operating gown with a spot of blood on the belly of it. He stepped over to Jack and asked him something, and Jack pointed to one of the beds, and John O'Leary went over to look at the patient.

Another of the O'Leary boys showed up, dressed like his father; what he'd been doing, Virgil had no idea, but he was wearing an operating gown and booties.

Wu, the doc who'd treated Virgil, came out of the back and called something to John O'Leary, who turned and went after him.

Virgil watched it all for another five minutes, and then when they were all occupied, slipped out the door.

TEN MINUTES LATER, he had his gear out of the hotel and back in his truck: they needed all the rooms they could get, and he wasn't that far from home; or, he could go into Marshall, which was pretty convenient. If he went to Marshall, he could be back in Bigham early the next day.

He drove out to the highway, to the stop sign, looked both ways.

He could be back the next day, to interview the O'Learys. The emergency would be over by then.

Or he could say, "Fuck it," and go home.

Let it go.

If the whole crew of O'Learys had resurrected one person, one kid, from the calamity of Victoria Plains, that would make up for any number of Murphys, wouldn't it?

Well, no, Virgil thought, it wouldn't. The O'Learys, he was convinced, had violated one of God's own natural laws: Thou shalt not kill.

On the other hand . . .

Virgil sat at the stop sign for five minutes, staring blank-eyed into the night. Remembering all those O'Learys, dark-eyed, bright, hardworking kids, hovering over the mass of injured and dying, doing what they'd been so well programmed to do. Would the knowledge of their crime be enough punishment? Would it haunt them down through the years?

What to do?

Five minutes.

Then Virgil sighed, said aloud, "Fuck it," and turned toward home.

THE NEXT DAY, the weather guys flew over what would be known as the Victoria Plains F4, the biggest tornado of the year in Minnesota. It had been on the ground for almost forty miles, knocking over a few farmhouses and outbuildings here and there. The storm killed twelve people in VP, and injured forty-odd more.

The track itself looked a little like a boa constrictor that had swallowed a pig. The southwestern tip showed a few downed trees, some messed-up fields; then the path got wider, and the damage more extensive. Then the trail got really fat, and in its fattest part, whacked Victoria Plains. After VP, it went off to the northeast, slimming down, and then, twenty miles farther along, lifting off the ground altogether.

The weather guys would have needed God's Own Camera to see it, but just where the trail had started to get fat, right at the head of the pig, the tornado had crossed a cornfield owned by a man named Alex Brown, and then barreled into an old woodlot, long neglected and overgrown with trees, brush, and not a little wild hemp; ditch-weed; marijuana.

If they'd had God's Own Camera, and had been able to see through the tangled mess of downed timber and layers of shredded brush, they might have seen the outline of a carefully dug grave, unexpectedly disturbed by the tree roots wrenched from the wet earth. And now, sticking up from between the roots of a dying marijuana plant, a few fingers.

One with a heavy gold wedding ring.

Dick Murphy.

Pushing up weed.